SHADOWS OF THE PAST

THE
CONTRA
ALLIANCE
TRILOGY

CREATED AND WRITTEN BY
TOM KOLEGA

BOOK I

SHADOWS OF THE PAST

STATE OF THE ART ENTERTAINMENT, LLC

CONTRA ALLIANCE

BOOK ONE: SHADOWS OF THE PAST

This is the State of the Art Entertainment, LLC premiere 1st edition 2009

Contra Alliance® is a registered trademark.

Creator and Writer: Tom Kolega

Editor: Alice Peck

Proofreader/Copy Editor: Jessica Swift

Interior Designer: Duane Stapp

Front cover artwork by Joe Benitez, Victor Llamas, and Edgar Delgado

Book cover design by Ian Shimkoviak

Copyright © 2009 by Tom Kolega

ISBN: 978-0-615-30202-7

For information regarding licensing agreements, bulk book purchases, special discounts, or toy, comic book, and movie production, or other business relationships, please contact Tom Kolega through one of the online Contra Alliance networks or e- mail: Kolega@ContraAlliance.com

Printed, manufactured, and produced in the United States of America

STATE OF THE ART ENTERTAINMENT, LLC

TABLE OF CONTENTS

SHADOWS OF THE PAST

PROLOGUE

"TROY!"

Troy watched a few more seconds of the Bruce Lee YouTube video before he swiveled around in his chair. He took two steps away from his iMac and jumped the double bed with practiced perfection. He slid across the wooden floor to the edge of his room and grabbed the doorframe to stop.

"Yeah, Dad?"

His father stood at the bottom of the stairwell wearing his business suit, even on a Sunday.

"Did you clean up your toys in the backyard?"

"Um . . . I was gonna . . . but the Redskins were on and I—"

"We have important visitors coming tonight, Troy. That battle scene of yours at the fire pit needs to go. I'm taking our guests out there for a talk. When I tell you to do something, you need to listen. Okay?"

"Yes, sir."

"Now, pick up those superheroes and come to the kitchen. I'll make your favorite hot chocolate." Joseph McBride gave his son a warm smile. "Our visitors will be arriving shortly."

Troy went to his bedroom window and peeked outside. Gusting winds tossed piles of yellow and brown leaves against the white fence that enclosed their backyard. The trees swayed over the rooftop and resembled monsters against the darkening sky. It already felt like Halloween. Only four days away, Troy could barely wait for trick-or-treating. He was going as Bruce Lee. His martial arts instructor had given him the idea.

1

Grabbing a bomber jacket from his closet, Troy sat on the bedroom floor and tied the laces on his black basketball shoes. He caught a glimpse of his mother's picture by his bedside. She was sitting on the porch at the family lake house in Montana smiling happily. This image was Troy's favorite. He stared for a moment. His mother looked so beautiful. A handful of photos and several videos were all he knew of her. Shaking his head to clear his thoughts, Troy jumped up and ran downstairs.

It was cold outside. A huge moon floated above the treetops, casting bright rays on the leaves. Troy collected Wolverine, Batman, and the rest of his favorite action figures from where he'd left them and placed them in an orange shoebox. He made sure he got every one, knowing how important his father's meetings by the fire pit were. They happened pretty often. Someone usually came knocking on the door after dinner. Dad would take them outside, no matter how cold or late it was. They always went to the fire pit. If it rained, they stretched a tarp overhead. When the wind howled, they wore coats.

Next to the pit, an old radio played music during the meetings. Troy never recognized any of the songs but it made it hard to hear what the discussions were about. After a while, Troy figured that was the point. The visiting men and women would meet for hours with his father, sometimes talking late into the night. Troy assumed they were discussing important war secrets. His father worked for the government and there were two wars happening somewhere far away, so that must have been what they talked about.

Troy finished collecting his toys and headed inside. As he came into the kitchen the smell of melting marshmallows was unmistakable.

"Thank you, Son. That's more like it." His father set down a steaming cup of hot chocolate on the counter.

"It's really cold tonight!" Troy exclaimed, sliding out of his jacket and reaching for the cocoa. He looked into the cup. Four white marshmallows were slowly disappearing.

"Careful now, that's hot."

"Better have a big fire out there tonight, Dad."

His father chuckled and returned to cutting a roll of salami next to a plate of cheese and crackers arranged for the forthcoming guests. He watched Troy blow the steam off the cup and take a sip. "How did the Redskins game end?"

"Twenty-five, seventeen—we won! You should have watched it with me."

"Maybe next week when they play the Steelers. It's a Monday night game. I had work to catch up on today."

"Do you ever miss Mom?"

His father abruptly stopped cutting the salami and carefully placed the knife on the counter. He stared at the cheese plate for a moment, as if looking for an answer among the crackers. A gust of howling wind outside rattled the kitchen window. He looked into Troy's wide-open blue eyes and then finally spoke. "Of course I do." He paused, as if about to say more, when the doorbell rang. "I think our guests are here."

Troy watched his father walk fast toward the door, sighing with relief at the interruption. Dad didn't want to talk about certain things; answering questions about Mom was especially hard. His father changed the subject whenever Troy brought her up, but he really wanted to know so much more about her.

Troy edged to the side of the kitchen and watched the front door. Two men came inside and greeted his father with handshakes. One wore a green army uniform with lots of medals covering his chest. The other, much older visitor, wore a dark blue suit and stood next to the soldier. That man caught Troy's gaze.

"Troy, come here please." His father turned to him. "I'd like you to meet two very important people." Troy winced to himself as he neared the guests, their stares hard to ignore.

"Son, this is McDaniel Jessup and Captain William Taylor."

"We've heard a lot about you, Troy," McDaniel said in an English accent, tilting his head slightly as he spoke.

"Really? I haven't heard anything about you."

The men laughed.

"Your dad tells me you're doing well at school and in karate." Captain Taylor bent low to Troy's level.

"I like martial arts. And school, that's easy."

"For you it is," McDaniel said. Troy did not understand the comment.

"I like your medals." Troy pointed to the collection on Captain Taylor's uniform.

The captain grinned and reached into his pocket. He opened his palm to reveal a gold and black coin. "This is for you."

"WOW! Really?" Troy grabbed the coin and inspected it closely. It had a bald eagle on the front and an inscription arching above and below it. "101st Airborne Division. Screaming Eagles," he read aloud.

"Good job." The captain beamed proudly at Troy.

Flipping the coin over, Troy ran his thumb over an engraved parachute with wings coming out both sides. He tried to read the back inscription. "Rend . . . e . . . zvo—"

"Rendezvous with Destiny," McDaniel helped him out.

Troy looked up at McDaniel. The man's deep eyes glistened a bit. His professorial English accent made him sound extra wise. There was seriousness about McDaniel that almost made Troy feel uncomfortable. Troy turned away from the captain. "It's cool. Thanks!"

"We're going outside now, Son. Be good in here." His father glanced at the men knowingly and led them through the kitchen. They took a bottle of wine and the appetizer plates outside.

Troy ran to the living room, turned on the television, and plopped down on the soft leather couch where he continued to examine the coin. He watched the Cartoon Network for a while, and then started upstairs with his shoebox full of action figures. He stopped cold in the hallway.

"Spiderman!"

The fire pit crackled and the radio played hits from the seventies as the three men sat close to one another, discussing Earth and their role in its future course.

"Captain Taylor's parents informed him of his heritage before the High Council resolution prohibited Nerrial children living on Earth from learning the truth," McDaniel said.

"So you know of the High Council's origins following the Nezdeth invasion?" Joseph asked.

"Yes, my parents taught me about the Time of Legend, War of the Star, and how the High Council was formed. They taught me about Nerrial's discovery of Earth in 1898 and why they were sent here as Emissaries. They sat me down for *the talk* the week before I enlisted in the Army. As you can imagine, it changed everything for me."

"At least you've been told . . . I regret that Troy can never know. The High Council feared Earth's technology was advancing too rapidly, which forced them to prohibit passing on our heritage and secrets to future generations. It's difficult . . . not being able to share the truth with my son. His mother and my youngest boy were in the last group permitted back to Nerrial. They left years ago, before Troy could even hold a memory. I'll probably never see them again. Troy doesn't even know he has a brother."

"I'm sorry, sir," Captain Taylor said as he put his hand on Joseph's shoulder. "I know what it's like to be without family."

"After Captain Taylor's parents passed, I tracked down his airborne unit in Iraq outside of Kirkuk," McDaniel said. "His performance in the field has been exemplary. I want to train him as one of us—an Emissary guiding the mission, influencing peace on Earth. I'm making arrangements for his deployment to NORAD[1] following his next tour in Afghanistan. At NORAD he will oversee the Starblazer program. I brought the captain here tonight to introduce the two of you. If all goes as planned, we'll be working together for a long time."

"It's my honor, Captain Taylor," said Joseph.

"Mine as well, sir."

"Nothing is more important than protecting the secrets of Nerrial," McDaniel continued. "Our mission to help Earth is sacred. We must enable this civilization to find its own peace by whatever political or, if necessary, military measures are required to defeat the evil presence that feeds wars, greed, and power lust. Nerrial will never dictate peace from afar, nor will it become an alien power of occupation. No matter how astonishing the existence of our shared human civilization is—that is not our way. We can *never* reveal the secret of our presence unless the High Council or Crown decides. That is the Emissary creed, Captain Taylor."

Troy put his bomber jacket back on. He tiptoed outside through the back door as a powerful gust of wind shook the fence. Night had fallen and thick clouds covered the moon. The glow of the fire pit illuminated the scattered leaves dancing around his feet. It was the only light in an otherwise pitch-black backyard. Troy put his hands in his pockets and walked across the lawn. His father and the men must not have seen him coming because they didn't stop talking when he got close enough to hear. Troy waited patiently; he knew better than to interrupt.

"One more thing Captain Taylor," McDaniel said.

"Yes, sir."

"While my government name is McDaniel Jessup, my true name is Magden.

---

[1] North American Aerospace Defense Command (NORAD)

6

Call me by my birth name in instances such as this. I prefer it."

"You can just call me Joseph," Troy's father added, getting a smile from the captain.

"I no longer have a family, but I know we will become close," the captain said. "Thank you for accepting me into the code. Our heritage—the truth—binds us. My dedication to the mission, to Nerrial, will never cease. I—"

"Troy!" Joseph interrupted. "I didn't see you come out here. You know better. How long have you been standing there?" His father sounded worried.

"I just came outside now."

"What's the matter? Are you okay?"

"I forgot Spiderman."

"What?"

"Spiderman is under the barbecue cover."

"Oh . . . right." His father got up and recovered the toy while Captain Taylor and Magden watched in silence. Joseph handed the figure to Troy. "I'll come check on you before bed. Go on." Joseph patted Troy gently along.

Troy ran back inside. He wanted to watch more Bruce Lee videos and get ideas for his costume. Halloween was just four days away. At seven-years-old, nothing else was more important to Troy McBride.

PART ONE
SECRETS

*"Peace will again fade and war will return. In time
of need, a new hero will rise. This I know."*
—Ciza, 384 AD on Adena

CHAPTER 1
BATTLESTAR
Hermosa Beach: April 20, 2035

At nine o'clock in the morning, the Hermosa Strand pathway in front of Troy McBride's beachside apartment was filled with people, just like always. Sunbeams broke through hazy patches in the marine layer hanging over the Los Angeles South Bay. Rays of warmth mixed with a fresh ocean breeze and created a magical atmosphere near the bustling pier plaza. Beach volleyball players spiked morning serves and kids bicycled along The Strand separating the oceanfront from rows of million-dollar homes.

Troy was deep in thought. He didn't feel depressed; he felt lost. Holding a declassified CIA report in one hand and a cold latte in the other, he knew his journey in life had grown muddled. Waves crashed against the shore as he rubbed the stubble on his chin—soon he'd have a full-fledged beard. Troy poured the remaining brown liquid from his cup into the sand and watched it swirl into a puddle. Lately he needed caffeine to fully awaken each day. Never liking coffee, he ignored the taste and drank it for the rush.

Gazing at the famous billboard overlooking the pier, Troy considered the controversy it had caused when going up. "Buy American" it simply read with an image of the flag waving in a background complete with red, white, and blue fireworks exploding across a composite skyline of the Space Needle, Statue of Liberty, and iconic Hollywood sign. He wondered at the irony of actually finding anything manufactured in America these days.

Early for work, he took his time as he walked on the pier. Troy didn't care about his current job. It was worthless. He thought of quitting everyday. Dishwashing barely covered groceries, but his problems weren't financial. Troy still had plenty of his hard-earned CIA money; he could afford living at the beach, but he needed something to keep him busy, something to keep his mind occupied away. So he worked a job of futility.

Mornings used to be so different. A long run, weapons training, weight-lifting or reading a book on top of a mountain he'd just conquered—those were the things that used to define a sunrise. Training. Always challenging himself to be the best or, as he preferred to think of it, stay the best. Whether for the military or for self-respect, being stronger, faster, and smarter mattered. He dedicated all of himself to it.

Troy used to feel that the world needed him. That somehow his path led to a destiny requiring total commitment and readiness. He never questioned the sense, believing a time would come when he'd make the difference in some unforeseen battle between good and evil. *How could one mistake take it all away?* His error haunted him still. It overwhelmed him and derailed his career. *I have to get over it.*

Troy reviewed the declassified CIA document he'd downloaded the night before. He'd contributed to portions of the original version, which remained classified and redacted for good reason.

Central Intelligence Agency (TOP SECRET)   Approved for Release
Date: April 2035

Summary Assessment of Threat Posed by The Revolution

The unprecedented nature of The Revolution's rise and successful attacks pose a significant challenge to the United States and international security. Popular comparisons to Al-Qaeda are unwarranted. The intelligence community is in agreement; The Revolution is not a terrorist organization—it is a global, interconnected criminal enterprise using a network of unassociated militia, mafia, and mercenaries from around the world to achieve its financial and anarchic goals.

The president has identified The Revolution as a direct and immediate threat to the national security of the United States. The Department of Defense is working closely with America's allies to form a cohesive strategy based on intelligence sharing, denial of safe havens, targeted apprehension, rapid reaction, and enhanced counter-narcotics operations to disrupt associated criminal networks and stem the flow of primary funding to suspected Revolution operatives.

Key objectives include optimizing the first line of defense against The Revolution beyond U.S. borders and alerting domestic law enforcement agencies to the presence of any active Revolution cells on American soil. Department of Defense actions will be integrated within the National Security Strategy of the United States.

Evidence indicates that The Revolution was behind three specific incidents, termed the "Critical Events," which have deflated initial doubts of the group's operational capabilities when the Revolution Declaration was received by various government agencies. The first event,

Second, the sophisticated theft and detonation of a stolen Iranian nuclear warhead near Isfahan resulted in the death of thousands of innocent civilians, bringing The Revolution under global scrutiny and onto the world stage.

Third, the brazen attack on NATO headquarters demonstrated the group's ability to conduct highly coordinated operations against a well-defended target in broad daylight.

The intelligence community is addressing the surprising rapidity by which the rogue group has been able to establish advanced technological and organizationally effective capabilities without detection. Several analytical assessments and corroborating SIGNT and IMINT suggest that state sponsorship of the group is likely. It is

The public was not allowed to know anything about the first Critical Event, or which state sponsors the CIA suspected were assisting The Revolution. Troy knew and was well aware of why the first Critical Event frightened so many in the intelligence community. Disturbing information was commonplace when one worked in the black world of intelligence affairs, but what the U.S. Marines stumbled upon deep in the Colombian jungle was different.

Built in a subterranean cavern, the Marines discovered a secret lab performing genetically advanced experiments that outpaced Western capabilities. The lab was outfitted with modern amenities, equipment, and information technologies. Recombinant DNA experiments where fusion between live humans and other mammals took place was successfully achieved. The evil draconian workshop earned the nickname "Demon Lab."

Troy remained baffled at how an obscure group calling itself "The Revolution" could develop the capacity and know-how to far surpass the finest scientific efforts of government and corporate laboratories in that same field. Finding and ending The Revolution became Troy's calling. Or so he had thought.

Troy strolled along The Strand, a cement pathway stretching twenty-two miles along the Pacific shoreline from Redondo Beach to Santa Monica. It provided joggers and bikers with a smooth track cutting across acres of white sand. The pathway gave solace to the many who called Los Angeles their home and who needed respite from crowded highways and the gridlock of city life. The Strand also led Troy to the Surfer Grill, the diner where he worked. He'd picked this basic form of employment on purpose. Nothing would ever compare to what he had lost, to what he was born to do, so Troy punished himself and practiced humility—the one trait his father told him he lacked despite all his skill and ability.

The truth was Troy had screwed up. Now he had to live with it.

Nearing the diner entrance, Troy pulled his golden hair back into a ponytail. The buttery, greasy morning food inside pierced the outdoor air with the unmistakable aroma of breakfast. His boss loved to fan that smell through the kitchen vents. It was the only marketing Trucker ever did for the Surfer Grill, and it worked. The diner drew a good morning crowd on most days. Bacon, eggs, and the blackest coffee available never got old.

Making his way inside Troy passed the daily protesters at the pier's central plaza. The protests had become so routine, the effects had waned on passersby. Serious media coverage only followed when violence broke out, and when that happened the coverage never focused on the protests' purpose. Hoodlums got all the attention. *Free to speak, but not many people listening.* Troy entered through the diner's side door, passing an older woman who smiled at him. "End Trade" and "Free California" buttons lined her yellow sweater.

"Would you like one of our new buttons, young man?" she asked, kindly extending a large red pin with the American flag on it. She gave Troy a friendly wink, apparently trying to entice him into the deal. Troy returned her smile and accepted. "Thank you, ma'am. I appreciate it." He had plenty of similar buttons around his apartment and didn't need more, but saying no to old folks was hard. They were doing their part to make a positive change. Hermosa was still a relatively safe place, wealth abounded. Protesters liked to congregate in its peaceful villagelike atmosphere, a sanctuary absent the cruelty infecting American inner cities.

Only ten miles eastward, Los Angeles crystallized the problem for America. The city battled a growing rebellion from within. Gangs and the impoverished rejected new food-rationing policies, security crackdowns, and curfews. New racial tensions belied the notion of acceptance. Troy had read about the 1960s and the civil rights movement, but that was over seventy years ago. America found itself in the midst of a modern phase of intolerance. It wasn't only about skin color this time. It was about the haves and the have-nots.

Troy washed his hands in the backroom and tied his apron on. Dragging his feet to the dishwashing station, he passed his boss without saying hello. Nobody knew if Trucker was his real name or not, but everyone knew he used to drive semi-trucks cross-country before buying the Surfer Grill. Trucker was burly and brash. He claimed to have fought a man in every state. A graying beard and large earrings gave him the air of a modern pirate. He rarely smiled and loved to lean over employees for intimidation when making them add an extra shift.

Once, a Surfer Grill waiter got fired for talking back. The waiter took a break during peak hours. Trucker got pissed. He tossed the scrawny man into the back alley like a sack of trash and told him never to return. All the employees feared Trucker, except for Troy. He didn't have to—underneath his apron whites, Troy maintained the physique of a human weapon and never forgot the martial artistry he'd mastered long ago.

"Son, you're a newbie here, so I'm expecting you to stay 'til closing time. A twelve-hour day never killed a man," Trucker had insisted on Troy's first day at the diner. Troy didn't respond, so Trucker tried the lean-in technique. Troy stared back into Trucker's eyes without saying a word. His message was clear enough.

"Ah, hell. Stay on if you want the extra money. Just let me know," Trucker had said after a moment of the stare down. He wasn't stupid; he knew Troy was no regular employee. It wasn't his raw strength, and he did not have a bad attitude. Troy was quiet and kind to everyone. Trucker never leaned over him again, though. Instead, he asked questions using extra-polite manners. Such out-of-character etiquette did not go unnoticed by Troy's coworkers.

This morning, Trucker stopped Troy.

"Good morning to ya, Troy. Would it be okay to stay a few extra hours? Someone just be quittin' again. Need you in the back kitchen later on . . . if you're feelin' up to it," Trucker requested, shrugging his shoulders sheepishly.

"I can manage that." *What else do I have to do? Clean my apartment? Start a journal? No, grilling burgers and fries would be best.*

The head cook, Carlos, greeted Troy with a breakfast omelet. A question accompanied the omelet every time. Carlos seemed to have an intense curiosity about Troy, who spoke little to anyone. Troy kept to himself, in his own world of lost potential. He knew the kitchen crew had bets on what he had done before working at the Surfer Grill.

"You look fabulous this morning, amigo! How do you keep the women away?" Carlos asked, trying to cheer the gloom off Troy's face.

"No women, Carlos. All I got is dishes, grease, and you. Thanks for the omelet, my friend."

"What do you think about the news?" Carlos asked before Troy could escape to his corner of the kitchen. Carlos brought up war stories with Troy constantly, probably because it was one of the few topics of conversation he responded to at length.

Troy paused. "More violence in Colombia, or is it another shooting spree in London?"

"Nooo!" exclaimed Carlos, realizing Troy hadn't heard. "This is out of China! We shot down fighter jets by Taiwan. China said our soldiers were there, in Taiwan. The Chinese say they'll do something back if we don't pay them money and stuff."

Intrigue flit across Troy's face. That *was* real news. Most mornings he checked the headlines before leaving his apartment, but not today. He had wanted to get outside early. *That has to be CONTRA.* The mission to uncover possible Chinese connections to The Revolution had been in the planning phase when he was decommissioned.

Excitement charged Troy up for the first time in weeks. He hurried to the back of the restaurant and turned on a radio next to the sink. Station One News barely came in on that radio but he wouldn't listen to anything else. Other stations were watered down. Corporations liked to keep the public in la-la land with stories about bullshit. Most of the stories weren't even real news anymore. Station One stayed independent. Former military personnel operated it and delivered Open-Source Intelligence news.

Troy rolled on his dishwashing gloves and turned up the volume. A reporter announced breaking news and a forthcoming Pentagon briefing. Troy strained to hear the words through the radio's static. Pressing the top of the soap nozzle, the green gel formed a blob in the palm of his hand. He caught a glimpse of his tattoo—the only tattoo he'd ever wanted and ever gotten. On the inside of his forearm between the top of his glove and the bend in his elbow, simple blue block letters read *BATTLESTAR.*

CHAPTER 2
ENGAGEMENT
Taiwan: April 20, 2035

The People's Liberation Army closed in.

"The sky is crimson like dragon's breath," Grace observed aloud with the eloquence of a true poet. "I'd feel better if Battlestar were with us."

"Get down, Major! And get that link up to PACOM!" Justice barked at her. He didn't fear the expanding battle with the PLA. Incoming rounds, explosions, and the constant peril of war never fazed him. He didn't worry about whether his parachute opened or if orders made sense. He didn't have time to contemplate all the nuances of combat; Justice was an Army Ranger—and according to everybody, a good one.

But the rumbling stomach cramps deep within his gut created an untimely distraction from the covert operation unraveling before Justice. As commanding officer of the First Company Counter-Revolutionary (CONTRA) Strike Force, or Blue Team, he needed to focus. This was the first mission for the unit. With each passing moment Justice ached with apprehension unrelated to the battle unfolding before him. There was something new in his life. Kate Hurst, the first woman Justice ever loved.

Justice and Kate met in Colorado Springs during the first phase of CONTRA training. Mobilized in secret to revive the failing alliance, NATO's new Special Operations battalion was advertised internally as the most elite, lethal, high-tech military unit ever assembled. Kate—codenamed Red for the vivid color of her hair—and Justice were nominated to be leading officers. Red was assigned to the Second Company, also called the Gray Team. The ongoing gun battle didn't disturb Justice, but the thought of never seeing Red again did.

"Firing!" shouted Gideon, the French lieutenant colonel and second in command. A seasoned veteran of the commando arm of the National Gendarmerie Intervention Group, his shoulder-fired missile cut free with a powerful burst, burning through the air toward the approaching PLA personnel carrier leading a convoy toward their position.

A dozen PLA troops from China's Thirty-first Group Army sat atop the vehicle. The group was charged with administrating the occupation of Southern Taiwan. Together with formidable Chinese Immediate Action Units (IAU), they assured the Resistance paid dearly for its counterinsurgency.

Two soldiers jumped from the vehicle before Gideon's missile struck. An explosion of orange flames engulfed the personnel carrier, sending it swerving to a fiery halt alongside the narrow dirt road leading from the Chinese military outpost on the outskirts of Chiayi. Their bodies on fire, PLA soldiers tumbled out of the carrier. They shrieked in agony as they tried to put out the flames that covered their skin.

The CONTRA Blue Team and their Resistance allies watched from a grassy slope, hidden from the road by green cypress trees on the foothills of the Alishan Forest. The now-smoldering vehicle ground the convoy of PLA armor to a halt.

"That should buy some time," Justice said, repositioning himself closer to Gideon. "Clearing that mess will take a minute. We'll need more firepower."

"From where?" Gideon's lip curled in anger. "I have but one missile left, sir."

"I'll consult with Rapidfire. The next mission we'll sneak the fire power in if we must."

"Take notes, a precision guided mortar system—which the windbags wouldn't provide us—could destroy that entire incoming convoy."

Justice understood Gideon's bitterness. Getting NATO agreement to deploy CONTRA in territory under Chinese control took strenuous political maneuvers. Hushed discussions in crowded restaurants, midnight parking lot meetings, back door promises—the whole gambit of bureaucratic wizardry was summoned. Only the guarantee of total stealth sold the deal to European Defense Ministers hungry for acquiescence.

Overcoming the consternation of NATO states unprepared to accept the risk of another open confrontation with Beijing was not easy. Internal disputes took months to detangle. For military commanders, the mission's secretive nature meant less capability on the ground, thus more challenges. The NATO Military Committee approved only half the CONTRA Blue Team for the Taiwan mission. No heavy tactical munitions were permitted.

The Chinese military outpost near Chiayi represented CONTRA's primary reconnaissance objective. Enough people at the Pentagon wanted to know if the Chinese were conspiring with The Revolution, as some intelligence analysis suggested. U.S. Navy signal interceptors off the coast of Taiwan confirmed a possible connection. There were enough believers to warrant a CONTRA team insertion.

Things were working according to plan before a PLA patrol detected them. Repercussions would surely follow *if* Justice and his Special Operations Blue Team escaped alive. His strict orders had been to keep the operation covert. That was the only acceptable outcome—Beijing could not find out NATO was in Taiwan.

Chiayi—the former agricultural center of Taiwan—served as China's Top Secret bioengineering hub, a sort of Silicon Valley for freakish breeding projects that supposedly furthered the study of advanced biology and genetics. Suspicions were that Chiayi's advanced projects found their way to Colombia and became the draconian human experiments U.S. Marines found in the so-called Demon Lab. Hard intelligence collected from Chiayi could prove Chinese involvement with The Revolution.

National Reconnaissance Office (NRO) satellites had confirmed the new construction of several large facilities near Chiayi. The buildings were alleged genetic labs erected after China secured its military takeover of Taiwan. CONTRA needed to find out whether these laboratories supported The Revolution's experiments in Colombia. If the PLA link was proven, then The Revolution would be unmasked as a Chinese puppet. CONTRA's mission would be declared a success. The conventional military brass and diplomats could take it from there.

Dug into moss-covered underbrush with cypress trees above, Justice overlooked the roadway and watched the firefight expand. The Special Forces operators of CONTRA at the front exchanged heavy gunfire with the PLA. More Chinese troops reinforced the patrol that had spotted the Blue Team and fanned out along the road, disappearing into the adjoining woods.

Justice pondered his options. He clutched his MP-5 submachine gun. Fighting intensified. The entire team could be captured or killed. CONTRA could try to fight their way back to Resistance hideouts in the Jade Mountains, or call for an emergency extraction. *Maybe the PLA hasn't identified us yet. Calling in the Shadowhawks would blow our cover.* The violent ongoing clash looked grim through the scope of his weapon. *Time to make the call. We're getting pinned. No evidence of The Revolution and our support to the Resistance might be exposed. Not good.*

There wasn't much time for him to decide. His heart pounded. Failure was not an option. *I'll get my team out and return to Kate.* Justice squeezed the trigger of his MP-5, ripping a targeted burst of rounds. Blood splashed from a PLA soldier's arm as he sprinted forward into the fight. The man spun as he fell to the ground. His body jerked from the shock of bullets, like he was being electrocuted.

Justice turned to Grace.

The brilliant Italian intelligence officer huddled quietly next to him. She appeared to be praying. Everyone knew faith was at the core of her being. Before joining CONTRA, Grace worked far behind lines of fire within Italy's

External Information and Security Agency. She had never experienced a pitched battle, yet she didn't hesitate to accept her position as Italy's leading CONTRA officer.

Her appointment irked many in the Italian chain of command who questioned her credentials. Most were surprised the "Holy Princess"—as they called her—ever accepted. They said she was too pretty and soft. Grace was proving them wrong. In the midst of the chaos surrounding their team, she appeared beatifically calm.

Grace marveled at the colors darkening the sky and prayed. Sunsets moved her, and behind the slope, the setting sun's tranquility inspired her. Even in the midst of war her creative passion persisted. At a very early age she had been nationally recognized in Italian literary circles as an extraordinary talent with adultlike insight and wisdom.

At fourteen, in an interview with Italy's primary online news source, *Corriere della Sera,* Grace had been asked to describe her gift. She rejoiced at the question, saying, "God provides inspiration to any man or woman, so I am only as talented as He decides." A smiling snapshot of the young Italian phenomenon accompanied her quote. She became an Internet sensation.

Another PLA personnel carrier exploded—the target of Gideon's second shoulder-fired missile. The concussion rocked Grace back into the moment, away from the postcard-pretty crimson sky. She met Justice's stare.

"It's time we leave, sir," she gently pleaded.

"Gideon," Justice commanded. "Make the call now."

"As you wish," Gideon replied.

At the front, Xxplosive watched the same darkening sky fill with plumes of smoke. To him, the sky looked disastrous and the situation on the ground even worse. Wreckage of burning PLA vehicles littered the roadway leading from low mountain Resistance hideouts to the city of Chiayi. Bullets traced across the forest—one hit its mark. A sniper put a bullet in Xxplosive's upper bicep, piercing through his battlesuit armor and drawing blood.

"I don't have time for this," Xxplosive muttered, wrapping medical tape around the bloody mess covering his black skin. Five years as a Navy Seal, and the last six with the Naval Special Warfare Development Group (DEVGRU), had taught him to deal with pain. The thin white tape would do just fine.

Dozens of PLA soldiers reinforced the patrol that spotted CONTRA. Hundreds more Chinese troops would soon follow. A large chain of PLA vehicles in the distance moved toward the Blue Team's position. The battle was getting out of control.

Next to Xxplosive, Nightscope let off clip after clip, frantically ducking while reloading conventional ammunition, venting his anger. He hated the PLA. The Communist superpower infuriated him, like many other things. The night their team was chosen for the Taiwan mission, Nightscope let loose in a way Xxplosive was now accustomed to seeing from his best friend in CONTRA. Three shots of Jack Daniels and Nightscope opened up on why America had fallen from its pinnacle. He blamed China.

"You name it: the espionage, our satellites, the Great Deception, and now—The Revolution. It's on them. I bet we'll uncover some serious shit over there."

According to Nightscope, everything was on them. "They stole from us. They lied and tricked us. I can't wait to get there." His words were sincere, but there was dread behind his patriotic passion. Only a fool would want to get into Taiwan, where assimilation campaigns read like horror stories. Nightscope reflected the disorientation of America's descent. The United States spent nearly a century as the preeminent world power. Most of the country blamed its downfall on someone else.

Xxplosive accepted that the world changed with time. America and the West had to find a way to keep pace. China used capitalism to build its wealth. Its wealth fed its rising military machine. After becoming an economic juggernaut came diplomatic weight and, finally, the emergence of a Chinese military superpower capable of taking on any nation—and it did.

Most history books said greed led to the transfer of power from West to East; profit without consequence when globalization first began. Enlightenment got lost in the gluttony devouring the old Western guard. Now new players were on the scene and they played by different rules. Everyone else had to live with it.

Bullets snapped overhead as more PLA troops took positions in the lightly wooded forest opposite Xxplosive's flank near the dirt road where CONTRA had first been spotted.

"They're coming in harder. Tough shit for us," Nightscope seethed, inserting another clip. "I can't hit them all. Check off down the road. On the path there's a platoon-sized unit creeping in on the tree line." Nightscope was a Delta Force operator and had been in even tighter situations. His hands were steady, trained to be quick under fire.

"I got multiples off my side too." Xxplosive let off a barrage of gunfire. "They're gonna cut around and split the team."

"Only if we let them. We have to fall back. These PLA maneuvers will pay if they cut around to our backside. We wouldn't be able to reach the rest of our team. You know what that means." Nightscope sprayed rounds into the midsection of a PLA soldier hiding behind the trunk of a thin tree. The bullets peeled the man away from his ill-selected hiding spot. He slowly fell backward, dropping his weapon in a horrified gasp at death.

Xxplosive rushed another spurt of gunfire. He turned toward the rest of the CONTRA unit on the slope behind them. Two incoming mortar shells exploded nearby, catapulting hot showers of dirt overhead and sending fragments of shrapnel into the torso of a Resistance fighter next to him. The man shrieked in pain, grabbing at his side in anguish.

"Light 'em up with laser fire and let's get ready to go," Nightscope said picking up his battlepack, loading a final clip, and preparing to move.

The laser weaponry issued to Xxplosive was untested in live battle. The Pentagon rushed its newest next-generation weapons to the battlefield before designs were stolen. In the past, too many designs had been stolen before they ever got used. China and Russia had penetrated the U.S. Secret Internet Protocol Router Network or SIPRNet and downloaded enough blueprints to reverse engineer everything from Air Force missile guidance systems to Navy railguns. Like much of the high-tech gear CONTRA equipped itself with, weapons testing took place in the field.

Xxplosive preferred traditional ammunition, but lasers packed precision killing power at the speed of light. They were the next best things to explosives. Dropping his M4 to the ground, Xxplosive unlatched the new high-powered Special Operations laser automatic rifle from his back shoulder holster and gripped the trigger.

"All right, last call for alcohol," he said glancing at Nightscope.

The two officers stood up and let their weapons negotiate.

An eternity in anticipation, mere minutes in real time. Justice scanned the horizon for the two Shadowhawk gunships dispatched to rescue the team. The gunships were inbound from the north where the USS Obama patrolled the southern coast of Japan. CONTRA's members would quickly fall under aerial assault from Chinese MiG's if they didn't escape.

"Shadowhawks will be here in seven," Grace reported. "They need us to move to the rendezvous now."

"Resistance fighters will have to hold the line," Justice said. "Getting our team over the other side of the slope is critical, before this gets ugly."

"It's already ugly," Gideon retorted.

Justice ignored the comment and looked down at the Resistance commanders CONTRA had been working with. He'd grown close to one of them, Chiang Chen, the leader of the Resistance. "I have to tell Chiang."

Grace nodded. She watched the rebel commanders shouting orders twenty yards below them. Used to waging a guerilla war, Taiwan's rebels were scrambling scared from the direct exchange with the PLA. Five years of occupation had taken its toll on their forces. The Resistance was much smaller than NATO intelligence estimated. Numbers in the ranks had depleted due to attrition of all types. Hungry, tired fighters had returned to their villages in droves over the past two years, trying to hide from the watchful eye of the Chinese military units and secret police that hunted them.

The Resistance welcomed CONTRA warmly upon arrival, though the NATO mission confused them. They didn't care about The Revolution— they'd never heard of it. Taiwan was fading into a forgotten history they bled to save. The Resistance needed the new weapons CONTRA delivered, but were reluctant to join in any reconnaissance or intelligence gathering against fortified PLA outposts. They supported CONTRA objectives because they wanted more help from the West.

The NATO officers listened to the constant requests for assistance— prodding and, at times, begging. The officers played along, knowing the free world had given up on Taiwan. To the disappointment of the rebel fighters, the CONTRA mission was entirely different from what they'd hoped. The West had already ceded Taiwan. Its liberation was no longer on the agenda. The defeat of The Revolution was.

Justice descended the grassy hill toward Chiang, his counterpart from the Resistance. A former major general in Taiwan's Sixth Corps, Chiang's commitment to repel the PLA occupation didn't waver. Chiang believed the Resistance would succeed and never lost faith. It was all Chiang had left; his entire family had been killed in the initial onslaught. Justice never told Chiang the realities shaping politics in the outside world. Mainland China had successfully blocked nearly all cyber- and tele-communications out of the island and misinformation was fed through government media channels.

As he neared Chiang, Justice felt responsible for the frantic situation. Chiang saw him coming and paid no heed. He continued directing the Resistance with the distinct authority of an active general.

"My friend," Justice said with a solemn look, forcing the issue. "We have to go."

Chiang paused from barking orders and held Justice in his gaze. He reached inside his vest and removed something. Chiang grabbed Justice by the arm, opened his palm and placed an object within it, then clasped the object into the American's hands.

"You look at that . . . what I give you . . . in America," he said in broken English. "Do not forget what we do." His eyes stared hard for a moment. Then the general turned and continued to bark his orders as if Justice had already left.

This is the end. Justice found it hard to go. Over the past two weeks he'd grown close to Chiang. The rebel commander passed along critical intelligence about China's activities in Taiwan. He told stories of execution, detention, and escape. The republic had planned its post-invasion strategy years in advance, in the days when the Red Army grew ominous across the Strait. Still, the Resistance could do little other than annoy Beijing's powerful military machine.

Justice tucked Chiang's gift into his own vest and ran back toward Grace.

"We're inbound. Hold on and get to the zone," the voice of a pilot from the incoming Shadowhawks shouted over the radio.

Grace slung her battlepack across her shoulders and trudged up the slope ahead of Justice, coordinating CONTRA's exact location. Years of training had made her stronger and tougher. Sometimes her angelic eyes and features overshadowed her military worth. Justice knew only time separated her from the recognition she sought. CONTRA provided her that opportunity to be taken seriously.

Having grown up a stone's throw from the Vatican, it was fitting that Grace looked angelic. Her soft complexion, bright green eyes, and warm smile always accompanied the cross hanging around her neck. She never removed it. Blessed by three Popes and passed down over generations in her family, the cross was cherished. Traditions held strong for fewer in Italy, but they fulfilled Grace and gave her peace in the continuum of time. That's what she told Justice.

Justice caught up behind Grace. The moss-covered slope made the incline tricky. Her legs must have burned under the weight of so much battle gear. She slipped and caught herself, palms to the dirt. She gritted her teeth and saved herself from a face plant. "Strength for the sake of peace. Make me worthy of service, Savior."

Justice panted orders to Gideon over his headset.

"How are we doing?" Justice asked passing Grace.

"Good, sir. 'In the hands of the Lord,' as my mother would say."

"I'm glad that's comforting. You wouldn't mind asking the Lord to tell the Chinese to stop shooting at us?"

"I can try, sir, but He might ask why we're shooting at *them*."

"Fair enough. Tell Him it's about trying to save the world. I'm sure He'd appreciate that."

"Yes, sir."

"The Shadowhawks, where are they?" Gideon asked, as Grace and Justice reached him at the peak of the slope between the firefight and rendezvous. "We're gonna be butchered like lambs."

"They're coming now," Grace huffed, breathing hard and sweating profusely. She balanced herself against the trunk of a large tree. Finding enough oxygen in the thick humidity was a challenge. It was difficult to talk.

"Gideon, let's make sure—" Justice began.

Machine-gun fire hammered in, clipping bark from the tree above.

"Assholes!" Gideon blurted. "Are you all right?" He looked to Grace, concerned.

"I think so." Grace examined the bullet holes inches above her head.

Justice wiped his brow. "They'll be coming hard 'til we're out. Now down the other side. Let's go. No rest here." He felt relieved as they descended the opposite side of the hill, out of sight of PLA guns.

"They'll have helicopters and fighters in the sky. Surprised they're not on top of us already," Grace said. "I wonder, sir, if the Chinese Ministry of State Security knows about the Shadowhawks or if they can pick up the gunship stealth on radar."

"Unlikely. That program was tight as the Moonwalk," Justice pointed out.

The Shadowhawk program had been designed in secret. The multi-role fighter-transport entered service three weeks earlier, in record-breaking development time, taking only two years from inception to production. The newest radar-evading materials, electronic warfare, and directed energy weapons outfitted the sharp one-winged crafts. Shadowhawks could fly faster and engage more targets with their weapons suite then any air vehicle ever produced.

CONTRA depended on them now for rescue from Taiwan.

Before CONTRA's arrival, no American personnel had been on Taiwanese soil in the past four years. Not since the peace talks broke down. The PLA closed off the island from the world in an effort to return Chinese culture to harmony, Chinese officials stated. Repeated attempts to send in observers from dozens of humanitarian organizations failed. The Red Cross, Doctors without Borders, and the United Nations were all denied access.

Taipei's fall was hard to take. Justice had watched with the world as live coverage of the attack streamed across television sets. His Ranger regiment was on call, ready to deploy.

Missile after missile had decimated Taipei and its defenses. The once thriving Asian democracy died in smoke, rubble, and human torment. The Battle of Taiwan was fierce but mostly one-sided. It marked the first war where strategic military exchanges of terrestrial and space-based weapons, directed energy, and cyber-war were the primary armaments employed. American tactical support couldn't stop the crushing mainland blitz.

U.S.-Taiwan defense agreements, relics of a time gone by, carried little weight when the balance of power shifted so far from the favor of the island to the mainland. U.S. fighters and joint military assets scrambled after the Chinese invasion commenced. Justice was on standby, so for him nothing was more dramatic.

For an intense ten-day period, the largest, most-advanced aerial dogfight and space-war the world ever witnessed raged above the Taiwan Strait. Squadrons of Chinese Sukoi and MiG fighters went up against Taiwanese KFX's, American and Japanese F-22's, F-35's, unmanned strike aircrafts, and long-range bombers. The skies and space over the embattled island, China's coasts, southern Japan, and Korea were the scenes of furious military combat. Advanced war technology and maneuvers led to swift escalation by both sides. America had the political and military support of all its major allies.

It hardly mattered.

China refused to bow out or back down. Highly coordinated counter-attacks against American military intervention were planned for decades in advance and proved very effective. Missile strikes and air raids annihilated U.S. military installations on Guam and Japan. The PLA launched sophisticated electronic warfare and antisatellite attacks against military ground stations, command centers, and orbiting intelligence, surveillance, and reconnaissance platforms. American commanders were blinded by the attacks, which disabled or knocked out many of the Department of Defense systems used for communications and targeting. The Pentagon reverted to operating at a low-tech tempo it had not envisaged since the mid-1980s.

An array of ground-launched antiship missiles, air-launched cruise missiles, and fleets of hard-to-detect submarines met four American naval battle groups dispatched to the region. After losing several destroyers and the first

U.S. carrier since World War II, the president ordered the battle groups to retreat. The war had already cost the world trillions of dollars. Cries for the Western allies to stand down grew far and wide. Plans to send in the Rangers and other U.S. Special Operations forces were rejected. Justice and his regiment were taken off standby—there would be no deployment.

China seized on the hesitation, demanding all Western forces to cease engagement at once. The PLA struck valuable Western commercial satellites with high-energy lasers, claiming they were military surrogates. Key components of modern infrastructure began to fail across the globe. The antisatellite strikes coincided with massive cyber attacks against civilian transportation and energy systems inside the United States, Australia, Japan, and Europe. Railways, airports, and power plants were shut down, leaving major cities blacked out and helpless for weeks.

The cost of restoring lost space and commercial assets alone crossed into the tens of trillions of dollars. Strategists argued the tide of war could not be overturned. The PLA had landed thousands of troops on the western shores of Taiwan and thousands more were parachuted in. America's Congress demanded an immediate cessation of U.S. involvement. The White House decided to pull the plug. Australia and Japan followed suit.

The dragon had risen, breathed fire on the hawk, and without question ended America's next century of domination. That was five years ago. Now, the small CONTRA strike force Justice led had intended to enter and exit occupied Taiwan without detection. They had trained for months to execute the operation. NATO was making due on years of promises to reassert democratic principles in Asia. It was finally happening. Whether or not The Revolution was a Chinese puppet didn't matter—new engagement was taking place and CONTRA was the tip of the spear.

"X-One to Blue Team, X-One to Blue Team, we are in the zone," a NATO pilot's voice came over the radio.

"Copy X-One, we are in the ring," Grace replied. Standing beside Justice and Gideon, she grasped the cross around her neck and softly recited the Hail Mary as she awaited their incoming rescue angels. Still miles away—and out of sight of ordinary human eyes—Grace saw the Shadowhawks clearly.

"While you spoke with the General I instructed a dozen operators to remain on the top slope," Gideon reported. "They'll defend our exit in case Resistance lines break."

Looking east through high-powered binoculars, Justice scanned the horizon. He couldn't pick the Shadowhawks up at first. He monitored the data links on the interior of his visor, then found them.

"Here they come," Justice announced. "When the first bird lands, direct all troops to board. Each gunship will have a cover team."

"Yes, sir."

Gideon started off. Justice grabbed him by the arm.

"We leave no one behind." Justice's hardened brown eyes were filled with the magnitude of previous losses.

Gideon nodded, respectful of the Ranger code.

"The rebels are retreating!" a CONTRA soldier yelled over the radio.

"Fall back and use up your grenades," Justice calmly instructed. "They'll do us no good on the ride back." He noticed Grace in prayer again, her lips moved softly between communications with the Shadowhawk pilots. Justice figured it was a good time for praying. The worst thing about fighting the PLA was their sheer numbers. The occupying force alone had more standing soldiers than most nations. Their nearest base was less than four miles away. It must have emptied by now.

Two Shadowhawks raced over the East China Sea at hypersonic speeds. They crossed Taiwan's coastline and swerved low through the Jade Mountains and over the Nantzuhsien River Basin. Hovering to a near standstill in seconds, the Shadowhawks vertically landed in their stealthy black skin at the rendezvous site within the Alishan Forest.

Engraved NATO insignias marked each side of the gunships. The winged fighter-transports would become CONTRA's trademark. Gunners manned laser cannons on each side of the exterior ports. A platoon of fresh CONTRA troops dismounted from each Shadowhawk to cover the operators about to board.

The soldiers from the Shadowhawks wore full-armor CONTRA battle-suits. The lightweight armor used nanotechnologies composed of flexible cloth that stiffened on kinetic impact. An outer layer of fabric could change colors to match immediate surroundings. Different lethal and nonlethal weapon systems were integrated into the battlesuits. Mini control panels at the forearms allowed operators to monitor battle management, intelligence feeds, and net-centric sensors at the push of a button or a verbal command. Strapped with the various tools used by Western Special Forces, the battle-suits provided a formidable advantage in the field. Exoskeleton variations offered superhuman strength.

"There's no way we can handle the garrison heading our way," Nightscope shouted. "As much as the Delta Force in me wants to stay, we need out of this mess—now."

"Between the devil and the deep blue sea, the Hawks are here," Xxplosive replied. "Kick the shift to high gear." Turning, he squeezed off rounds and ran up the grassy path toward the rendezvous. Nightscope trailed with several Resistance fighters keeping pace to either side of them. The men zigzagged through a lightly wooded patch of the forest.

Sweat ran from under Nightscope's helmet, mixing with smudged dirt on his face. Two Resistance fighters next to him took direct machine-gun fire to the chest. The fifty-caliber rounds ripped through their bodies. One man's arm severed and split in two at the shoulder. Blood splattered Nightscope's face. He sprinted faster, as did Xxplosive. The PLA followed them in their dash for life.

"Let's leave 'em a present," Xxplosive said, sliding to his knees. He thrust a detonator into the ground and got back up to full sprint within seconds—a move he'd practiced often in training. "Six, seven, eight, nine . . . ten." Xxplosive set off the detonation. The shaped charge blasted back toward the trailing PLA troops. An instant later a PLA rocket struck the Resistance front line, toppling a cypress tree. Xxplosive and Nightscope saw the tree fall as they crossed over the forested slope and headed down to the rendezvous site.

"Resistance is gonna have trouble," Nightscope uttered. A wounded Dutch operator struggled in front of him. He and Xxplosive helped the man as the entire CONTRA team hurried to board the Shadowhawks. Blood-soaked shrapnel wounds in the Dutch operator's arm drenched the Netherlands flag on his uniform and turned it deep red.

"You're gonna be fine," Xxplosive assured.

Justice ran up to Xxplosive and Nightscope.

"We gotta move. PACOM is picking up Chinese MiG's heading our way from the north. Go, go!"

"Got it, sir." Nightscope replied.

Justice continued giving orders as the last troops made it down the hillside. In full Ranger mode, years of training at the Fort Benning Army Infantry School kicked in to control his every motion, his every action.

Blue Team operators from the mission boarded the Shadowhawks while fresh CONTRA cover troops kept watch. Resistance fighters ran, wildly following the NATO retreat. Seeing their elite Western allies about to leave, they knew their lives were in great danger, their cause abandoned.

"It's a long way back to the Jade Mountains for those fellas," Justice said over the radio. "And the PLA won't be kind. Provide them cover where you can."

Nobody would return to help the Resistance.

Xxplosive dropped his battlepack and assisted the wounded Dutchman onto a Shadowhawk. Many other wounded were already on board. Grace was strapping herself into a seat as he picked up his gear and climbed aboard the opposite stealth transport, strapping himself in next to Nightscope.

"Picking up two fighters heading our way fast!" yelled one of the pilots at the boarding troops. "Get in now! If they lock on to us here, it's game over!"

"Everyone on! That's it—take off!" Justice shouted as he jumped in last.

As the Shadowhawks rose, Grace looked out the open-air side of the craft she flew in. A small group of Resistance fighters crossed the hilltop. They were heading for the forest line, east of the landing zone, where trails would lead them back to their hideouts. Just short of the forest one of the rebels unfurled the old Taiwanese flag before falling to gunfire.

"More death in another needless war," whispered Grace in empathetic sadness. That instant she felt a warm, tingling sensation flow throughout her entire body. It started from her core and spread to the tips of her fingers and toes. A blinding flash of light in her left eye followed. She plunged her head into her lap, covering her face with both hands.

It had been several years since the last occurrence. Grace had experienced the sensation often as a child. There was never any pain, but she could never understand *why* it happened or what it meant. The tingling and flash of light had scared her when she was young. It made Grace feel different, like something was wrong with her. She told her mother and father about it many times. They never seemed concerned and only smiled back, telling her, "You are Blessed." The sensation was more powerful this time around, like an earthquake shaking internally with perfect symmetrical force.

"Are you wounded? What's wrong?" Justice asked, coming to her side.

Grace lifted her head. Her hair fluttered from winds whipping through the interior of the Shadowhawk as the vacuum doors sealed shut and pilots prepared the thrusters. She regained her composure, holding back the powerful emotion that always followed the strange sensation and flash of light.

"I'm fine, sir." Wanting to change the subject, she asked, "Where are the Chinese MiGs? Is our escape clear?"

Justice hesitated before turning to the cockpit. "Pilot, any chance those MiG's get to us?"

"Can't be sure," the pilot spoke as if determined not to show fear. Perspiration leaked out of his every pore. Beads of sweat rolled off the back of his neck. His flight suit had turned dark green from all the moisture. "We have word a squadron of F-22s and unmanned interceptors have launched from Japan. They're nearing the zone and are authorized to engage anyone trailing our retreat."

An air exchange would have greater political implications that were harder to hide.

"So much for covert action," Grace muttered.

On the other Shadowhawk, Nightscope and Xxplosive slumped in their seats and let the adrenaline rush of battle dissipate. They watched several of the wounded CONTRA operators receive medical attention. Two Croatian soldiers across from them recounted the escape in their native tongue. English was the official language on any CONTRA mission, but the officers were too tired to enforce something so trivial.

Nightscope looked around at his fellow teammates. Everyone was dirty, panting, and beat. The exhaustion of two weeks of operating secretly, sleeping on the hard earth, and having no showers had ended. If none of the wounded died, the whole team would make it out alive. "Not bad. We could've all been buried down there," he said. His thoughts trailed off to the ground. "Wish we left on better terms."

Sitting next to him, Xxplosive leaned back and stared at the ceiling. A tired smile spread across his face.

"We brought the sting," Xxplosive said, rocking back a bit and putting up a fist bump. "They're gonna remember us at the front lines."

"Yeah, until next time," said Nightscope, meeting his friend's fist with his own.

"Until next time."

CHAPTER 3
APPROACHING DOOM
Panama Canal: April 25, 2035

Ripster bit into his lip and drew blood. The anticipation of avenging his pride and banishment intensified as a sinister plan, decades in the making, neared its fruition. Riding in the back of a plush limousine with Prowess and Likzi, The Revolution leaders headed to their most important meeting yet. For them, the deception on Earth neared its end. Soon open global war would commence and Nerrial's precious undertaking to bring peace would be over—a new beginning for Ripster and his cohorts.

"The diversion will work for us . . . and our masters," Ripster vowed, clenching his fist.

"You have blood on your chin," Prowess pointed out.

"Not as much as you have on your hands," Ripster chided.

Rain poured heavily. Starting at dusk, it came down harder as night fell. The full moon shined brightly on the Port of Balboa where large container ships from around the world docked. They had arrived several days earlier and awaited Revolution orders for loading. Several dozen additional ships lingered farther off the coast.

Ripster took steps to assure the vessels remained dispersed so as not to risk suspicion from the United States. Commercial tracking systems likely showed an influx of transports in the region, but most intelligence analysts weren't paying attention to what was happening in the Atlantic Ocean off of Panama.

American satellites and High Altitude Airships provided their intelligence community with persistent surveillance over the volatile South American region where violence, refugees, and death continued spreading—thanks to

The Revolution. Fierce battles raged in the jungles, countryside, and throughout small villages. Drug cartels and paramilitary forces were cooperating to outmatch and outmaneuver the military and law enforcement organizations of Latin American governments.

The fighting had spilled into the streets of larger cities including Valencia and Medellin, where terrified communities lashed out at failed government attempts to quell the surge of violence. Everyone called it the "Drug Wars," but narcotics were, in actuality, trivial compared to what was shaping the region.

Premeditated turmoil. Deceptive strategy. The Revolution.

Ripster, Prowess, and Likzi—known to both their superiors and subordinates within The Revolution as "The Three"—equipped rebel forces worldwide with the planet's most advanced weapons. Working with sophisticated criminal enterprises, they coordinated every complex aspect of The Revolution, recruiting lawless volunteers across the globe. Their nefarious mission dwarfed any previous activity the criminal underground had ever engaged in. Every available immoral soul was needed for the plan to succeed—a sort of Axis of the Underground was built to ensure it did.

The container ships inconspicuously encircling the Port of Balboa had arrived from around the world. Most ship crews came from Colombia where The Revolution made its home in the Southern Hemisphere. The Port of Balboa became an easy recruiting ground from among the numerous deckhands. Most nominees refused to join until they saw the loot offered as payment. More hard cash, jewelry, and gold were cast in front of hungry human eyes than ever before. The willing pool of drug runners and paramilitaries also cooperating with The Revolution grew exponentially.

Assuming control over several worldwide shipping companies represented a major component of the plan. Making a significant military, financial, or logistical contribution was a prerequisite to join the upper echelons of the secretive Revolution; that much was made clear when The Three asked new collaborators to unite. Human traffickers, drug smugglers, arms dealers, prostitutes, cyber-criminals, the Russian mafia, Colombian drug cartels, corrupt government officials—all worked in compartmentalized malevolence to profit from and gain power with The Revolution.

Remuneration from The Three came quick and in large quantity to willing accomplices. Nobody cared about what would happen next, they just signed on. The promised plan would be revealed at a time The Three chose. So the story went, over and over again to the various bandits and high-powered mercenaries around the world.

Secret networks of corporations and business fronts operating legitimate and criminal enterprises supported the effort, this much Western intelligence knew from bits and pieces of information collected over the past three years. How did it all come together? Who was behind it? These answers remained a mystery to the outside world.

The Three needed to keep their secrets for only a few more days.

The current operation was an important affair. Intensified Revolution recruitment brought droves of jobless and disaffected recruits searching for rumored payoffs that exceeded reason. Farmers, shop owners, and miners became willing criminals. Looking the other way was easier than watching their child go hungry. Like a cryptic evil rising from the mist, The Revolution's tentacles tightened their grasp over the region, upholding a clever shroud of secrecy from those who sought to destroy it.

In 1999, when America ended its control of the Panama Canal, it handed control of the waterway over to the world's largest shipping corporation— a Chinese company with the transnational infrastructure, personnel, and equipment to run whatever independent operations it deemed profitable. The Three paid off the company's executive board with millions of dollars in gold and bought open access to the canal for The Revolution. At the same time, they exploited the ongoing Drug Wars, using them as the perfect distraction for American leaders unconvinced U.S. preeminence had ended, even in South America.

The Three wanted diversions in any form. Mercenaries and the criminal underworld wanted to be paid. Colluding Chinese wanted the U.S. to focus its attention away from Asia.

Everyone got what they wanted.

The Drug Wars forced thousands of refugees to flee in every direction to escape the fighting. South American governments clamored for U.S. aid. American support came in the form of weapons, intelligence, and training to indigenous forces. The Drug Wars had entered an unexpected phase for participating conspirators. The scale and number of attacks against regional government forces and civilian centers were hard to track.

Hundreds of innocent people and security forces were dying in weekly battles. Various drug cartel and paramilitary commanders refused to take credit for the upsurge, unaware that The Revolution had large numbers of its own warriors. These red and black uniformed soldiers, who never spoke, provided security to The Three. Conspirators never saw the uniformed Revolution in large numbers and thought they were only a handful of guards who were ordered to keep silent. The truth was much different. The warriors numbered in the thousands. They carried out large-scale covert operations, performed all tasks in utter secrecy, and did so with fervent loyalty.

Thirty miles from the Port of Balboa, columns of uniformed Revolution troops moved alongside the southern edge of the Panama Canal. They marched just under the cover of the jungle on old transport roads once used by traders and merchants. By 2030, corporations and companies colluding with The Three owned most of the property on both sides of the canal, registering ownership under unfamiliar and untraceable names. The corporations were all different, but they had one commonality—they were part of a carefully orchestrated plan to permanently alter the balance of international power.

After decades of careful calculation everything had come together. Commencement would begin tonight for The Three. The players had bought into the promises and accepted the bribes—whether in the form of euros, dollars, diamonds, or drugs. The participants were never told the full extent of the anarchic plot. Most didn't care. It was big and it paid well. Some even understood that the world would *never* be the same after it was over.

Columns of Revolution troops stretched for miles into the deep jungle, winding around thicker parts of the forest, sometimes crossing through new paths created to avoid detection by the locals. The soldiers were clad in black armored battlesuits with red trimming. The reflection of the moon shimmered off their wet, futuristic helmets. Onward they marched, moving closer to the positions they would hold until final orders were given. The meeting taking place at Balboa that night would decide when those crowning orders would be executed.

Lee and Jiang manned the watchtower overlooking the Balboa port. They were part of a low-key PLA presence and knew something of great consequence was about to take place. Most evenings were dull and boring. The infantrymen would take turns napping on sleeping bags snuck into the watchtower, play cards, or surf the Internet.

In recent weeks, things had begun to change.

Their commanding officer ordered extra vigilance. He confiscated their diversions and told them to act professional. "No breaks, no food, and no smoking during shift," he had ordered. Lee and Jiang were not in uniform, but followed instructions as if they were still in their infantry unit on Hainan Island. They hadn't worn a PLA uniform since they arrived in Panama— they weren't even supposed to be in the country. A corrupted PLA officer colluding with The Revolution selected them for a "special mission" five months prior. Lee and Jiang were loaded onto one of the newest Chinese nuclear submarines and told they would be traveling to Taiwan to assist with hunting Resistance fighters.

The PLA was well known for deceiving foreigners. It treated its own soldiers with similar disregard. Both Lee and Jiang were smart enough not to question their assignment. They thought it was odd, being transferred to Taiwan on a nuclear-powered stealth submarine, but did not want to question orders. The fear of imprisonment and torture made saluting without argument the safest choice.

"What do you think is going on?" Jiang asked, peering down out of the watchtower. "The luxury cars have been arriving all day. We have been here for months and not seen one. Those people arriving last were white, not Latino."

"They spoke Russian," Lee said. "I'm almost sure of it."

"Why would they be at our base?"

"This is not *our* base, Jiang. We are never to speak in such terms," Lee snapped, trying to keep his friend in line. "The Americans might be listening," he whispered.

Jiang nodded to acknowledge Lee's effort to look out for their own good. Their commanding officers didn't like slip-ups and Jiang was known for his clumsiness. As he spit out the toothpick he'd been chewing on, a piercing shriek cut through the stillness. Lee and Jiang covered their ears to block out the shrill cry. It lasted several seconds before the night returned to silence. They looked at each other with wide eyes.

"What was that?" Lee whispered.

"I have never heard anything like it. It must have been a wild animal of the jungle," Jiang said.

"An animal! There are no animals that make such a noise, you idiot!" Lee exclaimed. "We would have heard that before, Jiang. Think!"

Jiang looked back at his friend and trembled. "Don't be frightened," he mumbled to himself. Two weeks ago, Jiang swore to Lee he saw ghosts outside their bunkhouse. There were three of them, he recounted, talking in a strange language, their eyes shining red. He told Lee they looked like demonic soldiers. Lee was uninterested, telling Jiang he'd been dreaming and couldn't tell the difference between his own dreams and reality. Jiang insisted, but to no avail.

The men sat in silence now, alternately staring at one another then looking back out over the sprawling port complex. A limousine approached. It passed through the gate as the other luxury vehicles had. At first it seemed there was nothing different about the newest arrival.

The limo parked and four figures exited. The last person barely fit through the door. His broad shoulders and long frame made him look nonhuman. "That one won't be sleeping in the bunk beds," Jiang commented. "He's far too big."

Lee ignored him. Neither of the guards could discern the nationality of the four. They wore dark cloaks and did not speak a word. Juan Carlos Hernandez, a powerful drug kingpin, approached the new arrivals and greeted them. Before the group disappeared through the main warehouse door, one of them turned to the large figure. The man leaned in as if to whisper something. He made a gesture toward the hangar on the opposite side of the port. Before whirling back around, an unmistakable flash of red light emitted from his left eye.

Jiang immediately put his hand on Lee's shoulder. He gripped it tight. "I was not dreaming. You saw?"

Lee had, and something deep inside him understood life at the port was about to change for the worse.

CHAPTER 4
FATE
Hermosa Beach: April 20, 2035

Sirens blared somewhere in the distance. Troy felt like they were going off in his head. Standing in front of his bathroom mirror he thought he looked different. Tired of the self-pity, his eyes were heavy. He saw the puffy, black bags beneath them, formed from the sleepless nights and guilt that infected him. The dedicated warrior lay dormant. Shutting off the bathroom light, he walked into the living room.

The decommissioning was on his mind again.

Troy stopped next to an enlarged photograph hanging in his hallway. Taken moments after returning from Africa in 2031, it captured the CIA director of National Clandestine Services (NCS) pinning a Defense Superior Service medal on Troy's uniform. The medal displayed a silver eagle gripping three arrows in its claws and brandishing the shield of the United States underneath an arch of thirteen stars and atop a wreath of laurel. Troy earned the honor by single-handedly rescuing two CIA operatives held hostage by Sudanese insurgents responsible for brutal murders and extortion plots against friendly governments in the region and attempting to blackmail the U.S. government.

In exchange for the CIA agents and the incriminating intelligence files they possessed, the rebels demanded $250 million dollars. The sensitive nature of the CIA operatives' mission and secret files raised the possibility of actually paying the ransom. The National Security Council recommended to the president a swift payment in exchange for the operatives and files before news of the hostage situation broke. The CIA protested the decision and requested the opportunity for a covert mission where plausible deniability wouldn't harm the ransom exchange if the mission failed.

Instead of paying the enemy, the CIA Special Activities Division (SAD) sent Troy McBride. Dressed as a farmhand, Troy snuck into a rebel safe house and killed eight guards with silent weapons. He reclaimed the precious intelligence files while tagging two additional adjoining insurgent complexes with GPS sensors. Unmanned Predator drones destroyed all three buildings as Troy led the rescued CIA operatives to safety through the outskirts of Khartoum.

Troy never failed a mission during his tenure with the agency. He became a hero within the CIA and a legend within the Special Ops community. Troy's military file listed him as an agent of the CIA Special Operations Group (SOG), the paramilitary wing of SAD. It remained Troy's official unit throughout his term of service and into CONTRA.

Troy slowly moved away from the commemorative photo and planted himself on the couch. With over a thousand channels available on Internet television, only Station One News, history programming, and documentaries about outer space really interested him. His father always watched shows about astronomy and the universe. Somehow, it became an interest of Troy's as well. He couldn't indulge in sports since his decommission. ESPN used to be his favorite channel, but he didn't care anymore.

Troy watched a Station One report on the destabilization of world affairs. A controversy had erupted over the declassified CIA assessment of the threat posed by The Revolution. Dramatic commentators from various cable news stations had demanded knowing why the first Critical Event remained classified. "The public wants answers!" they shouted. Troy knew the CIA wanted answers, too. He turned off the TV and sat in dark silence. Only the pre-funk partygoers making their way to the pier outside interrupted the quiet.

Earlier, his neighbor had asked if Troy wanted to head down for a drink. The Hermosa bars were busy on any decent evening. Maybe he'd still go. Right now, his mind was elsewhere—The Revolution. Troy had been instrumental in tracking its origins even before CONTRA's establishment. He could not forget the threat or his old habits of analysis.

Sitting in the dark, Troy considered the strength of The Revolution—its undetected rise to power shouldn't have been possible. There were too many mysteries surrounding the group to understand where it came from or who was calling the shots. At first, The Revolution was compared to an Al-Qaeda copycat that replaced religious zeal with economic contempt. They were assumed to be a new group of violent intellectuals aligning themselves with the renewed antiglobalization movement.

Most pundits speculated that the eleven-page Revolution Declaration sent to Western officials was a blatant attempt to gain attention. Dozens of grandiose references made to the "whole of mankind" and "untold histories of the universe" were preceded by a series of oddly construed caveats about world anarchy and threats against Western governments. It quickly led the Declaration to recycling bins.

However, the document didn't go entirely unheeded. Several sections of the Revolution Declaration referenced classified information on strategic defense systems inaccessible by the public. It disturbed a group of intelligence officials sufficiently to warrant further investigation. A small, secretive unit established within the Black Operations wing of the Pentagon—called Nightwatch—received the assignment under a joint CIA-Special Operations Command tasking. Troy was assigned to Nightwatch as the lead CIA-SAD agent.

Only after the first of three incidents—later termed the Critical Events—did top Pentagon officials become truly alarmed about The Revolution's nature.

The first Critical Event, still classified to the public and even to most government officials, occurred in 2033. On a counter-narcotics mission near Matarca, Colombia, U.S. Marines and multinational antidrug operatives stumbled upon a heavily guarded bioengineering laboratory deep in the Amazon jungle, nicknamed Demon Lab because of the hellish genetic experiments performed there. DNA strands of differing animal species were combined with human strands at the lab in an attempt to create a new breed of wickedly intelligent and menacing mammal.

An intense firefight ensued between counter-narcotics forces and fleeing soldiers who were later identified as belonging to The Revolution. The battle destroyed most of the Demon Lab. The Marines reported that several red and black clad Revolution guards directed the cartel guerillas and mercenaries protecting the lab. One of the guards, shot dead and burned by the retreating paramilitaries upon the Marine assault, did not appear completely human to medical teams examining the body. Speculation was that the guard underwent a genetic mutation of some sort, perhaps as a lab guinea pig. His skin was too badly burned to know for certain.

What The Revolution left behind startled many.

Significant amounts of collected evidence showed cooperation taking place between various criminal and paramilitary organizations around the world, as was suggested by previously declassified CIA reports. However, never reported and kept classified to everyone except the highest ranking U.S. officials, was the degree to which the Demon Lab was technologically advanced. Symbols on the lab's walls indicated it belonged to The Revolution. Photos of the labs interior showed several jagged patterns of symmetrically arranged diamonds, which matched markings included within the original Revolution Declaration.

The advancements in technology present at the lab were beyond any known Western capability. Speculation inside the intelligence community erupted. Troy worked tirelessly with Nightwatch after the Demon Lab's discovery and he tracked The Revolution in an attempt to uncover its origins. Mysterious references to three leaders began to surface. They were simply called The Three. Several witnesses identified two males and one female.

Fearful Colombian villagers and captured mercenaries insisted The Three possessed supernatural powers and wielded an endless trove of cash, diamonds, and weaponry. Intelligence on the leaders was hard to gather. Corroborated by captured guerrillas, rumors, and frightened villagers from the first Revolution attacks, anyone who'd ever seen the leaders feared them. They had reportedly built battlesuits far superior to the Western types just recently introduced into the battlefield.

The Three became Nightwatch's primary target. The covert CIA-Special Ops unit traversed the world, chasing clues and rumor. The Three were believed to either finance or direct the creation of the Demon Lab. They were hard to track or locate. Their trail went cold even though The Revolution became more active in its operations and connection to the criminal underworld. Once, Nightwatch was within six hours of raiding a Moroccan hideout where The Three had been meeting with arms smugglers. Only weeks later, the nuclear tragedy in Iran took place—the second Critical Event.

A group of thieves wearing the jagged mark of The Revolution stole several warheads from Iran's main nuclear site. When surrounded by Iranian troops outside of Isfahan the thieves detonated one of the warheads, causing over twenty thousand deaths. The event triggered worldwide panic and grief. The Iranian government had no idea why the theft had occurred on its soil, but it was clear to Western intelligence officials that The Revolution was a grave threat. When the third and last of the Critical Events occurred, fierce dialogue on the potential origins and dangers posed by the group was taking place.

In March of 2034, dozens of armed mercenaries brazenly attacked NATO's Brussels, Belgium, headquarters. The gunmen wore uniforms and the symbol associated with The Revolution. The consequent firefight and mortar barrage claimed the lives of eighty-two NATO personnel and wounded three times that number. Many of the dead and injured were high-ranking officials from various allied nations. For the first time, reports of a militant group called "The Revolution" surfaced on broadcast television and the Internet. American and NATO officials downplayed the new group's existence.

Simultaneously, the North Atlantic Council approved the creation of a

Top Secret strike force charged with searching for and destroying The Revolution. Since the mission was Counter-Revolutionary, the strike force was codenamed CONTRA. The Black Operations wing of the Pentagon dissolved Nightwatch and Troy transferred into CONTRA as the CIA Special Operations representative.

The transfer meant a lot to Troy. His father, Joseph McBride, was nominated as CONTRA's civilian director after serving a long career involved in transatlantic affairs. General William Taylor—who Troy had known since childhood—was named commander. Troy never worked with either of them, but he appreciated the keen, even fervent, interest both his father and General Taylor had in combating The Revolution and uncovering what was behind it. The honor of serving in CONTRA could not have been more absolute for Troy.

In the inaugural speech christening the first operational teams, Troy listened to his father say, "Never forget the Critical Events leading to the creation of this historic NATO force. You will protect history and bend the future back in our favor. In doing so, Western ideals will be reestablished in unity and the new Al-Qaeda will be destroyed. Beyond The Revolution, we must find a new enlightenment that guides the world away from war and fear. We begin by promising to end this scourge before it grows." Troy watched and listened to the speech with a sense of pride, understanding that fate had brought him to the right place.

The Revolution proved capable of carrying out complicated operations in preparation for what it called "the coming downfall of freedom on Earth." Nightwatch had uncovered disquieting signs that disturbed Troy: three mysterious leaders with a mythical fear among their followers; futuristic genetic experimentation transcending leading Western scientific capabilities; and a singular dedication to wreaking havoc by orchestrating an underground axis of evil.

These nuggets of information were shared with the entire intelligence community. The remaining Nightwatch revelations remained classified to U.S. Black Operations and CONTRA. After Nightwatch's disassembly, The Revolution remained an ill-omened mystery, demonstrating an almost surreal ability to appear, wreak havoc, and vanish like a shadow with fangs. Mercenaries, criminals, and rogue terrorists working together in disciplined cohesion, but how did the movement originate?

This question motivated NATO to form CONTRA.

Troy felt uneasy being off the trail of The Revolution for so long while its evil movement grew stronger. He had committed himself to exposing its origins and unmasking The Three. Sitting alone on his couch in the dark, Troy knew he still had a destiny to fulfill. Being wrongly decommissioned from the military could not be the end of his purpose.

He took out the Airborne Screaming Eagles coin General Taylor gave him so long ago and flipped it between his fingers. Troy never stopped believing in its inscription: Rendezvous with Destiny. He had to figure out how to recapture his purpose in life. Somewhere the world still needed him. That was the one thing Troy wouldn't give up on.

His destiny.

CHAPTER 5
ALLIED HONOR
Kadena Air Base, Japan: April 20, 2035

The Shadowhawks sped full throttle out of Taiwanese airspace toward Japan, carrying the CONTRA Blue Team. Justice faded in and out of an uncomfortable sleep during the flight. When the Shadowhawks landed at Kadena Air Base, he was the first off. He jumped onto the tarmac, his legs bent like licorice and it hurt to blink his bloodshot eyes.

Night had fallen and powerful floodlights illuminated the Shadowhawk landing pads. Justice did his best to look poised in front of the Blue Team, but the exhaustion and stress of a failed mission had caught up with him. Wobbling to the side of the Shadowhawk, Justice leaned against the hull and took in his surroundings. The smell of jet fuel was strong. Vehicles with flashing lights were approaching. Someone was shouting in Japanese.

Allied Base North Pacific, located at Kadena Air Base, was as good as home to CONTRA. One of three strike force command centers worldwide, it existed within a separate wing of the air base and served as a model for NATO's Pacific Integration Plan. NATO expanded military ties with all Pacific nations after the fall of Taiwan in 2030 and the United States provided its Pacific allies with access to almost all U.S. intelligence and weapons systems.

Washington didn't want Tokyo to become another Taipei.

At a secret North Atlantic Council meeting following the 2034 Revolution attacks on NATO headquarters, Japan and Australia were fully admitted into the alliance. Waning American power and European influence hurt more than just pride. For hundreds of years, Western nations had decided the course of human history—its future. Political authority was now spread throughout the world.

Decisions in India, China, Brazil, Iran, and Pakistan held great influence. Western economies and defense budgets had grown smaller. With the decline of America's military preeminence and the rise of China, forming new joint security arrangements through NATO trumped sovereignty concerns. Integrated joint forces could strengthen order and fill the American security vacuum. For this to happen on a large scale, CONTRA needed to succeed early as a test case. The strike force had to prove itself in the field.

Justice carried far more than the weight of a single counter-revolutionary mission in Taiwan.

Chinese MiG fighters had trailed the Shadowhawks on their escape. The MiGs refused to turn away over the East China Sea. An American F-22 shot one down. It would be an international incident the media would exploit. Justice had desperately wanted the operation to have a better outcome and he blamed himself. He'd been selected for CONTRA, but in his heart he was always a Ranger first.

He'd enlisted in the Army straight from high school, answering the call to serve with pride. Raised in the shadows of Mt. Rainer, he spent most childhood days running through the back trails, fighting imaginary battles with America's sworn enemies. He was nine-years-old the Christmas Eve his father told him pursuing justice was the best way to serve. The lights on the tree twinkled brighter in that very moment. It stuck with him and he chose his codename because of the memory.

General William Taylor—codenamed Patton and commander of all CONTRA forces—could have picked any number of more veteran officers to lead the Blue Team. Instead, he chose Justice. In the back of his mind, Justice questioned the decision. After all, he was the *second* choice. The original selection—Battlestar—was discharged in a scandal during the last phase of training. Justice wondered what he was up to. Troy should've been with CONTRA. They needed him.

Grace and Gideon trailed Justice off the Shadowhawk and leaned up against the hull next to him. Gideon tugged at the twirled ends of his black mustache, solemn. On the other hand, Grace looked fresh, as if just home from a shopping trip not a war zone.

"What now, Justice?" Grace tilted her head slightly in her empathetic way.

"Patton will want an overview. He can't be happy."

"Think he'll want that report tonight?"

"I'm certain."

The officers watched the rest of the dismounting CONTRA operators exit the fighter-transports and unload baggage and weapons. Some hobbled from injuries. All looked exhausted. Medical workers from the air base hurried the wounded into waiting ambulances. Lights flashing, the emergency vehicles accelerated toward the small military hospital next to the main hangars where Shadowhawks were kept hidden during the day.

At first, Justice hadn't noticed the torrent of medical personnel all around them. Now, he watched a Japanese nurse rush to the back door of an ambulance. Grabbing a fresh bag of gauze, she carried it to several troops sitting on the edge of a Shadowhawk and tended to their injuries. Justice gave silent thanks to be safe on solid ground; he briefly wondered if that counted as a prayer. Several CONTRA soldiers walked past him, saluting.

"Forget about what happened," Gideon advised. "We're alive. That's all that matters. Wait for the next mission, we'll make amends."

Justice nodded, fixated on the conclusion that the Blue Team's failure increased the chances of a groundswell in negative reaction from NATO officials already tentative about CONTRA's activation in the first place.

"Before we left . . . I was sure we'd uncover something. Wanted it bad on this one, Gideon."

"*Caro signore*. All of us do," Grace consoled. "This intelligence puzzle . . . it's a shamble. Nobody has the right answers on The Revolution. We'll find them. Believe."

Justice needed to believe. He and the Blue Team were part of a select few that understood The Revolution's magnitude. Justice had wanted to find answers in Taiwan. Even to those in CONTRA The Revolution did not make sense—a rogue group demonstrating a formidable capacity to awe in its brilliant atrocities rose to power without a trace of who guided it. If China were involved, things would make sense. The proxy force of a nation-state was understandable, but without one, the mystery of The Revolution continued.

The U.S. Defense Intelligence Agency assumed that because the 2030 invasion of Taiwan coincided with the release of the Revolution Declaration, there might be a link. Add in the advanced genetic experimentations found at the Demon Lab—similar to those seen in China—and many were convinced it proved state sponsorship or involvement of the Red Army. The Great Deception confirmed China was willing to go to great lengths to attain international power, but that did not present a plausible motivation for the PLA's orchestrating the Critical Events.

Justice needed more proof. He wasn't convinced of anything. China's erratic behavior was odd and aggressive to be sure. The country had also become well known for advancements in recombinant DNA—the same genetic bioengineering discovered in the Demon Lab—but still, why The Revolution? Was it more deception and diversion? But to what end?

The Chinese Great Deception leading up to the Battle of Taiwan fulfilled the Sun Tzu stratagem that "All war is based on deception." It worked. The brutal violence that followed sparked a new Cold War. The PLA administered its occupation with an iron fist, making the old Tiananmen Square massacre trivial in comparison. Nothing could have prepared Taiwan for what came next. China had seemed to become less hard-line in the years preceding the attack on Taiwan, but the invasion was one of those moments that changed the world.

Justice witnessed how the Resistance made things difficult for the PLA, however, the rebels controlled no territory and had to operate in ultimate secrecy—PLA spies were everywhere. That sordid occupation was not what brought CONTRA to Taiwan. A threat of even greater consequence did.

Western leaders were determined not to let another nongovernmental organization rise from obscurity into a global threat like Al-Qaeda had at the turn of the century. The Terror Wars ended after years of bloodshed. The historic peace in the Middle East was holding. Everyone wanted it to remain that way. The Holy Land Accords were the foundation for that historic peace and represented one of the greatest diplomatic achievements the world had ever known. Yet The Revolution posed far too many new problems, and officials did not want an old menace to return in a different form.

Justice had studied the electronic intercepts the Navy P-8 Poseidon surveillance aircraft captured from the PLA outpost of Chiayi. The stunner was when a Chinese intelligence colonel from the base spoke of "transferring more advanced shipments to the South American post for secret payments guaranteed . . . the rebels were performing well." Intelligence snippets such as that were hard to come by via signals or electronic intelligence. Fiber-optic cables and cryptic intranets transferred most of China's critical information throughout Taiwan.

CONTRA's mission had been to find out what cargo was being transferred to South America and to tap Chiayi's fiber-optic communications cables with NSA listening devices. CONTRA Headquarters asserted that uncovering China's role was key. Because the Blue Team mission in Taiwan failed, they might never know.

"If The Revolution is controlled by China, we will find out in time," Grace insisted, as if sensing Justice's thoughts. "There is nothing concealed that will not be disclosed, or hidden that will not be made known."

"Hope you're right, Grace. This war will define my life. Let's get inside."

Justice knew she was an idealist. Her poetry reflected that. In her file, Grace stated that witnessing the many tragedies, conflicts, and manifestations of greed driving the world toward its doom depressed her. Justice found that hard to imagine—Grace was one of the most positive people he'd ever met. Her upbeat attitude was contagious.

Xxplosive and Nightscope caught up to Justice, Gideon, and Grace as they reached the main entrance leading to the CONTRA Command Center. Guards from Japan's Central Readiness Force opened the doors for them. The Blue Team officers continued down a long, brightly lit hallway paved with white tiles gleaming from fluorescent lights overhead. The sound of squeaking military boots reverberated off the walls. Little décor lined the corridor except for an occasional poster of fighter aircrafts or armored vehicles.

The officers stopped where a NATO emblem made of embossed silver marked the entryway to the Command Center. Justice hit a code on the entrance panel and scanned his eyes into a biometrics reader that expanded outward from the wall. Unseen doors retracted into the sides of the corridor wall, splitting the NATO emblem into two symmetric halves and granting access to CONTRA command.

Each of CONTRA's three command centers—Kadena Air Base, Colorado Springs, and NATO Headquarters in Brussels—were designed exactly the same, so allied teams could operate fluidly at all three stations. The last time Justice and the other Blue Team officers set foot inside this operations center was the day before they departed for Taiwan. It seemed like ages ago to Justice although it had been only two weeks.

A gigantic flat screen covered the center wall of the command center's control room. The flat screen was dark at the moment. Half a dozen smaller ones surrounded it and were bright with Asian and American news coverage. The news was just breaking. Chinese state-run Xinhua reported that American fighter aircrafts opened fire on Chinese civilian and military jets off Taiwan's coast.

Station One was reporting a major military incident in the region, but could not confirm the details. CNN displayed stock footage of imagery from the Battle of Taiwan to conjure fears of another pending military engagement. The Pentagon was not providing any official comment or answering questions.

Two additional Blue Team officers—Sandstorm and Rapidfire—sat at a long center table beneath the giant central flat screen. A handful of NATO intelligence technicians staffed operations stations in the command center. Sandstorm and Rapidfire stayed behind on CONTRA Commander Patton's orders to maintain stealthier ground operations, process mission intelligence reports, and coordinate with regional allied forces supporting the CONTRA operation.

"Welcome back my brothers. It's a pleasure to see you again," Sandstorm said with sincerity and respect. As a Turkish Maroon Beret, Sandstorm rose to distinction serving undercover with anti-Jihadist Muslim forces called The New Brotherhood. The group sought to extinguish extremist factions during the final years of the Terror Wars. He recently commanded a peacekeeping taskforce in Palestine before taking his assignment with CONTRA.

"Glad to be back. Thank you, Sandstorm," Justice replied.

"I guarantee you I'm not staying back next mission. I can vacation elsewhere," Rapidfire said, clearly miffed. He was the Blue Team's advanced weapons specialist from the Czech Republic. He outfitted the team's battlesuits, making sure the new, conventional, guided, and laser weapons operated to spec. Rapidfire would add custom innovations where he could.

"I'll need a word with you on that next operation. We're gonna need some important changes I want you to oversee," Justice said. He thought Rapidfire looked pleased by the comment.

The returning Blue Team officers sat down in the plush chairs surrounding the center table and visibly relaxed. For several minutes they stared at the news monitors and satellite feeds. Sandstorm poured tea and set a welcome bottle of cold water in front of each returning officer while a NATO technician brought up the aerial view of the engagement that followed their retreat. Justice watched with great interest.

Lydia Lewis was reporting live on Station One. She happened to be the foremost media expert on The Revolution and sister of Nathan Lewis, a Gray Team CONTRA officer codenamed Satellite. Lydia's voice radiated with the understanding and preparation of a seasoned reporter. She confirmed unnamed senior Pentagon officials' authenticated reports of a military altercation near Taiwan. The secretary of defense was about to release a short statement denying China's version of the incident.

Sandstorm muted the volume. "I know you want to rest—and you deserve it—but Commander Patton is waiting," he urged, pulling up a chair next to Justice.

I'm sure he is, thought Justice. *I don't know if I'm ready.*

After taking another sip of the hot black tea Sandstorm had poured for all, Justice stood up to indicate he was ready. Sandstorm motioned to a technician and the giant center flat screen of the command center beamed to life, displaying a metallic NATO symbol against a blue backdrop. The screen quickly changed to a live image of Commander Patton in Colorado Springs, CONTRA's headquarters.

Patton wore a dark navy NATO service uniform and smiled genuinely. Prior to receiving his fourth star in transition to CONTRA, he commanded U.S. Army Special Operations. An old-school general with a big heart, Patton loved the troops and equally despised any adversary they faced. A hybrid warfare specialist whose combat experience began with covert cross-border operations between Afghanistan and Pakistan, he had studied counterinsurgency, counterterrorism, and the evolution of modern war for over thirty years. Patton revered the valor of the famed American World War II general from which he took his codename.

"Good evening, sir," Justice struggled to sound energetic.

"Colonel Justice, I've been following your every move, including your escape, as best I can. I'm proud of your team. Well done." Patton paused. "If a fighter does his best, what else is there?"

"Yes, sir, and thank you."

"No need for the long version. You need rest. I just want to hear it from you instead of reading it in a report. A quick assessment," Patton looked through the screen like a father wanting the truth.

"The first week and a half went according to plan. We delivered all weapons to the Resistance and were able to establish the desired rapport. They needed the weapons shipment. Unfortunately, the Resistance has entered a weakened state. They are being broken, contrary to some optimistic analysis."

"Tragic situation, I concur."

"We tried to pull any Intel they had on The Revolution. They knew nothing. I shared the Poseidon intercepts, but General Chiang seemed confused and didn't have much sympathy. Had different objectives nearer at hand."

"What of the fiber-optic cables?"

"We attached NSA sensors on two of the three main fiber-optic lines running out of the Red Base command zone near Chiayi. On our last sweep a PLA patrol spotted us and the firefight started. The third sensor would've been attached tomorrow morning."

"Any uniformed guards that looked like Revolution?"

"Not that we saw."

"A number on PLA casualties?"

"Dozens for sure, maybe upward of fifty or sixty. They were a mix of 31st Army and Immediate Action Units. That part of our Intel was correct. The IAUs ran that zone."

"Precious defenses for the PLA to put there. The IAU is reserved for critical operations. It could be to keep the Resistance at bay and away from Chiayi. Interesting though. If I was a Chinese military commander working with The Revolution, the IAU would get my vote to defend our secret."

There was a long pause. "How will this affect CONTRA?" Justice asked.

"I imagine it won't."

Patton's answer surprised Justice. *How could it not?*

"Get your team to rest. That's an order. We'll talk more when you return to base."

Grace rushed in front of the monitor before Patton could sign off.

"Commander, is the Gray Team active in theater?" she asked, her eyes wide with the eagerness that comes from genuine concern.

"Nearing their objective as we speak. My very best to you, officers." The NATO symbol flashed and the screen turned blue then went dark.

Justice and Grace stared at the blank screen. Sandstorm unmuted the news coverage. The purr from the excitable media coupled with the glowing TV monitors gave the room an urgent feel, as if the CONTRA mission defined a crossroads in the world's future. Weariness and stress did not overshadow Justice's dedication to ensure it was a better road. His mind shifted to what was taking place halfway around the world, deep in the Colombian jungle. His beloved Red was there.

"I'll say a prayer for her!" Grace shouted as Justice exited the command center, once again leaving him to wonder how Grace always knew his thoughts.

CHAPTER 6
JUNGLE'S PREY
Southern Colombia: April 22, 2035

"Shitty luck right now," Raption griped quietly, fresh out of water.

No matter how much he kept sucking on the rubber straw protruding perfectly out of his battlesuit, his body continually asked for more. The temperature control in his battlesuit broke soon after the Gray Team insertion into the Colombian theater. CONTRA battlesuits were heavy, the heat was a killer, and now, all of Raption's water was gone. Gasping for deliverance from the discomfort, he neared the point of begging for a water break. Raption only had one memory of being this thirsty, long before his military days, when rock concerts were everything. Back in the glory days Bruce Springsteen sang about…

The summer of his senior year in high school, Raption and two friends ended up in the California desert on a different mission of sorts. Mitch and Marcos showed up drunk at his parent's Santa Monica house with two tickets to the biggest rock event of the year, Coachella Summerfest. His best friends did not have a ticket for him but had enough guile to ask for a ride halfway across the California desert where the rock festival occurred.

"Why didn't you bastards get *me* a ticket?" Raption shouted, bummed out.

"Dude, they were sold out online. I already *told* you that. We got them from Mitch's fat-ass neighbor," Marcos said. "We're just drinkin' in the backyard and he was like, 'I can't go cause my wife is pregnant.' Ha! So he just gave us his tickets. Didn't even ask us to pay! Can you believe that?" Marcos laughed.

"Well that's great, assholes. What am I supposed to do?"

"We'll hook you up at the show…?" Mitch pleaded with an unconvincing shrug.

Raption did what any wild teenager would do—he borrowed his parents' car without asking.

The trio was somewhere between Los Angeles and Indio when the car battery died. It was July and over one hundred degrees on a dusty stretch of California State Route 60. They were out of water. Running late to the concert, the three longhaired, shirtless teens wearing baggy shorts and pierced lips and tattoos weren't prime hitchhiking candidates for picking up in the middle of nowhere. Finally, after two hours, a farmer told them to jump in the back of his rickety pickup.

With cracked, parched lips, Raption had stared up at the desert sky in the bed of that truck, thinking his parents were going to kill him. Then he passed out from heat exhaustion and dehydration. He woke to Marcos and Mitch pouring ice water over his head at a gas station and fighting over whose fault it was for being late to the concert. They eventually made it in time to catch their favorite band play. Raption got a scalped ticket and forever cherished the legendary adventure.

He had never been thirstier, until now—a lifetime away from that memory.

The Amazon rainforest was sweating like a sopping sauna towel compressing itself on Raption's body. Its suffocation was inescapable. There was not the slightest breeze or lapse in humidity within the mosaic of tropical foliage surrounding the Gray Team. Moving soundlessly through the thickness of leaves, branches, and tree cover, only the wild inhabitants stirred the depths of the pristine jungle. Fresh rain had not fallen for a day. Instead, a brutal heat bore down on the CONTRA strike force as they forged ahead twenty miles southwest of Matarca, Colombia, alongside the Caqueta River.

Second Company, CONTRA Battalion—or Gray Team—had been moving for almost forty hours straight after being dropped in by advanced Pave

Hawk II helicopters. The Gray Team searched in the area of the Amazon rainforest where the mystery of The Revolution had begun. The intelligence community thought there was more to find. The Gray Team was looking for a secret base of operations or a Revolution hideout for The Three, anything to justify the scientific investment uncovered two years ago in the Demon Lab. The continued escalation in Drug War violence around Colombia that started spreading from that exact vicinity was another indicator something was amiss in the jungle.

The Gray Team's commanding officer, a seasoned British Special Air Service (SAS) veteran codenamed Crosshill had assigned Raption as the point man on the search operation. He'd told Raption, "You'll take point. We got over fifty on the team. Stay tight. Never liked the way a place like this separates a unit."

Formerly a U.S. Marine jungle warfare specialist, Raption had been to Colombia on five diverse missions with a multinational counter-narcotics brigade tasked with disrupting and destroying expanding drug cartel operations in the Amazon. Raption was the only member of CONTRA who had witnessed the gruesome Demon Lab discoveries exposing the first real evidence of The Revolution's power and potential for evil. The detection happened near their current location and marked the first Critical Event leading to the creation of CONTRA.

Raption considered telling Crosshill that the team needed a breather. *He has to give the order soon. We cannot hold this pace much longer.* Raption looked back at the rest of the trailing unit. Many of them were obscured by the jungle's thickness. He could see Breakdown and Satellite on his left.

Sweat poured from under the perspiration-soaked bandana wrapped around Breakdown's head. Trickling down his face, the large drops actually fell to the earth. Breakdown resembled a runner holding on to finish a marathon. A Green Beret, action kept him on the move, regardless of any hardship.

Breakdown spent his free time driving a NASCAR replica on the hobby circuit and promoting Hispanic hip-hop music in neighborhoods most people would not dare visit. He thrived on his Mexican roots and wanted to make a difference in the lives of troubled young people. Breakdown had let Raption drive his replica racecar once at the Orange County Speedway; a rush he enjoyed more than skydiving.

Behind Breakdown was Satellite, an Air Force C4ISR specialist and the foremost technologist in CONTRA. Raption noted that Satellite wore his special control goggles to monitor incoming readings from a tactical drone—the Perceptor—which hovered somewhere above the Gray Team. The unmanned system fed intelligence to Satellite through its sensor array. Satellite had designed the Perceptor himself when he worked for the Defense Advanced Research Projects Agency (DARPA).

Raption enjoyed listening to Satellite expound on his love for gadgets and CONTRA was a playground for technological toys. Recognized as one of the most gifted inventors in the entire U.S. military, Satellite could have been making the big bucks at Boeing or Raytheon. There were guys like Satellite in the labs, but not many in the field, which is where he chose to be. Raption peered upward to catch a glimpse of the Perceptor.

The drone's situational awareness was priceless—it was CONTRA's eyes and ears. Every now and again Satellite would spot or hear something through one of the sensors. He would raise his hand and the team would stop. The sensors tripped often since the Amazon rainforest was home to one-tenth of the entire world's species. Up to this point the culprits had been harmless animals or one of those noises the jungle makes. Thanks to the Perceptor, no matter how thick the jungle seemed, CONTRA still had full knowledge of what lay around them.

Raption, Breakdown, and Satellite were in the lead with the Perceptor overhead. Crosshill and Diamond followed right behind them.

Crosshill commanded the Gray Team. He inspired with a charisma that fueled boldness. In his civilian life, Crosshill dressed in Armani suits and sipped expensive wines. Raption liked to call him "Bond." Inside of his military profession, Crosshill was a tough astute officer with combat experience in some of the world's roughest corners.

Diamond, the Gray Team's second in command, seemed least affected by the sweltering heat. Raption saw that as a perfect contradiction. He loved the contradictions about Diamond, but then again, he loved many things about her. A sniper from Iceland, she carried her AWM rifle with one hand and cared for it with a tenderness usually reserved for living things. Diamond soundlessly took each step—ready at all times for an impending ambush. Occasionally she stopped to look through her scope for possible targets, always craving the first shot. Diamond was NATO's best sniper and a former Olympic silver medalist in shooting.

She had told Raption that choosing a gun over the millions of dollars modeling agencies offered had been easy. The media had called her "the photogenic blonde capturing headlines and turning heads at the 2020 Olympiad." After a short stint on the runways of Paris and New York, Diamond had broken her contract and returned to her homeland in Hella, Iceland. She wanted to get the nauseating images of modeling out of her mind. Diamond despised the fashion industry's culture of moguls promising her a life of materialistic wonder. She had missed her weapon: her passion for shooting a rifle gave her a purpose and eventually led her to military service.

Red and Warsaw rounded out the Gray Team's officer core. They trailed far at the back of the company. Raption could not see them set between dozens of NATO Special Forces operators flanking the jungle march.

Red was a leading genetic and bioengineering expert; the only such specialist attached to an existing Western Special Ops unit. She had limited weapons training and no combat experience. NATO had to beg Canada's Joint Task Force 2 commanders to assign Red to CONTRA when the Demon Lab was discovered. Since the Demon Lab was a large-scale genetic engineering experiment combining the DNA sequences of animals with humans, Red's expertise was invaluable on the front lines.

From the back of the team, Red monitored the position of each soldier in the company and tracked each operator's location and health status through her battlesuit visor. Red ensured the team stayed in close formation and nobody veered off. Raption was particularly glad to have her along—several Marines were lost during the last sweep Raption's former brigade made into Colombia, only weeks prior to CONTRA's insertion. The Marines had completely vanished during a night mission.

Warsaw watched the rear of the unit, making sure no enemy forces trailed. Everyone avoided debating him. Raption liked his stubbornness and quick wit. A devout Polish Jew, his great grandfather was involved in the famous Warsaw ghetto uprising against the Nazis during World War II. He was tall and slim with an iron jaw and a big heart. Convincing him of anything was hard. Warsaw did not like jungles. He bitched about it, both under his breath and aloud. The Polish Special Forces officer cursed and cursed, following his expletives with expressions of loyalty to the mission. Complaining while remaining dedicated—that was Warsaw.

Together, the seven Gray Team officers led a company of fifty NATO Special Forces operators through the southern Amazon rainforest of Colombia. Most of the team was anxious for the mission, wanting direct action with The Revolution—the first real test after months of training. Hope and a sense of purpose motivated Raption and the rest of CONTRA.

The Revolution's grasp could be felt from South America to Eastern Europe, which raised new fears around the world. A possible Chinese connection made the group's threat level more dire. Officials outside CONTRA focused on that aspect of The Revolution—a possible ploy by Beijing to distract the world from its next move. The very select government officials and high-ranking intelligence officers associated with CONTRA had a greater fear, one that lay in the depths of the Colombian jungle that the Gray Team navigated.

Raption was all too familiar with the peril.

There was no doubting the significance of the discovery made two years earlier near the very place CONTRA now maneuvered. The Revolution's advanced technology struck alarm, even panic, into the hearts of America's toughest Marines who had witnessed the Demon Lab. Raption didn't like to think of what his brigade found as *creatures*. He could take many things, but the thought of humans forcibly mutated with animals made him sick.

Fighting and living on the edge came easy. Accepting the twisted malice found in the Amazon two years ago did not. Vomiting nightmares of mortified Marines who witnessed the Demon Lab surprised the therapists who were called in to treat them. Humans melded with animals in someone's sadistic process of playing God made any good man or woman sick. Raption hated The Revolution. Anticapitalist maybe, but the group was more like anticivilization. Stopping the movement before it spread any further was CONTRA's mission. Some thought it was already too late.

The final two Critical Events exposed The Revolution's dangers to a global audience. But the real reason CONTRA was in Colombia, and the reason its civilian director couldn't sleep at night, still remained Top Secret. The key to unlocking the mysterious origins behind the first Critical Event, the Demon Lab, lay somewhere in the sweltering Amazon rainforest for the Gray Team to rediscover.

"Stay quiet and keep low," Crosshill ordered, his British accent coming across heavily over the headset. "Five more minutes and we'll break."

Thank you. Raption silently rejoiced. To his dismay, unwelcome news immediately followed.

"The Perceptor is imaging a large clearing underneath tree-cover ahead," Satellite reported. "Can barely make it out. Taking her in for a closer look."

Crosshill halted the team.

Raption felt his muscles tense. One of the few aboveground clues Marines discovered at the location of the Demon Lab was a jungle clearing carpeted with an exotic grass. Raption's counter-narcotics brigade paid little attention to it at the time. Deforestation of the Amazon was a separate problem from the Drug Wars. The counter-narcotics mission had no intelligence on para-military forces either clearing wide areas of the Amazon or growing exotic grasses. The jungle clearing was thought unrelated to the drug harvest. The sign had been ignored.

Crosshill motioned to Satellite who glided over to his superior officer.

"What do we have?" Crosshill asked.

"Something odd. An Amazon jungle void of its undergrowth. Hard to make out 'cause the trees are still there, but underneath the trees… it's plain grass, like a front lawn in Florida."

Crosshill looked to Raption, wanting an opinion.

"Different from what we found. While the clearing near the lab had some tree cover, it was mostly a clear-cut with grass planted over the deforested area. No construction marks on the ground, not even when you stood next to the tree trunks. We checked all around. Whoever did it all left no impact. We couldn't figure it out . . . and it never made sense with what we found underground in the lab."

Raption peered ahead through the trees before them. He thought he could make out the edge of the clearing.

"Looks like our luck is changing," Crosshill said. Leaning in toward Raption he whispered, "We'll take a break next to that clearing. First, let's make sure it's clean."

"Roger that, sir."

The Gray Team moved forward. They stopped at the edge of the rain-forest where the thick Amazon jungle changed into a different kind of forest. Uniform exotic grass replaced the underbrush beneath the tropical tree cover. Raption drew a sharp breath upon seeing the familiar grass under the trees. About shin high, it shimmered a slight orange and blanketed the forest floor as far as the eye could see.

"Unnatural. Here we go," Raption whispered. His eyes focused beyond the trees to the flanks of the team. The well-planned ambush his Marine unit encountered last time in this jungle had caught him off guard. The waiting enemy struck without warning, hard and fast. Two of Raption's closest friends were killed. Now, that eerie feeling of being a bystander to horror crept back over him. The clearing appeared innocent, yet it seeped evil.

CONTRA's Gray Team crept alongside the clearing's perimeter for several minutes. Weapons drawn. Triggers ready. Crosshill ordered the team to split in two directions. Raption, Diamond, and Breakdown led half the company up the northern flank of the clearing. The rest of the company followed Crosshill and Satellite along the southern edge. The groups kept close to the inside of the natural jungle. They scanned for any presence of enemy forces within the perimeter where it was easy to see long distances.

This one's much larger, thought Raption as they marched. Removing all the thick jungle underbrush must have been a massive undertaking. In place of the thousands of varieties of Amazonian flora, the orange-glimmering grass rolled smooth, covering the jungle floor like a manicured meadow. Almost all the trees of the forest's emergent layer and canopy remained standing as if to hide the sprawling field of engineered vegetation from above.

Raption knelt at the forest's edge, surveying the area in front of them half expecting to see hired guns watching over the meadow as they would a cocaine pasture. He touched the soft grass with his bare palm. It looked harmless, but he knew it was a bad sign. *Enemy activity nearby,* he guessed.

"Who would go through the trouble?" Breakdown asked, kneeling beside Raption. "I hear of all the extravagant drug-growing operations, farmers making way more money off the drugs than with coffee or anything else. This doesn't make sense, though. It's so perfect looking, but it's worthless. It can't pay."

"Whoever did this put forth the effort for a reason," Diamond hypothesized, standing over the two men. "It holds significance, perhaps beyond monetary desires. There is value we don't understand: just like we don't understand a lot about The Revolution." She moved forward out of the overgrowth and into the clearing. "Let's go for a walk, gentlemen."

"Yes, ma'am," Breakdown said, with slight sarcasm.

Diamond outranked both Raption and Breakdown, second to Crosshill in the hierarchy of Gray Team command. She knew when to take the lead. It was never an issue between Raption and her. Their relationship wasn't a factor when it came to business.

"Crosshill, we are moving into the clearing from our side. All is well. No sign of the enemy," Diamond reported over the radio.

"Good. Same here," Crosshill replied. "We'll meet you in the middle."

Raption and Breakdown stepped into the grassy area behind Diamond. Walking in the cleared terrain was easier than trudging through the thick jungle foliage. The openness was a welcome change from the confined natural rainforest. A breeze passed over the strike force as they advanced to reunify. Raption saw one of the CONTRA soldiers taking a sip of water, which reminded him of his intense thirst.

"Breakdown, you got any spare H-two-O?" Raption asked. "I'm dyin' here, man. Couldn't stop drinking on the last hike. Know how I feel about carrying all the spares."

"Gotcha. We'll have to get back to the Caqueta River soon or we'll all be out." Breakdown tossed Raption an extra water pack. Their special-issued water packs could filter water from any source, purifying it and keeping it cool.

Raption popped the cap, thankful water existed. The clear liquid ran over his cracked lips and parched mouth. He swallowed hard on the first gulp. Grimacing he rehydrated the dry patch at the back of his throat. The second gulp went down much easier. Raption could've drunk it all. He took a deep breath and closed his eyes, daydreaming about a far-off beach. A strong fragrance permeating his nostrils cut his moment of solace short.

"Hey, Breakdown! You smell that?"

"Smell what?"

"Take a whiff."

Breakdown sniffed hard. He paused, sniffing harder. "Smells like the pot-pourri in my mom's bathroom."

Raption bent down and pulled a handful of the exotic grass out of the ground. He held it up close and inhaled. "It's the grass. Aroma like detergent or some fabric softener."

Breakdown laughed. "Need your clothes washed? Maybe there are chemicals in the grass? It has to smell for a reason." Breakdown knelt to the ground to pluck a handful of the grass for himself. The orange tint of the grass reflected in the sunlight.

"We brought back samples of this stuff to the labs," Raption said, studying his handful closely. "They tested it, checking for any substance worth selling. There wasn't."

"Maybe they were looking for the wrong thing," Diamond interjected, turning back to them.

"How do you figure?" Breakdown asked.

"This grass isn't indigenous. If it's not a narcotic, there's another use for it. Assumptions lead analysis astray. Raption's Marines were part of a counter-narcotics brigade. Their thinking was instinctively on drugs so that was the template given to the investigation. There's meaning behind the effort of planting this grass—and it's not drugs."

The other half of the Gray Team came into view through the sparse trees ahead. The company reconvened next to the foot of a large stump. The officers surveyed their surroundings in the peace of the incongruous landscape.

"Anybody want to brainstorm about what all this means?" Satellite asked, setting the Perceptor to hover mode above the center of the manicured field. The drone would search and sense for any sign of movement at the team's periphery.

"The real Amazon stops and a very different forest begins," Red responded. "Perfect geoponics. It's an achievement to create such a transformation of this large a cross-section so deep in the jungle. It's a masterful extraction of all the

Amazonian flora and replanting of this foreign grass."

"I can't imagine why. The clearing is a dead giveaway," Crosshill noted, checking his watch and looking toward the far side of the clearing.

"Maybe The Revolution didn't expect us to hunt them in remote parts of the Amazon when they set this operation up. Whatever it is," Diamond said.

The sun shined through the opening in the trees above, filling the grassy meadow with the nourishment it needed to grow. Raption was still amazed at the size of the newfound clearing. "Feels more like a state park than the Colombian jungle."

"It's time for a break. We can all use it," Crosshill announced. He ordered the team to move close to the edge of the thick rainforest where they'd be less vulnerable out of the open.

Raption stared back into the natural forest as they walked toward it. It was ominously dark. The sunlight came to an abrupt halt at the tree line. Anything could creep through. The team moved back about twenty paces where they could see through the forest again. Gear hit the earth. Tired soldiers on a mission didn't waste break time.

Crosshill put several troops on guard around the outskirts of the impromptu camp. The Perceptor above was good, but it couldn't catch everything. Nothing beat a pair of human eyes. Crosshill gathered the officer core together under the shade of a tree. Sitting in the soft orange-tinted grass, they planned their next move.

"The clearing goes on to the west as far as I can see. Why wasn't this detected by U.S. imagery intelligence assets?" Crosshill asked.

"Visibility from space or a fly-over is more difficult than it would seem," Satellite said, pointing up. "Whoever made the clearing left enough trees to provide cover. The Perceptor hardly made the distinction until it was right on top of the place."

Red felt the soft ground with her hand, brushing it back and forth. "The cultivation and cleanliness of the transplants are astounding," she gushed.

"The caretakers are expert farmers. They found a way to extract the natural Amazon underbrush and mold this tinted grass around the trees . . . flawlessly. There are no spaces left uncovered. It's miraculous really."

"The grass smells funny," Breakdown said. "What do you make of it? Raption told me the labs back home didn't find anything special about it."

"That's not *completely* true," Red corrected. "The labs tested for drugs to see if the vegetation was some kind of hybrid form of marijuana, similar to what was found in central Mexico years ago. No offense, Raption, but the assumptions brought back on this grass were related to the trade."

"None taken. Someone else noted the same thing earlier," Raption admitted, glancing at Diamond.

"The labs found no traces of known street drugs on initial testing," Red continued. "However, follow-up tests found there *were* high concentrations of a hormone-type substance, somewhat like a steroid for plants. The people raising these crops were putting a lot of effort into assuring they were healthy—"

"And concealed," Diamond cut in. "Seems like a lot of effort for some grass, even if it does have steroids in it. There's a purpose we aren't seeing."

"It's food," Warsaw said, in a quiet, casual voice.

The other officers turned around to him. Warsaw lay flat on his back several feet from the rest of the group. He was resting his head against his battlepack, staring at the cracks of blue sky visible through an opening in the jungle cover above. He held a long piece of the orange-tinted grass between his teeth, using it as a toothpick to nudge something free.

"Food for what?" Breakdown asked, uneasy.

"Experimentation."

"You think it's for what we found underground in the Demon Lab?" Raption asked, seeing where Warsaw was going.

"Maybe. Maybe not. None of us knows what else we *haven't* found. Those experiments weren't complete. They were far enough along to assume other genetic combinations did, or at least could have, accomplished the human-animal DNA mutations. There has to be a progression in bioengineering. Can't change a man into an animal overnight." Warsaw turned away from his intent stare at the sky. "Steroids in the grass—it's for feeding. Feeding something we haven't found."

Raption watched Red listen closely to Warsaw's theory. The genetically modified output created by The Revolution was termed "recombinant DNA" in bioengineering circles. Red fully understood the process of recombinant DNA yet had been as amazed as anyone by the progress The Revolution had achieved in the Demon Lab.

"While human guinea pigs used for the genetic experiments would have been easy to feed, finding a way to supplement the hunger of the large carnivores The Revolution was creating would have been much more difficult," Red professed. "Wolves, tigers, and panthers do not feed lightly. Hunting for their food or creating large farms nearby would have garnered unwanted attention. Reprogramming a meat-eater to consume steroid-rich grass seems a stretch, but so is everything else about the Demon Lab. If Revolution geneticists could perform complex recombinant DNA experiments successfully on animals and humans, there is no reason to think they can't turn grass into a steroid supplement."

Red proceeded, "Enter this exotic grass with no relation to the criminal narcotics trade. Essentially, if The Revolution can engineer a monster out of a man, it could find a way to feed that monster. Cruelty does not overshadow their evil genius."

"If Warsaw is right, we're sitting in a pasture of sorts?" Raption said.

"A pasture for what?" Breakdown asked, troubled.

"Either animals used for the Demon Lab or . . . the creatures they made."

Breakdown gulped hard. "I don't want to see them. I don't want to be a witness."

"If they bleed, they can be killed," Diamond said, following along with the conversation, caressing her rifle with a soft white cloth. "The Revolution can be anything. It can take any form. It doesn't matter. We can't be concerned with *what* it is. We know it's dangerous and that's why it must be stopped. If this is a pasture for their abominable creations, then we are in the right place."

"Speak for yourself," Breakdown muttered under his breath.

Raption stared at Diamond in veneration. She spoke like a general, cared for her weapon as if it were a baby, and still looked like a runway model. Instead of getting a snack or resting on the break, she had to make sure her rifle was competition ready. *A true sharpshooter forms a bond with their weapon,* she had told him once. *They become the same.*

Diamond looked up at Raption. Her eyes held his for a moment. She wouldn't smile openly to him on a mission, or around other officers, but she liked to sneak glances. Just that look communicated everything between them.

Crosshill stood up, sighing. He gazed out over the grassy clearing again. "This operation won't end until we locate something more than fields of grass," he said. "Headquarters is being pressured by the Pentagon. They want answers to what role this jungle plays in The Revolution. The Demon Lab was never forgotten and neither was the escalation of violence in the Drug Wars that followed its discovery.

"Before we left for Colombia, Commander Patton pulled me aside. He said finding who or what is operating at the heart of this jungle holds the key to unraveling the entire Revolution. The Demon Lab experiments were a scientific marvel, however sickening they might be. The Three had to run or finance the lab—if they even truly exist. If they do, the bastards are like Hitler or bin Laden." Crosshill folded his arms and appeared to be in deep thought.

As the late afternoon wore on, the Amazon's unforgiving heat abated. The spot where CONTRA stopped for a break was a serene escape from the jungle. A slight breeze provided relief from the hours of suffocation in the tight rainforest. The rest area had a noticeably calming effect. Grouped against the thicker jungle border, the unit relaxed and enjoyed the much-needed rest. CONTRA soldiers lay on the soft ground, catching up on sleep.

They had slogged and sweated for almost two days straight, searching for an evil shrouded in rumors and myth. Recognizing this, Crosshill decided to extend the break. They had moved nonstop since their insertion into Colombia and the troops were tired. He wanted to push on, but they could make up for the delay overnight.

Raption needed to catch some shut-eye. He drifted to sleep thinking about why the U.S. intelligence community believed The Revolution armed paramilitary forces and the cartels of the Drug Wars. The guerillas were well financed and trained too. They had outmatched regional military forces in pitched battles. The rebels seemed to pop up everywhere. The continued war changed the political dynamics of Central and South America. CONTRA needed to take down The Revolution's leadership. If they were responsible for the Drug Wars, killing or imprisoning The Three leaders were the best possible solutions to restoring peace in the region.

Red and Diamond walked to the outskirts of the ad hoc camp. Diamond kept a watchful eye around them and stared upward at the Perceptor hovering near the treetops.

"I wonder how Justice is doing...?" Red mused. She didn't feel comfortable talking to any of the male officers about him. The whole situation was hard to deal with. He loved CONTRA, but her heart hadn't been in it for some time.

Red liked to think she could connect with Diamond. They were the two female officers on the Gray Team, but Diamond was a lot tougher and more cut out for military service. The Icelander had genuine ladylike patience about her, too.

"Your man is a strong leader. An excellent selection for directing the Blue Team," Diamond said. "He'll be fine. Worry about *you* and *this* team. We're alone in this jungle. I don't know how long that will last."

"I'm in love!" Red exclaimed louder than she intended. She put her hand over her mouth. A nearby soldier lifted his head off the ground momentarily and looked over. Interested more in sleeping, he quickly turned away and rested back on the ground. Red lowered her voice. "I'm in love with someone I want to spend the rest of my life with. It's hard to ignore."

She thought she saw Diamond roll her eyes when she looked up to the treetops again.

"The Perceptor is gone. Satellite is probably maneuvering it around. How long will this tranquility last?" Diamond tightened her grip around her AWM sniper rifle.

"Not long I imagine," Red lamented. She struggled with her place in the military. An accomplished PhD with expertise in both WMD and genetics, she was the only CONTRA officer wanting marriage more than a promotion. And she worried about Justice constantly.

Unwilling to openly admit it, Red stayed on the team for him. Justice had once asked her to leave, seeing that she was unhappy. "You can teach at any university, live in the suburbs, and have a normal workday," he said. Red refused; her dislike of fighting was not as powerful as her desire to stay close to him.

Breakdown watched Raption fall fast into a deep sleep, his jungle hat pulled over his eyes. Breakdown thought of letting Raption dream away, but couldn't get what Warsaw said out of his mind. He needed to know more about the Demon Lab.

During the debriefing on the carrier, Breakdown paid attention to all the details. He knew how the Department of Defense shared sensitive information. They probably weren't getting the half of it. Rumors spread during CONTRA training about what the Marines found underground, the discoveries excluded from the official report. Raption was the only member from the Marine brigade in CONTRA. No others met the selection criteria. According to the medical records they all had psychological issues.

Breakdown bumped Raption's leg. He didn't respond. Breakdown nudged harder. Raption sat up with the look of an elementary student woken for the first day of school. He rubbed his eyes, staring blankly at Breakdown.

"Dude, what gives? Sleep is better than sex out here. You know that."

"The Demon Lab. We're in this stinking jungle. Tell me, what did you guys really find? Not the watered-down version," Breakdown said, his voice wavering. "Some people said you guys found monsters on that tour. Monsters are for nightmares, Raption. Tell me we're not in one." Breakdown's intensity lobbied for truth.

"Shit . . . since my last Colombian mission I've sat through countless consultations. Investigators and therapists of all kinds asking me to repeat what I'd seen. They tried to make me feel like it wasn't a big deal. I got so used to repeating the official version I haven't considered what's facing us. 'It's better to keep the flashbacks private,' the medical staff told me."

"*Loco mierda, hombre.* Sucks." Breakdown uncontrollably tapped his foot in anticipation of what Raption might say.

"CONTRA depends on me to have a better feel for the situation and provide insight about what might come next, but you don't need to be a genius to realize the evil could have gotten worse in the two years since we found that lab." Raption gathered himself. "I'll share what I shouldn't . . . after all, we might all die in this jungle."

"Don't say that, homie."

"You didn't want to be there, Breakdown," Raption said quietly. "Like a twisted video game or one of those low-budget horror movies, ya know, the fake kind?"

"The kind I hate."

"Some things people dream up come true." Raption looked away for a moment and started breathing hard. He turned to Breakdown and spoke earnestly. "Those things we found underground . . . they weren't people anymore. Maybe they once were, but not when we found them. They weren't people at all."

Nearby, Satellite saw Raption and Breakdown talking about something serious. He activated a listening device on his battlesuit to check the discussion, verifying the Perceptor readings were normal while performing friendly eavesdropping. The topic was the Demon Lab.

Rumors of what the Marine counter-narcotics unit found made it onto one of his sister's Station One reports. Lydia always seemed to have the inside story, and she got that one, too, even coining the phrase "ringleaders," which the public used in reference to The Revolution's mysterious leadership.

Satellite never shared his real job with Lydia. She thought he still sat behind a desk and developed technology for DARPA on assignment at Peterson Air Force Base. If his sister knew about CONTRA and that he was a member, she would flip. The FBI had interrogated Satellite once about Lydia. They thought he might be one of her sources. He passed the FBI polygraphs, so they left him alone.

He'd watched Lydia's original exposé on The Revolution countless times. She produced it before the last two Critical Events even happened. Everyone in CONTRA knew how close to the truth she'd been, though critics ruthlessly tore her credibility apart. Ultimately, it severely damaged her career. Despite the naysayers, Lydia became the go-to reporter on all things Revolution and tried to reclaim her status as a popular and respected field reporter.

Satellite positioned the Perceptor back into hover mode far above the team and walked over to Breakdown and Raption, taking off the UAV control goggles, motioning for Raption to continue.

"When we approached, it didn't seem any different from the other narco-hideouts we'd been finding and burning. Local farmers in that particular area were different though. Creeped-out bad, like they saw some spooky stuff happening. A lot of people disappeared, just vanished in the night, they said. Some were found murdered . . . their organs missing. The Colombians were still in control back then and were busting anybody helping the drug runners. We originally thought the deaths and fighting was about turf. The Drug Wars started raging around that time."

Raption shook his head and frowned. He paused and seemed to be retracing his thoughts, trying to picture the next moment.

"We came across nine hideouts on that tour, heavy resistance at each one. Those firefights, man . . . the guerillas had some weapons. They competed with us Marines. When we came across the last spot, there was nobody guarding the place. It was surrounded by a clearing like this one, but smaller. The hideout looked deserted. All of a sudden the fire started pouring in from all sides. They were waiting around the edges to see if we'd pass. You see, they didn't want us to find what was below—"

A high-pitched beeping from Satellite's Perceptor goggles cut Raption short. Satellite snapped his head toward the red flashing indicators. He grabbed his goggles and stood up while placing them over his head and focusing on the readings coming from the drone perched above.

He turned, calling out to Crosshill, "Problems!"

Raption and Breakdown stood too.

"What is it?" Breakdown asked.

"Readings of a large mass of thermal energy. Moving toward us slow from the west. I'm sending the Perceptor in for a closer check," Satellite said. "This could be something."

Crosshill ordered the team to strap up and get ready to move.

Warsaw awakened from what must have been a very deep sleep. He asked frantic questions, trying to collect his gear and find his bearings.

"How far?" Crosshill queried Satellite, checking his weapon and looking toward the direction the Perceptor moved.

"About five hundred yards or so."

Crosshill touched the radio-com on his ear. "CONTRA look sharp. We're moving. Be ready for a fight."

CHAPTER 7
FAITH

Colorado Springs: April 22, 2035

Grace held still, trying not to blink.

For the past ten minutes she'd examined her left pupil, searching for some explanation for the flash of light emitted during her team's escape from Taiwan. Her eye felt normal, same as her right one. Grace had performed this self-examination before. Her parents told her not to fear the eye sensation. Doctors never had an answer. Grace had felt foolish telling nurses and doctors about it growing up, so she stopped. Those hospital visits were embarrassing, especially because other peoples' thoughts had almost a physical affect on Grace.

Somehow Grace could detect people's spiritual and emotional rhythms. When directed toward her, the intensity level increased. She could visualize a connection between the psychology and actions of others, and then an experience of empathy followed, almost transferring information to her delicate senses. She didn't understand how it worked, but it did. Whether deceit, fear, or love, Grace could sense it. At an early age she learned to believe her intuitions, a gift her mother told her most people didn't possess. Grace wondered if her innate ability was related to the eye flash.

The first time it happened she'd been six-years-old.

Grace skipped ahead of her parents on a Sunday walk through the Vatican Gardens. The majestic dome of St. Peter's Basilica towered above the trees in the background. The sunny morning made her happy and full of energy. Medieval sculptures and fountains decorated every turn. Grace felt alive. As far as she was concerned, the magnificent gardens were better than any amusement park. Peaceful. Natural.

Surrounded by flowerbeds and lush bushes, Grace ran across the green lawn in front of a glorious marble statue of the Virgin Mother at the intersection of two small cobble pathways. Grace crossed herself and knelt, smiling at Mary looking down at her. She imagined the statue was cognizant of her thoughts. A lone, yellow wildflower springing up at the center of the next section of open lawn caught Grace's attention.

She ran toward it, hearing her mother yell something out about not wandering too far. Grace wanted to smell the sole flower sprouting up in the middle of the green grass. She bent down without disturbing it and inhaled carefully and deep. To her surprise, it had the scent of a thousand blossoms. Grace sat back on her knees, admiring the unique little wildflower. She couldn't imagine being happier than that moment.

A strange sensation flowed through her body and a bright glow flashed in her left eye. Grace leapt to her feet and covered her face. She ran back to her parents in distress and explained what happened. They weren't concerned. In fact, her parents seemed pleased. It was the first time Grace remembered her mother telling her she was Blessed.

"Dear God, whatever makes me different, let me one day understand," Grace said to herself, pulling away from the mirror. She didn't want to spend any more time staring at herself. After the latest incident in Taiwan, she'd been getting headaches from concentrating too hard on not blinking.

The Blue Team had arrived back at the sprawling military installation at Colorado Springs earlier that day. It was home of Peterson Air Force Base; NORAD; U.S. Northern Command (NORTHCOM); Space Command; and a nondescript building housing CONTRA headquarters. Commander Patton had delivered a memory card to Grace, which contained new classified intelligence derived from NSA intercepts and clandestine operations in Russia. Though she just returned, Patton asked her to extract pertinent data from over three hundred megabytes of information containing intelligence related to Revolution activity. Grace had to shift her focus away from Taiwan and the mystery of her eye.

A high-ranking general named Peter Nabokav, commander of Russia's Strategic Rocket Forces, had requested cooperation from NATO on matters related to Russian national security. Though CONTRA remained Top Secret, Russia's Federal Security Service (FSS) had moles everywhere and had informed General Nabokav of the NATO unit after he raised concerns of possible Revolution collusion with a powerful Russian mafia—Crvena Zvezda.

Nabokav, who was already an outspoken supporter of improving military relations with the West, had proposed crushing the growing influence of Russia's criminal underground. His bid to share intelligence and cooperate with CONTRA could accomplish both. An American defense attaché in Moscow agreed to review his initial request without confirming any knowledge of CONTRA's existence.

Grace barely settled into her room on base before she began to analyze the intelligence. Several documents on the memory card indicated Russia's Main Intelligence Directorate (GRU) was aware of and very concerned about Crvena Zvezda's cooperation with The Revolution. One internal report described a counter-intelligence operation coordinated between the GRU and FSS to apprehend a Revolution ringleader upon planned entry into Russia through Kazakhstan. Only Western intelligence referred to Revolution ringleaders as The Three, but Grace could assume that's who the internal report was referring to. The GRU-FSS operation failed after an unknown informant alerted the ringleader before he reached the Kazak border crossing. Two FSS agents tracking the leak disappeared without a trace.

The level of suspected Revolution activity within Russia stunned Grace. Both the FSS and GRU were concerned by mafia attempts to influence and bribe defense industry and military officials into stealing and selling highly advanced weapons. The list of arms believed compromised included tactical high-powered microwaves, thermo-baric warheads, supercavitating torpedoes, Electromagnetic Pulse (EMP) weapons, and an array of electronic warfare systems.

Grace found an elementary encryption in one of the FSS files. It identified a Russian location of great concern to the GRU where Revolution activity centered. Trained in the art of cryptology, she broke the code in less than an hour. The deciphered readout produced two sets of numbers: 53-32-56 and 58-34-57. Immersed in her work, Grace continued her analysis into the early morning—her tenacity paid off. Around 2:00 a.m. she finished a preliminary draft of her report that included new evidence of a possible Revolution plot in Russia.

Grace felt consumed by the complicating circumstances the Russian Intel raised. The stakes to stop The Revolution kept getting higher. If the group used any of the compromised Russian weapons, the outcome could prove devastating. When would there be peace?

Taking deep, slow breaths, Grace turned off the lamp next to her computer and stretched out on her bed, thinking of home. She valued the simpler things in life. Long walks. Wind in the leaves. Homemade pizza. Watching kids play soccer. She loved Rome evenings in spring when the feeling of warmth replaced the cold of winter. Simplicity always made Grace happiest. She knelt by her bedside and prayed, practicing what gave her most peace.

Faith.

CHAPTER 8
OPEN FIRE
Southern Colombia: April 22, 2035

The jungle clearing in front of the Gray Team maintained a symmetrical pattern of grass beneath the branches and leaves of tropical palm, sandbox, and nut trees. CONTRA advanced toward the mass of thermal energy the Perceptor tracked less than five hundred yards away. The orange-tinted grass stretched on, covering acres of massive ground between the CONTRA team and whatever life forms lay ahead.

The team walked straight through the clearing and among the surreal landscape of towering tropical trees. The natural Amazon jungle to either side of CONTRA disappeared as they closed the distance. The transplanted meadow took over, substituting the claustrophobic enclosed stiffness of the jungle with a refreshing openness. In some places the grass seemed thicker than in others, but nowhere was there a patch of dirt or indigenous undergrowth left over from the natural jungle.

A slight incline began as the team continued west. Their shadows grew longer. Dusk was settling in. The team moved at a good pace, reinvigorated by the short rest and the possibility of action ahead.

"Nearing thermals. Two hundred yards," Satellite reported over their headsets.

"Can you get an image feed?" Crosshill asked.

"Not right now. Too thick a jungle cover ahead."

"Keep trying."

CONTRA troops moved low to the ground, holding their weapons ready. Among the best-of-the-best in Special Forces from the most elite units of the

Western military alliance, there was a cockiness that whatever lay ahead would be no match.

"Our moment is near. Visuals soon. Don't fire until I give the order." Crosshill's order came across the headsets, breaking the quiet advance.

"The hell with that! If someone shoots at me first, they're dead," Breakdown mouthed.

The forest grew darker with each passing minute. Sparse patches of underbrush appeared, mixing with the exotic grass. The slight incline leveled off to flat ground. Crosshill ordered the team to spread out. Less of the tinted grass was visible with every step. The trees grew closer together in natural jungle form as the clearing came to an end.

Crosshill pointed at the ground and back at his eyes. Raption and Satellite nodded, acknowledging the change. "What do you see, Satellite? We're almost on top of those thermals."

"Hard to tell. I can't decipher it." Satellite sounded disgruntled. "There's a problem with the Perceptor. My screen's scrambling. The drone isn't responding to all commands."

"A glitch?" Crosshill asked, turning with concern.

"I've never seen it do this before."

"Interference is my guess," Warsaw chirped.

Breakdown shot a look of aversion at Warsaw. "Let Satellite deal with it. He invented that drone and knows damn well better than you what's wrong."

Warsaw pretended not to hear.

"I have a visual up ahead through my scope. It's a pack..." Diamond paused, "of *werewolves?*"

The CONTRA unit fell momentarily silent, not understanding exactly what Diamond meant. Crosshill flipped open the keypad atop his battlesuit forearm and activated SuperVision, a hybrid of night-vision binoculars with image intensification in all forms of light. The visor on his helmet shut over his face and he zoomed in for a closer look.

Without the aid of his battlesuit, Breakdown could see the outlines of the creatures grazing ahead. His jaw dropped. He'd never seen anything like them. Nobody had. "They look prehistoric," he gasped.

The most high-tech dinosaur exhibits at Universal Studios didn't have such realism. This was no set. The beasts were alive and they *did* look like werewolves. The name fit. Breakdown counted at least two dozen of them, moving slowly like some ungodly herd from the ancient past in the rainforest less than fifty yards away. The werewolves resembled a beastly creation from a mad scientist's basement.

"Jesus Christ," Crosshill wheezed, raising his visor with the press of a button.

"They've done it," Raption added.

Breakdown stared at the herd, studying it. He couldn't take his eyes off the creatures. The Revolution had clearly progressed in their unethical experiments. Breakdown shuddered to think human beings might be inside of those animals. He heard Satellite struggle nearby to maneuver the Perceptor, cursing to gain control of the drone. Satellite could usually troubleshoot the navigation and software on a moment's notice. Something or *someone* was interfering with it. There could be no other explanation. Perhaps Warsaw was right.

"What do you think they are?" Crosshill asked.

"They look like the ugliest dogs I've ever seen," Warsaw said. "Big dogs with lots of fur."

"They've gotta be ten to twelve feet tall. Upwards of twelve hundred pounds," Breakdown said. They looked like sabertooth tigers to him. He caught a shiny glimmer on the back of one of the creatures. "Anyone else see something on the back of the one to the far right? It looks like a metal plate."

"Not the only one that has it," Diamond pointed out. "They *all* do."

"Something's definitely wrong," Satellite said. He was frantically trying to control the Perceptor. "Want to use the drone's sensors to get a close-up. Sounds like walking up to them is outta the question. Can't control this any longer. It's failing."

"Keep trying! Bring it down softly if need be," Crosshill said. "You can fix it on the ground."

"It's . . . not . . . responding at all. Damn it." Satellite grimaced, his biceps flexed through his rolled up sleeves.

"Well, *damn it,* Satellite, let's not make it everyone's problem!" Crosshill commanded.

"These creatures are definitely mutations. An advancement of the recombinant DNA procedure The Revolution attempted in the Demon Lab," Red said. "Roving rats."

"It's what that lab was for . . . something like this," Raption said, swallowing hard.

"How can drug lords and crooks manage something so sophisticated?" Breakdown asked. His brown skin had gone pale.

"I don't know." Raption shrugged and turned back to face the herd.

Violent snapping of branches cracked nearby as the Perceptor crashed down into the trees north of them, lost in the jungle forever. Satellite removed his piloting goggles and threw them to the ground in disgust. "I've never lost a drone before," he said as he rubbed his eyes. "Werewolves," he muttered.

"Red, that device attached to their backs," Breakdown said. "What do you make of it?"

"Could be monitors of some kind if these creatures are indeed manmade. Maybe control mechanisms to alter their state of being? We've done it with dolphins on a limited basis."

There was a murmur from the CONTRA soldier corps. The officers exchanged concerned glances. Crosshill ordered silence and asked Satellite to ensure good recordings of the werewolves.

"Their backs are flashing!" Warsaw broke in with a loud cry. "Oh God, they see us . . . " his voice trailed off in terror.

One by one, the oversized creatures turned from grazing and began galloping in CONTRA's direction.

"They're attacking!" Breakdown shouted.

The werewolves charged with wild speed, covering fifty yards in mere seconds. Flaring nostrils and steak-knife teeth thundered in menacingly at a furious rate. The creatures' muscular build and strength became more evident as they rushed the strike force like hell-bent phantoms sent by the Antichrist.

"Fire at will!" Crosshill yelled.

As that order left his lips, the beasts were already only feet away from the team. Machine-gun fire erupted. Before the creatures reached the company, bullets peppered several of the werewolves. Some of them went down, the rest broke through the barrage of shots.

Breakdown dropped to the ground, selecting a werewolf coming straight for him. He ripped off a dozen rounds into its massive chest. The bullets' impacts sent blood splattering in every direction and the creature dropped in front of him. Breakdown felt the animal hit the earth like a small tremor.

He fired on another werewolf. Barely slowing its approach, Breakdown rolled to one side at the last instant and the werewolf fed on the arm of a CONTRA soldier behind him. Its sharp teeth sank into the man's flesh. The creature threw back its head, ripping through the man's arm like he was a rag doll. It clawed at the soldier's face and crunched his head between its paws with brutal power. The man's screams echoed through the jungle before he died in the horrific mauling. CONTRA troops fired on the werewolf until it fell dead on top of the soldier.

"Hard kills!" Diamond yelled.

"No shit," Breakdown panted, trembling. He aimed for their heads.

A loud clanging noise broke out in the background as the bloody fight went on.

More werewolves crashed through the CONTRA line and were atop the Gray Team. Two of the charging creatures leapt six feet into the air with astonishing grace, landing in the center of the embattled company. In a hail of gunfire, troops put them to death. Yet another beast grappled a tree and in one motion flipped itself backward onto a soldier taking aim. The creature roared as it crushed the man under its hind legs.

Close-quartered angles made it difficult for CONTRA to fire on the creatures once they were in the midst of the company. Two soldiers hit by friendly fire fell to the ground screaming in pain. Crosshill's orders were drowned out by the chaos surrounding the team. Several CONTRA troops were shrieking from injury and utter terror.

"Someone please tell me what the hell is happening!" Breakdown shouted to no one in particular.

"Settle down. Focus your weapon!" Diamond yelled back.

The clanging noise in the background grew louder.

Breakdown emptied clips faster than he could reload. A werewolf tried to pounce on Warsaw, knocking away his gun. Breakdown pumped the grenade launcher of his M4 and fired an explosive round into the beast's stomach. He hardly noticed the splatter of blood as he killed it.

"Thanks!" Warsaw shouted, unlatching a dagger above his boot and jumping onto the back of another werewolf.

"NO! That's damn crazy!" Breakdown yelled.

Warsaw stabbed it repeatedly in the neck and rode it like a bull. The beast jerked around, snapping at Warsaw. In one quick motion, its teeth cut through his shoulder blade and it held Warsaw in its jaw. The monster twisted and hurled him hard to the ground, shattering his collarbone with a sharp crack.

Breakdown unloaded another clip into the side of the creature before it again sank its teeth into Warsaw, who raised his arms in vain to protect himself from the ravenous assault. CONTRA soldiers put the beast to death with a torrent of body shots.

"Son of a bitch," Breakdown said, thinking Warsaw was dead.

The clanging noise that had been muffled by the sounds of gunfire, screaming, and pandemonium grew too loud to ignore. Breakdown, Raption, and Crosshill turned and saw the ground fifty yards in front of them open. An enormous metal building rose up at spellbinding speed. The structure unfolded into sections, expanding to form several platforms with ovoid shells on either side. Each shell had rectangular openings. Dozens of men wearing red and black uniforms ran up the platforms from inside the opening. These soldiers—who could only belong to The Revolution—took up positions on the platforms and began firing on CONTRA.

"Put fire back on that complex!" Crosshill yelled. "Satellite, call for air strikes, now!"

Breakdown realized the situation was life threatening for them all. A new pack of werewolves was released from a side door near the bottom of the emerging complex; they charged the team as the base continued to emerge from the ground.

"Get cover!" Breakdown yelled. He sprinted to a nearby tree and slid down while firing his weapon in the direction of the complex. The Revolution shot several CONTRA soldiers as they scrambled. Howls of pain and confusion filled the team's radio headsets.

Breakdown was at a bad angle. He stood up halfway, crouching to shift positions. Two slugs hit him in the chest with a *thud, thud,* sending him backward to the ground. Not able to catch his breath, he lay for several moments gasping for air.

Writhing in the shock of the painful hit, Breakdown forced himself back to his feet. He saw Raption's lips moving and could read the words *no, no* as his friend motioned him to get back down. But Breakdown couldn't comprehend what was happening. He looked down at his chest, feeling around and checking for blood. A searing pain struck his arm as the red flash of laser fire passed through him.

Breakdown blacked out.

On the USS Ronald Reagan, positioned off the Atlantic coast of Colombia in support of the Gray Team's mission, frantic calls for air strikes and help came through the Command Integration Center. Panicked voices shouted hysterical descriptions of the battle scene. Navy officers listened in confusion. Four Navy Joint Strike Fighters launched inbound over Colombia, heading for CONTRA's position.

"Someone get me a line to CONTRA headquarters," the rear admiral ordered.

Red ducked down next to Crosshill, clinging to his boot with one arm. She watched another werewolf pounce on a nearby soldier and rip through his body with predatory rage. The attack was unreal. It happened fast, but she observed it in a sick slow motion. A nightmarish blur of man against beast. Gore. Violence.

Though movement was hard, she forced her hand to grab her sidearm. Her main weapon was lost in the confusion. She fired relentlessly on the incoming werewolves, at first slowly pulling the trigger then she shot faster and faster, reloading as each clip emptied. After her fourth clip was spent, she crawled to the side of Warsaw who was bleeding profusely.

"Do . . . n' . . . let me . . . die . . . Red," he stammered.

"Try not to speak. You are going to be okay. Just breathe." Red attempted to wrap his gashed shoulder, which had received the worst of the attack. Red could see his insides. Warsaw's flesh hung from underneath his broken collarbone. Shock took Red over. Blood soaked her gloveless hands and small pieces of Warsaw's muscle stuck to her skin. She smelled body fluid and wanted to put on medical gloves, but could not remember where she kept them.

Another soldier cried out for help.

Red turned to see a werewolf devouring him. Digging its teeth into the man's midsection, it ravaged him with the efficiency of a bloodthirsty great white shark. The soldier's horrendous screams forced Red to cover her ears. Bullets whizzed over her head. Tears streamed down her face as she began crying helplessly. She stopped tending to Warsaw and tried to gather herself.

Wiping away the tears with her bloody hands, she focused on wrapping Warsaw's shoulder. He wasn't talking anymore.

"Joint Strike Fighters nearing!" Satellite yelled to Crosshill. "Suggest we clear now. We're too close to the strike area. They're coming in heavy."

"Very well," Crosshill answered. "Listen up, Second Company! Keep fire on the complex and fall back. Fighters inbound with heavy payloads. Repeat, fall back."

Red tugged Warsaw with all her energy to pull him out of harm's way, but she hardly moved him. She looked for help and called to a young soldier hopping in retreat while firing his weapon. "I need your help!" Red yelled.

"Yes, ma'am," the American replied in a kind southern accent, hopping her way.

Together, they pulled Warsaw backward. Red saw two other soldiers pick up Breakdown and carry him. They moved under heavy fire until reaching the cleared forest area. Bullets snapped overhead less frequently.

Covered in blood and soaked with sweat, Red pulled and pushed Warsaw's body any way she could. It seemed safe to rest for a moment, so she plopped to the ground in a pool of exhaustion. Soldiers came through from the front and streamed past her. Red knew she hadn't gone far enough to stop when Satellite rushed out from the front, low to her left.

"Get up and keep falling back!" he yelled. "I'll help with Warsaw. Just run! It's not safe yet." Satellite went to help with Warsaw and stopped. "I barely recognize him. His face and body's so mangled. Is he alive?"

"Still breathing, last I checked," Red said. She got up and ran, wanting to stay alive to tend the wounded.

Raption kept firing on the complex. He watched in amazement as the secret installation constructed itself into a mini-fortress of steel and metal. The structure raised four stories high with six hardened gunner positions at its corners. Each position was set on a platform protected by a wall making the gunner positions look similar to pillbox bunkers from the World War II Normandy invasion. Raption aimed for the helmets of the red and black clad soldiers moving into positions behind the bunker walls. Heavy gunfire rained down on the CONTRA team.

The Revolution's capabilities exceeded all rational possibility. "This cannot be happening," Raption muttered. The technology for the base he shot at was unheard of. They *had* to have help from China—or somebody. Up against something far more advanced and wicked than he'd feared, CONTRA had to survive now and get out of Colombia alive.

What was The Revolution?

Raption reached down and grabbed another clip from his belt buckle. Aiming for one of the ramps leading to the gunner positions, he released the full clip and hit several Revolution soldiers scurrying up the platforms behind the bunker walls. Raption breathed in deep, trying to remain calm. He picked off another enemy soldier running up the platforms. The soldiers were heading for the corners of the rising complex—the hardened gunner positions.

Laser fire began coming from the fortress. Raption was in awe, powerless to help his team. CONTRA couldn't keep up the firefight from their position. Strike Fighters were incoming. They needed that air cover—fast. He looked over to Diamond. She was crouched next to a tree sniping away, peering through her scope.

"Diamond, we gotta fall back with the rest," he said.

"I can see men exiting from the side of the structure. They appear to be heading around it and in the opposite direction from us."

"Did you hear what I said?"

"Hold on. One head shot. Let them know I'm watching." She pulled her trigger. "And yes, I hear you."

Raption loaded his last clip. Laser fire and bullets streaked overhead. Rounds were landing in front and to the side of where he lay, kicking up dirt and burrowing into the ground. So much ammunition laced the jungle that it trimmed the foliage like a crew of psychotic landscapers. Several leaves and small branches fell to the ground around Raption. He was in a very bad position.

The Revolution had him.

He peered up at Diamond. She kept her rifle trained forward on Revolution troops and continued firing. Several rounds hit the tree she used for cover, followed by several more. Raption crouched and pressed his back against the trunk he hid behind as bullets impacted the tree. He listened, waiting with strange patience for the slugs to penetrate all the way through. An enemy sniper must have spotted them. "It's time to go . . . NOW!" Raption shouted.

"Okay, cover me. You're coming right behind?" Diamond asked.

"Move fast. I'm almost out of ammo!"

Diamond slung her rifle over her back and dove into the underbrush, crawling swiftly from the front. Raption watched her push hard off the ground with both elbows, until she was out of enemy range. He fired madly at the complex, waiting to get hit until he ran out of ammo. Realizing he was the last member at the front, Raption turned to fall back. There, he saw the most terrifying sight of his life—a bloody werewolf blocked his retreat.

Incoming fire prevented Raption from standing erect or running in either direction. The beast snarled and growled in a deep gurgle. To Raption's amazement the creature lifted itself onto its hind legs and gracefully towered above him. Raption looked the werewolf in the eye and understood it possessed intelligence unlike other animals, an unsettling human intelligence. The creature's eyes were alive and showed signs of thought behind them. It watched Raption and seemed to smile in evil recognition of his predicament.

The beast was part human. Raption swallowed hard.

The mutated creature took a step toward him. Over the radio, Raption heard Satellite announce Strike Fighters were making their run over the complex. Crosshill shouted for everybody to get out of the zone. The roar of fighters came in low. Raption grabbed a grenade latched to his vest and tossed it toward the werewolf's head. Instinctively the beast caught the grenade in its jaws.

"Still more of an animal!" Raption thundered. Taking two giant steps, he leapt away from the creature. The werewolf attempted to follow him but its head exploded seconds before several four-thousand-pound guided bombs dropped from Navy F-35s above, landing right on target. Raption pressed his face hard against the dirt floor as the blasts reverberated around him. His ears rang painfully loud. A warm dust cloud rolled over him making breathing difficult. Several large chunks of the obliterated Revolution base fell to the ground near him. Small pebbles peppered his back. He questioned whether he was still alive and replayed the last minute of his life before poking his head up.

Raption coughed and grabbed a small cloth towel from his side pocket. Clasping it over his mouth he tried to make out the structure but couldn't see much of anything through the thick post-impact dust cloud. He *could* see partial remains of the dead werewolf. Half its head was propped up nearby—its eyes were staring right back at him. "This is a strange war," Raption quivered.

"Raption, are you there?" Diamond's worry was apparent over the headset.

He tried to speak but could only cough over the radio.

"We'll be right there. Hold on," she said.

By the time Diamond, Satellite, and a handful of CONTRA troops reached Raption, the smoke had cleared sufficiently and they could see the complete destruction of the complex. What remained was rubble, broken shards of twisted metal, concrete, and a large fire burning at the rear of the secret fortress. No human movement whatsoever.

Raption stood covered in dirt, ash, and sweat. He leaned against a tree. Diamond smiled at him adoringly—it was not time for professional distance. Satellite patted him on the back. "Blitzed the hell out of that one," he said, looking at what was left of the Revolution base.

"Good riddance," Raption managed.

CHAPTER 9
DOWN AND OUT
Hermosa Beach: April 23, 2035

"Thank you for shopping at Safeway," the cheerful girl behind the counter flirted. Troy should have smiled back and told her to have a good day. Instead he just stared at the grocery bags on the counter. Unshaven and without a shower, he hadn't slept more than two hours the night before. It seemed the world was moving around him and he was standing in one place. For the moment, he was.

Troy rolled out of bed and ventured into the midday heat to buy some bagels. He just wanted to get outside. Following Station One reports and sleepwalking through his dishwashing duties was all Troy could muster since hearing about the first CONTRA mission. He monitored what leaked out from the Pentagon and gleaned what he could from open sources.

"Excuse me, mister. Can you please move so I can slide my card?" a boy wearing a blue Dodgers hat asked while he popped his chewing gum.

"Oh . . . sure kid. Sorry about that." Troy shuffled forward. His flip-flops slapped loudly against his feet.

CONTRA had been in Taiwan. He knew that much.

Sitting on the picnic table in front of Safeway he yawned and dug into the plastic sack. A smile crept over his face, the delirious type reflecting a cruel sarcasm, the kind you get when hung over and functioning on fumes from a night of excess. Troy went out late to the bars with his neighbor the night before. They drank until the pier closed. He stumbled home after three in the morning, waking with a half-chewed slice of pizza in one hand and a phone number scribbled on the other.

For the last five months he'd longed for structure, camaraderie, and purpose. Without them he was alone. No purpose. All the while, the world continued along without him: The Revolution grew stronger—and he couldn't stop them. Today was yet another scorcher in Southern California—but he wouldn't be at the beach. Weather reports called for record-breaking temperatures over a hundred degrees. Troy scooted over to the shaded side of the outdoor bench and began reading the international headlines off his cell phone.

Warlords in Sudan and Nigeria were killing off villages and raiding warehouses full of international aid shipments. Europe was frenzied over street violence and continued shootings. There was looting in some cities. Fighting in South America worsened. Several car bombs exploded in Managua, a place previously untouched by the spreading Drug War chaos. China threatened to attack Japan for its purported role in helping NATO operate in Asia. Beijing demanded a whole slew of things and sent a carrier battle group off the east coast of Japan.

Troy unwrapped the plastic from his bagels and chewed into one like a hungry vulture. The growling from his stomach echoed loud enough for the clerk collecting shopping carts to turn and look at him. Two women skated by on rollerblades. No smiles from them in his raggedy state. After gobbling two more bagels, Troy paced around the picnic table running his hands through his hair and rubbing the stubble on his chin. He hadn't spoken to his father in months.

After the France incident, they talked every day for a while, but Troy grew tired of getting sympathy and reminders of his failure. Being the civilian director of CONTRA increased the awkwardness for his father. A similar discomfort used to occur when they talked about Troy's mother. She had left them when Troy was still a toddler. He slid the old picture of her out of his wallet and stared at it. *How different would life be if she'd stayed? She and Dad seemed happy in every picture. Why did she go?*

Troy should've been with CONTRA instead of in that parking lot. Leading the Blue Team felt like his destiny, his birthright. But then France happened . . .

A training day like any other, CONTRA was wrapping up the last of three phases before the strike force's operational initiation. Three companies of the battalion were split into color-coded teams: Blue, Gray, and Black. Seven selected officers commanded fifty Special Forces operators from each company. The NATO mission to hunt and destroy The Revolution was theirs. The first two companies were ready to deploy. Troy would command the Blue Team. General Patton would command field operations.

Missions to Taiwan and Colombia were planned.

The first phase of training had been in Colorado, the second in England, and the last in France. Troy performed at the top of the recruits throughout CONTRA training. His selection to lead the Blue Team during the England phase came as no surprise, but it was still the proudest day of his professional life. He didn't know then that it soon would be followed by the most humiliating of days.

Final preparations to launch CONTRA were underway at a French military base near Marseille. Troy finished a fighting simulation early and took his rented Ducati Superbike to the coast in hopes of catching the evening sunset, a must-see according to the French base commander.

In his rush to get to the viewpoint, Troy neglected to remove his battlesuit before leaving the base and broke a strict rule. He'd planned to change but it would have meant missing the sunset. Thinking nobody would see him, Troy put on a long jacket to conceal his futuristic battlesuit. He took a chance, which he'd believed held little risk.

After watching the spectacular sunset from Calanque de Sugiton, a vantage point between Marseille and Cassis, Troy began his return to base thinking it had all been worth it. On a bend in the winding road leading back, a branch flew into the wheel shaft of his Ducati. Troy lost control, banked to one side and almost crashed into a guardrail hovering above a one-hundred-foot drop. Breathing a sigh of relief, Troy inspected the damage. The bike needed only minor repairs.

Troy considered calling Breakdown or Justice to pick him up. A nighttime briefing on The Revolution was scheduled. He didn't want to miss out. The briefing would cover early planning on a possible CONTRA reconnaissance operation in occupied Taiwan. Troy decided against the call, not wanting to bring attention to his situation. Taking Top Secret military technology off base would not build confidence among his teammates. Troy felt stupid for his mistake and vowed never to repeat such foolishness.

He pushed the Superbike up the winding French highway to a trendy restaurant overlooking the ocean. Troy had visited the restaurant once before and knew there was a gas station with a maintenance workshop next door. Night was falling by the time he reached the parking lot. Nightlife in that area of France was lively. People were arriving in droves at the restaurant.

Troy tried to look inconspicuous, parking his bike under a tree between the gas station and restaurant. A Mercedes convertible pulled up next to him and an elegant woman wearing a black dress and red stilettos exited, giving Troy a friendly smile as she did. He watched her walk up the restaurant's stairs and enter the lounge, wishing he could follow.

Shaking off his thoughts, Troy jogged to the gas station and asked the attendant if he could borrow some tools. The attendant gave him curious looks and asked about the NATO emblem and peculiar uniform under his jacket. Troy explained he was a tourist and liked collecting different memorabilia. The attendee didn't buy the explanation. He provided the tools and watched Troy closely. The repairs took minutes. Troy started to leave, thinking if he sped to base he could make the Taiwan briefing on time.

The night was getting cold. He noticed the elegant woman had returned to the parking lot. Leaning over her Mercedes trunk, she collected a sleek cashmere sweater and folded it in her arms. While Troy thought of something clever to say, five college-aged males pulled up in another shiny convertible. Rowdy and drunk, they shouted obscenities and made rude gestures toward the woman. She hurried back toward the entrance of the restaurant. Two of the men jumped out of the convertible and blocked her way.

Troy could tell that the situation might get out of hand, but wanted nothing to do with it. Avoiding incidents with the locals was wise, especially considering he wore classified battlesuit technology not cleared to leave NATO installations unless on an official mission. Troy scanned for a restaurant employee or passerby. The back lot was empty except for the woman and drunken hoodlums. Three other men jumped out of the convertible and joined their friends in openly harassing and taunting the woman.

Troy dismounted from his bike. He kept waiting for someone else to arrive on the scene. Troy grabbed his cell phone and began dialing for police assistance. He'd make an inconspicuous exit when the police arrived and avoid trouble. One of the drunken Frenchmen noticed him dialing.

"Hey, we have a good boy with us. He probably wants to help the lady," he said in sarcastic French.

"Why don't you help yourself? Be a hero!" yelled another. He picked up a cobbled brick and hurled it toward Troy, who dodged it. The men cheered and laughed.

One of the men planted a kiss on the woman's lips. She yelled, pushing him away. Troy took a step forward and put his phone in his pocket. In a very commanding voice he said, "You will leave that woman alone and get about your business. You will do that *now.*"

The men stopped. They stared at Troy, then back at one another. Troy had spoken in English, not French.

"An American!" exclaimed one of the men.

"You are going to tell *us* what to do? I don't think so," said the man who threw the brick. "Leave, if you're smart enough."

Troy looked the woman in her eyes, sensing her desperation and fear. She wanted him to help. Leaving her to the hoodlums wasn't an option. Troy sized up the men. All were athletic. No matter, he could take them down with ease.

"Forget about the American. He's about to cry," said one of the men.

"*Laissez moi aller!*" yelled the woman. She spit at one of the men and kicked another in the shin. A hard slap landed across her cheek and reverberated in the parking lot.

Troy stopped thinking and ran toward them. The two nearest men tried grabbing him. Troy struck one in the face with his forearm while kicking the other in the stomach, sending him sprawling; both blows were restrained. Even though they were troublemakers and not the enemy he was trained to fight, Troy couldn't stand by and watch them harass a woman.

Two of the other hooligans lunged at Troy, throwing wild punches. He ducked both attempts, cracking one of the men in the knee with his elbow while delivering an uppercut to the other. Blood spurted from the man's mouth, his jaw crunching down on his tongue. The man fell writhing on the ground. Blood poured over his lips. He whimpered.

The last man threw the woman to the ground and pulled out a small pocket-knife. Behind Troy, two of the ruffians dusted themselves off. They weren't cheering or laughing anymore.

"You want to play with *me,* hero?" the man with the knife mocked. "Then come and play." He lunged forward. Troy jumped back and whirled around to block a fist about to impact the side of his head.

The men were athletic enough to keep up with Troy, even in their drunken state. Outnumbered five to one, they kept him busy and wouldn't go down easily. Troy would have to use more force. He jump-kicked one assailant, sending him over the hood of the woman's Mercedes. The man landed on the windshield, cracking it into spider webs.

Another wild stabbing attempt by the knife-wielding man nearly met Troy's chin. He avoided it in exchange for a fist to the center of his back. In a flash, Troy broke that man's arm at the elbow and shattered his nose with two rapid moves. The hoodlums were fighting an American Ninja and finding out the hard way.

Two men remained standing, including the one brandishing a sharp pocket-knife. The man without a knife drew a switchblade. He said something to the other. They both charged Troy. Instinct took over. He threw off the jacket concealing his battlesuit and activated one of the close-combat weapons, the Fang—a high-voltage electric whip with serrated blades designed to grapple into an attacker's flesh and shock him to death if the setting was lethal.

Troy released the Fang from below his wrist, injecting the weapon into the stomach of the nearest attacker. He pulled the cord, charging it with enough electricity to knock the man unconscious. The man dropped to the ground and lay motionless. Troy dodged a swipe from the switchblade behind him and recoiled the electric whip. He turned, facing the last attacker. The man dropped his switchblade and backed away mumbling apologies after seeing the battlesuit in action.

The abused woman picked herself up off the ground. Her knees were scraped, her chic black dress dusty. A red mark covered her cheek where she'd been slapped. She wept a "thank you" in English, touching Troy's arm softly, before running into the restaurant. A small crowd of onlookers had gathered at the back entrance. Someone announced a fight had broken out in the parking lot. The distraught woman pushed herself through the crowd not wanting any part of the aftermath.

Troy stared down the final hoodlum, angered that the drunken men had forced the situation upon him. Hearing police sirens approach, he walked to his motorcycle, deciding not to wait for the authorities. Returning to base would be best for him.

Later that night, under orders, Troy met with the local chief of police who arrived on base with questions about an American soldier with blonde hair. General Patton suggested they cooperate to clear up the matter. Arguments broke out with the police chief during Troy's reluctant interview.

The chief had interviewed the hoodlums first and accused Troy of lying about how the incident unfolded. The woman couldn't be located to confirm his testimony. To make matters worse, the hoodlums were members of *Olympique de Marseille*, a popular regional soccer team. Everyone in France worshiped soccer players.

CONTRA was operating under new NATO rules, which put Troy outside the traditional legal protection provided U.S. military personnel on home soil. The French police took him into custody. Wearing and using the NATO battlesuit put him in serious trouble under foreign jurisdictions.

Rumors spread through France that a drunk American soldier nearly killed several soccer players who were defending a woman in distress. The rumor-turned-fact made front-page news. There was outrage and little coverage to explain the context of Troy's actions. He was the villain and the soccer players were portrayed as victimized heroes.

An intense uproar of public anger spread, enough to get the French prime minister to demand Troy be court marshaled and jailed for breaking NATO rules and using classified military technology against French civilians. Patton defended Troy's actions, but to no avail. If the U.S. fully discharged Troy from military service, not just CONTRA, the French agreed to drop criminal charges. It became their best offer. The U.S. State Department negotiated a deal with NATO and French officials.

A week after the incident, the CONTRA Blue and Gray teams departed for Colorado Springs to prepare for their first missions. It was the last time Troy saw any of the other officers. It was also the last time anybody called him Battlestar.

CHAPTER 10
IN ASHES AND DUST
Southern Colombia: April 23, 2035

Midnight passed.

Crosshill had worried about the stories Raption told. The counter-narcotics operation uncovered barbarism and state-of-the-art terrifying and strange technologies hidden deep underground in the Demon Lab. The horrors were surreal. After the earlier encounter the Amazon forest seemed to curl and sway like a living organism, the shadows cloaking a living danger. Crosshill did not believe in ghosts, but he knew wickedness was real.

He reached into his pocket and grabbed his media locket. It held his most precious belongings, the pictures and videos of his family. He missed his wife and little girl, Margaret. They wanted him home. Sometimes he considered quitting for them. Margaret cried every time he left on a new tour. She'd hug him tight, insisting he stay. "Daddy, how are you going to watch my football game if you're gone?" she asked when he left for the CONTRA mission.

Margaret was growing up fast. Soon she'd be talking about boys, and even worse, going out to the London pubs with them. It seemed like yesterday Crosshill was drinking his first Guinness and watching Liverpool score goals at the corner pub. Now, he was a grown man with a family—one he missed deeply.

He closed the media locket.

Crosshill had planned on retirement in 2034 so he could work as a carpenter and be home. Seventeen years in the SAS was enough, until command briefed him on The Revolution. CONTRA was the only reason he stayed.

"It's time to move in," Crosshill ordered over the radios.

The remaining members of the Gray Team neared the underground jungle base on a cautious prowl. Small fires burned in and around the bombed-out complex. A low, misty haze hung above the tree line. Light from a full moon beamed down and illuminated smoke trails, giving the smoldering ruins of the secret fortress a ghostly feel.

Red and a half-dozen unscathed CONTRA soldiers had stayed back with the wounded in the forest clearing. Incoming search-and-rescue choppers would evacuate them. Six CONTRA operatives were dead from enemy fire or werewolf attacks. Another ten soldiers, plus Breakdown and Warsaw, were badly wounded and in critical condition. Warsaw's condition had worsened. He fluctuated between consciousness and unconsciousness because of vast blood loss. Death was imminent if he didn't get surgery.

The rest of the CONTRA team had orders to immediately investigate the wreckage of the destroyed Revolution base. Discounting the dead, the wounded, and the soldiers staying to guard those left behind in the clearing, the unit going back into the battle zone was at half strength.

Crosshill asked everyone to scrape together ammunition before the team began its sweep forward to explore the ruined base. Almost out, the officers and soldiers had to collect what they could from the dead and wounded. The admiral on the USS Reagan approved Crosshill's request for a SEAL team to assist his decimated company. The SEALs would meet CONTRA at the base. Unmanned Navy reconnaissance drones from the carrier patrolled overhead. Their sensors searched for traces of enemy activity below.

Crosshill wouldn't wait for the SEALs before inspecting the wreckage. He wanted to get there first. "How many enemy soldiers escaped from the side of the complex?" he questioned Diamond as they marched back.

"At least twenty."

"The soldiers on the opposite flank reported a similar number," Satellite added.

"We need to be careful we're not walking into a snare," Crosshill warned. "Nondetection by the drones doesn't guarantee a lack of presence below. After what we saw earlier, nothing is off the table. Watch for stray werewolves. We may not have killed them all."

The shock of their earlier battle hadn't settled. The Revolution seemed more menacing than ever. Unease weighed on Crosshill. He'd never dreamed of seeing creatures like the werewolves. The transforming base perplexed him further. None of it made sense.

NATO wanted an immediate report on how The Revolution managed the covert construction of the complex. If there was more to find underground, the expectation was CONTRA would uncover it while the trail was hot. Crosshill reminded himself that NATO formed the strike force for missions like this one. *This is our job.*

The werewolves etched a picture in his mind of the sinister creations their enemy had devised with diabolical success—a devilish reminder of what might await the Gray Team. The truth was, nobody wanted to find out what lay behind those wrecked walls. Not tonight.

The smallest noises pierced through the grim darkness. On several occasions, Crosshill spotted movement among the trees, but nothing came of it. CONTRA closed in on the post-bomb blast destruction: a sour smell seeped from the ruins—a nauseating greeting. Crosshill whispered over the radio for a squad of soldiers to inspect and cover the rear of the base.

"Open fire on anything that moves and shoot until it's dead," he said.

"Roger that," an Italian sergeant leading the squad responded.

Crosshill saw blazing fright in the squad members' eyes as they ran past him and Raption. Despite the intense training these Special Forces underwent, they were still nervous. "The SEALs will land any minute, team. They'll back you and help secure the perimeter. After the SEALs land, and you feel the surroundings are secure, find one of the dead werewolves to take back with us," Crosshill added, patting the sergeant on his helmet.

CONTRA needed more intelligence about the metal plates on the werewolves. Whether they were transmitters or control nodes, the labs needed a look.

The squad veered off ahead through the jungle and disappeared from view. The foot of the base was directly ahead.

"We're about the same distance from the base as we were when the shooting started," Diamond's voice came over the radio.

No movement or sound was detected from behind the pulverized walls. Only the flicker of burning ash surrounded the complex. The glowing embers filled the quiet night air with an appearance of candlelight in the jungle.

"A deceitful peace once again," Diamond whispered.

CONTRA edged to the southern side of the structure where Revolution troops had disappeared. The team moved slowly until they neared the corner end of the base and found the exit door. Crosshill motioned the company to approach. He jogged forward. Raption and Satellite trailed behind him with Diamond's rifle aimed at the entrance for cover.

Blasted half open, the bottom of the large metal doorframe was thrust deep into the earth and looked immovable. A space in the blown doorway provided enough room to walk through. Pitch-blackness lay behind the entrance. Crosshill thought of his family. His finger strained against the trigger as he jumped over a small mound of concrete. He closed his eyes for a moment than plunged into the entrance of the Revolution base.

Rubble blocked his way forward down a hallway. Crosshill spotted a ramp to his left leading slightly downward into the heart of the structure. He decided to take it. The other officers and CONTRA soldiers followed. A rotten scent filled the inside of the complex. Smoke mixed with the awful odor detected on approach consumed all clean oxygen, producing a toxic aroma. Diamond coughed, clasping her hand over her mouth to block the acrid stench.

The bombing run had demolished the upper levels of the base. The first floor aboveground, where the team entered, had withstood the force of the blasts. Crosshill realized the slanted walls of the broken hallway were in danger of caving in. Part of the moon was visible through a gaping hole above the two sides forming the fragile passage they walked through. If the walls collapsed inward, the ramp would be buried, preventing CONTRA from exiting. Nonetheless, they had a job to do and they wouldn't leave empty-handed.

The team moved single file down the ramp with expert speed, their weapons ready to rip into any threat. There were no dead bodies or signs of the enemy. Debris was everywhere. Still, the blast area seemed clean, like the earth had just swallowed up the top of the base. Strange.

The ramp wound in a semicircle to another floor beneath surface level. A different hallway, with the look of a corporate office building, lay in front of the Gray Team. Three doors lined each side of the hall. Crosshill gave the team hand signals to check behind each door. He kicked open the first, ready to fire. Two soldiers followed behind him. Papers were strewn about the floor from a buckled bookshelf at the center of the nondescript room. Aside from that, nothing seemed out of place... at first.

Ready to report the "all clear," Crosshill stopped himself when he noticed a large desk pushed up against the far side of the room. It had been wiped clean of dust. The shine from a fresh polish was unmistakable. Dust from the bomb blast covered everything else in the room—except for the desk. On it sat five white statuettes placed in a perfect circle, surrounding a sixth larger black statue.

Crosshill moved toward the desk and examined the statuettes closely, identifying most of them. They were well-known religious symbols, carved out of white marble: The Star of David, the Christian cross, the crescent moon of Islam, the OM emblem of Hinduism, and a Buddha, all arranged around a black centerpiece, which Crosshill didn't recognize.

Reminiscent of a gargoyle, or demon with wings, the black center statuette seeped wrathful wickedness. Though lifeless, Crosshill felt a definite energy from the object. "These sculptures were arranged after the blast occurred," Crosshill spoke to the CONTRA soldiers in the room with him. "Some sort of message." He snapped photos and stared at the arrangement for a moment, absorbed.

Crosshill exited the room and met Raption and Satellite in the corridor. They went ten paces forward before Raption put his arm out in front of himself and Satellite, bringing them both to a stop. The hall abruptly ended. The officers stood on a ledge hanging over a massive black hole. A hot stench blew up from the darkness. Satellite covered his nose, grimacing.

"Puke on me now," Raption whispered pointing down into the hole, holding his nose as well.

Crosshill gazed into the blackness, neither seeing nor hearing anything. Raption pointed the flashlight mounted on his weapon into the blackness. At first only the smoky haze reflecting back off the beam was visible. He increased the power and glanced over at Satellite, who was breathing heavily. The extra brightness of the flashlight made it possible to see a lower level of the complex.

A wicked shrill broke the night calm and sent the exploring CONTRA team to its knees. The dreadful high-pitched shriek lasted several seconds before the night returned to silence.

"What in the world was *that*?" Raption asked.

Satellite swallowed hard and shook his head.

Crosshill thought of the squad aboveground and those back with the wounded. He radioed to check on them. The squad reported okay. Red's voice came stuttering through an instant later. She rambled in fear, obviously shaken by the scream.

"There are noises in the trees . . . to either side of the camp," she said. "We're ready to fire but can't see or pick up any traces on thermal . . . I know there's something out there."

Crosshill considered going back. He would have, had it not been for Diamond calling the team to the room nearest the end of the hallway. Inside, a large staircase wound downward into the dark abyss of the base.

"We can't turn back, Red," Crosshill said. "There's something here we have to see. Keep the soldiers calm and wait for the rescue choppers. They'll be there shortly. *Don't* leave the area."

Crosshill took his first step down the staircase behind Diamond, Raption, and Satellite who had already begun the descent. Circling downward into the darkness, Crosshill found it odd that there were no dead bodies or any casualties from the firefight. He tapped Satellite on the shoulder at the bottom of the staircase, whispering, "Where are all the dead rebels? I must have killed at least ten during the fight. They didn't all escape or get up and walk away."

"I don't care. I'd rather we find none of them, sir. Fine with me. Tell you the truth, I just want to get the hell out of here and back up top," Satellite whispered back.

Diamond turned to the two of them, putting her finger over her lips to silence them. The team stood in a large cavernous room at the bottom of the staircase. The sound of dripping water echoed and puddles covered the floor. The nauseating smell of rotten fish continued to grow worse now that they were deeper into the underground complex.

Crosshill heard the faint sound of helicopters above. The Navy choppers must have arrived to pick up their teammates and insert the SEALs. More American troops nearby gave him comfort. At least they had backup.

As they got their bearings, the scope of the underground base started to set in. It was massive.

"Everyone stay tight. Enemy could be around any corner," Crosshill said. He felt his hand cramp from his unending squeeze on his weapon.

To one side the blackness continued down for at least another level. They were on one edge of a giant ovoid hole cut into the earth where the transforming fortress had been nestled deep underground and hidden. A walkway encompassed the inner edges of the immense hole it left behind. Partially collapsed wreckage of the base blocked parts of the passage, preventing the

CONTRA team from inspecting all the way around. Evidence abounded that the terrestrial complex they'd destroyed earlier was part of a much, much larger underground development.

Looking across to the other side, the slight outline of archways was exposed through shards of metal. Rubble and smoke made it difficult to tell what they were viewing, even with night vision. Unless they found another staircase on the opposite side of the aboveground level, there was no way to investigate the other side.

"Can you believe this?" Raption asked. "It must have taken years to build."

"They're going to have to send a whole division of analysts to check this out," Satellite said. "Talk about the Twilight Zone."

Crosshill mulled their next move. The Gray Team stood on one side of the walkway where two large metal doors towered behind them. Twenty paces ahead two huge archways led to dark pathways. The archways opened to the mouths of giant underground caves or tunnels. Inky black lay beyond. Crosshill motioned to several CONTRA soldiers to follow him to the foot of the archways. He used thermal and motion sensors to assess the presence of any life forms. There were none. Only dark stillness.

Satellite and Raption attempted to open the metal doors behind them. One door was locked. They could only nudge the other slightly. A potent stench of the sickening smell wafted through the gap. Raption turned, gasping, and fell to one knee vomiting in a nasty cough. He spit the puke out and licked his lips, spitting again.

"You all right?" Crosshill asked, running over from the archways and covering his face from the odor.

"Whatever's causing the smell, there's a lot of it behind that door."

"'Puke on me now,' huh?" Satellite smiled.

Raption looked up at him but did not laugh.

Cupping his hand over his face, Crosshill peered through the crack between the large metal doors. Something blocked it from opening fully. He shined his light in, revealing a plain concrete floor and wall. A dark liquid covered part of the floor. It looked like oil or blood. Crosshill starting feeling queasy and pulled the door shut.

"Couldn't see much. Something wet was covering the ground. Maybe it's causing the smell. Don't know, but let's move on."

The team moved toward the two archways where Diamond stood staring into the darkness. Everyone walked carefully with his or her back pressed up against the wall. The path from the stairwell to the archways was narrow. Only three feet separated the chasm in the earth from the wall. A stumble would mean sure death.

Crosshill marveled at the base's interior. Only the center part of the complex rose above ground level, the rest was built underground constructed of hallways, rooms, and tunnels. He knew the complexities involved in creating such a feat were astounding and he stopped to consider the magnitude of what they were witnessing.

"This can't be real. They cut this deep into the earth and built this thing . . . without detection. This isn't right. It had to be constructed over a long time," Crosshill said.

"The workmanship it takes to build something like this pushes my comprehension—never mind in secret," Satellite agreed.

"Must have taken more than a decade."

"It would mean The Revolution has been in power for many more years than we know of," Satellite said. "I find that hard to believe."

"I guess we have no choice but to believe it. We're here, aren't we? It's here," Diamond said.

"Underground though . . . " Satellite continued, questioning. "The landscape above. No sign of anything. If they hadn't revealed a presence we could've walked right by and never found it."

"They probably wouldn't have challenged us if that was the case," Raption said.

"Maybe they didn't *challenge* us. It could have been a time of their choosing," Diamond responded.

"What do you mean?" Crosshill asked.

The team turned into the mouth of the larger of the two tunnels, slowly creeping forward with their gun beams and flashlights bouncing across the dark walls around and above them.

"This enemy is far more cunning than we have given them credit for, let's be honest," Diamond said. "During training we were taught the likely truths of The Revolution. NATO's way of telling us the intelligence community's best guess. They were described as anticapitalists, drug lords, and businessmen gone bad at a time of political and economic upheaval, all working together," she paused. "Maybe someone's not telling us *everything*."

"You're suggesting Command doesn't want us to know something?" Satellite asked.

"What we've found proves the potential of that theory. There has to be cooperation, an axis arrangement of sorts. It's the only way they could ever achieve this feat."

Diamond turned away and pointed her gun beam down the dark tunnel. They headed deeper. "What Command taught made sense—what we're seeing is altogether different. I don't want to argue the point down here."

Crosshill picked a small piece of broken tile off the floor. It felt weightless in his hand and had an odd spongelike texture. He stuck the piece in a side pocket, saving it for the lab coats when he returned to headquarters.

"This tunnel is huge. We'll go just a little ways. See if there's anything worth reporting and head back to find those SEALs. We've seen about enough for one night," Crosshill said. "Headquarters can do what they want. We're not staying down here much longer . . . nothing good can happen. I'll sign to that in my report." Crosshill felt the team was vulnerable underground. The radios had patched out and there was far too much to explore for such a small unit.

CONTRA moved forward with caution. Their flashlights impacted the vast tunnel as much as fireflies did the night sky. The ground beneath their boots was dirt. The sides of the tunnels had small fixtures and piping visible in spots. The spongy tile covered some areas on either side. As they got deeper, only raw earth surrounded them.

Crosshill spotted a torch nestled in a lanternlike fixture jutting out of the wall. "Raption, why don't you see if that torch works? These flashlights are like pea-shooters in this place."

After a small tussle to unhook the torch, Raption managed to light a flame and bring brightness to the dark cavern. As the torch flickered to light, Crosshill glimpsed a man ducking into a bend in the tunnel ahead—without hesitation he fired three bursts from his semiautomatic.

"I saw someone! Right around that corner." Crosshill kept his gun barrel pointed in the direction he had fired.

"Me too," said a CONTRA soldier moving his way to the front.

Everyone stood motionless for a moment, straining to hear the slightest sound. There was nothing except the faint noise of dripping water behind them. The team moved forward, carefully rounding the bend in the tunnel.

Three men hung dead from the top of the cave. Nooses were tied around their necks and dried blood covered their bodies. Puddles of blood stained the dirt red below their feet. Each man wore camouflage and looked like the type of paramilitaries CONTRA had expected to find on this mission. Diamond gasped.

"Why do you think they were hung?" Raption asked.

"No idea," Crosshill said.

Twenty paces beyond the hanging bodies was a large iron gate with bars going from the top of the tunnel to the bottom. A small man huddled against the corner of the gate.

"Freeze!" Raption shouted. "Stay where you are!" He moved forward holding the torch, several CONTRA soldiers at his side. Their weapons were aimed at the man's head as they neared, ready to shoot if he made any sudden movements. The closer they got, the more harmless they saw the man was.

Raggedy clothes draped his frail half-naked frame. He trembled and mumbled incoherently in Spanish. He looked like a villager, but Raption didn't want to take any chances.

"Who are you?" he asked in a stern voice.

"*Silencio, por favor. Silencio, por favor. Silencio, por favor*," the man whispered repeatedly. He was unarmed. Raption took his eye off him for a moment to look through the gate. It was what they were searching for.

Another Demon Lab.

Crosshill walked past the whimpering man and up to the bars. Raption stood next to him with the torch. Gazing through the gate, Raption held the torch in front of them, shedding light across a room the size of a high school gymnasium. An iridescent glow came from the far back where dozens of large spherical vats of red liquid towered upward. Rows of examination tables and counters lined the middle of the lab. Microscopes and tools lay strewn across the countertops. The near wall ran parallel to where the Gray Team stood, covered with open cabinets full of high-tech gear, electronic equipment, and banks of computer screens.

On the opposite side of the lab was an unfurnished open space. Hay covered the entire floor where a half-dozen small wooden pens lined the wall. Next to the pens another cavernous opening led away from the lab down another tunnel. Above the entrance was a strange symbol similar to ones found previously in the Revolution Declaration, the first Demon Lab, and tattooed on several captured mercenaries. The symbol of The Revolution—a jagged arrangement of diamond shapes symmetrically spaced in a unique pattern.

The other officers joined Crosshill and Raption at the gate. Two soldiers tended to the trembling man. Diamond tapped Raption on the shoulder, pointing to The Revolution symbol. He nodded.

"This is what we came to find," Crosshill said, impressed by the lab's size and organization. "Never would I have imagined its significance would become secondary to everything else we've discovered."

"The effort for this . . . They could've outfitted an entire army with the best weapons for the money an underground facility of this magnitude costs," Satellite said.

"They have no shortage of weapons, my friend," Diamond pointed out.

Crosshill looked at the trembling man still mumbling nonsense at the foot of the gate. "Do you speak English?" he asked in a gentle tone.

The man didn't answer, just gazed back at Crosshill with lost eyes.

Diamond knelt in front of the quivering man. "He has the same look as The Revolution assassins in Brussels who attacked NATO headquarters. I was there when they unmasked a couple of those who survived. Most refused to talk. Those who tried didn't make much sense. They were under some kind of intense hypnosis from 'an undocumented psychotropic drug' the medics called it. There was no definitive conclusion."

"It was peculiar indeed," Crosshill said. "My commander at the time feared if The Revolution could perfect mind control, we'd be in for a long war."

"Should we try and cut through these bars and take a better look inside?" Raption asked.

Crosshill looked at the three hanging men behind them and checked his watch. "The sun will be rising soon. We could use a larger team and a whole lot more equipment to handle this operation. We've seen what we came for. Watch the villager close, Raption. He's coming with us. Cut the men down from the ceiling. We don't have time to carry them out, but we won't let them hang either."

The team began to make its way back out of the tunnel. They moved in surreal silence, the enormity of their discovery sinking in. Being CONTRA, they'd expected to engage in the unknowns The Revolution offered, but the last twelve hours were beyond anyone's expectation.

On most occasions Crosshill was able to draw logical conclusions. The more he considered what transpired, the more puzzling the possibilities seemed. The werewolves, the statues he found, the underground tunnels, the transforming base, and another Demon Lab. Extraordinary. Bizarre. All of it. There should have been dead bodies in the rubble, or for that matter, live enemy soldiers left in the complex. Instead, all had disappeared—dead and living.

Crosshill felt they were participants to something much greater than they could imagine. As CONTRA made its way back up the winding staircase, he radioed the squad guarding the back of the complex to ask if the SEALs had joined them and if they had located any dead werewolves. To his dismay, there was no answer. Crosshill tried again. Still, no answer.

"Maybe there's disruption of our signals here," Satellite said. "I'll try getting Red." Satellite connected to her as the team made its way down the hallway from which they entered. Red informed him that the rescue choppers had picked her and the wounded up as planned. They were already onboard the USS Ronald Reagan.

"We left a squad of soldiers behind when we went into the complex. Any word from them?" Satellite asked.

"No. I heard Crosshill give those orders and check in with the squad after that terrible scream we all heard," Red said. "There has been radio silence from them ever since."

The Gray Team exited through the broken door of the complex. The early morning sky brought welcome daylight. The fresh air was a relief from the nauseating, musty underground. Wisps of smoke still floated over the base from smoldering fires burning around the rubble.

"Be ready, we don't know if something is still out here," Crosshill warned.

CONTRA made its way warily, forming a defensive half-circle in front of the doorway they entered. They peered out at the rainforest around them, hoping to see a sign of their fellow troops. Only the sound of a fine morning breeze rustled the jungle branches.

"We have a missing CONTRA squad," said Crosshill. "Red, where are those SEALs?"

"They couldn't find the squad so they retraced a path back to the clearing. They are searching for them."

Crosshill continued to try and reach the men. The CONTRA soldiers disappeared like The Revolution combatants from the base. Crosshill caught Raption's gaze and shook his head in disgust. They both knew it couldn't be good. No one spoke for several minutes. The decision to proceed into the destroyed base before the SEAL team insertion seemed less compelling when considering the CONTRA squad's disappearance.

Finally the Gray Team met up with the SEALs. Together they searched the nearby jungle area for several hours. All they found was a sign nailed to a tree near where the CONTRA squad had been ordered to keep watch. On a wooden board, in red painted letters, the sign simply read:

Welcome to The Revolution

CHAPTER 11
COMMENCEMENT
Panama Canal: April 25, 2035

In a far off time and place, Ripster, Prowess, and Likzi had once been good, idealistic, and honorable people. That was decades ago. When introducing themselves to their recruits in The Revolution, they referred to themselves as "The Three" and never gave mention to their past lives or the complexities of their new calling.

Entering a large, unused port facility at the edge of the Panama Canal, The Three felt confident and proud things were proceeding according to plan. The core representatives of The Revolution awaited them inside. Old machinery and pieces of equipment that had outlived their usefulness lined the oversized stockroom. It was not an elegant setting. It did not need to be. The meeting would be quick and straight to the point.

A large round wooden table occupied the center of the stockroom. Men and women from different parts of the world filled its seats: gangsters from the streets of eastern Europe; important businessmen and militant leaders from Africa; espionage agents from China; cartel commanders from Colombia and Mexico; and the most influential members of the Russian mafia.

The meeting marked the first time all The Revolution's major members assembled in the same room, persuaded to attend—not by promises—but with large cash incentives, advance payments, and contraband. Independently, they were criminals looking to make a buck however possible. Together, they formed the backbone of The Revolution.

A handful of guards lined the inside walls of the facility wearing the customary black and red Revolution uniforms. One of them escorted The Three to their seats at the head of the table, the only chairs still vacant. A fourth, extremely large figure entered the room with The Three and remained by the entrance, not following them to the table. The figure received curious stares from the attendees, his size and demeanor capturing their interest along with the blood red cloak that obscured his face. The yellow hue of glowing eyes seemed suspended within the darkness of the cloak.

Ripster eyed the conspirators approvingly. Vladimir Polpotov, the leader from Russia's most powerful mafia, Crvena Zvezda, extended his hand in greeting. Ripster pretended not to see. An awkward moment ensued and the mafia leader abruptly sat down next to his brother Boris who was sweating uncontrollably. Boris dabbed a white cloth over his forehead and trembled in the presence of Ripster.

"We are ready to begin," Ripster announced still standing. His voice was deep and crackled like a firework. He led The Three. As far as any of the conspirators knew, Ripster commanded The Revolution. His bulging arms showed through the futuristic armor underneath his red cloak. Ripster held a commanding physical presence, always wore a mask, and never bothered with small talk. As was his habit, he addressed the conspirators with Prowess and Likzi flanking his sides.

"We are all gathered here because of recent developments most of you are not privileged enough to understand. I will tell you what you need to know. Firstly, there is an attempt by the pathetic alliance NATO to stop what we have already accomplished. They feed on information that means little. They assume simple things are difficult. They matter not."

Ripster began to pace. He removed his cloak while he walked, folded it carefully and placed it on the center of the table. High on the right side of his chest, emblazoned on dark red armor, was a jagged symbol made of diamonds. The conspirators seated at the table weren't aware of what the sharp symbol represented. Most had seen it before and accepted it as The Revolution's emblem.

"Our concern in the chance we have before us precedes your involvement in this great endeavor. The fortunes of your world, *our* world, are changing. Chaos will soon govern the weak. Those matched against us will suffer as conditions of life transform into something *we* control. To the rats attempting to stop us, only painful surprises await," Ripster said looking pleased.

He loved giving speeches to anyone interested, and when Ripster talked people always were because of the material rewards that followed. Early on, Ripster removed any doubts the recruited conspirators had about prosperity in joining The Revolution. He avoided empty promises and delivered on the ones he made. Ripster understood that human beings bit easily when the proper bait was cast in front of them.

"Serve others. Follow rules that benefit them," he continued. "Should we? NO. That is why we have guided you so graciously to become a part of the greatest glory you could never accomplish without *us*. The time has come— and we are ready for your final compliance. Prowess?" Ripster said, gesturing to his female cohort.

Prowess was tall and toned. Straight black hair touched her shoulders and contrasted with her pearly white skin, vibrant red lipstick, and yellowing teeth. Prowess always wore tight black clothing on her shapely body. She could have seduced most any man if not for her unflattering teeth. Prowess never shied away from staring with her gray eyes, reminiscent of shallow clouded pools. The toughness of a man embodied her boldness and venom poisoned her voice. Prowess showed no evidence of warmth or signs of compassion.

"One of our secret bases was recently discovered by a new NATO group called CONTRA. They formed to ruin our plans, so we must ruin *them*," she scorned. "Their persistence is forcing us to implement our plan sooner than anticipated. The outcome will be no less damaging to those they seek to protect." A cunning smile momentarily changed the coldness on her face.

"We have positioned Revolution forces and brought you here to set in motion the final chapter in human progression on Earth. New powers will bring gratification to your efforts. Tonight you shall be paid that which you've been promised. If you fail from here, *death* is promised—either by our foes or one of the persons sitting next to you."

The conspirators at the table glanced at one another nervously. Likzi watched without saying a word.

"If you do what we ask, if you merely succeed in finishing what you've started, we will reward you like kings amongst kings," Prowess continued, folding her arms across her chest. "Fighting in this region will continue. Let the nation-states be distracted by the Drug Wars. We will begin to board your ships with men and precious cargo. You are to follow our instructions in the regions where you will rule. Increase your activities and wait for the arrival of our main forces. The time has come for *invasion*."

Silence filled the room as the participants processed the pronouncements from Prowess and Ripster. Then the different groups began to murmur among themselves, annoying Ripster. Vladimir Polpotov stood up and annoyed him further. Ripster didn't like or trust the Russian mobster. Vladimir wore designer suits for every occasion and bragged about accomplishments Ripster found trivial. The young mafia leader was only in his early forties, having taken the helm of Crvena Zvezda after the former leader mysteriously died. Vladimir asked too many questions, had overstepped his bounds at previous meetings, and had a penchant for arrogance.

"May I ask a question before we continue?" Vladimir asked.

"If you must," Ripster said, grinding his teeth.

"How can we trust your plan will work on the scale intended? You have shown great capacity to make The Revolution work. Many of us don't understand how you've managed it. We don't care because we get what we want. Nevertheless, how will you have enough men to mount an invasion? We don't have enough ships or weapons to fight modern armies. We can operate in the shadows, but once open fighting begins we will be crushed. All of us can infuse chaos on a small, *local* scale. I don't see how this is enough. In the end we will be killed or imprisoned if we challenge authority so openly. There must be more to this plan."

Ripster put both his fists on the table and leaned toward Vladimir. His triceps bulged as he scowled and looked the Russian gangster in the eye, repulsed.

"That was more than a question. There is much you don't see or understand and we are not asking you to try. The Revolution is something more than what it appears. Understand this: you are but a small part. Any doubts will be removed once our full plan is set in motion. Ask the governments south of Panama if they thought the drug cartels could mount such aggression. There is reason for this. It is The Revolution. It is The Three."

Ripster stared at Vladimir with cold confidence. "Victory is assured," he continued. "Before you depart in the morning I will show you what more there is to our plan. I am certain you will find it comforting, just like the new payments for your loyalty." Ripster looked at all the conspirators, waiting for their greed to replace their doubts. "We need you to spread violence in the predawn of war. Our full power will be apparent once The Global Revolution begins. The *deception* we have created must last until real war commences. The world has seen nothing yet. We will meet in the morning to overcome any trepidation you might have. Once we have replaced your concerns with appreciation, your ships will begin loading."

Ripster turned and headed toward the exit, not waiting for concurrence. Prowess stared at Vladimir seductively as she left. The large figure standing at the doorway followed The Three as they departed, leaving The Revolution conspirators with more questions than answers.

The Three followed a path alongside the outer edge of the port facility until they came upon a larger warehouse. Two Revolution guards opened a gate at the front of the warehouse and the ringleaders entered.

Dozens of forty-foot containers were stacked high in the warehouse. To one side, red containers almost reached to the ceiling. On the other, black containers went about a quarter of the way up. The Three and the large figure walked around and inspected several of the black containers.

"We are prepared. The black containers will carry one Sentrix each," Ripster informed his cohorts as he looked directly at the ominous figure. "May the robotic war sentries of the heralded past return. Our only concern remains the reaction from those who are watching. If *they* become a part of this war, if Nerrial challenges us, as we anticipate they will, the outcome is uncertain . . . at least here on Earth."

"Let them come," Prowess hissed. "I wait to look into their eyes and kill." A red glow flashed over her left eye. She smiled at the large cloaked figure commanding The Three. He was a Nezdeth general—a member of the ancient demonic enemy of Nerrial.

Since the War of the Star ended with Nerrial's victory seventeen hundred years ago, the Nezdeth had been quarantined by Nerrial's Starforce to their home planet of Whorvz. Located on the opposite side of the same galaxy, the Nezdeth seethed in hatred and anger on Whorvz for generations, waiting for the right moment to reemerge, conspiring for revenge against Nerrial. They were now closer than ever—thanks to The Three.

The general was unmoved by the blabbering of Ripster or Prowess. He spoke in a hollow, low voice. "If Nerrial decides it is their time of revelation to Earth, they will not be pleased. For my entire existence I have planned for the moment to reclaim our freedom and make the people of Nerrial suffer. They do watch—here and *everywhere*. For too long they have decided how we should live. This universe is not theirs. Vengeance is near."

"Ours and yours," Ripster reminded. "We only want Earth, the sacred test of Nerrial's High Council will become our playground. They banished us from the Starforce. They've forgotten, but we haven't. Traitors. We'll spoil their precious experiment of peaceful influence. Do what you will with Nerrial. It's not our home anymore."

"What of the captured?" Likzi asked.

"Show them to me," said the general.

The Three led the Nezdeth general through the warehouse. They rounded a corner and came upon several Revolution troops standing over a doorway in the floor. Two werewolves crouched on either side of the soldiers. One of the Revolution soldiers bent low and grabbed a handle opening an entryway to reveal a staircase leading downward. Torches provided light to the underground passage.

The Three took the general down the stairwell and walked twenty paces to a small dungeon with dirt floors. Four Revolution troops guarded a cell with iron bars. Behind the iron bars, in tattered dark navy and black uniforms, sat the Italian sergeant and the six captured Gray Team CONTRA soldiers.

"These were the ones taken outside of our destroyed base in Colombia. When they came back to inspect it, we took them," Ripster explained. "There were more of them, but we decided not to bring greater risk to ourselves than necessary."

"They discovered the insides? Our tunnels and the chambers?" the general asked with concern, verging on anger.

"We believe their counterparts did, but they did not find the main tunnels and we've made sure they never will," Ripster replied.

"You've made sure of nothing!" thundered the general. "Your mistakes could cost us. I did not order the next phase. You were fools to reveal our presence!"

"One of your commanders was with us," Prowess protested. "He ordered us to battle."

"Then he is a greater failure than *you*."

"The CONTRA were atop us. They discovered our servants and moved in with their sensors. Initiation of defenses was ordered and we followed suit, *General*," Prowess fumed.

The general turned to the CONTRA soldiers. They stared at him, silent. Stripped of their battlesuits, their uniforms beneath were frayed from the struggle and maltreatment ensuing their capture. Several of the soldiers had cuts and bruises on their faces. The general approached the cell and sniffed the men like a dog might. He looked at a NATO emblem on the side of one of their arms and growled deep. The Nezdeth general pulled back his hooded cloak and exposed his face. Unmistakable pure fear was reflected in the expressions of the CONTRA soldiers.

CHAPTER 12
CLOAKS AND DAGGERS
Washington, DC: April 28, 2035

The busy streets below Joseph McBride's office window bustled as the cease-less business of the world carried on. Once the absolute epicenter of power on the globe, Washington, DC, seemed less magnificent than it had in previous years. When in its prime, the world followed the politics and policies ema-nating from America's capitol as if the decisions made by the United States affected the lives of everyone. For a considerable time, they had.

Joseph sat back in his chair rubbing his temple and watching the U.S. capi-tol glow bright in the night sky. He pondered his role in all that was happen-ing. The world had changed remarkably since he first came to Washington. Nothing was the same.

Joseph worked to protect the world from inherent wickedness and influ-ence it for the better. His official government titles kept him busy with as-signments plagued by the drudgery of bureaucracy, but they were necessary. Questing for something greater through those tasks remained his true calling, a legacy of those who came before him. Joseph kept his secret life well hidden, as did all the Emissaries.

The time neared when their great secret would be revealed.

Appointed the NATO allied command operations civilian director of CONTRA, Joseph endured a full plate of political patchwork, problems, and decisions required to hold an alliance together. Whenever a blip of uncer-tainty about the Top Secret unit came into question, Joseph was the first one on the phone or catching the next flight to Brussels, easing the apprehension of bureaucrats seeking reasons to give in. After only two CONTRA missions, new questions and disquieting international jitters were unending.

The political firestorm surrounding China's accusations of Western troops in Taiwan and the shooting down of China's newest MiG fighter raised internal fears that NATO's counter-revolutionary mission had wrought greater problems than it was worth. Keeping the strike force and its mission Top Secret became harder for both the civilian and military planners.

Until more understanding replaced the mysterious technological, scientific, and military advances of The Revolution, downplaying its significance remained Western policymakers' priority. Preserving a wavering public's confidence in global security depended on deemphasizing growing fears around the world. Government acknowledgment of alarm about The Revolution would only grant the group a force-multiplying impact, as was the case with Al-Qaeda.

Worse than the China mission was the discovery of a second Demon Lab during the astonishing CONTRA encounter in Colombia. Politics aside, indications of a real emergency abounded. Earth's security in the universe was vanquished. It made Joseph's primary calling that much more difficult. The risk of inserting a CONTRA unit into Taiwan was worth it if it proved The Revolution was an Earth-based threat directed from China. Those hopes were all but faded. The world was experiencing a different kind of danger—an intergalactic one.

What could he and the Emissaries do about it? Fear and indecision didn't bode well in unison. Joseph felt both. Prolonged unease made him think of family. Joseph hadn't spoken to his son Troy in weeks. Troy's decommission had put Joseph in a precarious position. As his father *and* the civilian director of CONTRA, Joseph was asked by NATO's secretary general to avoid involvement in the matter due to a conflict of interests.

CONTRA had lost its best officer and Joseph was forced to watch Troy languish in misdirection. He wanted to tell his son the truth about his mother and the world, to unload the burden he'd carried for so long. But the time hadn't arrived yet. Joseph would have to wait. The guilt was beginning to take its toll, as he knew Troy continued in a downward spiral while he stood helplessly by.

Sitting in his lightless office overlooking the Washington Mall, Joseph considered how things became so dire—the wars, the greed. Now, a likely Nezdeth presence on Earth. Throughout his life Joseph did his best to influence a better path for the world. He was an optimist, like the rest of the Emissaries who knew the truth. Some Emissaries said the hour of opportunity had passed. Joseph liked to think otherwise.

His oversight of CONTRA was about ascertaining if The Revolution represented humanity's worst enemy, the unimaginable dread of a distant past reborn on Earth. For the strike force to work, America's president had to uphold support between U.S. allies. Joseph had the president's ear but couldn't take credit for assuring transatlantic cooperation. The effort Joseph continued had been underway for over a hundred years. Emissaries had tried to create a means for Earth to survive on its own, independent of a Nerrial intervention and altering the status quo of wars and power struggles.

Emissaries were Earth's final hope for the planet to save itself.

Joseph had proposed the idea for CONTRA to uncover clues about The Revolution even before his worst fears of the Nezdeth had seemed probable. When the Marines found the Demon Lab, and Nightwatch tracked the origins of The Revolution and The Three, their connections to the oldest enemy of humanity were hard to ignore. Joseph had worked in government for his entire life, far removed from the cosmic developments of the universe, but certain truths couldn't escape him now. The evidence all but confirmed that the unthinkable was happening. Joseph sensed there wasn't much time left. Nobody knew how far The Revolution had progressed or what the Nezdeth role was. Joseph and the others had to move fast.

Magden walked into his office.

"Would you like me to turn on the light?" the chief of emissaries asked.

"I prefer the moon. Besides, we don't need to see each other."

Magden proceeded quietly to the window. The faint moonlight showed the wrinkles on his face and shimmered off the skin of his scalp. Magden still appeared younger than most men his age. Slim and in amazing shape, he moved with the energy of an athlete warming up for a competition. Magden deserved all of the respect he received. He'd kept his watch dutifully and influenced well, becoming respected far and wide.

"You've seen and read the reports from the latest Colombia operation?" Magden asked.

"Yes."

"And what do you think of it?"

Joseph didn't respond. He wanted to keep considering other possibilities. Magden was his superior and always expected a good answer, the right one.

"The evidence matches up with our gravest fears," Joseph began. "The analysts flown to Colombia after CONTRA left the new Demon Lab found *nothing*. That base was simply a destroyed structure. All things of value buried or gone. No passages or landmarks to inspect, only rubble and dead ends. What do I think of it? I think The Revolution got back in from underground and did what they had to to protect their secrets. We were watching from above so there is no other explanation. Tunneling of that scope . . . the technology of that magnitude doesn't come from *this* world. I suppose it doesn't make a difference anyhow. The proof came from the CONTRA Gray Team."

Joseph shifted uneasily in his chair and continued.

"Our suspicion makes sense, as we've discussed before, yet a Nezdeth presence on Earth should be impossible. And why would they conspire in the form of The Revolution? What could their ultimate goal be? The High Council has been hard pressed to accept any of it. They've set out to consider further, though I say it has taken too long for them to start! With the time delay between deep-space Starblazer transmissions, it might be too late if our fears are true."

Magden didn't flinch. He stared off through the window as if entranced by the nightmarish reality he and Joseph were facing. Silence held the room for several minutes.

Joseph couldn't wait any longer. "What of your understudy?" he asked. "Has he made the progress you've hoped?"

"*My* understudy and the progress *I've* hoped?" Magden turned with a stern gaze. "You were once my understudy, Joseph, and it seems that I must continue teaching for my newest understudy is also *your* youngest son and you should refer to him as such."

Joseph didn't want to have that discussion again. The inescapable truths of his family's own secret plagued him. Magden had little patience for Joseph's inability to deal with the situation. An undercurrent in their relationship, Magden wouldn't relinquish his persistent insistence that Joseph accept his path more gracefully. Magden was mentoring Lonthran, Joseph's youngest son, from Earth. The brother Troy didn't know he had was now chief of Earth intelligence on Nerrial.

"Lonthran is making progress, yes," Magden said, turning back to the window. "He believes it possible for the revealing of Nerrial to occur soon on Earth—and he is not alone. The new Princess of the Adena Monarchy, Shia, is a formidable ally. She is active and ready to reawaken the spirit if it has failed us. The High Council will eventually meet on the question I have posed so many times, but *never* under these conditions of near confirmation that the Nezdeth are present on Earth. I've made our opinions and the grave danger clear, even before CONTRA's Gray Team made these discoveries. The High Council will consider our message. It may be the only chance we have to save Earth from horrors worse than its own terrible imperfections."

"Good. I will inform Patton of the news," Joseph replied moving to the edge of his seat. "I'm proud of Lonthran. You know that."

"His standing is something to be proud of, for certain," Magden beamed, looking hard at Joseph.

The men remained silent for some time. They knew the actions they took and the knowledge they held could mean the difference between unspeakable tragedies and ultimate utopia.

"Have you spoken to Troy recently?" Magden asked.

"No. I can't help him," Joseph swallowed to keep his voice from wavering.

"I suggest you try. It remains far more important for him to become a part of the future then remain a bystander. The trivial process that followed his actions was in accordance with laws that are in place for good reason. That being said, those rules hold little weight in what's to come. We shall reinstate him and waste no more time. Troy is too important to the Emissary code and Earth. Should our ancient enemies truly be present on this planet, he will become a leader of the defense effort. If the French protest his return at this time, let them deal with me," Magden said resolutely.

Joseph shot up out of his chair, fueled by the excitement at the prospect of his son returning to CONTRA. This decision would change Troy's life for the better, bringing back the purposeful life he loved. Joseph had not expected this decision, at least not so soon.

"*Now* is the time to test the bounds and limits imposed on us from afar," Magden continued. "We are a part of this planet. Risk and reward will go hand in hand with how we manage the travesty befalling Earth." He continued speaking staring directly into Joseph's eyes, "You have accomplished everything ever asked of you, out of the good will of your own heart. There needs to be more like you, but do not forsake your own family for the cause."

"I'm better at some things than I am at others. When Elizabeth left us my world changed."

"She never *left* you. Remember, the decision was shared."

"Elizabeth is not here. I miss her and cannot speak to Lonthran for the first time in my life by space transmissions sent from NORAD," Joseph persisted, wishing he had a different answer. Service and total dedication trumped his personal life. There was too much at stake. After all, he and Magden could and would change the world.

Together, they led the Emissary mission of Nerrial on Earth.

"It's May third, 2035. I'm Lydia Lewis and this is a Station One Intelligence Report.

"Tensions in Asia are mounting. Sources at the Pentagon have informed Station One the Chinese military is carrying out major operations to root out Resistance fighters in the Jade Mountains and along the Taiwanese western shore. Satellite imagery shows large convoys of PLA tanks and armor moving toward suspected hideouts. There is still no confirmation whether an alleged NATO unit was behind last month's altercation leading to the shooting down of a Chinese fighter plane over the East China Sea.

"On the frontlines of South America's Drug War, rebels accused of having links to The Revolution ambushed a Brazilian army division en route to assist Ecuador's security forces. The ambush left twenty dead and over fifty wounded. Inside Ecuador, fighting raged near Quito where a dozen large explosions rang out early this morning.

"Brazil's minister of defense warned that the situation was nearing anarchy along its northern border as he ordered several thousand additional troops to secure hotspots alongside Venezuela. Already, an estimated ten thousand people are dead from fighting in Venezuela alone, and over two hundred thousand people have been displaced.

"Defense Secretary Auten released a statement defending America's policies in the region and voiced support for the South American Defense Pact signed last month in Rio de Janeiro. Auten declared the United States would increase its naval presence in the region and offered additional assistance for transporting food and much-needed medical supplies. The United States has sent over nine hundred million dollars in food and medical aid while taking in thirty thousand refugees left homeless from the Drug Wars.

"In the European Union, panic is spreading through many communities after street battles with police left more than one hundred people dead or wounded in Barcelona, Frankfurt, Prague, Milan, and several other cosmopolitan centers. The Italian interior minister said he'd never seen such blatant attempts by the mafia to openly confront state authorities. The EU issued a security warning to its member states and blamed most violence on criminal elements coming from outside the EU. The Revolution is suspected of either masterminding or supporting the spike in violence.

"In the United States, President Hawthorne is expected to sign into law the controversial new terrorism legislation granting the National Guard authority over U.S. gangs branded as terror organizations. Following the brutal execution of three more Chicago police officers that arrested powerful gang members, the bill has overwhelming public support.

"There is no word from the White House on whether the president will attend the historic ten-year anniversary of the Holy Land Accords in Jerusalem later this month. I'm Lydia Lewis and this has been your Station One, Open Source Intelligence update."

"Cut! Good job, Lydia," said Damien, the station program manager.

"Thanks, D." Lydia collected her notes, shuffling them into a neat stack on her desk. A technician ran up and helped her unlatch the microphone connected to her dress. Lydia didn't like being plugged in. The investigative part of being a journalist was what she loved. She'd been relegated to reporting from behind the desk since her exposé on The Revolution stirred so much controversy.

Her career never fully recovered even though recent events around the world gave credence to much of what critics had called "sensationalized hearsay bordering fabrication." Her inclusion of references to three shadowy ringleaders got the worst of it. Nobody would or could speak of them in detail, but Lydia believed they existed.

Lydia walked into her private office and thought about the report she'd just filed. *The world keeps getting crazier.* Never liking work clothes, she took off her Versace dress and slid into her favorite jeans. Throwing on a faded green t-shirt, she checked her messages. "Nothing new from Nathan . . . again," she said aloud. *What's he up to that's so important?* Ever since her brother started working at Peterson Air Force Base, there'd been less communication from him.

When Nathan was a liaison for DARPA in New York, they would go out on the weekends and have a blast. She started to climb the journalism ladder around that time, never thinking she'd become the biggest name in the field. Lydia missed the early days of her career when she'd just finished Berkley's Graduate School of Journalism. The action was more fun back then. She was ready for another field assignment . . . if Station One would approve it.

Lydia had been the first major reporter to bring The Revolution story to the public. Her exposé flopped when reviews from the critics turned it into a joke. "Too much science fiction," they said. The online *New York Times* skewered her, saying, "Lydia Lewis should stay behind a news desk where she belongs. Obviously in need of a thrill, the respected reporter lost a step and tarnished her image with her over the top documentary *The Next Al-Qaeda*. Someone should remind Ms. Lewis she works in New York, not Hollywood."

Bullshit.

After the CIA attributed the nuclear detonation in Pakistan and attack on NATO headquarters to The Revolution, people stopped criticizing. She'd fought so hard publicly defending herself live on talk shows with desk jockey's jealous of her success, it made her look desperate and Station One made a point to keep her grounded. Lydia never gave up her curiosity and still hadn't recovered professionally. It didn't matter, the time had come to write her first book: *The Revolution: Mysterious Conspiracy.*

There was more to The Revolution than the government let on. For over ten years Lydia had covered national security issues, first with ABC News and then CNN before joining Station One, which ended up giving her the most flexibility, allowing her to report everything from the signing of the Holy Land Accords to the invasion of Taiwan. She'd never before investigated anything like The Revolution, though.

When Lydia first started her research, most people thought the group was a tease, an attempt by bored intelligentsia to get some attention. The Department of Homeland Security likened the Revolution Declaration to college professors in need of a blog. Lydia remembered the first conversation she had with a ranking Pentagon official on the subject. The deputy director of the Defense Intelligence Agency (DIA) suggested she stop chasing fantasies in a world all too real. She e-mailed him after NATO headquarters was attacked by The Revolution and asked whether he'd "pulled his head out yet." DIA sources were harder to come by since then.

Lydia knew there was something more to The Revolution from the moment she started her research. She had never come across a subject so strange and interesting. Compelling rumors became mysterious leads into a highly organized underworld of antiestablishment forces bent on a fiendish conquest for power. Her first report on The Revolution kept the Pentagon hacking away at small errors to draw focus from the real story—the existence of a new nongovernmental organization far more powerful than Al-Qaeda ever was.

Lydia wanted to get back at those who took cheap shots at her. The false accusations and ridicule still stung. There were other tidbits of information Lydia had decided not to include in her original exposé—the most fascinating research to this day—creepy, cultlike aspects of The Revolution and the evil some said it cast over its followers.

She had interviewed dozens of villagers in Colombia and two of the captured mercenaries who attacked NATO headquarters in Brussels. Although the incidents had taken place in different parts of the world, the interview responses shared references to demons and a criminal underworld dedicated to an apocalyptic vision of Earth's future.

Several of Lydia's closest sources in the Department of Defense had not confirmed, or denied, the rumors of Revolution ringleaders. Now they wouldn't talk about The Revolution at all. Lydia's book would include all her previously unpublished research and link new worldwide developments involving the group. The project was moving slower than she liked and she needed to think of a way to jumpstart things.

In the elevator on her way to the ground floor of the Freedom Tower, Lydia dialed her brother Nathan's cell number. Third ring. *About to get his voicemail again.*

"Well hello, sis," Satellite said, picking up his phone and turning away from the CIA's assessment of CONTRA's discovery in the Amazon.

"I must be special. Are you a stranger or just too busy to talk with your boring sister?" Lydia asked.

"Ummm . . . I've been kind of out of the loop. Sorry. On some business travel and we've been working overtime. I meant to call you this weekend." The Gray Team would be departing within the hour from U.S. Southern Command headed back to Colorado Springs. Satellite wasn't about to inform his sister of that.

"You said that last time. I left you, like, three messages, Nate. What's up?"

"There's some classified program stuff I've been doing. It's . . . had me experiencing new things and visiting new places."

"Sounds exciting! Anyway, I just finished filing a news report and am heading back to the condo. Work is burning me out. I might take some time off and write that book I told you about. My brain can't get off it. What do you think?"

"I'd buy a copy."

"I talked with someone staffed on the National Security Council yesterday. I've known the guy for a long time. He's been a great source, but couldn't say much. Told me some things were happening with The Revolution—some real heavy stuff. I think I'm onto something again with this."

"A lot of crazy things going on out there," Satellite flatly responded.

"The Pentagon has its hands full. Something is definitely *going on* by the reactions I've been getting from all sorts of people." Lydia stepped out into the busy Manhattan sidewalk where a taxi awaited her in front of the Freedom Tower at the same time everyday. The driver held the door open and he smiled. Lydia looked at the dimming sky and swirl of clouds above the Manhatten skyline before stepping in. A storm was brewing.

"So have you heard from Mom? She must love the sunshine down in Florida. It's been ninety degrees every day this week in Orlando! Hope it's not too hot."

"Mom is fine, Nate. She plays Bingo twice a day and has read every book that little library has to offer." Lydia noticed her brother shifting the conversation *again* when it became security related. He wasn't always so secretive. Lydia talked to him for another ten minutes before arriving at her condominium. "You better be the next one to call!"

"You got it, sis."

As Lydia approached her door she noticed a package sitting next to her welcome mat. *Unusual.* Her doorman usually held everything that was too big to fit into her mailbox. There was no return address, but the postmark indicated the package originated in Panama.

Lydia wondered what it could be. The only contacts she had in Panama were fellow journalists covering the Drug Wars, but they never sent packages. None of those people even knew where she lived.

Nerves twisting, her hands suddenly felt clammy so she put them in her pocket to warm them up as she considered calling the police. *Maybe they should check this out?* As a journalist, she knew the need to be careful about certain things. Receiving odd mail shipments was at the top of the scary list. Her prevailing curiosity pushed past her thoughts of anthrax and letter bombs.

Lydia didn't want to be paranoid. *Just pick it up and take it inside.* It was probably nothing.

Lydia bent down, putting her hands underneath the package.

CHAPTER 14
REGROUP
Colorado Springs: May 3, 2035

Justice held the silver trinket General Chiang had given him before the Blue Team fled Taiwan and reminded himself of the promise he had made. Strangely, Justice already felt detached from that operation. Political fallout erupted and continued making the headlines, infusing the talk-show circuit with renewed criticism of America's military-industrial complex and conspiracy theories about secret wars concocted to revitalize ailing defense firms.

Several U.S. senators were openly requesting a federal investigation into whether President Hawthorne approved of American troop participation in combat operations against the PLA. Senator Huckson from North Carolina, the powerful Foreign Relations Committee chairman, demanded answers. He appeared on cable talk shows all week, blasting the White House administration for its recklessness and accusing the president of sending American forces into battle under the guise of NATO.

For its part, the Hawthorne administration refused to comment on any American or NATO involvement. CONTRA remained Top Secret, but the controversy threatened a wary American public not wanting to risk open war with China. The prospect of conflict over Taiwan, or anything else, was unpopular to a public tired of financing wars and sending troops overseas. Clamor began about using taxpayer dollars for new dangerous military adventures. Public opinion polls favored a "Fortress America" strategy for national security and an end to overseas deployments.

The National Security Council and members of the Pentagon who knew about CONTRA grew concerned that anti-NATO sentiment would gain a foothold in Congress. It put President Hawthorne in a difficult position to support any covert operation and became the primary reason he requested an emergency briefing from CONTRA Director Joseph McBride and Commander Patton. The meeting would focus on what transpired in China and Colombia. According to White House staffers, both operations remained sensitive. Everyone braced for a leak about the secret strike force to hit the networks.

Of greater concern, though, was how speedily The Revolution had reached the advanced stages of military technology CONTRA had discovered in the Amazon rainforest. The futuristic infrastructure, access to laser weapons, and bioengineered creatures baffled everyone. The latest Colombian encounter raised the stakes, guaranteeing the continuation of CONTRA, regardless of any Congressional protests.

For Justice, observing the battle video feeds from Colombia trumped the Sino-U.S. sensationalism on all of the twenty-four-hour news networks. CONTRA was at war. The conflict had escalated to the point where Justice was fairly certain the problem went far beyond just China. Something *else* was at work. He viewed the imagery and listened to the digital feeds, replaying them repeatedly, not trusting what he was witnessing. Anticipating the Gray Team's return to Colorado Springs, Justice twirled the memento from Chiang, contemplating how The Revolution pulled it off.

The Gray Team would be landing soon. He wanted answers almost as much as he wanted Red.

After spending nearly a week at SOUTHCOM recovering from their encounter with The Revolution and debriefing the task force in charge of monitoring the Drug Wars, the Gray Team was heading back to CONTRA headquarters. SOUTHCOM monitored all of Latin America, but what transpired on the CONTRA mission caught the command off guard. The absence of evidence found by inspection teams sent to examine the new Demon Lab caused aftershocks throughout the intelligence community. Tons of earth had somehow buried the underground tunnels within the crater of the destroyed base after the Gray Team left and before DoD inspection teams arrived.

The Revolution must have used its large advanced network of underground tunnels to maneuver and operate out of sight, setting off detonations and backfilling its secret base of operations while demolishing the aboveground remains. Several large underground explosions registered with the Air Force Applications Technical Center (AFTAC) Auxiliary Seismic Network. Four AFTAC seismic stations were located in South America to collect measurement and signature intelligence for the Air Intelligence Agency. They reported the strange findings to the CIA and DIA.

Both agencies passed the intelligence on to the National Security Council and CONTRA headquarters. The Revolution had somehow assured that the Gray Team's findings underneath the Amazon rainforest in Colombia—the tunnels, lab equipment, statues, and dead bodies hanging from the ceiling— would never be seen again. Nobody outside of CONTRA would ever get to explore the underground Revolution base. Video evidence and firsthand accounts would have to suffice.

Justice marveled at the The Revolution's ability to operate so effectively in secret—it was almost enough to distract him from the excitement of his love returning to Colorado Springs unscathed. He would see Red for the first time in a month. They'd spoken over the videophone and she'd told him about the horrific jungle battle, stopping to cry a few times. It was so hard to believe. Too much had happened since Taiwan.

"Red will be here soon, partner," Xxplosive grinned, taking a swig of cherry cola and leaning up next to Justice on the hood of a Joint Light Tactical Vehicle (JLTV). They waited off the main runway at Peterson Air Force Base. "What do you have in your hand?" Xxplosive asked seeing Justice staring at his palm.

"Something General Chiang gave me before we left that day," Justice said, continuing his gaze.

"Sorry to hear about what happened."

"Yeah." Justice couldn't say much more.

Xinhua news was reporting PLA forces had killed Taiwan's Resistance leader the day before. The PLA had issued a death warrant for Chiang following the skirmish with CONTRA. After Chinese commandos raided his hideout, pictures of the dead commander broadcasted on Chinese television, much to the delight and self-congratulation of occupational authorities.

Justice gazed at Chiang's silver trinket and wondered what it signified. He tried to prod the locket that looked like a miniature pirate treasure chest. No luck. He rotated it in his hand, feeling disappointed that he'd never understand the importance of Chiang's last words. Then he saw it: a small circular disc blended into the bottom of the chest. Justice wound the disc and paused, listening to the bells twinging and twanging inside.

"The Taiwanese national anthem," Grace said, walking over to him. "Patton had me watch footage of the last days before the invasion. I remember that song. It's beautiful."

Justice thought of Chiang's final words: *Do not forget what we do.* The chest represented his symbolic treasure of lost freedom. Chiang died for that memory. Justice would honor him by remembering. They were from different countries but they were the same. He turned the musical gift around in his palm and it slipped to the pavement, breaking in two.

"Shit!" Justice cursed, upset with himself for being clumsy.

"Hey, wait a minute . . . look there." Grace pointed and bent down to pick up the pieces. "Something popped out." She tugged on a tiny piece of paper bulging out from the bottom of the trinket.

"What is it?" Xxplosive asked, setting his soda on the JLTV.

"This is yours. You open it." Grace handed the tightly folded paper square to Justice.

He carefully unraveled it. His eyes widened at what he saw. "It's a map . . . of Taiwan? That's odd. Multiple locations are marked."

"Seems most are in the Jade Mountain area. Could be Resistance related?" Grace guessed peeking over his shoulder.

"There are a lot of Asian characters on here, especially down at the bottom." Justice flipped the map over. "Nothing on the back. We'll have to get this translated. Grace, can you see this gets done through the right channels ASAP?" Justice felt good about finding the map. It gave him closure to think Chiang did not die in vain.

"Will do," she responded. The State Department Bureau of Intelligence and Research, Office of Analysis for East Asia and the Pacific, has the best translators. I'll get it to them." Grace took the map and gently placed it in a document folder she'd been carrying.

Justice tried to stay in the shade of the JLTV and out of the burning afternoon sun. All of the officers eagerly anticipated reuniting the two teams. CONTRA needed to regroup. Things were not going according to plan. The strike force seemed farther away from understanding The Revolution. Too many new questions and complexities loomed, indicating a drawn-out struggle for the elite battalion.

Two Shadowhawks appeared on the horizon. Justice's heart pounded harder as they approached the runway. The gunships landed and a mix of CONTRA soldiers and officers from the Gray Team exited. Several wounded troops hobbled off, some requiring assistance. Justice scanned for Red. Instead, he caught Crosshill's gaze as he came down the ramp, his equivalent in rank from the Gray Team.

"Welcome back, Colonel," Justice said with a salute and a smile.

"My American friend, it's a pleasure to be here." Crosshill's baggy eyes made him look older than when they last met. Justice could see the strain he'd experienced. Crosshill clearly blamed himself for the disappearance of the seven CONTRA soldiers. Justice knew how he felt.

Next to Justice, Nightscope and Xxplosive welcomed Raption back in less formal ways, nearly tackling him while trading obscene remarks.

"Now, why can't a lady get such a sweet welcome back?" Diamond said, standing with her hands on her hips in front of Xxplosive. He towered above her.

"Because we actually like *you*, Diamond. Don't cha know?"

Diamond laughed. It looked like the first time she'd felt at ease in a while.

Satellite was next out. He set his battlepack next to the JLTV.

"How are you holding up?" Justice asked, wondering where Red was.

"Happy to be alive. Ready for the next episode . . . I guess."

"Good, 'cause it's comin' around the corner." Justice looked to the top of the Shadowhawk where Red stood. Simultaneous smiles spread across their faces. Breakdown was at Red's side. She tried helping him down the ramp. His arm was wrapped heavily in bandages, still healing from the laser fire that burned through it.

"Look who's here," Nightscope said seeing Breakdown. "I thought you were staying back at the hospital a few more days?" He ran up the ramp to assist Red.

"I couldn't bear to stay away from you any longer," Breakdown rapped, with a fake pucker for a kiss, cut short by a grimace.

"Save the kisses for the ladies. I don't want 'em," Nightscope said. "Hello, Red."

"Hi, Nightscope," she smiled.

"I think someone is waiting for you and you better not make him wait any longer. He's bound to shoot someone." Nightscope took Breakdown's arm from her. "Let me help Breakdown here. You go on."

She didn't have far to go. Justice made his way up to her and took her in his arms. Their embrace exuded desire and their deep kiss conveyed their need. Talking was unnecessary—the warmth from their bodies communicated unspoken emotions.

Breakdown rolled his eyes. "Let's let these two *catch up*."

"That's probably a good idea."

Patton stood firm and listened to Joseph McBride over the secure transmitter, carrying on a conversation he never thought he'd have. The words Joseph spoke, the meaning behind them, didn't seem real. There had to be another explanation but all the evidence showed otherwise. Deep in his heart, Patton knew it was true.

"Commander, we will need to prepare CONTRA for the next phase of the war. Magden has already agreed that if The Revolution is what we think, this step forward makes sense. It's something we have to do. There aren't many of us now. Those who are here and active must find a way to prepare and protect Earth. Inform Colonel Vickers," Joseph said.

"And what of our request?" Patton asked, swatting at the fruit fly annoyingly circling his head.

"Lonthran will bring the question forth to the Council."

"I still don't understand how it's possible."

"Neither do I. The scope of our endeavor has multiplied a millionfold, and not just for *this* alliance. There is much more than Earth at stake. One more thing, Magden spoke to me about Troy." Joseph paused for a moment. Patton could tell the words were hard for him. "We must bring Battlestar back into the fold. We can't afford not to, especially if this war expands. All Blessed with military experience will be called up and he's the best. Magden will handle any bureaucratic objections among the allies."

"Good! I agree with that decision, as you know. I'll see that it gets done," Patton said with dignity. He swatted at the fruit fly again, crushing it in his palm.

"Thank you, Commander."

Patton never wanted to lose Battlestar in the first place. He knew Battlestar's true identity. Being a Nerrial descendant and Blessed mattered in the field. Patton removed the digital earpiece and pondered the discussion. As an Emissary, he wished they were wrong about The Revolution. Being who *he* was, his senses told him otherwise.

When Patton smashed what he thought was a bug, the hovering Micro Electro Mechanical System (MEMS) drone—indistinguishable from a fruit fly—

was destroyed, sending a loud screeching noise through the headphones of the Secret Service agent sitting in the NSA Microsystems Technology Office in Fort Meade, Maryland. The agent threw off the headphones, cursed, and rubbed his ears. Two NSA technicians next to him laughed.

The main CONTRA briefing room was alive and noisy with activity. Chatter among the officers hit a fever pitch of competing war stories. The upbeat vibe from being together again was palpable as the two companies waited for Patton's briefing.

CONTRA operated as teams of unique but balanced chemistry. The officer cadre knew each other well. Leading the most high-tech, agile strike force ever created required effortless relations between the multinational officer corps. The Blue and Gray Teams had spent the previous summer and fall training and living together. They ate, drank, and partied with one another, studying the scattered clues collected concerning The Revolution. They shared worries and some even fell in love. Bonds were formed—the kind that last a lifetime.

"Still ticking my fellow innovative wizard?" Rapidfire bellowed, slapping Satellite on the back and sliding into the seat next to Xxplosive. Rapidfire and Satellite were the two senior technical experts on CONTRA and often shared ideas on innovation, technology, and weapons.

"Round one over. Good news for most of us," Satellite said frowning a bit. "Wish we could say the same for our Gray Team." Nine soldiers from the company of fifty were killed in battle. Three more died at SOUTHCOM's hospital following emergency operations from wounds sustained during werewolf attacks. The seven members who vanished in Colombia were still missing in action and seven more remained severely wounded, including Warsaw, who was in critical condition.

"Our side got lucky in Taiwan," Rapidfire leveled.

"We didn't have to deal with werewolves . . . or transforming bases, thank God," Xxplosive admitted.

"I won't be staying behind in any control room on the next mission—werewolves or not," Rapidfire added. The CONTRA advanced weapons specialist was itching for field action.

"How is Warsaw?" Grace asked, sitting across from them.

"Not good," Satellite said. "Critical at SOUTHCOM's hospital. They think he'll make it out, maybe with full function in his limbs but they're not certain. That thing tore into him brutally," Satellite shuddered.

"Atrocious beasts," Grace cringed.

"Worse up close," Diamond went on, leaning her rifle against the wall. Nobody else brought their weapon into the briefing room except her. She took the pins out of her hair and pulled back the silky blonde locks coiled beneath her blue NATO beret. "Whoever made those creatures is as evil as their creation. Stopping them is paramount. I hope we don't sit around this base for weeks again. Both teams should deploy back to Colombia together."

Grace noticed Raption across the room. He couldn't take his eyes off Diamond. There was something between them. Grace sensed it during training and more so now. Diamond was beautiful but there was more in Raption's eyes than physical attraction. Grace glanced around, wondering if anybody else noticed. Their connection was obvious to her but, then again, she had an above average ability to perceive such things. Grace remembered when someone used to stare at her like that.

Crosshill dialed up a video feed on the center flat screen, which displayed the room containing the statues in the underground Revolution base. "Grace, I wanted to discuss this recording with you. I understand you're versed in religion and symbolism."

"Somewhat."

"The Revolution took the time to set these statues up *after* the F-35s completed their weapons drop. I think there is a clue here . . . especially this demonic figurine in the middle. Damn thing's been giving me nightmares, the bad kind. The other statues surrounding the devilish middle figure are recognizable," Crosshill said pointing at the screen. "They obviously represent the world's religions. The centerpiece, though . . . Have you ever seen it before?" he asked Grace who studied the video feed with him.

Grace sensed Crosshill was more troubled by what he saw than he let on. "To me this arrangement communicates a message of good versus evil, a symbolic introduction—of sorts—to The Revolution. They've written about it in some of their obscure statements, including the Revolution Declaration," Grace articulated, having read many times the original pronouncement sent to Western governments.

She continued her assessment. "The statues reflecting Christianity, Islam, and the like are positive, sculpted in a lighter material. The black demonic figure in the center oozes evil. Could it represent the devil or some other dark manifestation of worship? Sure. I'll have to check with some university folks on this. There are unique features on that . . . thing. We could be missing a specific message."

"I agree," Crosshill interjected.

"The Revolution wants us to know they're anticivilization and antiestablishment. We know that from their writings. It seems they want to tell us more . . . as if they believe that our traditional world of faith will surrender to something new and dark that they represent."

"Hence the statues of global religion surrounding the demon?" Crosshill asked.

"Yes, perhaps it gives The Revolution a sense of power and larger purpose. It could be their psychological war paint," Grace assessed. "This evil aura builds on their mysticism and fear instilled in their followers."

"And in us!" Breakdown bellowed, cupping his freshly bandaged arm. "Maybe the one in the middle is one of the creatures they've created? Or maybe The Three are just damned possessed!"

Patton stopped at the briefing room entrance and listened to his officers discuss the images they were viewing. He was all too familiar with the mission footage. Nothing was more perplexing, more astonishing, than the statue at the center of the desk Crosshill had found. It was no hybrid bioengineering experiment. The figure was all too realistic. By itself, the statue was enough to turn everything Patton knew about the universe upside down. He hadn't recognized it at first. Magden had. The figure was the reason for Joseph's call.

Patton entered the room. All the other officers moved to their seats and stood at attention.

"At ease," Patton said, standing behind the podium in front of all his active CONTRA officers. He felt this address was more important than those in the past. He couldn't say everything he wanted to, but he still needed to prepare them.

"Welcome back, everyone. We've learned much from your first missions. Some of what we know is hard to understand. There is no question that the enemy is . . . " Patton paused, considering his next words carefully. "They are something other than what we expected. I know many of you feel less informed than you'd like about the challenges ahead. As you've witnessed, or watched, the surprises deep in the jungle . . . "

Grace listened suspiciously to Patton. He was keeping something from them. Grace couldn't ignore her senses. Patton was holding back something very big but he wouldn't, or didn't know how to, tell them. Grace wasn't sure which. As she continued listening, it became clear that Patton was not altogether fazed by the discovery in the Amazon. He was not shocked by the Gray Team's findings.

As Patton continued his briefing, Grace tuned in and out. She paid more attention to her emotional read of the CONTRA commander. She'd never felt such strange emotion from Patton before and didn't like it.

"These werewolves and the enemy base you found in Colombia are clear indications our enemy is of a scope we'd rather not admit. The mystery we face may be greater than any our nations have ever encountered. There remains no certain answer as to what The Revolution is capable of. Yet there can be no doubt that the gravest of all dangers will become empowered the longer these questions remain unanswered. Myself and Director McBride were summoned by the president to discuss both your missions and CONTRA's future, perhaps expanded, role the world.

"As you are all aware, NATO is considering the possibility of designing up to a dozen more battalion-sized units under the CONTRA framework, perhaps entire divisions. Whether our first actions have helped or hurt this cause remains uncertain. The president has questions he wants answered personally. I look forward to meeting with him and telling you how it affects our future together in the fight we were formed to win.

"What I want is for all of you to remain highly concentrated on your teams and next missions. We are doing our best to locate the missing CONTRA soldiers in Colombia. The secretary of defense ordered a large unit of Marines and Army Rangers to continue the search. They will be leaving from Fort Hood tomorrow morning. Does anyone have any questions?"

Endless ones, Grace thought.

"Is there any word on how it was possible for that base to be built undetected underground or how our surveillance and space assets were unable to identify any of the activity?" Satellite asked in a frustrated tone.

"These questions are being looked at by American and European intelligence communities. Space Command is working closely with them to review all forms of information collected from the South American region over the last two years. This topic will be a primary talking point with the joint chiefs, who will also attend the White House meeting. The president was not pleased to hear of your discovery and our intelligence community's ignorance of it. I've had many discussions with directors from the NSA and CIA who are assigned to support the CONTRA mission . . . They have a hard time accepting that base was a reality."

"Commander, forgive me, we have so many active Responsive Space and

Near Space systems we've reconstituted since the Battle of Taiwan, and everyone has been watching the Drug Wars. It's not as if this part of the world is off the map. There is *no way* that construction could have gone unnoticed, but it did. Maybe a clearing in the jungle could be missed, but not the construction of the entire base. It's otherworldly what we found," said Satellite.

Satellite's line of questioning was on target and Patton knew it. Satellite was an expert in space technology, as his codename suggested. He'd worked for the NRO and DARPA before assignment to CONTRA as an Air Force C4ISR specialist. He understood how American and allied technical assets worked. The issue didn't even require expertise. The U.S. military and commercial space industry monitored virtually every square foot of global territory; common knowledge to most news observers. Many systems destroyed by China during the Battle of Taiwan had been replaced by now.

Patton felt the weight of dissatisfaction in his officer corps growing. He couldn't even look at Grace, whose eyes were burning through him, analyzing his every emotion with her precious senses. CONTRA wanted answers from him. He wished he could say more and tell them everything. That decision wasn't his to make.

"Answers will come. Not as quickly as you'd like, but they will come," he promised.

After the contentious afternoon briefing, Patton gave the teams the rest of the day off. Red hadn't left Justice's bedroom since they returned several hours ago. They talked and talked while laying in each other's arms, their bodies touching for the first time in weeks.

"I thought about you the whole time we were apart," she turned over, looking at him. "I know you don't like to talk about stuff. I just like to hear it from you though. I need to hear it."

Talking about *stuff* wasn't a problem. The only thing scaring Justice was

Red's desire for them to quit the military. Red was more important, but the military was his way of life. Justice couldn't work in an office. He tried to picture himself getting ready each morning: straightening out his tie, grabbing a briefcase off the counter, sitting behind a desk and e-mailing away until the phone rang. Torture.

Red brought it up often, living a *normal* life, the nine to five, which made Justice cringe. He didn't want to consider anything but the military, not for another twenty years. Ever since he was seven and saw his parents exiting a Blackhawk at Fort Lewis he had known his dream. He was living it.

"I love you, Kate. You know what I want. It's for you to be happy, for *us* to be happy together. I think about it too . . . a family."

"You do?"

"I just don't know when it can happen . . . but I want it to."

Red sat up. She pulled the covers up to her chin and stared at Justice. Her dazzling red hair lit up against the white pillow.

Justice moved closer and slid his hand under the sheet. "We'll have the biggest Christmas party on the block. I'll cut down our tree myself." He knew she loved that kind of talk.

"Nobody has real Christmas trees anymore! You're just saying things to get your way with me." She slapped his hand hard.

"I'll get a tree from Saskatchewan or wherever you're from."

"I'm from British Columbia you stupid American!" she sassed, straddling him while playfully pushing the pillow over his face. Their discussion would have to continue another time.

Justice woke to the sound of his work cell phone buzzing. He'd been in such a dream state he thought it was morning and not ten past midnight. He leaned over and picked up the phone.

"Hello," he whispered, not wanting to wake Red.

"Justice, I'm sorry to disturb you." It was Patton. "I'm leaving for the Capitol in a couple of hours instead of tomorrow afternoon. Something has come up. I need to get going, but before I do I need to speak with you. Can you be in my office in a half hour?"

"Yes, sir. I'll be there even sooner."

"Good."

Justice slipped out of bed. He stood for a moment, looking at the woman he knew was his future wife. He scribbled a note and left it on the pillow next to her. He dressed quietly and grabbed his leather jacket off a chair, then slipped out of the bedroom. Making his way down the staircase, Justice wondered what the commander wanted to talk about at this late hour.

Justice shared the spacious three-story house on Peterson Air Force Base with CONTRA's other male officers. The downstairs living room was dark. Someone had left ESPN on in the game room. He peeked in. No one was there. *Probably tearing up the town.* He stepped out to a crisp, clear May night.

Taking a deep breath of the fresh air, Justice gazed up into space. There were so many stars. He used to stare at them when he was a kid. Late at night in his backyard, he'd lay flat on the cold grass and just look up, sometimes for hours. He would marvel at the distant suns, twinkling so far away. Justice stopped wondering long ago if anyone else was out there, but he still loved looking at the night sky. He jumped into the front seat of his jeep and drove across the base.

Patton's luggage was outside his office door, ready for his departure. Justice knocked softly on the open door. "Can I come in, sir?"

"Ah, yes. Please do, Justice. I'm just trying to finish here. Shuffling some last minute analytical reports and imagery my trusty executive officer, Decon, delivered minutes earlier. You know, even though I've done it before, meeting with the president of the United States is something you can never be too prepared for."

"I can imagine, sir. I've never had that honor."

Patton looked up at him. "You keep up your leadership, Colonel, and you will. I guarantee you."

"Thank you, sir."

"Do you remember what I told you the day I called you into my office in Marseille?"

Justice thought for a minute. "You told me about courage and how it was more than bravery in battle. That it required perseverance to assure its true form."

"Precisely. And why is it so important to persevere?"

"It's what brings light to the good side when the road is unclear. You persevere because anyone can show moments of bravery, but courage requires the act of never relinquishing. Not when it's hard, and not when it's easy."

Patton nodded, clearly impressed. Justice remembered their talk almost verbatim.

"There is a man I know who is of the most courageous kind," Patton said, folding his briefcase shut and laying it on the desk. "It appears that these times require the best men in the fight."

Justice thought he knew what was coming next and hoped he was right.

"It's time Battlestar came back where he belongs."

A grin spread across Justice's face. He *was* right.

"I want you to retain command of the Blue Team. Battlestar will rejoin your unit as a leading officer. We'll see where it goes from there," Patton said, staring out the office window over the grounds of the base, his back to Justice. "The Black Team is getting close to finishing their training," Patton said referencing CONTRA's third and final arm.

"He could lead any team, sir. How did—"

"The orders came to me today. After the Colombia discovery, the France incident isn't worthy of holding back our mission in any way. Battlestar is technically already reinstated . . . he just doesn't know it yet. I want you to find him and tell him in person. He deserves that much. It's why I called you here tonight." Patton picked up his briefcase and walked out into the hallway. "Get him back to base by my return, you hear?"

"Yes, sir. I'll start tracking him tomorrow."

Before Patton rounded the corner, he turned to Justice. "One more thing. Take Breakdown with you. He knows where Battlestar lives and that arm of his isn't ready for training yet. He'll enjoy a little So-Cal time."

Justice nodded. "Good luck in Washington, sir."

"Thank you, Colonel."

CHAPTER 15
THE PACKAGE
New York: May 3, 2035

Lydia eyed the package she'd placed on the dining room table. She read the note that came with it one more time:

> *You'll want to see.*

Part of her wished she'd left the parcel on her front step and let the police take care of it. The fact that an anonymous visitor dropped it off right at her door scared her. Unsettled, Lydia didn't open the package right away.

She thought of the recently murdered investigative reporter in Poland: he cut into a letter bomb. That reporter's specialty was covering the rise of mafia activity spreading throughout Europe. An *anonymous* person shipped the letter bomb to *his* apartment. The small explosive device inside detonated when the reporter ripped into the top of the letter. It killed him instantly.

Was she being a fool?

Lydia tossed her keys onto the kitchen counter. She took a minute to glance around. Her doorstep was behind the security gate so whoever left the package either jumped the gate or piggybacked in with a neighbor. Most tenants in her complex knew better than to let the latter happen.

"I'm being paranoid," she said aloud, trying to allay her fears. "It's probably nothing to get worked up about. *C'mon* Lydia."

She grabbed the small knife used for opening mail and brought it to the glass dining room table. Lydia sat in front of the package for a moment. Taking one heavy breath for bravery, she cut into the top and tore away the exterior tape. There was a plastic bag within. Lydia stopped suddenly and fell back against her chair gasping.

Dried blood smeared the inside of the bag.

She folded her arms close to her chest and sat frozen. A pitter-patter of fresh rain tapped against the kitchen window outside. Lydia raised her knees so that the heels of her slippers were on the edge of her chair. She closed her eyes hoping there wouldn't be a body part in the bag.

After building courage, Lydia lifted the plastic bag out of the torn mailer. To her relief there were no visible body parts, or anything of the like, inside. She shook the plastic bag and its contents around to study them. The bag contained a blue beret, a headset, some letters rubber-banded together, and what looked like a purple velvet pouch.

Lydia jumped up and ran into the kitchen. A mixture of excitement and danger swirled in her head. Lydia slid across the kitchen floor on her knitted red slippers her grandma made long ago and opened the cupboard under the sink. She grabbed a pair of yellow dishwashing gloves, not able to think of anything else to use to protect her hands.

The rain started to pour outside, beating hard against the sliding door of Lydia's balcony overlooking the city street below. She put on the rubbery smelling gloves to protect herself from the dried blood and grabbed an old magazine out of her recycler. Lydia sped back to the table and tore pages from the magazine, spreading them over her placemats. She ripped open the plastic bag, shaking its contents over glamour shots taken of Disney's latest idol turned teen princess.

The blue beret was the first thing Lydia inspected. Caked with dirt around the interior as if someone stepped on top of it in the mud, she flipped it over. To her surprise, a shiny silver NATO emblem was pinned to the front. Lydia set the military beret to the side and shuffled through several unopened letters addressed to someone in Germany. She picked up the purple velvet pouch.

A small circular military patch was stuck to it. The patch also had a NATO emblem, woven into its center and surrounded by the many national flags of the North American-European alliance.

Lydia noticed an oddity in that the patch featured the Japanese and Australian flags. She inspected it more closely, bringing it up to her eyes to read the small text woven around the outer edges. The top portion read:

NATO Response Force - Gray Team

Her eyes went to the bottom where it was harder to make out the words obscured by what appeared to be dried mud or blood. After a second, Lydia was able to see:

Counter-Revolutionary (CONTRA)

The hair on the back of her neck rose. "What is this?" she whispered. A million thoughts and questions passed through her mind. *Had NATO created a task force of some kind to engage The Revolution? Why was it kept a secret from the public?*

Lydia looked into the velvet pouch that reminded her of the Crown Royal cloth sack her grandfather's favorite whiskey came in. She unraveled a tiny black string wrapped around the pouch's opening and lifted a small flap to reveal a collection of photographs. Lydia took them out.

After seeing the first, her hands felt numb. She flipped to the next and swallowed hard. Looking at another and another, Lydia began trembling. It was difficult to make it through all ten. Some of the pictures didn't even look real, but she knew they probably were. Her stomach turned. Confusion gripped her mind. NATO was in a war that it didn't want the world to know about. Lydia understood why.

As a reporter she had seen many mysteries and heard gruesome stories. She'd traveled the world and reported on everything from gory massacres in African villages during the Resource Wars to the front lines of attempted genocide in southeast Asia. Lydia was also one of the last reporters out of Taiwan. Never in her time of witnessing the world's tragedies had the gravity of a story been more horrifying than this one. Her hands continued to tremble as she set down the stack of pictures.

Lydia closed her eyes and concentrated on taking it all in.

The stories, those tidbits she couldn't include in her original report on The Revolution, they were true at an order of monstrosity greater than she could have imagined. Even *she* thought the Colombian villagers might have just been spooked, scared of the drug cartels that governed their land. People usually exaggerated—it was human nature. That didn't seem to be the case in this instance. Lydia had to do something. The contents of the package would dominate her life for the next weeks and maybe even months. *I need to find answers.*

The rain had stopped. A serene stillness quieted her condo. The silence helped Lydia contemplate what was more than a news story. It was an international cover-up, a secret war—and perhaps something that would alter humankind. Those monsters in the photos weren't the kind of animals you could find in an online encyclopedia.

There had to be people high up in the government who knew about this. They would try to disgrace her again. Lydia looked back into the velvet pouch to see if there was anything else. She didn't see it at first: A small cigarette-sized paper rolled tight and held together with a red wax seal. Lydia pulled it out and cut into the seal, unrolling the paper to reveal a note neatly written in silver ink:

My name is Prowess. I am one of The Three.
Everything you know about your life, your world, is a lie.

Go to the Holy City at the site of the coming anniversary. I will find you there. The Revolution will prevail.

CHAPTER 16
WHITE HOUSE
Washington, DC: May 4, 2035

They say the White House used to be a different place. That going there was like stepping into the throne room in an emperor's kingdom. They once called America's kingdom the "city on a hill" for all to witness and admire. Those days of wonder were in the past. The glow and shine of America's supremacy and legacy had faded faster than most predicted. The admiration and strength projected for almost a century distanced itself from memory. The city on a hill was shrouded in a fog of lost dreams.

The corridors of the White House remained the same and the Oval Office was still the president's mainstay for business. Old traditions continued, and when world leaders came to America's capitol, they visited 1600 Pennsylvania Avenue. The features hadn't changed, but perceptions—and the times—had.

Magden had watched it all happen from a distance.

Staring through the tinted bulletproof windows of an electric BMW, Magden thought about it all. Sitting next to him were Joseph McBride and General Patton, his fellow Emissaries. The neatly tended grounds and groomed lawn of the White House seemed picture perfect—a contradiction with the madness unleashing itself on the world. He'd never been to the White House before, not in the glory days or in the new era of struggle. Magden had his chances, of course, but he never needed to go. Things were different now.

A Secret Service agent opened the sedan's door and the Emissaries exited. Joseph led the way into the White House. His government title made him the highest ranking in the civilian world of Earthly affairs, though Magden was indeed their leader. Magden felt the hot sun on the back of his neck. The burn of the yellow star seared; it felt so different from their Blue Sun of Nerrial. A soft spring breeze blew the scent of freshly planted flowerbeds across the White House lawn.

Another meeting must have just adjourned—several congressional representatives and senators exited the West Wing. As they passed Magden listened to them talk about votes for a new initiative to gain them bipartisan support. He recognized most of them, though he didn't look at them. Magden didn't care much for their kind. When elected, most became people of missed opportunity.

Senator Huckson, chairman of the Foreign Relations Committee, was among them. He had become a thorn in Magden's side. Huckson lobbied hard against NATO operations and the allied initiatives Magden chaired. The men surrounding Senator Huckson were prisoners of campaign promises they never intended to fulfill, seeking to extend their power and usefulness by serving competing agendas against others seeking the same.

There was still hope for some politicians, one of which they were about to meet. President Hawthorne was a political rarity in modern times. Sincere. Trustworthy.

A Marine guard stood firm at the door. Another guard guided the men along the red carpets of the White House. The halls bustled with activity. A small group of college men and women hovered around an orientation tour guide showing them through the most famous house in the land. Administrative staff members scurried in an out of rooms. The air buzzed. The administration preached action, Washington's responsibility to serve the people. Known for working long hours with their sleeves rolled up, President Hawthorne's staff attempted to turn the ruinous tide of America's fortunes.

Magden spotted the president's energetic national security advisor, Sandra Bethlem, clutching her thick leather notebook and practically running down the hall to greet them.

"Director McBride, I apologize for not seeing you in," she said. "Things are a bit hectic today. Back-to-back meetings all day long, although I must say—yours is the most pressing." She gave Joseph a forced smile and handshake.

"No worries. It's quite all right, Dr. Bethlem," he said.

Only in her midforties, Sandra had a seemingly endless wealth of knowledge about global events and America's place in history. A graduate of Georgetown's National Security Studies Program, she was well published and spent several years on the Joint Intelligence Staff. Known for being open minded, she wore pointed black eye glasses and kept her dark blonde hair pinned up in a well-groomed twist.

"I would like you to meet General William Taylor of the strike force in question, and this is McDaniel Jessup, director of NATO Allied Partnerships, our counterpart from the United Kingdom," Joseph said, quoting Magden's official government name and title.

"Oh . . . yes, I'm happy to meet the both of you," Sandra said, giving two firm handshakes, though she lingered with Magden's and gave him a steely look. Magden sensed she was searching for something in him at that moment, something important, but he couldn't guess what.

"Let us get to the Oval Office. The president awaits!" Sandra declared.

With that, the national security advisor turned and walked down the elegant corridor furnished with paintings of America's grand history and bygone presidents. The red carpet and white walls brought an exalting radiance to the hall. It was magnificent. Magden admired the interior décor as he listened to Sandra speak frantically of new reports streaming in from intelligence sources around the world monitoring China, the Drug Wars, and growing European unrest. She seemed rattled.

None of it was good news.

They reached the Oval Office and the door was open. They walked in, greeted by a surprising collection of some of the planet's most influential people. Magden had planned on an intimate discussion with the president and joint chiefs of staff on issues related to CONTRA, but the scene was different than expected. The vice president, secretary of defense, and directors of the CIA and NSA all waited in the Oval Office along with President Hawthorne.

The president greeted Joseph, Magden, and Commander Patton as they entered the room. He asked them to have a seat at a table set in the center of the office. The layout lent an overly formal air. All three of the Emissaries sensed an intensity in the room even more blatant than the vice president's overuse of cologne.

Magden and Joseph exchanged a quick nervous glance—anxiety a rare emotion for both of them. The president wasted no time getting straight to the point. He stood at the front of the table and looked each Emissary in the eye.

"Gentlemen, we have a problem. It appears there are things you are not sharing. I won't bother with the details because I think you already know them. *What* are you not telling us? And just *who* is directing this conspiracy? That is what I'd like to find out today."

The president's tone was sharp. The room was deathly quite. Magden could hear his heart slamming against his chest. He couldn't believe the question. The secret, theirs to protect, the one Nerrial had guarded for over one hundred and thirty years, had been compromised.

CHAPTER 17
NEW BEGINNINGS
Hermosa Beach: May 4, 2035

"Damn this haze! I wanted to feel some good ol' Californian sunshine," Breakdown complained peering out the rental car window at the morning sunrise over the Hermosa Pier.

"How's your arm?" Justice asked.

"Feels like I got a big fat needle burnin' through the middle of my bicep. The doc told me their lasers are different than ours. The energy pulses were set at wavelengths to make the bio-effects more potent. It hurts like a mother."

"The Revolution got its hands on laser weapons. Explain that to me," Justice said stopping at a streetlight.

"Would if I could, sir."

"Maybe you can just tell me which way to turn at this light."

"That I can. Take a right here on Hermosa Ave. There's a parking garage about a block down to your left."

"You're sure Battlestar is out here? I'm rolling the dice on this trip, Breakdown. I mean, it'd be a cryin' shame if we came all this way and he moved to Memphis."

"Trust me, he's here. Last we talked, he was gonna start working a sloth job at a restaurant I know. Said he had to cleanse his pride. He was in the doldrums, man. I've never seen the guy like that before. Anyhow, we'll find out if he's still there quick enough."

"Can't wait to see the look on his face *if* he's there," Justice said, his tone noting it had better be the case.

Justice enjoyed the thought of surprising Battlestar as much as Breakdown did, but he worried about finding him since Patton's orders were to not return empty-handed. Battlestar had stopped communicating with anyone from CONTRA months ago. Justice heard that even his father, Joseph, hadn't spoken with him in some time. Battlestar shut himself out from the rest of the world, turning off his cell phone and not answering e-mails. Finding him might not be as easy as Breakdown thought.

Justice parked the rental car and the CONTRA officers walked toward the famous Hermosa Pier. Because it was still a relatively safe area for pedestrians, this area of Los Angeles was considered one of the last bastions of normalcy—unless you had the money to live in the glamour of Beverly Hills, but no one called that a *normal* lifestyle. Justice and Breakdown passed a stretch of restaurants and storefronts through a plaza bordered by rows of palm trees. The men attracted stares from morning coffee sippers and beach bums who were not used to military officers in full service dress, especially their unique blue uniforms and matching berets.

Breakdown stopped at the end of the plaza in front of a rundown restaurant. A faded Surfer Grill sign, shaped like a surfboard, protruded from the top of the eatery on a mock tidal wave. Dust caked the diner's windows and half the plastic tables outside had cracks from the sun's daily abuse. In scribbled green marker a handwritten paper sign taped atop one of the empty tables read "Broken."

"What a dump," Justice said shaking his head in disbelief. "I can't see Battlestar working here."

"It isn't the nicest place in the South Bay," Breakdown confessed.

Justice knew Breakdown and Battlestar went way back—they'd first met at a party in Manhattan Beach six years before their CONTRA selection. At the time, both officers were enrolled in secret weapons training programs at Boeing's Laser and Space Systems complex in Redondo Beach. The Boeing Future Force Lab was built to develop and test the next generation of America's growing arsenal of laser infantry systems and battlesuits. They were some of the first soldiers to test the future gear, some of which was now part of the CONTRA armory.

Justice pushed open the screen door to the Surfer Grill. The door creaked loudly and almost fell off its hinges. He stepped into a swirl of sweet-smelling bacon and eggs that overcame his nostrils like the aroma of a freshly carved turkey on Thanksgiving. The five patrons at the front counter stopped eating their morning grub to stare at the well-dressed officers. Justice walked to where a man who looked like a retired NFL lineman—in an apron smeared with grease stains—stood with a pot of coffee. He gave Justice an unfriendly stare.

"Excuse me, sir," Justice said in a polite voice thinking the man must be the diner manager. "Does a Troy McBride work here?"

The man didn't respond right away. He stood motionless in the same spot then slowly set the coffee pot down and wiped his hands on the apron, adding to the stains. Sweat ran down his large forehead. His gruffness didn't exude the essence of customer service. He eyed Justice and Breakdown with suspicion.

"Troy McBride quit a couple weeks ago. Son of a bitch said he had things to attend to. Kind of a funny fellow if you ask me. Kept to himself and didn't say much. Maybe he went looking for you two guys?" the man yawned, checking Justice out from head to toe. "Either way, is there anything else I can do for you boys? Maybe cook you a morning special?"

Justice looked at the man's nametag. *Trucker.* He was either attempting to act helpful or skirt the real issue. "Thanks for the offer, Trucker, but we're not hungry. Perhaps you can tell us the last contact information you had on file for Troy? That would be of great assistance. It's very important we find him."

"I don't keep records of employees after they quit. Information gets recycled in this business pretty quick."

Justice nodded, unconvinced. He looked around the diner. He got the sense that if Trucker *wanted* to provide more information, he would be able to offer something. He appeared as the type of person who despised an officer or authority figure on principle. Justice wanted to ask someone else about Troy but did not see any waiters or servers about. They could not come all this distance to be turned away by someone named Trucker. For now they would have to think of other options. Justice looked at Breakdown and rolled his eyes in disgust. The officers walked out of the diner on the famous Hermosa Strand next to the pier. The sun started to break through the morning haze.

Justice was about to lecture Breakdown about confirming Battlestar's exact location before driving down to Hermosa Beach. As he opened his mouth to begin the reprimand, a young Hispanic worker ran toward them from the side of the Surfer Grill. He looked over his shoulder nervously, and then motioned for Justice and Breakdown to come toward him, away from the front of the diner.

"You are here for Troy?" he asked with a look of excitement as they walked over.

"Yes, we are. Can you help us find him?" Justice asked.

"Of course I can! My boss is an asshole!" he sounded off with glee. "I heard what you asked inside and he lied. Troy still works here. He's on a break, probably somewhere there on the pier." The worker pointed down the walkway, past a large lifeguard tower.

Relief surged through Justice. The thought of revisiting Trucker and giving him some Ranger love flashed through his mind. "Thank you kindly. Your help is truly appreciated."

"My name is Carlos. I am Troy's friend." The man extended his hand. "Troy will be going then?" he asked.

"Yes, he will be coming with us," Justice responded.

"I'm sad to hear that." Carlos looked to the ground.

"You are a true friend, Carlos," Breakdown said trying to cheer up the worker who obviously admired Battlestar. "I'm pleased to see Troy had good company in his time away from us."

The officers bid Carlos a gracious farewell and told him not to mind Trucker. Breakdown handed Carlos a business card and NATO command coin, telling him, "Problems can be referred our way."

Carlos examined the coin curiously as the CONTRA officers strode away.

Justice and Breakdown proceeded down the pier, past the lifeguard tower, and toward a row of benches overlooking the sandy stretch of Hermosa Beach where surfers rode incoming waves and girls sunbathed. Near the center of the pier where the ocean met the beach, they saw a lone man sitting on a bench.

Troy watched the sun crack through the morning haze.

He contemplated walking out on the rest of his shift. Troy didn't need the diner's escape anymore. Whether volunteering or working for a government contractor, his life had a purpose. The time he took to recover from his de-commission disgusted him. Troy had never been in such a freefall but now the hopelessness and despair were lifting. The meaning he'd found in CONTRA and Nightwatch would return. It was his last day of answering to Trucker. He chuckled at the thought.

Troy suddenly felt someone's presence behind him—*right* behind him. He whirled around, ready for action. "What the hell?"

The blue service dress CONTRA uniforms with light gray trim were unmistakable. There stood Justice and Breakdown, his old friends and most trusted allies. They looked the prime NATO officers that they were.

"Have we caught you at a bad time, sir?" Justice asked sarcastically, flippantly checking his watch.

"We could come back on a different day?" Breakdown persisted, playing along.

A flood of emotion raced through Troy. He shot up off the bench and ran his hands through his hair, perplexed, not trusting his eyes. They were in uniform—on business. CONTRA officers didn't travel around the country in full military garb to make friendly house calls. The strike force was active. They were in the news. The mass media didn't know it was CONTRA, but Troy did. He stared, grinning at his friends and former colleagues, unable to speak.

Justice didn't wait long. "We're not here for you . . . Troy," he said, pausing to let the moment build, "We're here for Battlestar."

Breakdown would later swear he saw a distinct spark in Battlestar's left eye at that moment.

"What took so long?" Battlestar beamed. He had planned on a long road back to service, perhaps months. Now this; suddenly CONTRA wanted him back. An unexpected gift—destiny. Purpose. Still astonished he wanted to know everything about the first missions. "Have The Three been located?" he asked easily slipping into officer mode without trying. "How nasty is it out there?"

"No and bad," Breakdown confirmed, extending his healthy arm for a lengthy shake.

"Worse than feared," Justice added. "You look in better shape than I thought you'd be in though."

"I haven't worked out once since the decommission." Battlestar's body naturally stayed strong. He never questioned it. "I know the first mission went off. Is everyone all right?"

"Not *everyone*, but we're holding," Justice replied.

"What happened to your arm?" Battlestar asked looking to Breakdown.

"Enemy fire."

"Revolution?"

"Yup. They're a bit more advanced than we anticipated," Breakdown said, stone-faced. "You're not gonna believe—"

Veep. Veep. Veep. Veep.

The signature sound of CONTRA's emergency receivers buzzed to life on Justice and Breakdown's belts. They unlatched the tiny earpieces and inserted them while pressing on the communicators.

"Officers Justice and Breakdown here," Justice reported.

"This is a command request for immediate CONTRA Blue and Gray Team reconstitution for new deployments," Decon's voice came in a strict military tone. "Orders coming straight from NATO in Brussels. You are to return to base *now*. This is a Code Seven order, Colonel. New missions await."

"Roger. We're on our way."

"Did you locate Battlestar?"

"Yes, we're here with him."

"Bring him with you to the military terminal at LAX. There will be an executive jet waiting in fifteen minutes."

"Got it, Decon. On our way," Justice said removing his earpiece and latching it back to his belt.

"What's up?" Battlestar asked.

"We need to get to LAX—and I did say *we*," Justice noted.

"Mission time, *primo*," Breakdown added, winking.

Just like that, the deal was sealed. Battlestar was back.

The officers ran down the pier and crossed the Hermosa Strand. Several bystanders watched the CONTRA officers dashing into the main plaza. Trucker was one of them. He stood right outside the Surfer Grill shaking his head.

"We have a rental car a few blocks down. Do you need anything before we leave?" Justice asked.

"My stuff can sit here. All I need is CONTRA."

"I got a better idea than that rental," Breakdown raved.

"Hold on one second," Battlestar said. He spotted Trucker and broke off toward him ripping off his dirty apron.

"I won't be needing this anymore, Truck," Battlestar declared, holding out his apron.

Trucker wouldn't take it. "I'm gonna mess up that Carlos real good for telling those frat boys of yours where you were."

Battlestar stepped within kissing distance. "You better think twice about that. You'll fare much better by giving him a raise—understand?" The fire in Battlestar's eyes caught Trucker off guard. He trembled and surprised himself by nodding along. "I'll be checking in, too," Battlestar asserted, tossing the apron on the ground in front of Trucker. "For what it's worth, thanks for the job."

Battlestar caught up with Justice and Breakdown at the edge of the plaza. They were arguing about leaving the rental car behind.

"I don't know why I listen to you," Justice said.

"I was right about Battlestar, wasn't I? You gotta trust me. I come through, boss."

"You better hope so, Captain, because we don't have time for any bullshit mistakes."

A woman in a beach skirt and bikini top crossed the street in front of the officers, temporarily distracting Breakdown.

"Breakdown!" Justice hollered.

"Follow me this way, sir. It'll be worth it."

"It better."

Battlestar knew exactly where Breakdown was taking them.

The officers jogged two blocks up to a garage with a flashy red sign reading Tricks and Sizzle. A bulging, muscular Hispanic man wearing a Lakers jersey stood at the entrance. His jaw dropped when he recognized Breakdown.

"Chavez! Cousin, what the—? Why didn't you tell me you'd be back in town?"

"Pedro, I'm sorry, but I don't have much time. Work stuff. We're in a bind. I need the car."

"*Your* car?"

"Is it ready?"

"You don't plan on driving it in the streets?"

Breakdown tilted his head to the side. "We gotta roll fast, Pedro."

Justice stepped in between the two relatives. "Whatever our cause, it needs to proceed fast or else we have to get on with the rental." He sounded impatient about the detour they'd taken.

"Oh, *hell* no to a rental," Pedro said, waving the men forward. "Follow me."

They walked through the garage where a classic jukebox gleamed in the corner playing "Highway to Hell" through its refurbished speakers. Budweiser pinup girls formed a sort of gallery of admiration above the jukebox. Pedro took them through a set of swinging doors into a larger area of the garage adjacent to a showroom where the floor sparkled in cleanliness reserved for upscale department stores. A row of Ferraris and Lamborghinis lined the showroom. A handful of mechanics polishing a freshly waxed Bentley stopped to stare at the military officers visiting their workshop of exotic autos.

At the end of the dream row of automobiles was a red and white NASCAR, branded with the number thirty-three. It was Breakdown's converted Chevy Camaro. Not a standard racecar, given it had a backseat, but as close to the real thing as one could get with racing wheels, an engine, and redesigned body built to professional specs. Pedro stopped in front of the NASCAR and watched his wide-eyed cousin caress the machine.

"You did good with the paint. The NASCAR folks will be proud," Breakdown praised.

"She's looking beautiful," Battlestar affirmed. He knew thousands of dollars had been invested into altering the Chevy Camaro, making it ready for the junior NASCAR circuit, Breakdown's racing hobby.

"So this is your idea you assumed I'd love?" Justice asked.

"Yes, sir. It is."

"This vehicle is impressive, Breakdown. What do you suppose we are going to do with it?"

"Headquarters said Code Seven, sir. I didn't want to risk our chances on not getting to LAX on time in the rental," Breakdown replied as he ducked away to inspect the inside detail.

Troy knew Breakdown was friendly with Justice and could get away with being a smart ass, but he was pushing the limits. Justice just wanted to get to

LAX—it was obvious. "It'll take more time to go back for the rental. Maybe we should give it a try?" Battlestar coaxed, trying to ease the situation.

Justice sighed, examining the car. "Where are your keys? We have to hurry the hell up. I'm driving."

"Oh, no, no, no. I'm the only one that can drive my baby."

"Your *baby*?" Justice seemed to have had enough. "Damn it! You have a wounded arm and can barely lift a glass of water."

"*Breakdown*?" Pedro said, appearing confused by the use of codenames.

"My other arm is just fine. Besides, you can shift. C'mon, let's go." Breakdown speed-walked to the driver's side before Justice could argue.

"Don't be so pedantic, Colonel," Battlestar jested.

"Get in the back, Battlestar. I'll only take so much," Justice said, giving in to the scene.

Battlestar hopped in with part of his mind on Decon's message. Reserved for pending threat-intelligence, Code Sevens require immediate action. Battlestar wondered what happened to merit the emergency call.

"Hurry this up. No time for experimentation. We have a plane to catch," Justice ordered.

Breakdown settled into the front seat as if worshiping the car he loved. He gripped the steering wheel with one hand and pushed hard on the gas pedal. Black rubber burned into the white showroom floor as the engine roared to life, sending black smoke funneling behind the NASCAR.

"Chavez, you son of a bitch!" Pedro yelled, throwing his hands in the air at the sight of the black marks on his pristine showroom floor.

"Sorry, cousin! I'll take care of the cleaning bill!" Breakdown shouted out his open window.

"I miss you, bastardo!" Pedro yelled, smiling as he watched his cousin speed away.

"We need to have a serious sit down," Justice said, "but right now, get us to LAX in one piece. Drive this beast without crashing. That's an order!"

"Sir, I'm happy to fulfill it. I just need you to shift right about NOW!"

Battlestar exploded in silent laughter. He couldn't have dreamed a better return. Breakdown took the first corner tight and accelerated toward the Pacific Coast Highway. He ran several stoplights and broke a dozen more traffic regulations as he swerved around corners, dipped through backstreets, and sped to the airport.

As the officers drove toward the reserved military entrance at LAX, Battlestar felt his focus shift as his warrior mind took back over. Air Force guards at the gate waved the car through after scanning the officers' biometric readings to confirm identities.

Battlestar stepped out of the car and felt proud. Breakdown tossed his keys to an agent from the Air Force Office of Special Investigation who greeted them with a sealed folder of classified preliminary briefings for the upcoming CONTRA missions. "Park this over in the special weekend zone. I'll have my cousin come pick it up at the gate," Breakdown said.

The CONTRA officers hurried up the stairs of the waiting jet. Battlestar turned to gaze at the mountains beyond LAX. Little did he know, it would be the last time he'd ever set eyes on California soil.

CHAPTER 18
THE HIDDEN SECRET

Washington, DC: May 4, 2035

"I want to know," the president demanded.

Joseph McBride perspired with a chill that made him flinch underneath the tailored lines of his suit. The president of the United States looked him square in the eye, questioning his loyalty. The CONTRA meeting wasn't arranged to discuss the state of The Revolution; it was a meeting to confront three of America's most trusted leaders—leaders more important to the world than anyone in the Oval Office could realize.

Somehow, the Emissaries had been put in jeopardy.

"Mr. President, I'm not sure what you're getting at. All our information was processed through the regular channels for intelligence sharing and reporting. You know everything." Joseph tried to sound unmoved, realizing the president's questions weren't aimed at operational matters. He continued, "We came prepared to discuss plans for the next CONTRA objectives and to assess how The Revolution's technical advancements took place without detection. These were the talking points given to us for preparation and we've done so."

President Hawthorne took his time to reply. He spoke carefully, choosing each word with precision. "I read through each of your bios this morning. All three of you have served your country and the alliance with great patriotism for the duration of your adult lives, which makes this more difficult. Nevertheless, when serious concerns are raised they have to be evaluated, and I want answers."

The president folded his arms and began pacing around the room.

"The Presidential Daily Briefing is the top current intelligence product anywhere in the world. I hear everything we know, every morning, over strawberries and waffles. There was never a hint in one of those briefings that The Revolution had laser weapons. The underground base, and those monsters you call werewolves, are a completely different degree of surprise altogether. Before we can discuss *these* crucial matters of our national security, we have to talk about *your* connections to them."

Patton shifted forward in his chair. "With all due respect, sir, *we* are not affiliated with The Revolution," he said, in a tone reflecting his wounded honor and subdued anger.

The president turned to Sandra, and nodded. She set a small digital player on the center of the table. She announced to the group, "This is an audio recording of a conversation that took place between *Magden* and Joseph McBride the day after the CONTRA firefight in Colombia."

Joseph stiffened. Sandra had used McDaniel's given birth name. Nobody outside the secretive community of Emissaries ever called Magden by his true name. McDaniel Jessup was on his driver's license, his fake birth certificate, and all other official government forms.

Sandra hit play.

It has been sent then?

The transmission was delivered through the channels last night. I only hope it reaches the Council with enough speed to influence a change.

That is my concern. We hold the power to end The Revolution, yet must wait for approval from the very Council created to assure such travesties as the Dark War never repeat. We are running out of time! There is more than enough evidence now. There can be only one answer to what's behind this. We know what that is.

Joseph, our best guess is not fact, and you know we cannot reveal anything until we have authority. Our main loyalty cannot be forgotten. We have become acclimated here, but our born allegiance must remain predominant. It is the way. Remain patient.

My patience is running low.

Sandra stopped the audio, leaving the Oval Office in uncomfortable silence. One of the joint chiefs leaned forward, the slight creak in his chair echoed throughout the room. The Emissaries sat stunned.

Revealing the secret by mistake was the oldest concern. Someone tracked them. Eavesdropped. Measures were taken from the beginning to prevent such an occurrence. Joseph realized how foolish it was to speak as they had. He remembered the conversation well.

The president and government officials waited for an explanation. When they saw it wasn't coming, Sandra spoke.

"We have over four hours of recorded conversations between the three of you over the last four months. An anonymous informant said you were hiding information and tipped off the Defense Criminal Investigative Service. An investigation was launched. I was against it at first, telling them it was a waste of time, but when the case officer shared these conversations of code words and talk of *councils* and *transmissions,* we became concerned. We still don't understand exactly what you're talking about. You are careful never to say too much. We cannot wait any longer though. It's too important."

Sandra spoke with a soft seriousness that tugged at Joseph's heart. They were on the same side, but Sandra wouldn't believe them even if Magden *could* tell her. It would take weeks or even months for their accusers to fully comprehend Nerrial and its relationship with Earth.

Joseph looked at Magden, questions burning in his eyes. Magden knew he wondered if he, the chief Emissary in charge of the entire legion, would reveal, in this moment of need, the truth.

However, Magden also knew it was neither the right time nor his decision to make.

In his appointment as director of Allied Partnerships in the NATO Division of Political Affairs and Security Policy, Magden helped build CONTRA's groundwork along with Joseph and Patton. Working for the alliance was a distinct privilege for Magden. Influencing the creation of CONTRA was the perfect contribution for him to make. His service continued his family's dedication to the cause on Earth that began long before his time, on the eve of the Second Great War, when the threat of conflict crept slowly over Europe and the Pacific.

Magden's grandfather, Calliden, had watched the imminent wickedness loom. Powerless to stop it or intervene, he recognized the Nerrial role needed to transform from *observation* to *influence*. Calliden pushed for the change. Things on Earth were going wrong. The dangers were too great. The elusive, unseen evil persisting on the planet like a plague would overcome all that was good if left unchecked. Emissaries needed to act.

The tragedies of World War II shifted the Emissary role. Influencing events to prevent future horrors and tragedy became their mission, no longer observation. Many Nerrial Emissaries worked themselves high into the governments of good men. Calliden was one of them. He strived patiently to advise and recommend the creation of a peacetime military alliance. On April 4, 1949, the mission succeeded and NATO was born.

Calliden knew a third World War between the Soviet Union and United States would mean the end of human civilization on Earth. The risk of annihilation was real. He persuaded the High Council to debate the greatest question an Emissary could ask: When would Nerrial reveal itself to Earth? A Triad was held at the outset of the Cold War. A Triad brought all of Nerrial's political pillars together to decide on an issue of grave importance, but the hope for revelation was denied and again delayed. The revelation question still burned among Magden and the other Emissaries today.

Emissaries were ordered to protect Europe and America through the newly formed peacetime NATO alliance that they helped create. The shield held successfully. After the fall of the Soviet Union, many Emissaries believed a window to achieve true longstanding peace had opened. But war returned as it always did on Earth. The Wars on Terrorism, Resource Wars, and the Battle of Taiwan followed. National struggles, strife, murder, and death continued to haunt Earth's people and pit one against another for money, power, or hatred. Following each war, hope for peace dwindled more rapidly than the Emissaries anticipated.

Hope drove the Emissaries, then and now—the hope that Earth's final days were not at hand.

The three men called to the White House had been tasked with countering The Revolution as government servants *and* as leading Nerrial Emissaries on Earth. Their fathers had been friends and the primary voices continuing the mission during the Cold War. Now, Joseph, Magden, and Patton led the mission and fought against a peril larger than the traditional worldly threats facing Earth. The first signs appeared deep in the Colombian jungle when the Demon Lab was uncovered: signs from Nerrial's past whispered of doom, the Nezdeth.

Horrors from history, no matter how terrible and no matter how well documented, could easily be forgotten. Magden thought the newest transmission to Lonthran would strike the right chord with the Crown, Nerrial's key leadership figure. The evidence of a Nezdeth presence on Earth was all but fact. Saving Earth depended on action from afar.

"So gentlemen, what is it you're not telling us?" the president asked, growing impatient with their hesitation. "How is it that *you* hold the power to end The Revolution?"

Each of the Emissaries waited for the other to speak. They were in a position none of them, or those who came before them, had ever encountered. The situation was without precedent. Magden thought of a proper response. Like Sandra had mentioned, the DCIS and likely other government agencies had probably trailed their every move since CONTRA's operational phase began. Suspicion oozed from the group gathered in the Oval Office, denying the Emissaries an easy escape. To honor the Nerrial Emissaries' code, Magden would do his best.

"Mr. President, our dedication to the promotion of peace and unity between nations has always been paramount. We are the most devoted people to the cause, now and forever. That recording, and others like it you may have, implicates us for actions that appear to contradict our commitment. Let me assure you they do not. It is—"

"Then tell us what the hell you are talking about! It's that simple, *Magden*," Sandra said cutting him off.

"Sandra, please. Let him finish," the president said. "We haven't found anything implicating them beyond words." He turned toward Joseph, Magden, and Patton and continued. "However, even if you men have been working in this country's and NATO's best interest within some kind of independent association, vigilante group, or cult makes no difference. The chain of command is a requirement eluding no one. I would like to understand what it is you have been up to. What is the High Council? Who is Lonthran?"

The president locked Magden in a dead stare. His questions were specific.

Magden studied the shiny table in front of him, seeing his reflection in the polished wood. He wondered *who* the informant was. The broader mission of caretaking the great secret seemed secondary. He cared about Earth. He sighed quietly, knowing life would never be the same. "Sir, I am sorry. For the first time in my career of service, I cannot follow your order. I am not able to give you the answers you want." Magden expected his response to mean imprisonment.

"*Can't* or *won't*?" the president asked.

"It is an answer that would require more time than remains in this day. What I *can* tell you is that we have never disavowed our service to this country, the alliance, or the good causes we work to promote. We are as concerned about The Revolution as anyone; in fact, *more* concerned."

Magden's sincerity did not alleviate the conundrum he and his fellow Emissaries were in. Clear disappointment and surprise carved President Hawthorne's face. He'd expected nothing less than a full explanation. Nothing Magden could say would make the situation better. Their mistakes were on record—dishonor and failure in the noble endeavor to save Earth without intervention. He wondered what the remaining audio might contain. It probably didn't matter. Nerrial intervention had to happen to stop the Nezdeth.

"Joseph . . . General Taylor, is this your position as well?" President Hawthorne asked.

Patton barely moved his head to nod.

"I have nothing to add, sir," Joseph said. "Other than we are not traitors."

Magden's emergency receiver vibrated on his belt. He peeked. A Code Seven coming in from NATO headquarters. *Damn.* He couldn't respond.

President Hawthorne put his hands in his pockets. Biting his lip he walked over to the window behind his grand desk that held a commanding presence in the Oval Office. He folded his arms and looked at the pleasant green lawn everyone called his front yard. The White House never felt like home to him. The place was a large office space—a very decadent one—but there was never time to relax.

The men behind him were hiding something very important. His gut told him to leave them in their positions, that they weren't a threat. He wished he was alone with them and contemplated sending the rest of his advisors and military counsel to wait in the hall. Everyone agreed there had to be a logical answer to the code talk used, but nobody who listened to the recordings could decipher the lexicon.

The codes and conversations baffled investigators on the task force appointed by the president. The Secret Service had overseen the investigation with support from the DCIS and NSA. The purpose of the task force was to brief the president on what the men were hiding. The task force had followed the men wherever they went, listened to every phone call, and read every personal e-mail over the last four months. Their findings amounted to a laundry list of codes that resembled fantasy references. Sandra was the first to pose the idea that there might not be code at all. "If not, where does that leave us?" the president questioned. She had no answer.

Sandra had argued that the men would divulge everything if confronted. The meeting's format was by her suggestion. To Sandra, the concealed information was a national security issue—her territory. She wanted to know the men's secrets. To the president, Sandra seemed plain obsessed. She had listened to all the recorded conversations, memorized the key words and often-repeated phrases. She replayed the recordings for the president, took notes, and lost sleep in her search to find some meaning behind the codes.

Even though the NSA recordings implicated the men for hiding *something*, they also showed their dedication to winning the fight—impressively dedicated in fact. The president and Sandra did agree they were good men.

The room stayed quiet as the president pondered. He dreaded what he had to do next. As he walked back to the table, he said, "Alexander Hamilton, one of this country's most decisive and influential founding fathers, once said, 'The direction of war implies the direction of the common strength; and the power of directing and employing the common strength forms a usual and essential part in the definition of the executive authority.' Gentlemen, without your total and complete loyalty, we have no common strength."

The commander in chief met the eyes of each of the three Emissaries.

"Each of you is released from duty. This will be considered your last official meeting as CONTRA officials and furthermore as government officials of any position. My disappointment in your withholding information couldn't be greater. You are suspended without pay. I will order the investigation to continue and I expect your full cooperation under the law. I don't care for this 'I can't tell you' bullshit!" The president pounded his fist on the table with a flare of anger in his voice and his eyes. He collected himself after the moment of rage.

"Now, we do have other matters to attend to. Your termination officially begins after this meeting is adjourned. Hard as it may be, let's follow through with your planned briefing. Not that I can trust everything you say, but tell me, gentlemen, just what, in God's name, happened in Colombia?"

PART TWO
REVELATIONS

*"The suffering brought upon us by the Nezdeth
can never be forgotten, or it will return."*
—Exa The Great, 367 AD on Cellcia

CHAPTER 19
THE HORROR COMETH
Beirut, Lebanon: May 3, 2035

"The war begins upon the completion of this task," Ripster vowed while leaning over the vat of dark purple liquid.

"Our task is already complete. The unfolding is all we await," Prowess boasted.

"Once it starts it won't stop. The time for reward will come fast."

"We shouldn't even be here to take part," Prowess snapped. "The Revolution elements from this region should manage this operation. Your backbone is weak when taking orders from the Nezdeth."

"These are my decisions, not theirs," Ripster shot back, whirling around. "You gossip; *I* know what is necessary. Assuring that hate returns to the holiest land *is* our interest. The beginning of glory over our brethrens' beautiful discovery will be fueled by it. *Oh, how wonderful Earth is in all its rare magnificence and imperfections.* Let them suffer! Let them crawl and die like pigs! And they will die and crawl, oh yes they will . . . won't they, Likzi?" Ripster berated, spitting into a corner in the dark Beirut basement of the abandoned building where The Three convened.

Likzi sat on a small wooden stool in the opposite corner and watched his partners. They'd been here for the past twelve hours. The closer they came to realizing *the plan*, the more Likzi felt removed from the ultimate objectives. He couldn't even recall why they were doing it, but he knew the three of them were sick, poisoned by the Nezdeth, their former enemy. A faint remembrance of his life before The Revolution, before serving the Nezdeth, pulled him toward goodness once in a while—perhaps the only difference between himself and the other two. Ripster and Prowess couldn't realize it, but Likzi did—all three of them were doomed.

"They will suffer . . . and they will die," Likzi admitted halfheartedly. "I can't imagine there is much chance once the second stage begins, unless the—" he stopped abruptly. He couldn't say what was on his mind or call them by name. The mere thought of the celebrated Nerrial Starforce sent a wave of intense fear to his soul. Facing them would be unthinkable. Likzi's only fear was fighting and killing his brethren.

Before falling into the hypnotic poison of the Nezdeth, Likzi had been a noble Starforce officer along with Ripster and Prowess. They served under a defense fleet assigned the mission of ensuring that Nezdeth military forces remained confined near their home planet of Whorvz. Likzi sat on the stool and strained to recall what went wrong on their last fateful mission. Ripster and Prowess waited for him to continue.

"What is the matter with you again?" Prowess complained. "I look forward to it if they come. Let Nerrial show itself instead of hiding behind closed doors. Their efforts will not make a difference on this hopeless planet. We are better than they. Power will be ours, as it should be." She kicked a wooden table hard against the wall. The frame snapped in two.

Prowess couldn't wait. Her heart burned for open conflict. No longer would they have to live in secret shadows of Middle Eastern basements and underground tunnels in the Amazon rainforest. The Three would stand revered for their achievements. Nezdeth promises for their service would soon be realized. Pitiful mankind, near and far, would know The Three's names and true origin. The Nerrial secret, kept for so many years by the Emissaries, would be destroyed forever. Prowess lusted for the moment.

The war would start in Jerusalem tomorrow, when good nations would meet for large celebrations and festivities to mark fleeting accomplishments of bringing peace to the Middle East. For so long, peace was deemed impossible, but the Holy Land Accords were working. The Three would shatter that progress in one day. They were well aware of Jerusalem's historic importance and what mid-East peace meant to the global community. The Holy Land Accords created a way toward permanent peace and had held up, but not for long. Saved as the final disruption following: subversion of the Chinese government, fanning the Drug Wars, and spreading violence in the EU—The Global Revolution was truly ready to begin.

"If indeed Nerrial chooses to reveal itself, Prowess, we cannot assure the delights of our reward without a great battle," Ripster said.

"A fight only we can win."

"Your confidence is foolish!"

"The Nezdeth have become more powerful because of *us*!" Prowess eyed Ripster with a mixture of approval for getting them this far and hatred for bowing to every demand of the Nezdeth.

"Realize, my dearest, that in Jerusalem the aftermath of open war will become the test," Ripster pointed out. "The heavens will be shaken."

"Not even the great Etralin or Ciza could stop us from doing what we will in the Holy Land," she argued.

Once, when Prowess was eight-years-old, she had gotten lost in one of the many museums paying tribute to the millions who died during the War of the Star. Her mother found her standing at the memorial of Etralin and Ciza, the heroic brother and sister who fought in the legendary struggle against the Nezdeth. Prowess wanted to grow up with as much purpose as they had, like so many of the young who were Blessed.

When she came home from the war museum, Prowess prayed that never again would Nerrial fall under the aggression of the Nezdeth. As a teenager, she learned to use her High-Senses as the gifts they were. Her remarkable speed, tenacity, and intelligence made her the best female fighter in her Star-force class—she was ripe for a leadership position. Prowess knew then it was her calling to serve. She just never imagined that it would be for Nerrial's ancient enemy. The poisoning led to a morbid fascination with evil and vengeance, which replaced her morality and the cause of righteousness she had possessed as a Starforce officer.

That Blessed Nerrial military officer Prowess had once been was dead and gone, lost forever to the effort of assuming power for power's sake. Spells of hatred changed her. The same Nezdeth toxins used on her so many years ago were about to befall the people of Jerusalem in The Three's last act of diversion before The Global Revolution. Prowess would oversee the operation's success followed by her ascension to greatness.

Several Nezdeth warriors dressed in the customary black and red battlesuits of The Revolution entered the basement to ensure the poison was ready before it was sealed for later use.

"The chanting will be for a different cause when we finish with Jerusalem," Prowess beamed.

"May the rains fall heavy," Ripster added.

Over one hundred thousand spectators—including dignitaries from around the world—were expected to attend the celebrations for the tenth anniversary of the Holy Land Accords. The Israeli, Palestinian, NATO, and United Nations Security Forces would be patrolling virtually every corner of the city. The presence of a powerful Earth security apparatus didn't matter to The Revolution. Starting the takeover of the planet in dramatic fashion suited the Nezdeth purpose well. Pandemonium at the outset of a large, expanding battle with Nezdeth warriors was what the generals wanted in order to capture the desired Nerrial attention.

Diverting Nerrial's Starforce's attention to Earth would split its defenses, allowing the reconstituted military industrial complex of Whorvz to launch its rebuilt space-force incorporating stolen Nerrial war technologies provided by

The Three. Altogether, *that* diversion would accomplish the Nezdeth's multifaceted purpose—revenge for losing the War of the Star and occupation of Nerrial to consume its precious, abundant resources fueled by the magical energy of its Blue Star. The secret invasion strategy would not remain hidden for much longer.

"Everything is ready, Prowess. Carry out the plan as we've agreed," Ripster said.

"I intend to," Prowess lied, enamored by her own cunning.

She didn't intend to follow orders from *anybody* once global war on Earth commenced. Prowess would do as she desired, tired of both Ripster and the Nezdeth. Maybe she was a gossip, but it gave her pure pleasure. She had already arranged for famed Station One News reporter Lydia Lewis to meet with her. Secrets were overrated. The Revolution could not be stopped now, so Prowess would gossip freely of her accomplishments. Spreading fear was more important than following Ripster's constant orders. The truth would spread fear and what better way to sow panic than through a reporter?

Prowess didn't request permission from Ripster or the Nezdeth; she didn't need it, the same way she didn't ask when tipping off the Americans about Nerrial's Emissaries. Because of Prowess, those behind CONTRA's creation would have to operate under the watchful and suspicious eye of those they came to protect.

My wickedness is beautiful.

"It's time we depart and go our separate ways. You and the Nezdeth guards will handle the rest of the Jerusalem operation," Ripster went on. "Tonight I leave with Likzi for Kazan, Russia. We will meet with our Russian counterparts and receive their main delivery for the global campaign."

"I don't see why the Nezdeth couldn't have brought it from Whorvz. Earth technology is primitive compared to what we should be using. It forces us to depend on the pawns," Prowess fretted.

"The *pawns* have proven useful."

"Are you carrying out the termination of the Russian contract?" Prowess asked.

"Even useful pawns have a limited life," Ripster hinted. "When next we meet, our plans will be in full motion. The wait is nearing its end, as is all goodness of life on Earth."

CHAPTER 20
BATTLE READY
Colorado Springs: May 4, 2035

The chartered CONTRA jet would arrive at Colorado Springs in minutes.

After Justice and Breakdown debriefed Battlestar on the first CONTRA missions in Taiwan and Colombia, he scanned through a stack of classified CIA reports. The reports contained information the mainstream media did not know—happenings around the world that mattered but the government kept secret to avoid panic among the populace. Battlestar read, occasionally glancing out the plane's window at the Rocky Mountains below. Snow cover was sparse and forecasts called for ongoing droughts to worsen. Strict water rationing policies were already in effect across most of America.

Significant new intelligence about The Revolution had been uncovered since Battlestar's decommission. More than anything, the developments puzzled him, making the counter-revolutionary mission seem extraordinarily daunting. *The more we discover, the less it makes any sense.*

An intelligence memo given to Justice by the Air Force Special Agent at LAX outlined new CONTRA missions. During the flight, Decon called Justice with more updates and Justice relayed the information. The memo and updates were in anticipation of The Revolution's next moves and the plans for CONTRA to stop them. Each of the CONTRA teams would deploy: one to Israel, the other to Russia. The missions were the result of new intelligence collected by the NSA and provided by the Mossad indicating The Revolution was ratcheting up its organized vision of chaos on two separate continents.

In Israel, agents from the Institute for Intelligence and Special Operations, or Mossad, believed The Revolution was preparing for a major attack during the Holy Land Accord celebrations. Seized weapons shipments and an array of fugitives entering the country with Revolution ties cast concern over the signing's anniversary. A United Nations Stabilization Force (UNSFOR) Brigade stationed at the Golan Heights was placed on alert and relocated to the outskirts of Jerusalem, a move that hadn't happened in over five years. NATO requested one CONTRA team deploy to the region and follow up on intelligence leads regarding Revolution activity that had the Mossad concerned.

On the Russian front, new NSA intercepts of encrypted messages from mafia leaders uncovered a key Revolution meeting scheduled to take place outside of Kazan, approximately four hundred fifty miles east of Moscow. NSA shared the intercepts with CONTRA, and NATO liaisons shared them with Russian intelligence services. One of the decoded messages mentioned ringleaders attending the gathering where an advanced weapons transfer would take place involving ultra-powerful, non-nuclear electromagnetic pulse (EMP) weapons. The weapons were being smuggled out of a secretive Russian military complex called Yamantau.

The transfer site was in Kazan at an abandoned military base placed under the watchful eye of the Russian FSS and General Peter Nabokav, commander of Russia's Strategic Rocket Forces and the *same* general who had previously requested CONTRA's assistance. The meeting in Russia coincided with suspected Revolution actions in the Middle East and represented a dangerous increase in global activity.

"I'm not too late to stop the ringleaders," Battlestar muttered as he watched Breakdown rewrap his arm. "You gonna be able to join us?" he asked.

"I'm not sittin' on my ass at home."

"Your arm hasn't healed yet," Justice reminded. "I know it's not what you want to hear, but you're wounded."

"Ain't stayin' behind. I can operate on two feet and my good arm can still pull the trigger," Breakdown burst out. "I drove us well enough, didn't I?"

Justice smiled. "We made it to LAX."

"This pinprick is no excuse to keep me back. I'll have words with Patton if he tries. Put me on site, that's all I ask."

"That decision doesn't come from me," Justice answered. "But I'll support your wish the best I can."

"I doubt Patton will argue," Battlestar reassured. "By the way, if I forgot to say thank you in L.A., know that I'm forever grateful to the both of you. You can't imagine how I feel."

"We know," Breakdown said.

The emergency receiver on Justice's belt buzzed. "Colonel Justice here." He spoke little and mostly listened to someone on the other end for ten minutes before putting the receiver away. "That was Grace with some very interesting information."

"What's that?" Battlestar asked.

"Before we escaped from Taiwan, General Chiang—who I told you about—gave me a trinket. It was a music box with a map hidden inside. Chinese characters were written all over the place. Grace had the map translated. Turns out, most of the information is related to Resistance hideouts, but at the bottom, Chiang included a string of intelligence related to The Revolution. They *did* know something about it.

"The Resistance knew of PLA soldiers and equipment being transferred to South America in support of an unknown operation. Chiang noted that a captured mainland officer admitted this while being tortured for information. Of no use to them, Chiang thought it might interest us and be connected to The Revolution we informed him of."

"And of course it is," Battlestar beamed.

"Grace is following up with Pacific Command. See if we can get anything more out of this."

Their jet descended toward the strategically important Peterson Air Force

Base, home to NORTHCOM, NORAD, Space Command, and CONTRA Headquarters. A feeling of nostalgia came over Battlestar. The return to adventure was upon him.

"I haven't talked to my dad in about three months," Battlestar acknowledged.

"He's in a meeting today with Patton at the White House," Justice put in. "Things are shakin'. Maybe it's just these new missions, but Decon told me there was something big coming out of their talks. Said it had to wait 'til we were on the ground."

"Are they still in DC?" Breakdown asked, massaging his arm.

"Decon didn't say. We're about to find out."

The jet touched down and the officers exited to a waiting jeep. Red and Grace got out wearing their service dress uniforms. Grace smiled and ran to Battlestar. He didn't know why, but she always felt like family to him.

"Well, *ciao*, stranger," she sang, pulling at his long hair. "You haven't changed a bit except for this long hair, *mio dio*. Hope you enjoyed your off time 'cause we got work to do."

"From what I read on the way here, it appears so." Battlestar hugged the Italian intelligence officer. He'd shared many long talks with Grace during their time in CONTRA training, on subjects ranging from religion to war to cooking. She was easier to get along with than most women.

Red welcomed Battlestar cordially, then she tossed Justice the keys and kissed him on the lips, putting her hands on the back of his head. "You outrank me, honey, so you get to drive. The new mission briefings are waiting on us."

"Let's get to it then, babe."

Battlestar entered the old briefing room and the CONTRA officer corps gave him a rousing welcome. While he made his rounds greeting the other officers, Crosshill pulled Justice and Grace to the side.

"You wouldn't believe what just came through about an hour ago," he whispered to them.

"I'll believe just about anything these days," Justice said.

"Patton is no longer in command of CONTRA. President Hawthorne removed him today, citing insubordination."

Justice cringed, saying nothing for a moment. "How can that be? He's one of the most respected generals in the whole U.S. Army."

"It must be something serious," Grace uttered.

"That's not all," Crosshill said, glancing at Grace. He motioned her to come nearer, looking over his shoulder to see where Battlestar was. "Director McBride was also removed. Same reason given."

"No!" Grace put her hand over her mouth.

"What does this mean for our teams? Who is in command?" Justice asked.

"The Pentagon will select a new interim appointee from NORTHCOM or Space Command until someone else is named."

"Perhaps you should tell Battlestar?" Justice proposed to Grace. "You two were the closest friends before his decommission."

"He needs to know right away. Before this meeting begins. Everyone else has been informed," Crosshill added.

"Okay . . . fine," Grace hesitated. "I'd rather not. Our connection is a strange one . . . sometimes I feel as if we've known each other since childhood. It's the same with some other Italians, but Battlestar is a pure American."

"You'll need to hurry," Justice insisted.

Grace walked over to where Battlestar was talking with Xxplosive and Sandstorm. She tapped his shoulder. "Sorry to interrupt. I need to talk with Battlestar about some company business." She led Battlestar into the hall and waited for two military policemen to walk by.

"I guess . . . I guess that—"

"This is some bad news? Don't tell me I'm *not* in after all."

"No, it's not that, but you're not going to like it just the same."

"Go ahead, Grace. Say what you need."

She blurted it out in one quick breath. "Crosshill told me Patton and your father were removed from their positions today during a meeting at the White House."

Battlestar paused, perplexed by the news. "What do you mean, *removed*?"

"I don't know anything else. Crosshill did say it was something about . . . insubordination."

"My father removed by the president? He's spent his whole life in service! He's never even been reprimanded during his career."

"I don't get it either."

Battlestar shook his head at the crude timing of the news. Several Space Command officers rounded the corner heading toward the meeting room.

"We better get inside, Grace," he said.

"Are you okay?"

"I'm fine."

As the Space Command officers passed Battlestar and Grace in the hall, Battlestar noticed one of them, a colonel, eyeing both him and Grace intently. The colonel made eye contact with Battlestar and gave him a strange look. Battlestar glanced at his name—Vickers—and followed Grace into the briefing room.

Everyone took his or her seats. The acting CONTRA commander, Air Force Brigadier General Michael Brownberg, was sensitive to the situation. He was a friend of Patton's and a respected strategist. The teams didn't know much else about Brownberg, but they did know it wouldn't be the same without Patton.

Throughout the briefing, Battlestar thought of what might have happened to warrant the president dismissing his father and Patton. He tried to put it out of his mind. He was about to go on his first official CONTRA mission. Two days ago he had been sitting on his couch unable to shake the plague of guilt and failure. Now, Battlestar was back on track toward a destiny he hungered for. "They'll be back . . . just like me," he whispered under his breath.

The teams geared up, ready to load the four Shadowhawks that waited on the runway. The mission briefings had been grim. General Brownberg elaborated further on the new Revolution threats and CONTRA missions in Russia and the Middle East. There was no time for the teams to consider what caused the removals of Commander Patton and Director McBride at the White House. Less than twelve hours had passed since CONTRA had received new orders. The strike force was prepared to move out. The officers and troops made their last phone calls before departure. They were battle ready.

Satellite hung up in dismay, sliding both palms over his forehead.

"What's wrong buddy?" Breakdown asked, passing by.

"It's my sister, man. Last week she tells me she's going to write a book about The Revolution. Now she calls to inform me she's vacationing in *Jerusalem* of all places—right before we're heading there on a mission."

"Vacationing? If I know anything about your sis, she's there to work."

"Lydia thinks repairing her career because of that Revolution exposé is necessary."

"That report was good."

"Yeah, I know. Thanks." Satellite hadn't expected Lydia to be in harm's way. She hadn't mentioned going to Jerusalem before. After hearing new threat briefings on The Revolution's activity in and around Israel, he wanted her to leave but couldn't say anything. Classified information was just that. This time Lydia was too close to the action.

Satellite latched several ammunition clips onto his battle suit while worrying that terror might return to the Holy Land. He was frightened for Lydia. "Damn the job, it's not worth it. I know you're there to work," he grumbled.

Over the roar of Shadowhawk thrusters, Crosshill called for the Gray Team to board their craft, destination Israel. The CONTRA mission: defend the Holy Land Accord legacy, Israel, and Palestine from a pending Revolution attack.

Justice looked over the Blue Team. They would be deploying to Russia to connect with a company of Russian Special Forces, or *Spetsnaz*, to prevent an advanced arms transfer of strategic grade EMP weapons to The Revolution. Their secondary objective was to try to kill or capture one or all of The Revolution ringleaders. Preparations were swift. Being armed and ready in less time than most people need to plan a trip to the grocery store was a requirement for a CONTRA strike force.

Justice hoped this mission would end better than Taiwan. A warm hand touched the back of his neck. He turned to find Red standing beside him.

"Crosshill wants us to board," she said.

"Yeah, I heard." He sighed as they stared at one another. Justice regretted leaving her to danger once again.

"My team, we'll see action first." She squeezed his hand.

He kissed the back of her fingers. "Follow your team closely and keep your eye out for snipers. There will be thousands of people packing those streets. Whatever The Revolution tries to pull off, they'll do it in a crowd. I wish I could be there to watch your back."

"That's probably all you'd be doing," Red laughed. She put her arms around his neck and pulled herself close, squeezing in tight.

Justice could feel her heartbeat through the CONTRA battlesuit. His throat started to tighten. Pulling away, he could tell she fought off crying.

"I'll be seeing you," Justice assured.

"Maybe have that talk about *stuff* when we come back?"

"I'd like that."

Battlestar repeatedly tried to reach his father, but couldn't.

Grace was with him at the weapons bay. She had a gift for him.

"I wonder if we'll encounter any of those werewolves," Battlestar pondered, making sure he had everything, snatching whatever he needed from the bay.

"Never do I wish to see one of those evil beasts. Should Satan build an army, those creatures would surely join." Grace grabbed two more grenades and latched them to her battlesuit.

They were the last ones to gear up. Battlestar knew Justice would be calling the Blue Team any second.

"I've got everything but my old sword. I guess that's not standardized CONTRA equipment yet," Battlestar ventured half-seriously, while he inserted extra batteries into his battlepack then strapped a serrated survival knife onto his thigh.

Grace pulled back a blanket sitting in the corner of the weapons bay and cleared her throat loudly. "I had one of the armament guys get this." She held out a sheathed blade. "It's samurai. An authentic *katana* blade."

Battlestar unsheathed it. The flawless silver reflected the light that streamed in through the nearby windows. "You know me well, Grace." Battlestar had taken an interest in martial arts as a boy. As a man he became well acquainted with the underappreciated potency of silent weapons and achieved mastery of Ninjutsu. "It's perfect," he said admiring the sword.

"I don't know what you're gonna do with it, but you're welcome."

CHAPTER 21
BLACK WIDOW
Jerusalem: May 4, 2035

"How long will you be staying ma'am?" the bellboy asked as he led Lydia to her hotel room.

"Just for the celebrations . . . I think." She tried to sound cheerful and mask her mounting fear. The bellboy rambled on about how he'd been to New York and seen her on the big screen in Times Square. He may have even asked her a question, but Lydia just nodded, not really hearing his words. Unable to stop glancing at her watch, she considered the envelope she'd been given at the front desk.

Lydia thanked the bellboy with a sizeable tip and began unpacking her essentials, not expecting to be in Israel for more than three days. If all went well with tonight's meeting, Lydia would spend the rest of her time in Jerusalem working on The Revolution book, fresh with new information. She removed her working manuscript and set it by her bedside, along with a list of questions to ask "Prowess."

Soon Lydia would meet with one of The Revolution ringleaders; at least, she thought that's who Prowess was. The contents of the package delivered to her apartment had to be from someone high within The Revolution. After viewing the photos from the package again, meeting with a Revolution ringleader forced Lydia to question her sanity. These were criminals and terrorists of the worst kind. They had created monsters in the Colombian jungle, were fighting a war, and held NATO troops hostage. The pictures proved it. *What would stop Prowess from taking me hostage?*

Reaching into her purse she pulled out the envelope from the front desk. Her name had been scribbled on the plain white envelope. It had no other markings. Lydia sat on the edge of her bed, assessing the situation before her. She regarded herself as a true field reporter, one who didn't run from a good story. Lydia had been on dangerous trips before, but usually with an entire crew or at least a cameraman.

Once, in Nigeria, at the outset of the Resource Wars, an African farmer offered Lydia's translator one thousand dollars to *buy* her. The translator agreed to the deal and shook hands with the farmer. Thankfully, Lydia's cameraman fought off the farmer who claimed she now belonged to him. The network fired the translator. It was the last time Lydia visited the African countryside. This time around, Lydia was alone. Nobody even knew she was in Jerusalem. Her producer approved her request for a much-needed "vacation." Lydia told friends she might visit her mother in Florida or go on a cruise. She didn't want any official reporting duties, but if Prowess decided to kidnap her, nobody could trace Lydia.

I could go missing for days before anyone would notice.

"This is stupid," she said aloud. She picked up her cell phone and dialed her brother. It rang three times. "Come on Nate, pick it up. Someone's got to know where I am."

"*Hello, you've reached Nathan Lewis—*" Lydia hung up, not wanting to leave a message.

You are a crazy fool.

She ripped open the envelope. "If I don't do this, who will?" she asked, recalling the famed cliché, "If you want something done right, do it yourself" her Grandma Dorothy used to recite.

Lydia felt this was one of those times.

Unfolding the single sheet of notebook paper from the envelope, she said a prayer asking for protection—another thing she learned from Grandma, prayer—every night at supper and every Sunday at church, no excuses. Unfolding the single sheet of paper, her eyes scanned the page. Underneath the East Jerusalem address written in scratchy penmanship was a clear message in bold letters:

BRING NO ONE ELSE

Lydia's cell phone rang at just that moment. She checked the caller identification: Nathan was calling back.

"Nathan!" she exclaimed, immediately comforted.

"What's up, sis? These are odd calling times you keep!" Satellite yelled through the phone. She could barely hear him.

"Are you standing in front of a lawnmower? I can hardly hear you, Nate. Can you call from anywhere louder?"

"Can't help that. I'm about to board an aircraft for a trip! I could tell them to power down, but I doubt they would . . . even for you!" he hollered, laughing loudly into the receiver.

"Okay, well, I just wanted to let you know that I'm in Jerusalem on a working vacation," Lydia blurted, relieved someone finally know where she was. Nate was silent on the other end. She waited a moment longer, but only heard the loud engines of the revving aircraft. "Nathan, did you hear me?" she asked.

"I heard you!" he shouted back. "Listen Lydia, you know things have been crazy around the world. You need to be careful over there. Very careful. You hear me?"

"I do. You too . . . wherever it is you're going." There was another pause on the phone and Lydia began to worry. It wasn't like Nathan to hesitate so much. *What isn't he telling me?*

"I love you, Lydia. I'll talk to you soon. I really have to go now!"

"Nathan, wait!" she said, but he'd already hung up. She couldn't remember the last time he'd said *I love you*. Lydia's cell rang again. She picked it up instantly without checking the number. "Nathan!"

"This is Prowess," said an icy, stiff woman's voice.

Lydia's heart skipped a beat. Caught off guard, she tried to say something fast, "Oh . . . nice. How are you tonight?" Her forced cheerfulness was blatant. Lydia couldn't believe how weak her response sounded and punched herself in the knee.

"Kindness means nothing to me, Ms. Lewis. You have the note I sent with my location for our meeting. Are you coming? I don't like disappointment."

Lydia sat up straight to compose herself. The voice on the other end was snakelike. She felt uneasy but, at the same time, hearing Prowess helped Lydia realize things were moving forward. She hadn't come to Jerusalem for nothing. *How did Prowess get my cell phone number?* "Yes, I'm coming. I just had to get some of my things together. Where is the location we're meeting? I'd like to know it's a safe place, where I do not have to worry about my personal safety."

"Sorry, it's in a part of town where tourists don't visit, on a street where little girls don't play at night."

Lydia tensed. "*I'm* not a little girl and that's why I ask certain questions. What safety guarantees can you afford me?"

"None."

"Then why should I come?"

"Because I'm the biggest story of your life."

"That's not much assurance, Prowess." Lydia needed to protect herself without losing the story.

"Ms. Lewis, if I wanted you dead it wouldn't be difficult for me to see that through, but you would be of no value to me then, would you? People listen to your news station and you in particular. I have chosen you for this reason. There is a message The Revolution would like delivered—which *I* would like delivered. Whether you'd like to be the one reporting it is up to you. Don't waste my time. I will be at the location in one hour. Show up or tell me now that you won't."

Lydia paused, knowing her answer. "I'll be there."

"Good." Prowess hung up leaving Lydia listening to dead air. She kept the phone against her ear as if expecting Prowess to return on the line and provide more explanation. Lydia was scared, truly scared. It was time to go if she was going to make it in an hour. This meeting was her chance to reclaim her career in the field. Lydia grabbed her notes and took one last look at her hotel room, praying Grandma Dorothy would be watching over her.

CHAPTER 22
INTO THE HOLY LAND
Jerusalem: May 5, 2035

"Everybody look sharp. We land in thirty!" Crosshill yelled over the radio headset.

The team slept as much as they could. Time for stretching out the travel kinks would be limited. The Shadowhawks neared their destination. Each fighter-transport carried nearly thirty Gray Team members in modular rows designed with secure Intranet stations built within each chair, linking passengers to battle command and control.

"Colonel Crosshill?" Breakdown asked, trying not to show pain from his laser wound, holding his weapon straight with two hands.

"Yes."

"What are the chances we get ourselves some smoking hot gyros before we get into the messier side of things? I vote taking time for some lamb and local dessert. It might put the troops on the right footing, if you know what I mean."

"Wishful thinking. The Israeli military has a team on the ground waiting for us. We are to rendezvous with them, some blue UN helmets, and our regional commander. They got somewhere for us to go if *you* know what *I* mean."

"Right. So that means no? Okay then, just thought I'd check."

Crosshill appreciated Breakdown's humor. He felt stiff: on edge. He hadn't been able to reach his wife when they touched down in England. No one picked up at home and she didn't answer her cell. It bothered him. Crosshill had told her he would call around that time. Talking to her always helped before a mission. Something in a woman's voice, whether a mother, girlfriend, or wife, gave a man the comfort and confidence he needs before going into battle. If death should meet a soldier on the battlefield, there'd always be that last talk to hold on to.

"Diamond, what is Warsaw's status? You remembered to check in as I requested?" Crosshill asked.

"Still hospitalized. He'll fly back to Poland in a week and rehabilitate in the home city he codenamed himself after. It will likely be months before he can return to CONTRA. He is going to live, the medical staff assured me of that. Also, the search for our missing squad of CONTRA troops continues turning up dead-ends."

"Keep checking in on that. I want to know first if that status changes."

Crosshill moved down the center aisle of the large lead gunship, making sure the team was in check. Flying nonstop from Colorado Springs to Lakenheath Royal Air Force Base in the United Kingdom for a refueling stop, the company made good time to Israel.

CONTRA would join the multinational security force assembled in Jerusalem for the Holy Land Accords' ten-year anniversary—called the greatest security detail ever. It was three times the size of the security at the last World Cup in India. The increased precautions and extra surveillance paid off for the Mossad. Warnings of a possible Revolution attack were shared among security forces but kept from the public's attention so the celebrations could continue unimpeded and without fear.

The intelligence briefing provided by Brigadier General Brownberg at CONTRA headquarters appeared damning enough. Two containers seized a week earlier at Tel Aviv's main port had shipped from Colombia via South Africa, supposedly loaded with coffee beans. In actuality the vessels carried large amounts of weapons. Well hidden, the weapons were only discovered through a random inspection. The shipment was traced to Panamanian financier and cocaine trafficker Juan Carlos Hernandez, a man on CONTRA's list of most wanted suspects connected to The Revolution.

The container bust coincided with dozens of Latin American and Russian "tourists" being detained by Israeli security at different points of entry along the border. Fake passports and corresponding forms of identification were confiscated. Most of the detained had criminal records or ties to organized crime. Several of the Latin men had tattoos matching the jagged symbol found on Revolution mercenaries killed or captured in previous engagements. The Israeli Defense Force (IDF) alerted multinational peacekeeping commanders who reported the findings to NATO Allied Command Operations who in turn alerted CONTRA.

The Gray Team's mission was to corroborate new findings on the ground with classified intelligence concerning The Revolution. The strike force would support planned IDF raids on three safe houses where persons of interest were under surveillance in possible connection with the confiscated weapons shipment and detained tourists. Determining whether The Revolution posed an imminent threat to the scheduled celebrations was critical to avoid a security catastrophe and setback for regional peace.

At least that had been the plan. Things were moving fast on the ground.

"Damn it to hell," Crosshill fumed, reading a new mission report off his digital flip-screen attached to the forearm of his battlesuit. "This changes our plans . . . thirty minutes before landing. Swell." He checked his watch twice and pressed his radio on. "Satellite. Come see me."

Crosshill was struggling to make sense of the newest intelligence and its impact on their mission when Satellite reached him.

"What do you make of this new Intel we just got in?" Crosshill asked.

"Wasn't able to read all of it. I'm attempting to harden the Perceptor software components against enemy jamming and—"

"*This* mission, *not* that drone is the priority! Understand?"

"Yes, sir."

Crosshill put his hand over his forehead and blew a sigh of frustration. "Sorry, Major. That was uncalled for. I couldn't reach my wife, Diane, in England."

"I understand."

"Satellite, according to this latest report, Hezbollah has provided the Mossad with a hot new lead on The Revolution. It leaves us about . . . " Crosshill checked his watch again, "twenty-five minutes to make sense of it. And I don't get how, two days ago, a possible Revolution hideout is uncovered in one of the most populated Lebanese ghettos, and we don't know about it 'til now." Crosshill pointed erratically at his watch.

"Twenty-five minutes before we land in Israel," Satellite joined in.

"Neighbors complain of a terrible smell. They call in authorities. An investigation finds a makeshift chemical weapons facility in the basement of a vacant building owned by men with ties to the *same* arms smugglers involved in the shipment of weapon containers seized from that Juan Carlos Hernandez asshole. How's that for bad news? I'd say it's a bloody red alarm!" Crosshill bellowed out.

"It gets worse . . . I noticed in my initial scan," Satellite agreed.

"Yes, it does. The missing building owners were traced to a rented home in Beitan, a town outside of Jerusalem, and that's where they were found— dead. The cause is undetermined but appears to be poisoning, according to IDF HAZMAT teams who scrubbed the place clean. In their inspection, 'not a drop of oven grease or loose hair was gleaned.' I thought that was a cute insert. Let me read this shit verbatim." Crosshill scrolled down on his mini-digital screen.

"Okay, here we go. 'The carpet, floors, and cement garage of the rented home were stained white from industrial-strength solvents. There was no furniture, electronics, or even food in the house—only three dead men sprawled naked on the living room floor, their mouths gaped open, as if frozen in shock. Their skin had turned an awkward dark blue. Whoever murdered the men took great care in leaving no evidence behind in *most* of the home. A jagged blood-soaked symbol splattered on one bedroom wall seemed to send a message, the meaning of which is unclear at this time.' This look familiar?"

Crosshill pushed his screen up to Satellite's face so he could see the symbol.

"Matches the same Godforsaken diamond pattern we keep finding at Revolution sites," Satellite acknowledged.

"Yeah, and get this. 'Blood from the symbol matched the DNA of one of the deceased men, though no punctures were on his body. Security forces in the region were placed on a heightened alert.' Thanks. Now so are we . . . twenty minutes prior to landing."

Crosshill looked up at the television monitor tuned to Al Arabiya news. The murders hadn't made the headlines. IDF officials wanted to keep it that way for certain. Nonstop coverage focused on the preparations for celebrating the Holy Land Accords. Dignitaries were arriving and there was a buzz throughout Jerusalem. A massive parade later that day would signify the unprecedented unity marking a once-torn region of the world.

Crosshill stared back at the digital readout he and all officers on the Gray Team had received. He didn't like late-breaking information. It meant things weren't going according to plan, even at the start of the mission. Coupled with the intelligence briefing they received before departing, there was no doubt The Revolution was planning something big.

Red came and sat next to him. She was moving fast, her face animated like she had news. Crosshill scooted over as Red flipped through the newly received intelligence files. "Sir, the IDF analysis of the chemical weapons facility in Beirut is incomplete or incorrect. I'm trying to make sense of it."

"What's the matter?"

"The chemical compounds listed within the report aren't the common cocktail of nerve, blister, or choking agents. The Revolution may have been trying to hide its real ambition . . . I don't know . . . Perhaps they were working on something else? I'd like a word with the analyst who compiled this report. The ingredients checklist provided doesn't reflect a weaponized threat. It needs to be clarified or we could be hunting for fairy dust and not chemical weapons."

"The Israeli's have provided us a contact on the ground. A Colonel Ranin from the IDF *Sayeret Matkal*. I'll see if Ranin can get someone from the IDF Intel branch on the line."

A breaking Al Arabiya news story flashed on the monitor. A reporter shuffled a stack of papers with a disturbed look on his face. Rough news footage streamed in showing police beating down a frantic man in front of a bus station while onlookers watched in horror. Below the bright red *Breaking News* icon on the screen, the crawl read: Police Report Widespread Incidents of Violence Across Jerusalem.

"What now?" Crosshill questioned, pressing his radio headset. "Pilot, open up the side gun ports."

Each side of the craft opened as the Shadowhawk's descent took CONTRA over the rooftops of old Jerusalem. Diamond and Raption joined Crosshill and Red looking down on the historic city as the thrusters slowed the engines for landing. Crosshill scanned the streets below for any signs of mass violence. He saw nothing unusual—until the pilot switched to hover mode and brought the gunship lower.

"Look there! Is that a riot?" Diamond asked, pointing to a soccer field where a ruckus had broken out. Emergency vehicles were skidding onto the grass and personnel were scrambling to disperse a large crowd that appeared to be engaged in a brawl. Some of the crowd began fighting the arriving police and firefighters.

"Could just be a fight?" Red proposed.

"It ain't part of the celebration plan, I'll tell you that," Raption quipped.

Crosshill shook his head as the Shadowhawks touched down. "Doesn't look right."

The raw power of the gunship thrusters kicked up a small dust storm as the team emerged in full battle gear. A waiting contingent of IDF, UN, and NATO personnel greeted CONTRA's rapid exit from the Shadowhawks.

"Do you get the sense people around here think we're important?" Breakdown asked Raption who jogged next to him toward the welcome party.

"Like we know a hell of a lot more than they do."

"I guess it doesn't hurt to let 'em think it." Breakdown tightened his trademark black bandana and blinked away the whirling dust.

Crosshill recognized some of the people meeting them. "Good day," he said, saluting each. "As I understand, there is reason to believe the situation is becoming more fluid."

"Colonel, we don't even have time to discuss it," said Lieutenant General Arnold Taggert, the regional NATO Commander and lanky U.S. Marine Corps veteran with defined wrinkles and a sharp face. Crosshill had worked with him on one other occasion, on a transatlantic training operation in Italy several years back. General Taggert wasn't much for small talk and lacked the customary cordial nature of most general officers. He was about the business of the day, and only that.

"You get your team all ready to depart. I'll inform you about the disturbances on the way into the city," General Taggert said.

"*Disturbances*?" Crosshill asked.

The general looked at Crosshill. For a moment, fear flashed behind his hardened military demeanor. "We're still trying to get a handle on it. Reports started coming in from all over the city less than an hour ago—right after that Intel you got was filed. Some kind of group hysteria is taking over. Fights. Shootings. Coming in from every direction. Like someone just lit a madness match."

"We watched the news on the way in—"

"Mossad thinks it's The Revolution. I want *you* to tell me what it is. That's why you're here. I don't like this guessing shit. There's been too much of it the last week. CENTCOM stationed me here three months ago and there wasn't a peep out of The Revolution, not until ten days ago. Now trouble is starting. You're the experts, right? Do what you need. I'll support any request your team has."

"Appreciate it, General. We'll do what we can, sir," Crosshill sputtered back, trying hard to match the general's confidence in CONTRA.

General Taggert turned and started waving a convoy of armored vehicles forward. "More changes," Crosshill grumbled. First he couldn't get a hold of his wife in England, and now multiple last-minute alterations to a well-planned objective. He exchanged brief greetings with the UN's deputy commander and the IDF's Colonel Ranin—CONTRA's primary Israeli contact on the ground. Crosshill had a difficult time concentrating and masking his frustrations.

The mission was not off to a good start.

The CONTRA team loaded into ten waiting heavy Mine Resistant Personnel Carriers (MRPC) supplied by the IDF. A NATO JLTV led the MRPCs from the small peacekeeping base directly through the streets of Jerusalem. An Apache Hellraiser attack helicopter hovered overhead. The convoy made its way to the multinational command base in the heart of Jerusalem where CENTCOM urged General Taggert to return.

Crosshill sat inside the lead MRPC with Diamond, Satellite, and General Taggert, who handed him a headset patching him into local military radio communications. Crosshill heard a barrage of different languages, all speaking excitedly about various incidents suddenly erupting throughout the city. He heard gunfire in the background. The operators tried to calm security personnel in the field and issued instructions to use nonlethal force to end the spreading calamity. Everyone was talking at once.

"—a man just killed him—"

"—shots fired near the temple—"

"—But why are they attacking the shoppers?"

General Taggert barked into his headset, "Patch in CENTCOM! I want

General Jackson on the line when I get back to base. CONTRA is here. Let him know."

"Sir, I ask permission to launch our Perceptors to get a direct look at what's happening around us," Satellite requested, leaning over to Crosshill.

"Sure, Satellite. On the next stop," Crosshill said waving him off, trying to pay attention to the radio.

Raption sat next to Breakdown and Red in the rear-armored vehicle listening to the same cacophony as Crosshill in the lead vehicle. Their driver had tuned in the radio transmissions over the vehicles' speaker system. It crossed Raption's mind that they were already too late on the scene.

"Something is definitely going down," Breakdown said. "We need to get out on foot. I don't like being stuck in this box."

"Things are amiss. We're not surprising anyone with a raid today," Red guessed. "Whatever was supposed to happen is happening. We're another step behind."

Raption looked at her, agreeing internally. "Plans change fast, that's all," he said halfheartedly. "We'll get it straight."

The convoy continued for several minutes, weaving its way through tight streets and picking up speed before turning up an alley to avoid the large celebratory parade route. After making another hard turn, the convoy ground to a halt. The officers heard screaming outside. Raption peered up into the driver's area to catch a glimpse through the front window.

A mob of civilians was running down the street on either side of the armored convoy. They streamed past both sides of the vehicles, forcing the drivers to stop to avoid running the civilians over. Many of the people wore traditional Jewish and Palestinian garb. They carried flags and signs with positive messages in Arabic and Hebrew. The fleeing crowd blocked the armored convoy's route.

"Looks like the parade is gonna be cancelled." Breakdown frowned in dismay. "Request permission to step out of our vehicle. Do you copy, Crosshill?"

"Permission granted," Crosshill responded. He and the others in the lead MRPC were already out on the street. The convoy was nowhere near the peacekeeping command center.

Crosshill ordered CONTRA to exit the armored vehicles and move toward the parade route where IDF security personnel were radioing for assistance. It was hard to march against the crowd, but the troops tried to organize themselves in the mayhem. Raption saw a young mother fall to the ground clutching her crying baby. With Breakdown's help he and three CONTRA soldiers pushed the stampeding rush back to protect her from being trampled.

"Are you okay, ma'am?" Raption asked the woman, helping her up. She looked no older than nineteen. She nodded and mumbled, "Thank you" in relatively clear English.

"What is everyone running from?" he asked.

The woman was breathing hard and checking to see if her baby was hurt. Raption repeated the question.

"We were sitting in the stands, watching the parade. It just started. A group of five or six men came running. They stabbed the people marching in front of the parade. I don't know why. May I go?" she asked, clearly distraught and about to start crying.

"Of course," Raption said. He motioned the woman to move on, wishing her well and patting her baby gently on the back.

Satellite pushed his way back through several civilians and grabbed Raption by the shoulder.

"You gotta come see this!" he shouted.

Raption, Breakdown, and Red followed Satellite through a thinning crowd of onlookers who were dispersing from the scene. The officers passed the point where the lead armored vehicle in their convoy had stopped. They turned up and jogged a block, following the parade route. Several wounded civilians bled in the street, some receiving medical attention from a local response team.

The wounded were members of a marching band. Their instruments lay broken next to them. Three men, shot dead, lay nearby. Small pools of blood formed from their bullet-riddled bodies. A half-dozen IDF soldiers stood above the corpses, looking at the violent aftermath in helpless disgust. Raption assumed the dead men were the attackers, but quickly found something different.

"Farther up," Satellite asserted, leading the officers another half a block to where the street veered slightly toward the east in the direction of Palestine. There stood Crosshill, Diamond, and General Taggert with Colonel Ranin and the UN deputy commander. They were staring into the sky where a purplish haze mushroomed over East Jerusalem, expanding across the horizon and starting to obscure the bright sun.

"What is that?" Raption asked.

"God knows!" General Taggert exclaimed. "I can tell you it ain't good. Crosshill, move your team in that direction. See where in the Lord's good name that crap is coming from. If it's chem-bio, we'll know before you get there. I want that rainbow fountain put out!"

The UN deputy commander stopped a passing UNSFOR SUV. Thick-skinned with black armor and iron grills, the Range Rover roared down the street and came to a screeching halt in front of the group. General Taggert and the UN deputy commander jumped into the backseat and sped off toward the joint peacekeeping command center, leaving Colonel Ranin and the CONTRA team behind.

"Back into the armored vehicles. Time to find some fight," Crosshill ordered as Satellite launched the unmanned Perceptor drones.

Raption jogged with Breakdown and Red back to their vehicle. As he entered, the Apache helicopter overhead pulled away to assist in protecting the British prime minister's entourage from a mob.

CONTRA headed toward the source of the purple haze—the East Jerusalem ghetto. They moved fast through a city unraveling in a slow madness.

Wild dispatches now overloaded the radio operators, confirming the worsening situation: a large fire burned near the Dome of the Rock, four gunmen held dozens of hostages in the Mahaneh Yehuda marketplace, multiple incidents of civilian rage played out. Voices over the radio became more frantic as CONTRA crossed into Palestine and closed in on the target location.

Then, sudden radio silence. It was as if everyone stopped talking at once.

Technicians tried to fix the communications system while the convoy rolled up to a roadblock. Several large commercial transport trucks were parked across an intersection and stopped traffic in both directions. A jam of vehicles backed up two city blocks. Some of the drivers waited in their cars, others got out and walked about looking for help. The CONTRA team was the first on the scene. No IDF or local police were visible. The team exited their vehicles, this time with battlesuit protection activated against chemical weapons.

Purple haze billowing from a building darkened the sky right above them. Raption stared at the strange, thickening cloud as Colonel Ranin unsuccessfully tried different radio frequencies. The communications net was down. The IDF colonel slammed his headset against the side door of a red pickup. The driver pretended not to notice, not wanting trouble with the angry Israeli officer.

"Seeing anything?" Raption asked Satellite who was wearing his Perceptor goggles, allowing him hawklike vision from the high-powered optics of the soaring drone.

"A very dark East Jerusalem neighborhood for this time of day. Found the building of interest in the slums. Strange how the purple funnel is coming out the top. There's activity—shit! You're not gonna believe this, Raption. I see black and red uniforms. It's unmistakable. It's them . . . in the open."

"*Jackpot.* Here we go again." Raption instinctively checked his weapon.

That's when it happened.

First, the screams, like a movie theater full of people shouting at the climax of a horror film. Raption spun and saw a swarm of civilians running madly into the traffic jam from a side alley. They looked frightened, their eyes fixed wide, but not dangerous. Suddenly, in a violent burst of rage, they started attacking the passengers in the idling cars and on the sidewalk. That's when Raption realized CONTRA and Jerusalem were about to face an onslaught that would fill the worst chapters of human history. He could only imagine what the Blue Team would find.

CHAPTER 23
COLD BLOOD
Russia: May 5, 2035

Battlestar lingered impatiently. The Blue Team had been waiting for over an hour at the Kazan airstrip where a Russian cargo plane had dropped them off. The team had limited time to complete their objective. The chance of stopping the advanced EMP weapon transfer to The Revolution faded with each passing minute. EMP weapons could have devastating effects on Western city centers or entire countries if used properly.

Designed by Russian scientists to mimic a high-yield nuclear electromagnetic pulse, the effects of the EMP weapons in question would create a geomagnetic storm. Releasing an intense electric field, they were capable of destroying all computer, communications, and electronic systems within miles of detonation. Recovering the systems would take weeks, months, or even years. Meanwhile, every facet of modern life would grind to a halt.

Worse than losing satellites in space, and worse than cyber war, EMP could ravage the electronic infrastructure humanity relied on and leave a scattered wake of unstable electric fields behind, causing long-term complications in restoration to pre-attack norms. No Internet. No refrigerators. No stock market. No cell phones. No nothing society had become accustomed to, and no telling how long it would last.

Battlestar felt the hilt of his samurai blade. *Revolution ringleaders might be on the receiving end tonight. Just give me one swing.*

The Kremlin didn't want the NATO force landing at any major airfields; they wanted to keep the cooperative mission secret. White frost covered the grounds of the small hangars lining the auxiliary Kazan airstrip. The coldest May on record had hit abnormal lows a day earlier. Mother Nature was more than sick, she was in a death spiral. Oddities of global warming delivered freak weather patterns of hot and cold at random times throughout the year. The state of Russian diplomatic transparency was quite similar.

Russia and the West were going through another series of political wrangling that shifted relations back and forth between trust and distrust. Fear of retaliation by powerful Russian mafia elites persisted. Organized crime despised order and rules, so Russian politicians wanting to strengthen ties with the West had to stay quiet and work behind the scenes. Many good people died for proposing openness or challenging the mafia underworld. Thus, a Russian request to NATO for assistance in preventing the mafia EMP transfer to The Revolution was altogether unexpected.

General Peter Nabokav wanted to bring down the powerful mafia infrastructure meddling in military and security affairs. Crvena Zvezda had become a thorn in his side. According to the CIA, when the criminal underground began influencing matters of state security, Nabokav lobbied for their destruction. Made aware of CONTRA's existence through Russia's FSS, he reiterated a request for cooperation through supporting a joint operation to kill or capture whoever attended the forthcoming Revolution meeting. The second time Nabokav requested it, NATO approved. The invite was welcome news to Alliance Command.

General Nabokav convinced his superiors at the Kremlin they needed NATO expertise for the mission. Suspicious activities involving The Revolution and Crvena Zvezda led Nabokav to insist that CONTRA help under the auspices of NATO-Russia cooperation. Something had spooked the general while he oversaw surveillance of the industrial zone east of Moscow near the abandoned military base in question. He wouldn't explain, claiming it was a state secret.

Battlestar stood in the outer doorway of the airport waiting room where CONTRA anticipated the arrival of General Nabokav and a *Spetsnaz* company. They should have already been there. Battlestar gazed over the barren land surrounding the airstrip and sipped on the last cup of hot chocolate provided by the local police officers who seemed unprepared for CONTRA's visit. Dressed in mismatched police officer uniforms and oversized hats, the police openly stared at the NATO force and talked quietly among themselves, providing little direction or information on what would happen next.

"Not the reception I expected," Justice said, leaning against the doorframe opposite Battlestar. "General Nabokav was supposed to be here with that *Spetsnaz* unit to greet us. We were supposed to leave for the target objective immediately. He's been held up in Moscow by some late developing bullshit."

"Last minute reconsiderations?" Battlestar questioned.

"Spoke to his deputy. Nabokav was unavailable. Not sure what the deal is."

"We can't have come here for nothing. If that meeting takes place tonight, we don't have much time. How far are we?"

"The base is less than twenty miles east of this airstrip, but we have no transportation. If they don't get their act together . . . we're going to miss out."

Battlestar looked at the CONTRA soldiers bunched together in the airport waiting area behind him and Justice. The high-tech Blue Team seemed out of place. Their heavy battlepacks lay on the ground next to their weapons, most of which were laser-based for this mission.

"Decision time's getting thin. If we stick here for another hour, we won't be able to stop the EMP transfer," Battlestar declared, seeing if Justice understood what he was thinking.

"You mean . . . if we hike it?"

"We can cover twenty miles pretty fast, we'd just have to get going soon. Can't walk up and knock on the door. We'll need some recon time to prep the field. Who knows what they'll have protecting the transfer, especially if Revolution ringleaders show," Battlestar reasoned, knowing the myriad problems such a decision brought.

"A heavily armed NATO company moving through the Russian countryside *without* escort. Probably wouldn't get reprimanded for that," Justice said sarcastically. "Hell, we could come under attack from the Russians themselves. They could say we moved illegally, and they'd be right. *NATO trespassers in the motherland.* I don't like the idea. That being said, it's an option. Winners don't wait for chances, they take them. If our Intel is correct, we can't sit this one out."

Battlestar nodded his approval.

Grace and Gideon walked over to them.

"A herd of sheep without a local shepherd," Grace sighed. "Troops are starting to use up the batteries in their battlesuits to stay warm. That's not good. We'll need them in this weather."

"The Russians knew our schedule, Grace. This is unacceptable," Justice concluded. "We can't sit around drinking stale hot chocolate while they figure things out. I want you to make a call to Brussels and see if headquarters can get this cleared. Let's call back our contacts at the State Department and in Moscow. See if we can get some movement. One way or another, we're making an interception tonight. With or without the endorsement of our hosts, CONTRA's leading the way—all the way."

Recognizing the Ranger motto, Battlestar cheered, "Hoohah!"

"'Stupid is what stupid does.' How does that saying go?" Nightscope asked, spitting his watermelon gum toward a garbage can, not caring that he missed and it stuck to the wall.

"Somethin' like that. Heard it before . . . from you I think," Xxplosive recalled.

"Ready to move and can't get some coordination from the home team. Hurry up and wait. Do they have a tourist bureau? Maybe get some Greyhounds out here? Take us for a tour of the local vodka plantation while we freeze our asses." Nightscope continued letting off steam. "How come we never get sent to the Caribbean for a mission? Somewhere nice. Next you know we'll end up in Antarctica. The Revolution will have declared the continent theirs and we'll have to build an igloo for our operating base. At least we'd have some chairs!" Nightscope raised his voice in the direction of the two Russian police officers watching over them in the crowded waiting room.

The officers looked confused, recognizing that their Western visitors weren't happy.

Nightscope shifted, trying to get comfortable on the floor. "I bet these guys haven't seen a beautiful woman, or the sun, for months. Look at them," Nightscope pointed unabashed with the barrel of his weapon.

"Easy now. We won't be here for long. Plans are in the making," Xxplosive cautioned, loading the cartridge of his laser cannon. "This night won't end here, Nightscope. Count on that."

"Good, 'cause we didn't come here to kick back in this lonely, nowhere room. Let's look at that satellite imagery again. I need to do something productive. Take my mind off this cold tile. I hate waiting, you know."

"I know."

Escorted by two guards dressed in heavy fur coats, Rapidfire and Sandstorm strode into the room toward Nightscope and Xxplosive. The guards peeled away. The CONTRA officers had asked for a tour of the small airport in an attempt to collect intelligence while the rest of the team waited.

"We counted eight vehicles outside," Sandstorm disclosed. "Not enough seating to make it worth it to the team. I imaged the entire perimeter and uploaded the mapping while talking with our escorts. There isn't much of anything useful out there."

"Sounds about right," Nightscope mumbled.

"Weather report is calling for snow around Moscow tonight," Rapidfire added, placing his hand over the laser turret at his side. "I'm willing to melt some."

Twenty miles to the south, a light flurry of snow had already started to fall. Three trucks moved in a small convoy over pot-holed back roads toward an old ranch in the distance. The ranch sat on the outskirts of an abandoned military base that had once housed a mobile missile brigade belonging to Russia's Strategic Rocket Forces. No lights were on in the main house. Behind it, in an old barn where farmers kept expensive equipment during the brutal winters, lanterns glowed.

The farm equipment had been removed from the barn. In its place were crates of stolen electronics, designer apparel, and advanced weapons. Half a dozen men in expensive black suits and trench coats waited in the center of the barn, pacing and speaking to each other softly in Russian.

Vladimir Polpotov was one of them. From disbelief at early offers made by Ripster to hunger for vast opportunity in the most lucrative criminal enterprise Vladimir had ever been a part of, he had come a long way as a member of The Revolution. He promised his sidekick brother Boris that after the EMP transfer succeeded, they could retire from "the life" and start anew—somewhere far from Russia where their old enemies would never find them.

For each of the Russians involved in The Revolution, the culminating point had arrived. They carefully prepared for the transfer that was about to take place.

Vladimir and his fellow mafia bosses had brought half a dozen bodyguards with them to the barn, mostly to assist with logistics. One hundred well-paid gunmen stood ready at the abandoned military base nearby in case Ripster failed in payment. The gunmen were a mix of retired soldiers and professional criminals turned into highly trained loyalists for Crvena Zvezda. Each had killed before and was on call to do so again.

Black and red clad Revolution Guards patrolled the outskirts of the ranch. They stood watch for the incoming convoy or any unwelcome guests. The Revolution troops moved awkwardly when they walked. These weren't the mercenaries or lightly armed guards the mafia regularly dealt with. These troops wore premium grade uniforms akin to cutting-edge Western battlesuits.

Vladimir didn't like the presence of The Revolution troops. He had not expected them to be at the ranch. Vladimir operated with a smooth confidence gained from years of success, control, and expensive tastes. Tonight, he was edgy. Meeting time was approaching and soon the most important transfer in black market history would occur.

"I can't get you that approval," General Peter Nabokav stammered, his voice coming through the receiver nervously. "It's not up to me, you understand? There are other generals and members of the Duma who want you out of my country. Pressure . . . threats from our shared enemy . . . it goes deeper than even I feared. The cargo plane will return for you. It will be there in thirty minutes."

"What about the transfer?" Justice asked. "Are we supposed to pretend it won't happen, General Nabokav, because some crooked superior of yours is scared of the mafia or some other political nonsense I'm unaware of? We're already here! You know this is important to *all* of us."

"I'm sorry, comrade. As much as I'd like to, I can't do anything to help," were the last words General Nabokav spoke before the line went dead.

Justice peered over at the Russian police officers and thought about what CONTRA had to do. The strike force couldn't walk away from an operation where both Revolution ringleaders and strategic EMP weapons were involved. He motioned for Battlestar, Grace, and Gideon to come closer. "All right, time to have our police friends take a little nap. They can't make *any* calls."

"Are you sure?" Grace worried.

"I'm *not* sure. I think it's a terrible idea," Justice paused, "but we can't turn back. If it costs us everything, we have to accept it."

"It's a gamble," Gideon added. "If The Revolution gets those weapons though, the outcome is too dire. Grace, you know military defeat or civilian catastrophe becomes a real possibility with those EMP weapons in the hands of The Revolution."

Grace nodded.

"Pick your friendly police officer and tag him," Justice ordered. "Upload your tags prior to my go and we'll stun simultaneous in two minutes. Be casual. Raise no alarm."

Grace distracted the guards while Justice relayed the news to the rest of the team. The Russian police went down without any chance to retaliate. CONTRA soldiers checked them over to make sure none had a bad reaction. They gently moved the officers into the waiting room and covered them with blankets.

Grace scribbled an informative note and taped it to the front door. The police would wake soon and find themselves locked in without any means of communication. The incoming cargo crew would find them, and if not, CONTRA would call it in. Eventually.

"We gotta move fast. Twenty miles to the objective," Justice announced over the radios. CONTRA immediately set out, wasting no time. They would approach the abandoned base through farm country. The route added an extra three miles according to Sandstorm, but Justice decided they'd do it anyhow. Risking detection wasn't an acceptable alternative under the circumstances. CONTRA had to get to the base, stop the transfer, and apprehend any Revolution ringleaders before the Russians caught wind of their actions. They didn't have much time.

They strapped on their battlepacks and were off.

Rapidfire and Sandstorm showed Justice a path winding around the back of the airstrip. It curved away from the main road and out across the barren flat terrain that stretched out for miles around them. Vegetation was sparse; so was tree cover. Dusk hadn't set in yet, but the day was growing late and the sky gloomed with lumbering clouds. Nightfall couldn't come fast enough. The closer to the airstrip they remained, the easier it would be for the Russians to find them.

Justice wanted to push hard. If they could make good time early, and get far enough from the airstrip, disorder on the part of the cargo plane crew would probably allow them to reach the objective. Only a handful of officials knew CONTRA was in the country. Less knew what their mission was. Russian terms for the mission included the assurance CONTRA would cede command and control of the operation to General Nabokav. Since Allied Operations Command wasn't patched in to CONTRA radios, Justice could make the call to move forward without clearance or direct consent from NATO.

"What would your dad think of this?" Justice asked Battlestar.

"He's not the civilian director right now, so it doesn't matter. Saves me from getting in trouble at home, I guess," Battlestar forced a chuckle that didn't quite reach his eyes.

The bitter cold nipped at the team as they marched quietly in two single-file lines, keeping a pace somewhere between speed walking and light jogging. Justice flipped on the temperature control in his battlesuit. A wind picked up from the east.

There were no major roads crossing their path. In the distance, headlights from passing cars occasionally flickered. The drivers would have needed binoculars to spot the unit against the dark backdrop of frozen gray tundra. Patches of snow crunched beneath CONTRA boots and small snowflakes appeared every few seconds.

Battlestar considered the pending operation. He wondered who would be guarding the base and what firepower they'd bring to protect the EMPs. Something didn't seem right. He hadn't given it much thought with all his excitement about being reinstated, but his mind shifted to the Kremlin's initial approval of the joint *Spetsnaz*-CONTRA operation.

Most Russian war planners considered investing resources in ground forces a waste of money. That was General Nabokav's rationale for calling in CONTRA, but there was more. Moscow's thinking was hard to understand, but it occurred to Battlestar that something else must be at play. It dwelled heavier on his mind with each mile they covered.

The only thing breaking his chain of thought was Grace. She crossed over from the parallel marching line to talk with him. He hadn't spoken to her for months—until his arrival back to Peterson Air Force Base—and had forgotten how much he liked her and the closeness he felt to her.

"This is certainly an adventure. I don't care for the odds, but I'll admit I feel a little safer with you here," Grace said, smiling.

"How much difference one man can make, I'm not sure. I would like a shot at a ringleader. This might be our best chance."

"Perhaps you are here for some special reason. We shall soon find out what the future holds."

"Grace, before our trip to Russia, you briefed the intelligence on this mission very well."

"*Grazie.*"

"What more can you tell me about General Nabokav? I understand his reasons for wanting us here given the EMP scare and The Revolution. However, there has to be more. What isn't he telling us?"

"There is more," she said, seeming grateful for an opportunity to share her insights. "First I'll tell you what I know, then I'll tell you what I think. I did perform intelligence work on Russia before joining CONTRA and was as surprised as anyone when mission plans called for an operation into the belly of the great bear.

"General Nabokav grew up in a city called Mezhgorye," she continued. "That city was constructed from two large settlements organized by the Russian Ministry of Defense during the Cold War. Over fifty thousand workers were brought in on rail from around Russia to settle at the highest peak in the South Urals. They worked for years building a gigantic underground military complex deep within that mountain, called Yamantau. They carved square footage over four hundred square miles, according to reports the DIA has on file."

"That's gargantuan!"

"Nabokav's family helped manage the massive food, clothing, and fallout systems warehoused inside Yamantau, which could shelter up to sixty thousand people for months at a time."

"In case of nuclear war?"

"To *win* that nuclear war. It's still policy, that's why Yamantau remains Russia's primary strategic command and control center. The whole national leadership has classified briefings on how they'll be evacuated to the Yamantau complex if Russia is attacked or if the Kremlin decides on a first strike."

Snow flurries fell heavier and stuck to the ground as Grace continued telling Battlestar what she knew.

"After we came back from Taiwan, I deciphered a code from electronic FSS files the NSA had captured. It gave me positioning coordinates. The location—Yamantau. Recently, secret testing and experimentation of all kinds have ramped up there. EMP, directed energy, you name it. NATO and U.S. intelligence have been watching and that's how the NSA picked up on the EMP transfers from Yamantau to Kazan. The Revolution just happened to be involved as well. This I know."

"Impressive."

"The reason I *think* General Nabokav called us has nothing to do with the state of the Russian army, like he said. I think it's because the Main Intelligence Directorate, or GRU, cut him off from whatever is happening at Yamantau."

"Why?" Battlestar asked.

"Apparently, Nabokav didn't like what was going on for some time. The mafia—maybe even The Revolution—was given access to the site. The GRU looked the other way and Nabokav had a major blow up with someone at the Kremlin. Then they blocked his access to the complex, which is unheard of since he commands Russia's Strategic Rocket Forces! Nabokav hates the mafia and criminal underground."

"And The Revolution too I suppose . . . and now they're about to get the most powerful nonnuclear weapons in the world if we don't stop them," Battlestar agonized.

"One more thing."

"What's that?"

"A hunch . . . I get them sometimes. In Colombia, the Gray Team discovered that The Revolution used a network of large underground tunnels. What if—"

"The Revolution tries to use Yamantau the same way?"

"Exactly," Grace nodded

"Their mere access is troubling. Nothing seems farfetched anymore. We need to bring this up to NATO command."

"Got a vehicle just ahead to the right, folks," Justice informed over the headsets. "Looks like a couple of locals might just need some alone time. Keep moving." The Russian teenagers never noticed the fifty-seven heavily armed NATO troops marching within yards of their car.

The military base was less than ten miles away. CONTRA's objective neared.

Ripster stepped out of the lead truck. Likzi followed. Russia's four most powerful mafia kingpins waited by the barn door. Slicked hair, fancy watches, and shined shoes made them look like Wall Street stockbrokers at a board meeting. The elegantly dressed criminals were clearly surprised that so many Revolution troops accompanied Ripster.

Two dozen Revolution troops had been waiting at the ranch when the mafia leaders arrived, now there were twice that many. The Revolution troops never spoke a word. One passed a note to Vladimir with instructions for the handover.

The planned exchange was critical.

The Russian mafia alliance operated under the auspices of The Revolution. Though the gangster factions had historically clashed over territory—often by murder—the existing truce between the crime families held and it paid dividends. The truce was Vladimir Polpotov's idea. He offered it in the name of profitable cooperation between Crvena Zvezda and the other clans. Lucrative payments from The Revolution made it easy to ignore the once-contested field turf.

"Good evening, Ripster," Vladimir said.

"How is our precious delivery?" Ripster asked, gazing over Vladimir and his cohorts. The EMP weapons would perform a key role in the launch of The Global Revolution. The early phases were already beginning around the world. Ripster wanted to complete the handover quickly so that he could monitor developments.

"The goods are here," Vladimir stated. "Everything is in order as promised. As for your end of the bargain?"

"You may see for yourself," Ripster replied pointing to the trucks parked behind him. "But only after we complete our inspection."

Ripster didn't intend for Vladimir or any of the mafia bosses to see the empty truck beds. There would be no payments on this night for a job well done. Ripster had gotten word Vladimir had an uncle serving in the army officer corps. Coincidentally, a high-ranking army general named Peter Nabokav had recently been asking questions about EMP weapons and strange happenings at the secret Yamantau military complex. That same general had even attempted calling in a special NATO strike force to disrupt that night's exchange.

Ripster had guessed—incorrectly—that Vladimir and Nabokav were conspiring against The Revolution. As a consequence, Ripster planned on a different kind of payment this time around. He had no mercy for traitors and would guarantee whoever betrayed him never saw the light of another day.

Likzi kept silent as usual, waiting for Ripster's commands. The murders about to take place seemed senseless to him. He felt no pity, but was tired of the evil game he'd become a part of. Ripster and Prowess hungered for The Global Revolution. Likzi was apathetic. He followed Ripster into the barn, catching a glimpse of the two Nezdeth generals exiting the last truck. They had a vested interest in seeing the night went well, so two of them had come.

Likzi had watched the days go by as if an accomplice and prisoner inside his own body. It came easier for Ripster and Prowess, they had fully changed and never hesitated, never cared.

For Likzi, it was different. At times, he felt the rush of hatred controlling his mind and the enjoyment of plotting revenge. Kill. Vengeance. Hate. Malice in every waking moment couldn't overcome the truth he still remembered before he became a minion and his servitude to the Nezdeth began. Those memories felt like a distant dream he could see but never touch.

Likzi wasn't sure exactly how many Nezdeth were on Earth. There were thousands replicated from the warrior class, waiting for their moment. They dressed in red and black Revolution battlesuits designed for combat on Earth and to hide their scaled maroon skin from humans. Nezdeth warriors were fearless. They kept a low profile, multiplying underground like roaches for years in the tunnels and caverns built to house their kind. Their time aboveground was near. All hell was about to break loose—literally.

Vladimir led Ripster and Likzi into the barn, a simple setting for transferring the world's most sophisticated EMP weapons. Ripster planned to use these to destroy America's military Global Information Grid, which was why Vladimir and the mafia kingpins were so important to The Revolution from its outset. Ripster recognized they had access and power.

At the center of the rickety barn stood a stack of sixteen metal tubes. Each tube held a self-contained strategic-grade EMP weapon created in Yamantau's military research laboratories. The weapons were easy to transport and use. The EMP weapons were designed by Russia's scientists for use either before the nuclear option or for conventional defense against high-tech militaries invading Mother Russia. The Kremlin had wanted the capability to pull the plug on the electronic lifeblood of an enemy. Since electronics controlled virtually every piece of modern military hardware and software, strategic EMP weapons could make an opposing military's instruments of war useless. Checkmate.

"Where is Prowess?" Vladimir asked Ripster as he inspected the EMP tubes.

Ripster knew Vladimir was intrigued by Prowess. She was strong and evil. It attracted him. "She's on another mission of equal importance."

Two large cloaked figures entered the barn. They were massive in size and dwarfed the huge mafia guards standing watch by the door. The men let the figures by without question, which bothered Vladimir.

"Are these your friends?" Vladimir questioned, motioning toward the cloaked Nezdeth generals. "I remember one of them from Panama. Who are they and why the need for cloaks?"

"You ask too many questions," Ripster lashed out. A red glow in his eye startled Vladimir, who stepped back. "They are neither men nor friends of anyone." Ripster covered the EMP weapon he'd finished inspecting.

He knew that the Nezdeth generals were aware of the staged Russian betrayal. Providing a message of allegiance to the rest of The Revolution was more important than letting these pawns live. The Russian mafia served Revolution planning well, but they were now expendable.

When the Nezdeth removed their cloaks and stepped forward, the Russians realized things were not going to proceed according to plan. Ever.

Vladimir's eyes opened wide at the sight of the unexplained beings in front of him. Their cloaks were off, their wings spread. He muttered, "Shit, man," before recoiling and hitting his beeper for backup.

CHAPTER 24

DEVIL'S BREATH

JERUSALEM: MAY 5, 2035

Lydia sat in the cold, dark room, wondering how she ended up there. She now understood the undeniable foolishness of her decision to meet an anonymous source from The Revolution alone. Her desperate attempt at getting the scoop for her book, and redeeming herself in the eyes of her peers, had Lydia trapped at the mercy of Prowess. Twice she asked Prowess if she could leave. Twice she got no for an answer.

The men guarding her cell were Arabs. They wore camouflage gear like any soldier, but on their heads were red and white checked head covers with a black band surrounding the top. A Shumagg and Ogal, distinct marks of the Arabian culture. Lydia didn't speak fluent Arabic, but did enough reporting on the region to follow a conversation. The guards talked about something happening outside. The effects of a plan were unfolding. She needed to get out and tell someone what she'd seen earlier . . .

Fear had pulsed through Lydia's body the moment the taxi left her in East Jerusalem, the Palestinian side of the capital, where Prowess had directed her to meet. Palestine was still catching up to Israel. Much of the nation lived in poverty. Conditions had improved, but slowly. Decades of neglect couldn't be reversed overnight. Many of the poorer neighborhoods received only a trickle of the financial assistance supporting the construction of new schools, hospitals, and even shopping malls. The uneven distribution kept certain areas stuck in the past. The East Jerusalem ghetto remained the worst.

Lydia noted the empty streets as the taxi sped away. She waited for Prowess to make contact. Three men dressed in black appeared from the shadows, startling her. She dropped her purse and found it hard to speak. The men didn't say anything, their faces hidden behind dark cloaks. Their eyes glowed yellow in the night. One of the men held his arm out in a clenched fist; he slowly extended his index finger toward an alleyway off the street.

Lydia shook her head, but complied when the man lifted his black jacket to reveal a gun the size of a chainsaw. The men followed several paces behind Lydia, silent as she made her way in the darkness, her heart jackhammering with raw fear. She questioned whether the men were even the right contacts and tried to pray, but couldn't focus on anything except for walking straight.

The alley smelled of trash and human waste. The old apartment buildings to either side were in desperate need of repair. Graffiti covered the walls and only a couple of windows were illuminated. Places like this were generally full of people crammed in unwanted housing for the cheap rent—this area should have been a lot louder, humming with life and activity. Instead, only the heavy footsteps of the men following Lydia echoed in the air.

There was nowhere to run, no way for Lydia to escape. They neared the end of the alley. An empty field sprawled in front of her. Alongside it ran a dirt street, hardly wide enough for one car to pass at a time. Lydia turned to face the men for further instructions, and was startled to find she was alone. She scanned the alleyway, curious as to their silent departure.

"Ms. Lewis," rasped a voice that Lydia recognized.

To her right, leaning up against the last apartment building in the darkness, was a slender, tall woman. Lydia took in the straight, shoulder length black hair around a pale face and eyes an odd gray color. Prowess wore a black leather full-body jumpsuit, a weapon-laden belt, and military-grade black boots. The only other color on the woman was the bright red of her lipstick. Her lips glimmered in the moonlight when she gave Lydia an evil grin, which revealed yellow stained teeth.

Prowess stepped out of the shadows. "You came alone. I'm glad."

"Yes . . . of . . . course," Lydia stammered.

"You would have watched your companions die if you didn't," Prowess cautioned, studying Lydia closely. The reporter stood frozen, waiting to see what would happen next. Prowess approached closer, not stopping until they were eye to eye. She was tall enough to look down on Lydia. She surveyed Lydia's face and sniffed at her. Pulling out a large knife from her belt, Prowess pointed the tip to Lydia's chin so it pricked her slightly, drawing blood.

"If you should find bravery and try to run or do anything other than what I tell you, this knife will find its way into a place of my choosing. I promise it won't be a pleasant selection. Do I make myself clear, Lydia Lewis?" Prowess spoke, moving her head to emphasize the threat, her voice heavy with an accent Lydia didn't recognize.

"Yes, I understand." *I couldn't run if I tried. You are a freak of nature.*

Evidently pleased with herself, Prowess put the knife back into its slot and made a growling sound before instructing Lydia to follow her. She walked briskly down the alley without looking to see if Lydia had obeyed, but Lydia did, her legs shaking uncontrollably, feeling like jelly crutches.

Prowess darted to the left, into a doorway hidden from view. Lydia barely caught the door shutting behind her. When she stepped through, Prowess was already halfway down a flight of stairs. Lydia hurried to catch up with the mysterious woman. A small lightbulb flickered above Lydia's head as they descended a second staircase, then a third, and a fourth. Finally, a square cement hallway not large enough to stand up in arched like a tunnel in front of them. They were far beneath ground level now.

The sound of distant moans terrified Lydia. She kept pace with Prowess, not wanting to lose her in a maze of hallways. They passed several closed doors and, occasionally, a tunnel running in the opposite direction. Lydia spotted several people down one of the tunnels but could not tell who they were. Torches attached to the walls lit the way, spaced perfectly so that when darkness started making things difficult to see, another torch provided illumination. The sheer magnitude of the underground construction amazed Lydia.

No one knows this is down here. This isn't supposed to exist.

They came to a place where the tunneling no longer appeared on either side. The hallway became much wider and Lydia could stand up straight. More torches lined the walls. Up ahead there were guards who opened a gate as the women approached. Lydia caught herself gasping, sure she was at the heart of The Revolution.

The guards at the gate were dressed in red and black battlesuits. They wore helmets with tinted visors, black gloves, and boots. None of their skin was visible. Lydia couldn't see their eyes through the visors, and she dared not stare long, but she had the feeling they were watching her attentively as she passed.

This part of the underground complex bustled with activity. Armed Revolution soldiers were everywhere, carrying crates and moving boxes. Some were pushing tanks of what looked like fuel in dozens of spherical tubes resembling fire extinguishers. All wore battlesuits with exotic looking weapons strapped to their gear-laden ammunition belts. They looked like the army of a massive superpower, not a group of rebels.

Prowess stopped at a metal door built into a sidewall. She looked at Lydia for the first time since they'd descended from the alley. Prowess held her in an ice-cold stare filled with a malice Lydia didn't understand. This woman was different from anyone Lydia had ever come across. She'd interviewed hundreds of people with strange or unique backgrounds, but when Prowess had stood face-to-face with her in the alley above, it was like encountering a different species or breed of human. Prowess carried herself in an odd way. Her gray eyes were dead and deep like space.

Prowess turned to the metal door and opened it with a clang, revealing a warehouse-sized room lit by bright fluorescent lights shining from high above. Lydia couldn't decipher the extent of the place and it took a minute for her eyes to adjust. When they did she saw an arrangement of large transparent cylindrical containers of dark purple fluid. The cylinders stood at least ten feet tall and were equally wide. They went on as far as she could see.

Prowess stared at Lydia, as if waiting for a comment or assessment of some type. Lydia could only blink. She was speechless and tried to think of something inquisitive to ask. All of the strange, new information was difficult to grasp. She didn't feel scared anymore, just helpless. Prowess must have sensed this.

"You've lost your fear. I expect the same won't be true for the rest of this city tomorrow," Prowess threatened.

Lydia forced herself to speak, not as a reporter, but out of dread for humanity. She suspected the cylinders of liquid were worse than bad news.

"What do you mean to do with all of this? Nobody wants to hurt you. Who are you angry with?" Lydia asked.

"I wouldn't take the time to explain, even if I cared," Prowess replied.

Prowess looked past Lydia, who turned to see a towering figure shrouded by the dark maroon of a heavy cloak. The figure had hidden eyes cast in glowing yellow that menaced from within the concealment. The demonic thing moved closer to Lydia. She saw scaly, burned skin covered its face. Panic and dread beyond all nightmares overtook her before the blackness of human unconscious.

Lydia didn't know how much time had passed since her collapse. She awoke to the darkness of her captivity, a prisoner of The Revolution like the seven NATO soldiers in the pictures sent by Prowess. She could see the black and red uniforms of Revolution guards through a small slit in the door.

Lydia didn't know if she was still underground, or why Prowess was keeping her. All she could think of was the being's menacing face she'd seen. She tried to convince herself it wasn't real. *My mind played tricks on me. The devil himself couldn't make such a monster.*

She wept in her cell, knowing the truth.

CHAPTER 25

NIGHTMARE SURPRISE

Jerusalem: May 5, 2035

"Those with lasers, tune to stun!" Crosshill shouted.

Caught in the middle of civilian-on-civilian violence in East Jerusalem, CON-TRA was stuck in a traffic jam, diverted from their objective of shutting down the bizarre fountain of purple haze emanating over the city several blocks away. The mob entering the gridlock from the alley was rabid and malicious. Their eyes would not shut. Drool foamed on the mouths of some and they did not converse. They only attacked—people on the sidewalk, passengers in their cars—breaking windows to pull the innocent into the street then beat them violently.

Those waiting in their parked cars saw the brutality, and everyone began to panic and flee their vehicles, running away from the crazed mob. They crashed into CONTRA troops heading toward the scene. There were screams of terror from the civilians trying to escape. A car accelerated in the traffic jam as it tried to get away. It smashed into the pickup truck behind it. Turning and accelerating forward the car crushed a man, pinning his legs between the fender and the car in front. The pinned man screamed in agony. The driver reversed and watched the man fall on his hood in pain and tears.

The Gray Team didn't know who to help first.

"Raption, Breakdown! Get up to the front of this mess and unblock the road. We need it cleared," Crosshill ordered. Next to him Colonel Ranin didn't move. He seemed paralyzed by shock as the scene unfolded.

Red watched a middle-aged woman in a pretty blue spring dress beat a man with a crowbar. The woman resembled a housewife but she hit her victim with the frightening ferocity of a prison escapee who didn't want to go back to Death Row. "What am I doing here?" Red whispered. *I shouldn't be at the front. I'm no warrior. Who am I kidding?*

Red took her eyes off the woman for a moment and tuned her laser from kill to stun. People in the street were being brutalized. Red ran toward the mob, weaving through frightened civilians. She wanted to save the man from the woman's assault. CONTRA soldiers perched on top of cars and trucks took aim at identifiable demented civilians, stunning them with non-lethal laser bursts.

Diamond flipped up the battlesuit control panel on her forearm and acti-vated the close range Active Denial System (ADS). Built into the wrist sock-ets of some battlesuits, the ADS directed microwave radiation at low power, delivering a burning sensation to human targets up to fifteen feet away. The effect was not fatal, but painful all the same. Aiming the ray, Diamond jumped atop a car and hopped from hood to hood toward the crowd.

The mob took hits from CONTRA. Momentarily stunned, they fell to the ground from the laser shots but quickly recovered and continued attack-ing their victims. Most of the time, when a military laser stun took people down they stayed down. Red tried reporting over her radio, but remembered that nothing transmitted. She saw Diamond moving from vehicle to vehicle. Though not as athletic, Red propped herself onto the hood of a car and man-aged to jump over three cars until she reached the sidewalk as well.

A young teenage boy wearing jeans and a plain white t-shirt came straight at her with a deranged fury in his eyes. He was scrawny and unarmed. "Stay back!" Red shouted. The boy ignored her. Red shot him twice. He winced from the pain and continued forward. Red fired again, burning four black holes in his shirt before the boy threw himself at her. He screeched and clawed at Red's face, cutting her chin. She held him back with her gun and finally knocked his front teeth out with the butt of her weapon. Face bloodied, the boy didn't slow his attack

Another man in his fifties came at Red from the side. He was dressed in a business suit and much bigger than her teenage assailant. The same maniacal rage of a wounded animal burned in his eyes. Red couldn't fight both of them off. She cursed at them to stop, backing up against a storefront window. The larger man tried to take Red's weapon. He pushed her to the ground as they fought. Red's head struck the pavement hard. Even with a helmet, the fall shook her wits. Her vision blurred and she felt weak. Helpless to stop him, the man took her gun. Red saw him raise the weapon to strike her.

Gunshots rang out.

Red closed her eyes waiting for the pain. It never came. The boy and man fell dead next to her on the pavement. Diamond lowered her rifle and came to Red's side.

"These people are not in control of themselves. They're like the ones in Brussels," Diamond said, extending her hand to help Red off the ground. "Don't hold back. The Revolution is here. Let's go find those who started this."

Red took Diamond's hand and slowly raised herself off the ground. Dizzy and dazed, she leaned against a light post for a moment and looked at her dead attackers on the sidewalk, wondering what would've happened if Diamond hadn't saved her. Red was fairly certain she had a concussion from the fall. She pried her weapon out of the man's limp hands and stumbled forward.

A news helicopter passed above, capturing the violence on the street.

Red stood rubbing the back of her head above the woman in the blue dress she'd spotted when the mob first attacked. The woman's dress was stained with blood; her blonde hair was neatly styled and her green eyes looked alive. She still clutched the crowbar in her dead hand. Her wedding ring sparkled. Next to her was the man she had beaten to death. Red turned and vomited on a parked car.

Raption and Breakdown reached the row of semi-trucks blocking the intersection.

The back and front ends of the trucks were smashed together. Whoever erected the roadblock did it fast, not caring about any damage. The CON-TRA officers climbed on top of the trucks to get a better look down the street, expecting to see a similar traffic jam on the opposite side.

The street was empty. No cars. No people.

Raption heard a crack and saw a yellow flash extend through the sky. A surface-to-air missile streaked from somewhere several blocks away and made a direct hit on the news chopper above. The chopper exploded in a ball of flame and came down—right toward Breakdown and Raption.

"Jump!" Raption yelled as he tumbled off the side of the semi.

The officers lunged to opposite sides and hit the ground rolling underneath the truck as the helicopter crashed directly on top of it and the one behind. A lava of hot debris and metal hurled everywhere in a furious rush of power and heat. A sea of flames surrounded them and the sound of crushing metal, breaking glass, and the rotor blade ripping apart roared in their ears.

Raption pressed himself hard to the ground willing himself to survive. The intense blaze started melting through Breakdown's fire-resistant battlesuit. He yelled as his flesh burned underneath. Raption pounded out the flames around them, gashing the side of his face on the bottom of the truck. Heat and fire engulfed the entire truck above them.

"We're gonna burn!" Breakdown howled, struggling to pound out the flames around his boots.

Through the embers and smoke, Raption spotted Crosshill and two med-ics running toward the inferno. Medic battlesuits contained built-in fire extin-guishers instead of close-combat weaponry. They quickly sprayed fire retar-dant over the blaze giving Raption and Breakdown a chance to stumble out of the conflagration. On their knees, coughing hard, they crawled to Crosshill and the CONTRA medics who helped them away from the wreckage.

Raption's entire face was covered in blackened ash except for a dark blood trail oozing from the side of his forehead.

"We'll get you some stitches. Lay down for a minute," Crosshill instructed. One of the medics arrived and prepped the wound with disinfectant before he started closing the cut, wasting no time.

Satellite and a tech specialist from Germany navigated two Perceptors in close range of the large industrial target building ten blocks from their position. Revolution troops were on the rooftop and on an adjacent apartment building. The dark purplish smoke was festering from the apex of the industrial building obstructing their view.

Satellite left the Perceptors with the German technician at the controls and sprinted over to Raption and Breakdown as they emerged from the smoking crash scene.

Jesus," Satellite mumbled, kneeling next to his coughing friends. Crosshill handed him a small can of first-aid coolant spray. Satellite applied it to Breakdown's shins. "You guys are lucky to be alive."

Crosshill continued to tend to Breakdown. "You're really burning it up wherever you go, Breakdown."

"That's pretty funny, sir. Thanks."

After another moment, Satellite grabbed Crosshill's arm to get his attention and make sure he was heard. "Sir, we got the building of interest not far from here. Revolution troops on the rooftop."

"You're certain it's Revolution troops?"

"One hundred percent."

"We'll rush the target after this situation is brought under control. Report that to command once our radios—*if* our radios—start working again."

Satellite weaved back toward the German technician. Behind him the burning semi-trucks launched black smoke high over the tangled heap of metal, releasing a powerful charred smell across the street. Nobody on board could have survived the helicopter crash.

CONTRA soldiers finished fighting the wild mob and the madness calmed.

Some of the possessed throng had been killed. Most were stunned multiple times with the highest nonlethal laser and ADS settings to strike them unconscious. Colonel Ranin stressed to CONTRA that every civilian being zip-cuffed was a victim of the strange happenings. Passengers from the cars stuck in the traffic continued to scatter, fleeing the fiery wreckage.

Satellite reinitiated the control display on the inside of his goggles. He looked to the German technician who stood shaking his head. Both Perceptors were offline.

"Shot down?" Satellite asked.

The soldier nodded, appearing upset.

"Both of them . . . ? That quick?"

"Yes, sir. Sorry."

"Damn Revolution," Satellite kicked the tire on an armored vehicle hard. "OUCH!"

CONTRA troops cordoned off the area, helping those hurt in the attack and keeping watch for more maddened civilians. The only other security personnel arriving on scene were three Palestinian security officers. They had heard gunfire and ran straight over from several blocks away. Sweating profusely, they stood in awe of the CONTRA team—wearing their battlesuits and geared with high-powered weapons, the Blue Team looked like futuristic warrior angels.

The Revolution soldiers in the nearby East Jerusalem ghetto would be less impressed.

The civilian prisoners and injured were handed over to the care of the three Palestinian security personnel who fretted about not having enough men for the task.

"Just watch over them until help arrives." Crosshill spoke authoritatively. The Palestinian security officers didn't argue.

Crosshill split the CONTRA team in two to approach the industrial building that was exuding the purple haze. Crosshill assumed the purple haze played some kind of a role in the city erupting into insanity. Before they were shot down, the Perceptors imaged Revolution troops surrounding the area. Everyone briefly viewed the uploaded images on their battlesuit visor displays.

"That's them," Diamond said, checking her ammunition clips.

Crosshill indicated that he would lead Raption, Breakdown, Red, and half the team's troops beyond the burning roadblock where they would cut around from the west. Diamond, Satellite, and Colonel Ranin would lead the other half of the team down an alley and approach the target building from the east. The CONTRA force would meet in front of the building and forcibly enter, kill whomever they had to, and snuff out The Revolution operation. Their radios were still dead. Both Preceptors were down. No help was in sight.

"Too many hot spots in Jerusalem. We're on our own," Colonel Ranin grunted.

"It should take us ten minutes to get to the building from here," Crosshill guessed, before the teams parted ways. "Watch your flanks down these streets. Shoot to kill if you see Revolution."

Raption walked to Diamond before the teams split. He grabbed her hand for a moment, saying nothing. She wiped some of the black ash off his face then watched him stride away with Crosshill. Diamond cocked her rifle and turned to follow Satellite and Colonel Ranin down the alley with the CONTRA troops they guided east.

Other fires burned across the horizon of Jerusalem, filling the air with a fog of despair. The darkness grew as smoke mixed with the dark purple haze turned the sunny afternoon to an indistinct gray. Armageddon had arrived in the Holy Land on this day of celebration.

Passing the burning roadblock that almost took his life, Raption touched the tender, stitched wound on his face, thinking that most people would need a week to recover from the trauma alone. He and Breakdown were going on for more. Raption turned to see Breakdown hobbling and carrying his weapon with his one good arm. The bottom of his battlesuit was charred. Accessorized by his black bandana, and now his limp, Breakdown vaguely resembled a pirate.

Small shops and apartment buildings lined the quiet street beyond the downed chopper. CONTRA officers were on the near side of the block with Crosshill. On the opposite side of the roadway ten CONTRA troops moved parallel to them, watching the rooftops and balconies. They operated off hand signals with all eyes on Crosshill.

After the next block, Raption could see the street they were supposed to hang a right at, which would lead them to the target building's front door. This part of the city should have been bustling with people, but it was abandoned. There was no movement or even a sound. The burning roadblock behind them created an eerie backdrop as they entered what seemed to be a ghost town within Jerusalem.

"Where is everybody?" Raption asked aloud.

"Either they got the notice this was a bad day for parades . . . or we're walking into the badlands," Breakdown replied. "Either way, *bad* is the key word."

At the intersection where they were supposed to turn, a CONTRA soldier across the street started firing at something on the rooftops high over Raption. He knew it was the enemy because most of the soldiers across the street dropped to one knee and took aim, peppering gunfire above his head. Shots were returned. A mix of lasers and bullets flashed both ways.

Raption strained his neck, his weapon pointing upward, to see if he could get a bead on a target. He glimpsed the unambiguous outline of a grenade floating down from the rooftop instead. It landed on the sidewalk and bounced back near several troops behind Breakdown. Before anybody could react, the grenade exploded, sending two soldiers through a butcher's store window, killing them instantly. Another soldier tumbled into the street writhing in pain.

Raption kept his weapon pointed directly above him. He saw the visor of a Revolution soldier peer over a balcony two stories up. Letting off two rounds, Raption hit the soldier square in the forehead. He slumped over the balcony and must have dropped another live grenade because the explosion at his feet cut the balcony in half. It snapped forward, flinging the dead soldier onto the street below. There was a crunching sound and his body crumpled to one side on the road, five feet in front of Raption.

This was the closest that Raption had ever been to an actual Revolution soldier. He'd engaged uniformed Revolution troops in the Colombian jungle but always at a distance. Up close, he could tell their uniforms were well made, similar to CONTRA's own battlesuits. He crouched low and watched the CONTRA soldiers across the street let off full clips at enemy gunners above. Two soldiers took hits and fell to the ground: neither got up. Gunfire was heavy from above and dust rained down from the bullets piercing the walls overhead.

"We need to get around the corner!" Crosshill shouted.

Two Apache helicopters approached and swooped around the block, letting their high-powered machine guns rip and shred whatever unlucky souls were shooting at the NATO force from the rooftop.

"Finally some air coverage. Thank you!" Breakdown shouted at the attack choppers, giving them an enthusiastic thumbs-up.

Raption ran into the street and pulled the wounded soldier back while the Apaches fired away overhead. A NATO medic began working on him to stop the bleeding. The soldier—a Slovenian man—was in shock but alive. His badly cut left arm twitched uncontrollably at his side. A six-inch shard of glass stuck out from his forearm. The sharp tip protruded through the back of his elbow. It was difficult for the medic to stop the bleeding without hurting the soldier. He shrieked as the glass cut through his sensitive nerve endings.

"The pain is unbearable," the medic said to Raption. He didn't need to be told.

Ahead of Raption, Crosshill moved fast around the block, taking a position at the corner of the intersection. He kicked over a trash can, bullet tracers zapped overhead. Raption joined him and downed three Revolution soldiers in twenty seconds. The target building was only four blocks away. Obviously The Revolution didn't want CONTRA to reach it.

Raption darted bravely past Crosshill through the intersection. He took cover behind a green van. Two CONTRA soldiers slid on the ground behind him. Machine-gun fire kicked up dirt inches away from them. Raption saw enemy movement in doorways and windows down the entire block. CONTRA had picked a wicked street. It would be a harder fight to the building than they had planned.

"Ten minutes my ass," Raption whispered.

Diamond, Satellite, and Colonel Ranin were halfway to the target building before they saw any movement in the alley. They heard gunfire erupt in the direction of Crosshill's team but decided to stick with the plan and keep moving. They came to the final block before needing to turn north and make their approach from the east side of the building.

Diamond spotted three Revolution soldiers down a street no more than twenty yards away. Two of the soldiers stood above a row of seven civilians lined on the ground. The civilians were face down, as if an execution was about to take place. Diamond dropped to one knee and focused her scope on the head of one of the Revolution soldiers, ready to fire and kill.

The soldier carried a cylindrical tube in his hand. He sprayed a purple mist over the civilians' heads in a slow back-and-forth motion. Diamond didn't like what she saw. She pulled the trigger and dropped him. Before the other two soldiers knew what happened they were both on their backs, one bullet from Colonel Ranin and another well-placed shot by Diamond.

With their weapons swiveling upward and to the sides searching for hidden enemy positions, the team moved cautiously toward the civilians.

"Why aren't those civilians getting up or moving?" Satellite asked. The seven lay still in the street like they were dead.

Colonel Ranin shouted, "I am an Israeli military officer. We are here to help you." The seven bodies shifted slightly on the ground, as if rousing themselves from a deep sleep.

One of them, a blonde teenaged girl with a backpack slung over her shoulder, lifted her head up. Her pack looked heavy with books. Sitting up in the street she bobbed from side to side like a doll, her eyes glazed over.

Diamond peered upward at an open window and saw—in her peripheral vision—Colonel Ranin bend low to determine if the girl was okay. Diamond shouted, "Stop, don't get so—" but it was too late. The teen snapped her head forward. With a vicious bite she tore a chunk of flesh from the side of Colonel Ranin's face. He doubled back in agonized surprise, falling to one side.

The girl jumped to her feet. Her backpack slid off to the ground and mania filled her eyes. She crouched low and prepared to pounce on top of the IDF colonel. Diamond took aim at the girl's arm and fired a nonfatal shot. The bullet hit with an ugly red splash but didn't stop her. The teen recoiled back then attacked Colonel Ranin's face again, biting wildly. The colonel protected himself with his forearms and screamed in agony. The teenager—surely someone's sweetheart—bit into Colonel Ranin's wrist, stopping only when she hit bone.

"Aghhhh!" the colonel shouted. He kicked her hard in the stomach and flung her away. A CONTRA soldier fired several laser stuns into her back. The girl writhed as two other soldiers cuffed her. The rest of the civilians who had remained on the ground started to get up. The CONTRA team restrained them before they could hurt anyone else.

Diamond could tell Colonel Ranin was enraged. Flesh hung from his bloody face and wrist as he got to his feet, wincing. Diamond wondered why The Revolution was using civilians to stir chaos in the city.

Satellite did not process what just happened to Colonel Ranin. Instead, he crouched next to one of the dead Revolution soldiers Diamond had first shot. When the soldier hit the ground, his helmet rose slightly off his neck. The helmet pushed up and created a separation from the rest of his battlesuit, exposing the enemy soldier's skin. Despite the altercation, Satellite focused on that skin and a crack in the soldier's visor. Satellite was hypnotized and numbed by the reality of this nightmare.

He knew what he was looking at.

It wasn't genetic engineering coming from some combination of pre-existing species. The scaly maroon skin and fiendish yellow eyes of the dead Revolution soldier were *alien*. Satellite was certain. There was no semblance of humanity or earthly creature in what he saw. It was unearthly. Wicked. From somewhere else. A being like no other natural living thing he'd ever imagined seeing outside of science fiction.

Diamond broke his concentration, calling out to him as she moved back toward the alley. "Satellite, let's go. There'll be more Revolution to deal with before this day is over."

Satellite gripped his weapon and trotted forward in a blur. He looked back at the dead alien soldier. Things made more sense to him now. He wanted to tell the others but couldn't bring himself to do it. His voice failed him. Satellite felt like anesthetic was injected into his brain. A comalike lethargy engulfed his thoughts accompanied by the strange feeling of being abandoned on some far off desert in the galaxy. Satellite drifted knowing the team would find out soon enough. They proceeded down the alleyway, now only a couple blocks from the target building.

Five men appeared from around the corner, heading directly toward them.

"Hit the ground or die!" Diamond yelled. She couldn't tell if they were friendly or possessed by the madness spreading across Jerusalem. The men got down on the ground in fear of the blonde NATO officer expertly pointing her rifle at their heads.

Colonel Ranin approached, more cautiously this time, holding blood-stained white gauze to the side of his face. He asked the men where they came from. The garbled mess the men blurted out in fearful half Arabic and English was hard to interpret. They repeated that "red devils" were in the building CONTRA moved toward.

"Take us to this building," Diamond demanded.

The men refused, shaking uncontrollably from pure terror. CONTRA let the rattled men go, telling them to head away from the fight. It was obvious they could be of no help.

Encountering the men disturbed some of the CONTRA troops in a way the gunfight hadn't. Several murmured to one another that something strange was happening, but still they continued forward.

The street ended at a narrow dirt road, an empty field to its right. A metal fence ran alongside the edge of the field. Broken cars lined the fence providing little room for the team to navigate toward the industrial building. There was no sign of Revolution troops on the dirt roadway or in the field, but Diamond could see the target building less than a hundred yards up. Gunfire and explosions were ringing out blocks away. Crosshill's team must have gotten themselves into a hell of a fight.

Diamond looked to Satellite for an opinion. "Proceeding to the building was our plan. Seems we should. Either that or we go reinforce Crosshill. What's the report gonna say?"

Satellite stared ahead with a blank gaze. Suddenly, he turned to Diamond. "Lydia. My sister, she's in this city. Nothing's for sure . . . but I need to find her."

CHAPTER 26
CAPTURED AND CAPTIVATED
Jerusalem: May 5, 2035

Something big was happening in Jerusalem.

For what felt like hours, Lydia had sat on a single wooden stool alone in a dank concrete cell. There was a lot of running about and commotion in the hallways near where she was being held. The Revolution guards standing in front of her chamber left moments ago, just after a loud explosion shook the building.

A mix of strange voices and languages communicated excitedly in the halls outside her cell. Lydia still didn't know if she was underground or on the top floor. There were no windows or hope for escape. The shooting and explosions seemed to be nearing, the concussions getting louder and closer. *Perhaps security forces had found The Revolution's hideout?*

Lydia heard the gunfire and bombing outside as Prowess opened the door to her cell. Too calm for danger to be at hand, Prowess didn't seem worried at all. Light from the hallway silhouetted The Revolution ringleader. She stood shadowlike before Lydia.

"You see, some are more sensitive to it than others," Prowess pronounced with a smile. She held a small transparent vial in her palm, opening up her hand so Lydia could see it. It was the same purple liquid Lydia had witnessed The Revolution soldiers carrying.

"What is it?" she asked.

"It's our special potion for the world to feast upon. To do The Revolution its favors," Prowess gushed. "Do you want a taste?"

"No, thanks."

"If I wanted you to have it, you would," Prowess snapped, tucking the vial away in her pocket.

Lydia was terrified of Prowess. At the same time, though, nobody else seemed to have any authority; Prowess represented the only chance Lydia had for possible release. Lydia thought about bringing up the demonic creature inside the large room full of The Revolution's potion. *Maybe Prowess will mention the horrid creature?*

"Will you tell me what this is about?" Lydia asked.

"Redemption. Jerusalem is the first city on our list to experience what's to come. This is your future. This city was chosen first because of its historic importance, but don't assume happenings in Asia and Latin America were not our doing. More cities will fall as our plan unfolds. The Revolution owns this area of East Jerusalem we're in. Anyone living here either works for me or is under Revolution control. It makes things easier, you see."

Prowess explained the dark purple potion was a psychotropic drug. In aerosol form, it effected people in different ways. The Revolution perfected it to implement their master plan, she boasted. Some people were uneffected by the potion, but most ended up going berserk. "Raving madness is the intention," Prowess told her, smiling wide. Inserted into select ventilation systems the night before, the potion was now activated throughout the city. Lydia could tell that, despite all the info Prowess was sharing, there was so much more going unsaid.

"Our potion is having the desired effect and will only get worse. Hear the reaction outside? No trumpets of celebration and speeches to speak of today," Prowess laughed. "A dark purple cloud gathers above the city. After it condenses into a mist and falls slowly downward like a beautiful rain, corruption will touch everyone, except those of us in The Revolution. You see, we're already depraved. There's no stopping it. Not CONTRA, not anyone."

"You still haven't told me what The Revolution wants or why this chaos is necessary? Why did you call me here if I'll never get to report on it?" Lydia appealed.

"You'll go when I let you—*if* I let you." Prowess paused, looking directly at Lydia. She took a step closer and bent to one knee in front of the stool. The gray coldness in her eyes swirled like a storm.

"The Revolution is a brigade of pawns that buy time, Lydia. Your planet is under invasion—Earth *itself* is a pawn. Far away, deep in space, there is a perfect solar system called Nerrial. Powered by a rare Blue Star, its people live in a utopia with environments as plush as your best refuges. Why do we cause chaos here? So they will come to help you just like they always have. This time it won't be in secret. When they arrive Earth will see a war like no other and Nerrial will be vulnerable to attack—they're Starforce divided. We will have destroyed what they built and cared for here. I will then be redeemed."

Lydia sat dumbfounded.

"Take mental notes, child. This is important. Enough distractions will force Nerrial to take its eyes away from what's really coming. They think Earth is precious. What they should really be worried about is *far* worse."

"Are you . . . from . . . there?" Lydia's mouth flapped like a fish out of water.

"Wouldn't you like to know?" Prowess taunted. "I used to be. One day I will return, perhaps—when it's mine. What you saw—"

A large explosion nearby shook the building hard. Dust from the ceiling scattered on top of the two women. Prowess looked concerned for the first time. A Revolution soldier ran to the cell door and spoke in the strange language Lydia had heard earlier.

Prowess nodded to the soldier, then turned to and Lydia said, "Follow me out. And like I told you yesterday, stray and you die."

Lydia was relieved to be in the hallway. She could see they were in fact on the upper floors of the building. Through a window she caught a glimpse of the darkening day outside. The blaring sounds of gunfire and war rang out around them. Prowess led Lydia to a row of windows where Revolution soldiers poured heavy fire down on the street below. Lydia had a front seat on the wrong side of the trenches. Prowess walked to the windows and looked down. She stood motionless for a moment evaluating the scene.

Lydia had been in war zones before: she knew this fight was at a climactic point. The soldiers around her were frantic. Prowess gestured for her to come closer to the windows. Lydia refused. Prowess took two steps toward Lydia, grabbed her by the hair and dragged her across the floor.

"Stop it!" Lydia begged.

Prowess slammed her face against a window, which cracked from the impact.

"When I talk, you listen!" Prowess shouted in her ear, keeping Lydia's face pressed hard up against the glass.

Bullets shot through the glass above Lydia's head. Someone from below must have been aiming for her. Shards flew everywhere. Tears welled up in her eyes from fear and Prowess's brutality. Lydia saw traces of bullets and lasers streaking in every direction. There were bodies lying on the sidewalks. The building's attackers were dressed in dark navy battlesuits. Lydia recognized these as NATO troops, the same kind she'd seen in the pictures Prowess had sent her. Prowess pulled her back and threw Lydia to the floor.

"I will be busy now and have no more time for you. I showed you all you need to see. Go ahead and report what you will. See if they believe you this time. It won't matter either way," Prowess asserted.

With that, she turned back to the window shouting something to The Revolution soldier next her. He gave Prowess a large advanced-looking machine gun containing an array of glowing red plasma cartridges. The weapon appeared too big for Prowess to handle but she did so with ease. Clearing away shards of glass in front of her, she fired down onto the street shouting and laughing at the same time.

Prowess was crazy. Nobody in the room seemed to be paying any attention to Lydia. The soldiers all concentrated on the fighting below—shooting, ducking, and reloading. Scrambling to her feet, she staggered out of the firestorm. A Revolution soldier ran into her and knocked her over. Lydia picked herself up off the ground again and tried to find an exit. Every few minutes the building shook from the impact of a rocket or bomb.

Shouting and shooting escalated. A hazy smoke filled the hallways.

Jerusalem had thousands of troops and security forces in the city for the Holy Land Accord celebrations. They were probably all converging outside.

Lydia's face was swollen from the slam against the window. She touched her numb cheek and ran confused down the hallway, not knowing where she would end up. Lydia veered to the right and took a flight of stairs two at a time. Revolution soldiers stared at her as she passed. Surprisingly, they did not try to stop her on the stairwell. Lydia kept her chin low, trying not to look at them.

She raced down several more flights of stairs, slipping in places slick with blood. The closer she got to the bottom, the more violence surrounded her. There were bleeding Revolution soldiers crawling about and no medics to help them. Lydia thought of the dreaded demon figure she'd seen before and wondered where it was.

She stepped over a wounded soldier writhing on the staircase with his hands clasped around his neck, thick blood seeping out. Lydia heard a gurgling deep in his throat. She walked with her back pressed hard against the opposite side of the stairwell. The dying man reached out for Lydia and grabbed her cream-colored sweater with his blood-soaked hand. The soldier tried pulling her toward him.

"No!" Lydia yelled. Her sweater tore and she yanked herself away, fleeing for the next flight of stairs in mortal terror. A red stain covered the front of her ripped shirt.

Hysterical now, Lydia ran for her life. She reached the bottom of the last staircase and tripped over a broken chair, landing hard on her right knee. It popped loudly and she rolled in pain on the floor of the building's lobby. Spinning on the ground—momentarily numb from the pain—Lydia could see the large space had couches and chairs with walls pockmarked by bullet holes. Dead or dying Revolution soldiers were everywhere. She heard more yelling outside. This time, the voices were shouting in English.

The chance to withstand the horror of Prowess and The Revolution lifted Lydia's spirits and provided a final rush of energy. She needed to get to someone to share what she knew, but she wasn't sure how to get outside without dying. At least The Revolution soldiers in the lobby were not in any shape to fight.

Lydia struggled to her feet. The wall to her left exploded inward. The force of the blast thrust her hard against the concrete lobby wall, almost knocking her out. She held on to her will to live with everything she had left. Smoke filled the room. Cut badly from shrapnel, her hands burned with pain. She cried, whimpering, trying to cling to survival. Through smoke, dust, and a gaping hole in the side of the building, Lydia could see outside. Two NATO soldiers entered the building through the hole.

One pointed a gun at her face.

CHAPTER 27
WARRIOR CLASS
Russia: May 5, 2035

The Blue Team closed in on the deserted military base near Kazan. Their back-country detour was about to end. The team's objective grew near as night fell.

Battlestar peered out over the cold, open terrain. A ranch of some kind was up ahead, between CONTRA and the abandoned base. Battlestar saw Revolution soldiers on the outskirts of the ranch and radioed the rest of the team to get low. He saw at least a dozen enemy soldiers in position. Nobody else had spotted them yet.

"Proceeding in with caution. Activate SuperVision," Justice ordered over the radios.

Battlestar had discovered The Revolution soldiers without the help of any technical sensors. He often disliked them because they hindered the acuteness of his *natural* senses. He followed instructions nonetheless, turning on all sensors in his battle helmet when instructed.

Shooting erupted inside of a barn just down from ranch. Gun blasts flickered through the wooden structure, poking holes in it. Battlestar heard cries for help. Revolution troops on the outskirts of the ranch turned toward the shots. Several ran toward the barn.

"Stay put until we find out what's going on," Justice ordered.

Battlestar wanted to engage, hungry for a good fight.

At once, gunfire poured over the barn from the direction of the military base. Battlestar zeroed in on the base with his battlesuit's optics. A large group of men wearing black jackets and cargo pants charged with heavy machine guns—the Russian mafia. The guards surrounding the ranch wore red and black uniforms—the official Revolution troops.

"Maybe the weapons exchange isn't going to take place after all," Battlestar whispered to Grace. The Revolution must have been in the midst of an internal struggle. He crawled to Justice and Gideon who were deliberating on whether CONTRA should enter the fight.

The uniformed Revolution soldiers and charging mafia traded fierce fire. The exchange quickly erupted into full-blown combat. Gunfire and lasers lit up the fields and frozen tundra. The night filled with red and yellow tracers volleying back and forth in violence.

"This is gonna end fast," Battlestar said. "They're killing each other off. Pleasant for us, but we shouldn't wait 'til it's all over."

"Let's make this a three-way contest." Justice agreed. "On my mark. Take out all sides moving toward that barn. We'll secure the EMP and get the hell out of here. Give them another few minutes to kill each other off. Whatever weapons might be there, the mafia is getting screwed tonight. Not our problem."

"I want the uniformed Revolution," Battlestar answered.

"There are three trucks parked outside the ranch," Gideon advised, pointing. "They've either unloaded or are gonna load from inside that barn where the shooting started."

"When the order is given, we'll end this before they can," Battlestar replied.

Sandstorm knelt next to Xxplosive and peered through his Turkish-made semiautomatic rifle, marveling at the advancing Revolution soldiers. He respected a tough enemy, and that's what The Revolution was. Even though they were vastly outnumbered they were easily winning against the rushing mafia mercenaries. Sandstorm shifted to the inside edge of the fence that ran alongside the outskirts of the entire ranch. Staying on its outer border, CONTRA hadn't been spotted yet; the enemy was too distracted.

The officers were on a slight ridge about one hundred and fifty yards above the barn. The military base was to their right. They had a perfect vantage point to watch the unfolding drama while awaiting orders from Justice.

"Interesting, don't you think?" Nightscope asked, sounding amused.

"They ain't so tight anymore," Xxplosive affirmed.

"Thankfully. Them killing each other gives us less to do. *Sakra revolce*, lots of lasers," Rapidfire remarked, also impressed by The Revolution's weapons' capabilities.

"Time to hit 'em," Justice's order came over the radio. "No one gets out of that barn. What we're looking for is inside. It can't leave with them."

The entire Blue Team crept twenty yards up, picked targets, and opened fire.

Sandstorm, Nightscope, Xxplosive, and Rapidfire led two squads against the mafia side of the battlefield. They would secure the perimeter of the ranch opposite the military base and eliminate any threat coming from that direction. Justice, Battlestar, Grace, and Gideon would move against the uniformed Revolution with the remaining CONTRA troops advancing toward the barn.

Inside the barn, Likzi surveyed the dead bodies in front of him. He heard the incoming machine-gun fire. "They didn't come alone," he said to Ripster. He was standing behind the Nezdeth general who had just extracted his axe from Vladimir Polpotov's dead body.

Vladimir had gotten one shot off into the Nezdeth's shoulder, his life's final accomplishment. The shot drew blood and soaked the cloak of the brooding alien figure. It did little else. Ripster had killed Vladimir with six laser shots to the chest and the Nezdeth general had further maimed him with his battleaxe, merely for the pleasure of it. Axes were preferred killing weapons for the Nezdeth who possessed far advanced tools of warfare.

Ripster and the two generals obviously reveled in the murder of all the mafia leaders. They had been biding their time on Earth for months, yearning for the war to begin. Fighting was in their blood.

Likzi stepped over Vladimir's mutilated body to look outside.

He pondered how this battle would affect The Global Revolution. He supposed it didn't matter. He served on the monsters' side. They had Sentrix, after all, and droves of Nezdeth warriors bred underground for the upcoming war. In addition, a massive buildup of their four-legged bioengineered beastly counterparts under the control of The Three would execute an all-out attack on Earth. Thousands of the Nezdeth warriors were now being loaded onto container ships in the Panama Canal, headed for the world's largest ports. The evil that Likzi was a part of would soon destroy all goodness in the world.

Two bullets cracked through the side of the barn near Likzi and penetrated a wooden crate, obliterating the dozen razor-thin Internet mirror panels inside. Likzi instructed several Revolution troops inside the barn to load the EMP weapons onto the waiting trucks. The Nezdeth wanted them out of harm's way fast.

Blessed with Nerrial High-Senses, Likzi picked up a threat from outside. Although the sharpness of his natural-born special abilities had become less powerful since he turned evil, they remained. Several conventional rounds entered through the barn, as did laser fire. The mafia did not spark Likzi's internal warning system, he'd been expecting them. Someone else was outside, either the Russian military or, perhaps, the CONTRAs. Likzi suspected the latter.

The Revolution handled the mafia with relative ease. Nezdeth warriors maneuvered to an advantage and had far better marksmanship and tactics. The Russians, who could, turned and ran in retreat soon after the failed assault. Several dropped their guns and withdrew to the base after watching laser fire liquefy their comrades.

Boris Polpotov was among the first who fled. Without knowing his brother Vladimir lay dead inside the barn, Boris had tried to save their first cousin, Sergio, who was bleeding to death on the black leather of his sedan. They had rushed the ranch with everyone else, getting off two clips before Sergio slumped forward, cursing in pain. Boris pulled him back and saw the mess of melted flesh where Sergio's torso used to be.

Boris wanted none of the suffering. He dragged Sergio out of harm's way and now was peeling out of the base. Breaking through a gate, Boris sped toward the nearest hospital to save the cousin who taught him checkers in grade school. He'd known Sergio since birth. Boris hoped Vladimir was okay, but what happened with the mafia didn't matter anymore. That part of Boris's life was over.

Battlestar attacked The Revolution soldiers, catching them off guard. He killed nearly a dozen on a first or second shot. Battlestar had his eyes on the barn. He saw things differently when the adrenaline rushed. The world slowed and he got faster. Pumping rounds in step, Battlestar darted forward.

"Give him cover!" Justice shouted over the headsets.

Battlestar knew what he needed to do. Courage came naturally. He crossed a hundred yards—never running so fast. Battlestar sensed a Revolution soldier honing in on him and sent a barrage of bullets into the chest of the enemy without even looking in his direction.

He stopped at a small toolshed fifty yards from the barn. The military trucks weren't far away. Revolution soldiers were loading them full of large tubes. Battlestar presumed the tubes held the EMP weapons. He looked back to the rest of the CONTRA team before cautiously moving forward.

"Our perimeter is secure," Xxplosive reported over the radio. "Our squad had success against the mafia front. The area between the ranch and military base is quiet. Most of the mafia elements are dead, wounded, or gone."

"Hold that line. Don't take your eye off the base," Justice ordered.

Nightscope reached up, clicking his radio to mute. "So what, we gotta just sit and wait here?"

"I guess." Xxplosive eyed the base for any movement. "They got out fast. I don't think they'll be coming back."

"Doesn't mean we can't still shoot up some Revolution!" Rapidfire boomed, squeezing three pulsed laser rounds in the direction of Revolution soldiers outside the barn. All three passed just over their heads through the wooden structure.

Three laser rounds from the direction of the military base flew over Ripster's head. He knew those were not mafia weapons. He peered outside. The troops surrounding the barn were not Russians either. Ripster had seen their uniforms before . . . in Colombia.

CONTRA was outside.

Grace wanted to catch up to Battlestar at the front, feeling compelled to fight next to him. She veered in a wide angle to keep out of Revolution gun sights. A laser tracer zapped above her head. Her helmet sensors picked up the heat. Grace dropped to the ground and tracked its point of origin, spotting the enemy soldier hunkering down and firing another laser round toward her. The second shot missed Grace by inches. It would be the last action from her Nezdeth enemy.

With one squeeze of her laser rifle, Grace fired a shot traveling at the speed of light toward the visor of her opponent. The round melted through his face and exited through the back of his skull, killing him instantly.

Grace scanned for Battlestar. He'd been next to the toolshed up ahead of her, but wasn't there anymore. Grace clicked a button on the side of her helmet, loading the visor on her battlesuit. She searched for Battlestar on the battle management display.

A hand reached under her visor and covered her mouth, smothering the scream she tried to let out. Whoever held her from struggling had a firm grip, but was gentle, not hurting her. The hold eased. It was Battlestar. His gaze was intense. He slowly released his hand from her mouth, giving her the signal to be quiet. Battlestar pointed at her eyes and then out across the frozen grounds.

At first, Grace could not tell what Battlestar was pointing at. Then she saw it.

Standing at the back corner of the barn was a large figure. The shape seemed human at first, until her eyes adjusted. The figure stood taller than any man Grace had ever witnessed. It could have been the largest body builder she had ever seen but that's not what sent dread through her soul when the being turned around. It was neither the height nor the bulk that petrified Grace. Arching from the back of its looming frame, underneath a dark red cloak, two sharp tips protruded skyward. The demonic face, scaly maroon skin, and what could only be folded wings made Grace realize this war was about something entirely different than evil forces found on Earth.

"*Cielo ci protegga* . . . That's not a man," she uttered, terrified.

"No, and it's not a werewolf either," Battlestar replied.

"Then what is it? The devil?"

"It's going back inside. I'm gonna find out," Battlestar whispered.

"Let's wait for the others," Grace shuddered.

"Might be too late by then. Trust in me."

"Let's wait for the others," Grace shuddered.

"Might be too late by then. Trust in me."

Grace nodded, unable to disagree much with Battlestar. She could feel his thoughts clearer than anyone's. He wanted inside the barn and crept toward the back, disappearing from view. Grace tried to find a fitting prayer, remembering only a scripture: "Thou believest that there is one God; thou doest well: the devils also believe, and tremble."

Escaping without the EMP tubes was not an acceptable option for Ripster. The Nezdeth general would sooner kill him than allow him or Likzi to flee. The planning had taken far too long for failure. The EMP weapons played an important role in the wider Revolution agenda already in progress. Ripster conferred with Likzi and the general. "We have nine Revolution soldiers remaining in the barn. Less than a dozen still fighting outside. The remaining will load the cargo. If they die in the process, it will still be worth the effort," Ripster sneered. "Likzi, you and I will defend the trucks on departure. Activate Sensory Controlled Weaponry. May CONTRA feel our power before the barn is surrounded. We'll enter the fight and hold off the NATO force. Load the tubes!"

Battlestar turned off his radio and snuck into the barn. He hid behind a stack of crates. To his surprise, *two* of the large beings were inside. He stiffened, fearless on most occasions, but not this one. *What are you?* These creatures were not men, and they weren't werewolves either. Unless Lucifer sent them himself, they were some type of bioengineered mutants . . . or they were aliens.

One of the demonic figures was cloaked. The other's hood was down. Battlestar could not remove his eyes from the unmasked creature. It stood like a human, had arms, legs, and a head. All similarities ended there. The being was twice the size of a man. Its yellow reptilian eyes shimmered with a haunting evil. Large batlike wings bowed from its back. The undisguised creature spoke to its counterpart in a raspy incomprehensible language. Neither carried visible weapons.

Bullets were hitting and traveling through the barn at all angles. The creatures ignored the gunfire. Battlestar counted fewer than ten Revolution soldiers inside, all taking orders from two humans wearing highly advanced battlesuits. Battlestar recognized them—the ringleaders of The Revolution.

Some analysts thought The Three did not even exist, alleging the stories were just that—created to build the mythical power of The Revolution into something more than it was. Those analysts were wrong. These two people matched descriptions Battlestar had collected himself while with Nightwatch. A supposed third ringleader was female. They were the most wanted of all The Revolution. Battlestar had been waiting for this chance.

It could all end tonight.

He watched the ringleaders preparing to make an exit. Battlestar gripped the hilt of his samurai blade, waiting for the right time to make a silent kill. Revolution guards threw a flash grenade of some type outside and grabbed the EMP weapons tubes. The ringleaders and Revolution soldiers rushed outward providing cover fire as a last desperate attempt to escape with their prize.

Battlestar leapt from the shadows of the barn to its center. In two quick strides he was at the throat of one of the creatures. The samurai blade cut through its neck to the sounds of a high-pitched shriek. The decapitated demonic being fell to the ground with a shuddering thump. The other creature jumped back, turning to stare at Battlestar. It reached into its cloak and pulled out a five-foot-long axe. With a move that seemed too quick to be real, the creature swung the axe at Battlestar who ducked and stumbled backward to avoid his own decapitation.

The creature rumbled something in its strange language and gurgled grotesquely. Battlestar quickly recovered and reached for his gun. The creature catapulted toward him. In a fury, it hacked the weapon from Battlestar's hands, slicing it in two, and took another swing at Battlestar's head. The axe and samurai sword met in midair in a spark of metals. The force of the creature's strength sent Battlestar backward again. He somersaulted away to create distance between himself and his enemy.

Outside, Gideon had watched the barn intently. Moments earlier, Revolution troops loaded several tubes onto the back of one of the trucks before incoming fire became too heavy for them to continue.

Gideon briefly recalled his dream of opening a restaurant on the Seine in Paris. What a different life than war. He loved the beauty of France. "Prosciutto and wine when we return . . . I'll survive this for that," he muttered to himself. "So far, so good, eh Justice?"

"It's working," Justice answered.

"Estimations on how many we have left inside?" Gideon asked over the radio.

"It's hard to say for sure. Maybe a dozen or so," Nightscope responded. "Can't tell from here, but can't be much more than a dozen, sir. They're pinned."

A burst of white light exploded from inside the barn, sending a blinding flash into the eyes of CONTRA. Gun and laser fire came heavily from the barn. The remaining Revolution troops rushed from the wooden building, shooting.

Gideon covered his eyes, protecting his face from the flash grenade's searing light. When he opened them, two men wearing battlesuits followed behind the Revolution troops. The men sent hundreds of pulsed laser rounds from their battlesuits across the field.

"Damn flash grenade! SuperVision made that worse. Can't . . . readjust . . . my eyes. Can't see anything," Justice panted sounding frightened.

"Give it a moment, Justice," Gideon consoled.

"Revolution's trying to load the trucks!" Xxplosive yelled over the radio, "And we got new players on the field. Are those potentially the ringleaders?"

"Likely," Gideon confirmed over his headset. "This is it. They match the descriptions we have on file from Nightwatch."

"Concur from my vantage point," Rapidfire reported. "Who built those battlesuits?"

"Hit them with everything now," Gideon urged, focusing on the heavily armed ringleaders. Their capture or killing could make up for any troubles the team's decision to push forward into Russia would bring.

Grace dared not move. She was too close to The Revolution ringleaders exiting the barn. She listened to the radio chatter, watched, and waited. A red glow came from one of the ringleader's eyes. Her muscles flexed tight.

Suddenly, like watching computer-generated imagery, Grace saw his futuristic suit come alive. Laser canons transformed out of his battlesuit in one rapid but fluid motion of automatically shifting parts. Gun barrels popped up on both his forearms and lit off a flurry of laser shots, scattering the CONTRA team for cover. The strike force returned fire, but the ringleader did not flinch. Grace watched in amazement as conventional bullets collected into piles on the ground in front of him. Incoming rounds dropped in mid-air *before* impacting him, like some invisible force field was actively deflecting the projectiles.

Grace could not see the large being or Battlestar. After several moments of second-guessing, she asked for heaven's protection, got to her feet, and followed Battlestar's steps into the back of the barn. As she did, a CONTRA soldier pulled the pin off his grenade and lobbed it toward one of the emerging ringleaders.

A grenade struck Likzi, knocking him back through the side of the wooden barn. The ringleader crashed in between Battlestar and the creature, his face cut from shrapnel. The circuitry inside Likzi's armored battlesuit caught fire and started frying his flesh. He struggled to his feet and removed the battlesuit, screaming in agony as he peeled it away. The skin on his back sizzled from the scorching metal. Likzi grabbed a small laser gun from the battlesuit and staggered forward. He froze as he spotted the dead Nezdeth general. Likzi then watched in amazement at the dexterity of the NATO soldier in the barn.

Grace entered the back of the barn at that moment and witnessed a Revolution soldier running inside. Battlestar threw a knife through that soldier's throat while keeping a wary eye on both the creature before him and the wounded ringleader.

Two other Revolution troops backed into the barn, firing at CONTRA positions outside. Before anyone could react, Battlestar instinctively attacked, contorting his body as he jumped. Turning and slashing, he cut through both enemy soldiers in one strike with his sword and landed on his feet.

Battlestar's left eye flashed for a moment.

"*Santa Maria,*" Grace gasped. His eye had flashed in the same way hers had countless times. She'd never seen that in anyone else but herself. They shared something inexplicable. Grace needed to find out what it was.

The remaining Nezdeth general and Likzi recognized the flash—Battlestar was of Nerrial. The Nezdeth general angrily rasped something to Likzi. Likzi pointed his weapon at Battlestar but could not pull the trigger. Killing someone from Nerrial was unthinkable to him. Distant memories of his life in the Starforce kept him from following the Nezdeth orders. The demonic creature shouted irately, but Likzi could not squeeze the trigger. Instead, he watched the end of his life come at him in the form of a samurai blade, thankful his evil and suffering would end.

Battlestar struck downward with his sword in a deathstrike through Likzi's upper chest. The Nezdeth general jerked his head around, noticing someone behind him. Grace.

Battlestar grabbed two more throwing knives from his belt. With a flick of his wrist, the two sharp blades streaked across the barn aimed for the Nezdeth general's head. The general blocked the knives with his axe and stared at Battlestar for a moment.

The creature cooed one last indiscernible sentence before spreading his wings from underneath his cloak. The tip of each wing was dagger sharp. The creature bent low. Battlestar prepared to engage. Grace aimed her weapon to fire. In two powerful swoops, the being broke through the barn roof and was lost into the night.

CONTRA surrounded the barn outside.

"Something just shot out the top of the barn," Gideon yelled over the radio.

Sandstorm, still watching over the abandoned military base with a squad of soldiers, turned to see the outline of prehistoric wings spread out across the night sky. The clouds had parted to reveal a full moon. The alien wings—like an ancient pterodactyl's—crossing in front of the moon was a creepy image he would never forget.

There was room in the truck for one more EMP tube. Ripster had peered back into the barn and seen Likzi cut down by a sword. Suddenly, a laser burned through Ripster's right hand and the two Revolution soldiers on the truck fell dead in a rupture of machine-gun fire. Ripster located the CONTRA soldier who shot him and unloaded multiple laser shots into his head and stomach, liquefying the man. Four or five Revolution troops remained, about to be mowed down. There was no way to get the last EMP weapons out.

Ripster's battlesuit sensors indicated no human life to the east of him. He ducked behind the trucks and ran fast without looking back. The night was supposed to end differently. It gave him solace to know that more than forty container ships in Panama loaded with thousands of Nezdeth warriors and what CONTRA called "werewolves" were heading for the world's major ports. Best of all, each ship contained five mighty Sentrix. The stolen robotic warrior technology that had saved Nerrial so long ago would now—under Revolution control—wreak destruction over Earth.

Battlestar, Justice, Gideon, and Rapidfire stood next to Grace inside the barn. They stared at the dead thing lying in a heap of devilish flesh. The officers snapped photos, recorded the being, and rubbed their foreheads, speechless. Other dead bodies were strewn across the barn in what had already been a gruesome murder scene before the three-way gunfight started.

"It kind of looks like that statue Crosshill found underground in the Colombian base," Justice finally said.

"That's because it's the same creature," Battlestar replied.

Sandstorm, Nightscope, and Xxplosive collected evidence to ensure positive identification of the mafia leaders. Their deaths were a big deal. The EMP weapons were secured. The CONTRA forces achieved the mission they set out to accomplish in Russia. On any another night, it would have been victorious news in the fight against The Revolution.

But now none of it mattered. The NATO officers tried to make sense of what they were looking at. Had they removed the helmets of the rest of The Revolution soldiers, they would have seen even more strangeness.

Battlestar walked to where Likzi lay. Sandstorm had pronounced him dead moments earlier. No one paid much attention to the deceased ringleader—they were consumed with curiosity about the demonic figure at the center of the barn. Battlestar knelt down by Likzi. He ran his hand over the exotic armored battlesuit on the dirt floor next to the man. There were weapons nested on the inside of the suit crafted in a highly sophisticated form of technology that Battlestar had never before seen.

Likzi's head moved, startling Battlestar. The ringleader looked up with a smile and tried to say something. Battlestar moved closer, sensing no reason for fear, but he placed his hand on the hilt of his sword just in case.

"The light in your eye is a sign. You are Blessed . . . and of Nerrial," Likzi whispered in soft clarity as his eyes closed a final time.

Battlestar stared at the ringleader, feeling for a pulse. There was none.

"Is he still alive?" Grace asked, appearing next to Battlestar.

He couldn't answer. Thinking hard, he stared in awe at Likzi. There was a familiarity to that word he'd used—*Nerrial*. Battlestar had heard it once before, he was sure of it.

Unknown to Battlestar were the final images in Likzi's mind. One of the best days of his life; standing in front of a mirror with his mom who smiled with pride as he wore his Starforce uniform for the first time. Remembering that moment, Likzi felt happiness. It gave him peace. The sickness had ended.

The sound of helicopters echoed outside. "The Russians are here," Justice said. He patched into Allied Command Operations, getting orders on how to handle the situation. America's ambassador had just begun a meeting with the Russian prime minister. News was breaking worldwide about the tragic events unfolding in Jerusalem.

"Take what you can!" Justice shouted. "Upload files now. Synchronize everything with the grid and get it sent. We don't know how friendly they're going to be," he ordered, in reference to their Russian company overhead.

Russian *Spetsnaz* troops scaled down ropes suspended from eight helicopters hovering outside and shouted for all NATO personnel to drop their weapons and cease communications. The *Spetsnaz* immediately surrounded and secured the EMP tubes.

Battlestar followed their directive in a slow daze. He took off his helmet, holding it for a second. Then he recalled where he'd heard the word *Nerrial* before. Battlestar let the helmet drop out of his hand. It rolled for a second before it stopped next to Likzi's dead body.

CHAPTER 28
TAKEDOWN
Jerusalem: May 5, 2035

Crosshill's Gray Team unit was in a pitched street battle in the ghetto of East Jerusalem, four blocks away from the industrial building that emitted the frightening purple haze. A garrison of Revolution troops impeded the CONTRA objective, picking apart the NATO team. Laser tracers streamed over the street where two wounded CONTRA soldiers were being dragged to safety. The soldiers had taken serious hits. One looked fatal.

A cluster of bullets slapped into the wall above Crosshill's head. The Revolution sent volleys of gunfire at Raption who hunkered helplessly behind a van across the street. The vehicle was peppered with more bullets, windows shattering.

The Apache helicopter providing cover overhead took multiple small arms hits. Its Active Protection System destroyed three surface-to-air missiles in midair with counter-projectiles before a laser shot found its way through the cockpit. The attack helicopter wavered and pulled away. Were it not for the air cover strafing Revolution positions, CONTRA would have already been overwhelmed by the enemy.

Watching the attack helicopter depart, Crosshill sighed and leaned back against the wall. They'd been stuck for the last twenty minutes trading shots with a dug-in enemy perched on rooftops running down the entire four blocks to the target building. The other half of the Gray Team was probably already in position, waiting. Either Crosshill's unit needed to push through or pull back. They couldn't stay where they were.

Breakdown took Red and a squad of men through a restaurant adjacent to the intersection to get on a rooftop of their own. Inside the Syrian diner they found a stairwell winding upward. Breakdown gave Red a hand up the last step and they crept onto the restaurant rooftop three floors above the fight. Breakdown poked his head up to get a look around.

He saw Raption clinging for cover directly across the street and a group of CONTRA soldiers trying to circumvent the main fight a block away. The soldiers were moving toward the intersection through an alley one block north to get better positions in the fight.

Several Revolution soldiers on a balcony eyed the Gray Team troops coming back down the alley. They were waiting for the NATO troops to get closer for an easy kill. Breakdown tapped Red on the shoulder and pointed to the ambush about to unfold. She nodded. Breakdown and Red did not hesitate. Synchronized, they opened fire on the balcony, spraying it with bullets until all The Revolution soldiers dropped. Their shots broke a glass sliding door behind the soldiers. One of the enemy fighters fell backward onto a large, jagged shard—his hideous death shriek did not sound human.

Two miles away, Diamond, Satellite, and Colonel Ranin got their team into place at the eastern perimeter of the target building. They saw little resistance but could hear the gunfight raging to the west. Diamond instructed the troops to hold their positions. She would take Satellite, Colonel Ranin, and five soldiers to recon Crosshill's position.

"We'll cut across the back streets and see if the others need our help. If so, we'll send a man back and wait for reinforcements to take this building," Diamond said before they broke off jogging through the ghetto, staying close to the sidewalks and walls.

As Diamond led them two blocks down, they turned upward on another deserted street. "Where are all the people?" she asked.

"It's peculiar," Colonel Ranin said. "I noticed the silence on our way through here prior."

"Maybe everyone is aware of what's happening and they've locked themselves inside?"

"Thousands of people live in this ghetto. I don't see how everybody could've gone into hiding so quickly."

The small group continued for two more blocks, making it halfway to the ongoing gunfight and Crosshill's team. Satellite did not speak a word.

"We're getting closer—" Diamond began.

Suddenly, in an area of the slum lined with rows of coffee shops and cafés, gunfire showered them. They dove for cover by a café, hiding behind whatever they could find. Relentless bullets laced the café's windows and door.

Diamond crawled to a table stacked with menus. Colonel Ranin slid next to her, lowered to the ground. The hail of bullets did not cease. One of the CONTRA troops lay hit on the sidewalk. Diamond looked around the café table. There were over a dozen Revolution troops firing on them from down the block. "They're everywhere," she muttered.

"Bastards came from nowhere," Colonel Ranin added

"How does The Revolution sneak such an army into Jerusalem? How does that happen under the IDF's watch?" Diamond was outraged and confused. "I thought security was at a maximum."

Colonel Ranin appeared angry. "We got the whole bloody world securing this city with us. It's not just the IDF. There's a gunner in every window. I—aghh!" Colonel Ranin cried out reaching for his shin.

"What's—Are you hit?" Diamond asked.

"Don't know. Sharp pain . . . like someone's pushing a nail through my bone." Red blotches formed on his pant leg. "Yeah, I'm hit."

Diamond spotted dark visors peering down from a window across the street and fired on them. Near her, Satellite was shooting at anything that moved. She heard a thud and Satellite's hard grunt. Something knocked him over and sent his gun into the middle of the street. Satellite was gasping for breath crawling on all fours toward his gun.

Diamond grabbed his collar and pulled back.

"You'll be killed! Stay back and get your bearings," she insisted, kneeling down to check if he'd been shot. "You're hit but it didn't penetrate your armor. That's a large caliber round. It'll give you a nasty chest contusion if nothing worse happens." Diamond pulled his side arm out of its holster and put it in his hand. "Use this for now."

"Okay."

Diamond leaned up against the café table, aiming her rifle at an enemy soldier in a doorway thirty yards away. One shot. The dead man fell sideways, onto the sidewalk. Bullets zapped over her head shredding the menus with a *phfffft* and sending ribbons of paper flying in every direction. The CONTRA soldier next to Diamond took a bullet in the neck and fell face first on the pavement between her and Satellite. She shot three more Revolution soldiers and ducked for cover.

A dead Revolution soldier was sprawled out less than six feet from them on the pavement. Satellite must have gotten his bearings back. He reloaded the side arm she'd given him and shot another enemy soldier coming out of a side door in the coffee shop behind them.

"This is no good," Diamond said, calling out to Colonel Ranin. "We need to try a different way. Getting killed won't help Crosshill."

"Let's get the hell back," Colonel Ranin answered. His shin was a bloody mess. "I have enough scars for the day."

"Satellite, can you help Colonel Ranin?" Diamond asked.

He nodded.

Diamond ordered the three unscathed CONTRA soldiers to provide cover. One of them had an automatic grenade launcher. "On my mark we all go. Let it rip, and then you three fall back. I'll help our wounded soldier. We'll have to come back for the dead," she said. "Okay, unload!"

Running for their lives, they provided each other with cover and scrambled back out of The Revolution's gun sights. Diamond worried The Revolution would trail them. "Don't stop until we make it back to the eastern perimeter of the target." Only blocks away, it seemed like forever before they reached the dusty narrow road. The waiting CONTRA troops looked dismayed at their return—three of them wounded and one soldier dead.

Diamond almost threw down her sniper rifle in disgust. She panted hard and wiped the sweat off her face, leaving dirt marks. She looked up at the apocalyptic purple darkness imprisoning the sky and continuing to spread across the city.

Colonel Ranin sat on the dirt road. He looked beat up and exhausted as he wrapped his shin with medical tape. A chunk of his cheek was missing, the girl in the alley had gnawed his wrist, and now his shin had a bullet in it. Diamond gave him a fresh roll of tape. "Use it all. You need it," she said. A small metal round jutted out slightly from his shinbone.

He ran a finger over the round. "Only surgery can remove this."

As a result of Colonel Ranin being ravaged with injury, and Satellite acting distant, Diamond felt she needed to make all of the decisions. There was confusion over what they should do next. Their radios were still jammed. The CONTRA troops waited for her to give an order.

As a female commanding officer, Diamond felt more pressure to have a quick answer. She could not find one. The truth was Diamond had no idea what they should do. Wait there? Hold the perimeter like the original plan called for? Or go and try to support Crosshill again? Satellite needed to get involved and help her out. He was third in command of the Gray Team, after all.

"Satellite?"

He rubbed his chest, but didn't respond.

"Satellite, damn it!" Diamond repeated to get his attention.

"Yeah."

"What the hell is a matter with you? Are we going to stay on this dirt road or what?"

"Scattering farther won't do anybody any good. We should wait here."

Diamond eyed him closely, not liking his monotone. She studied his face and awkward mannerisms. Satellite was not acting like himself.

"Look up!" a CONTRA soldier yelled.

Three IDF attack helicopters flew in low and stopped several hundred yards from their position. The multinational joint command center must have gotten word NATO troops were in trouble. As the fresh attack choppers hovered, their gun turrets pointed toward the ongoing Gray Team battle blocks away. The helicopters unleashed a cache of missiles and cannon fire for well over a minute without any let-up. It brought cheers from the CONTRA troops.

"Get those son of a bitch bastards!" Colonel Ranin shouted.

Those are his boys up there, thought Diamond. *It's about time the cavalry arrived.*

On the restaurant rooftop, Breakdown nudged Red and pointed east to three incoming IDF helicopters. He could see them through the haze emanating from the top of the target building, which looked like one of those large smoke bombs he remembered from Fourth of July parties. This smoke bomb wouldn't go out by itself: extinguishing it would be CONTRA's job.

The attack choppers hurled a burst of firepower down the street at the target building.

"Get down!" Breakdown shouted.

Missiles, explosions, and heavy gunfire bore holes through the dilapidated apartments lining the blocks between Crosshill's team and their objective. Yelling and destruction lasted for what felt like an eternity before the blazing cannons finally stopped.

"Looks like we might get somewhere after all," Breakdown said to Red who crouched next to him. They crawled back to the edge of the rooftop and peered through the smoke and dust to get the full picture. Every window on the block was blown out. Glass was everywhere. There were pockmarks the size of grapefruits all along the walls and an entire apartment building had collapsed two blocks down.

"Is everyone okay down there?" Breakdown shouted.

"Fine . . . I think!" Crosshill yelled back. He went forward into the open street, motioning for everyone to follow. "Now is the time!" he shouted.

Raption obeyed orders with several CONTRA soldiers right behind him. They moved fast, shooting Revolution soldiers who'd fallen into the street and were stumbling out of half-destroyed buildings hit by the helicopter gunships.

"We need to join that forward rush," Breakdown said doubling over for a moment, almost tripping over an exhaust fan on the roof.

"Let's get down there!" Red exclaimed with an excitement that caught Breakdown off guard. Justice would've been proud.

The CONTRA team progressed for two blocks, making it halfway to the target building without pause. Crosshill was at the lead. He shot his sixth Revolution soldier on the surge and then two more who were slumped on the ground. "Make sure they're all dead!" he yelled.

Crosshill could see the front of the target building now. From the street it looked like any other apartment building—except for the ominous dark purple smoke spewing from its top. A haggard Revolution gunner staggered out of the doorway at the edge of the third block. Crosshill was reloading. He and the soldier saw each other at the same time. Crosshill dropped the MG4 automatic in his hand and grabbed the shotgun off his back strap. Cocking it quick, he shot the enemy soldier's head off. The decapitated body thudded to the ground like a bag of rocks.

Crosshill inserted the shotgun back into its holster and picked up his MG4 off the ground. He reloaded it and fired at a gunner sniping at the team from his perch atop a burning apartment complex to his right. As the shots rang out, splashes of blood burst between Crosshill's shoulder and neck. A second armor-piercing bullet went through his right thigh. The bullets made impact at virtually the same time, sending Crosshill to the pavement in a slow fall.

He heard Raption cry out behind him and rip a dozen rounds in the sniper's direction. Smoke must have camouflaged a second shooter that Crosshill could not see. He found himself staring at the pavement from an odd side angle. Smoke, rubble, and shouting surrounded him. It took a moment to realize what was happening. He thought of his daughter, Margaret, in their London home watching him leave for missions, not crying, not waving, and just watching Daddy go. Then he saw the cross on the hill in Tibet where he'd buried Winston Blair, his best man and first mate on all things.

Up until Winston died, Crosshill had thought death implausible for men like them. They'd lived through so much in the Special Air Service. Death happened to other soldiers but he and Winston were the best. Untouchable. When he buried Winston on that rocky, cold Tibet mountaintop, all his bravado dissolved. Crosshill's best friend was gone. His CONTRA codename represented the cross he'd carved at the burial site.

Unable to lift himself off the ground, he kept feeling around his neck in disbelief. Warm sticky blood was thick between his fingers. A slow panic for survival washed over him. He wanted to see his family again. All these thoughts passed in clear perfection within mere seconds, because Raption was on top of him that fast.

"Crosshill! Stay down," Raption begged falling to his knees. He pulled Crosshill's gun gently over his head and out of the way. Crosshill was panicking, Raption could tell. He tried keeping him calm. Crosshill gaped at the blood on his hands.

"We're gonna need to get you out of here. MEDIC!" Raption yelled frantically.

There was fighting on both sides of the street and a tornado of action around them. Gunfire, screaming, fire, smoke, explosions, rubble, and troops engaging at all angles on the narrow ghetto block of Jerusalem's Palestine sector. CONTRA soldiers rushed forward. Their radios were still mysteriously jammed and the bizarre purple smoke covered the entire skyline above them. It was crazy, but oddly, Raption didn't want to be anywhere else.

A CONTRA medic ran to Colonel Crosshill. "We'll take care of him," the medic said.

"I'm fine . . . Just wrap it and let me be on . . . I . . . am fine . . . really," Crosshill slurred. He was in shock, confused, and pleading to stay in the fight.

"You're losing lots of blood. It's best to get you out, sir," Raption agonized, eyeing the pools forming under Crosshill. Raption wasn't a trained doctor but he'd seen enough wounded men to know when bullets hit a main artery. Raption looked to the medic. "You take him out of here, you hear me? He's wounded bad enough to get out of this fight. No bullshit about him hanging around."

The medic looked at Raption as if he was stating the obvious.

Raption checked the name badge of the medic. Kenny Montano. He knew him from training. Nice kid, and the youngest of the medics in CONTRA. Kenny was already at work, immune to the fear of being killed by the bullets snapping overhead.

Raption grabbed Crosshill at the forearm. "I'll see you back at wherever we end up."

Crosshill swallowed hard, unable to reply.

Raption took one last look, hoping he would see Crosshill alive again. There wasn't much time to think about it. He hopped over some rubble in front of him and tried to get a bead on the action. The Revolution fortified around the main building as CONTRA closed in.

As they made it out of the diner's front door, Breakdown spotted Raption kneeling next to someone in the street. He wanted to catch up and be at the front. The rest of the team had already advanced halfway to the building in a fighting sprint. The pitched battle had turned in CONTRA's favor since the IDF helicopters blasted The Revolution.

Breakdown couldn't tell what was happening in front of the target building nor could he see Diamond's half of the Gray Team. He did not know a Revolution soldier aimed and fired an Anti-Tank Guided Missile (ATGM) from a gaping hole in the apartment building cattycorner to him. The ATGM headed in his direction, trailing smoke. Red bull-rushed him into the street as the missile struck the front side of the restaurant they'd just left.

The missile exploded. Its impact knocked the restaurant's large neon sign off its hinges, sending it crashing toward the sidewalk in a burst of sparks and electricity. Breakdown watched the very top of the sign, shaped like a sandwich, topple down toward Red. The sharp tip was coming right for her head.

He grabbed Red's collar with his good arm and heaved her out of danger as the sign collapsed and ruptured in a shower of thundering wreckage next to them. Sparks danced burning speckles on their faces. Part of the sign jabbed out hard, hitting Breakdown in the ribcage of his battlesuit.

The Revolution soldier who fired the ATGM round was loading another missile. Breakdown spotted him. He rolled over on the ground, grabbed the trigger of his M249 and unloaded an entire clip, letting the rounds continue to hit and tear the enemy soldier to bloody shreds after he was already dead. Breakdown's finger still pressed hard against the trigger when the rounds stopped spitting. Red put her hand on his shoulder. He looked up.

"Thank you," she said.

"Nice tackle," he managed.

Two CONTRA soldiers ran by carrying one of the wounded away from the front. Red's eyes lit up. "That's Crosshill. Wait!" she yelled, getting up and running to his side. Breakdown dragged himself up and followed.

He looked Crosshill over but couldn't find a comforting word.

Crosshill stared at them both. "I'll be fine. Just need to get some more bandages," he whispered. "It doesn't even hurt."

Breakdown held Crosshill's hands with both of his, looked him in the eye, and nodded encouragingly to his friend and leader. The medics rushed him out. Crosshill was fading to sleep. "C'mon Red. We gotta go." Breakdown tugged at her arm.

While the IDF attack choppers dumped their ammo, Diamond shouted for the CONTRA troops to move forward toward the target building. "We are taking that building and we are taking it now!" she yelled, ferocious and confident in her orders. "Move!"

CONTRA would obey—or die trying.

Next to her, Satellite still seemed detached, as if it wasn't his battle to deal with. Bad timing given he was in the midst of the most intense combat of his career. So much was at stake. The ground beneath them shook from the rocking of explosions, heavy cannon fire, and machine guns unleashing their wrath from the attack helicopters on a single three-block stretch infested by The Revolution.

Multiple rockets, small arms, and lasers traced back to the three hovering gunships. Diamond thought the choppers were too close to the scene. They should have been positioned farther back. As she rounded the corner in front of the industrial building, Diamond shot three Revolution soldiers who were firing at the helicopters.

Incoming rounds from the top floors riddled the ground near her feet. Laser fire came close to hitting her face. A hot tracer singed a blonde strand of her hair. Diamond felt the heat pass and hit the ground for cover, rolling next to a wall twenty yards from the front entrance of the building. Diamond's unit successfully turned the corner and engaged with The Revolution. The IDF choppers let their final missiles fly behind them, completing their destruction of the entire street block in front of the target building.

A CONTRA soldier in front of Diamond ducked near the same broken wall. Leaning his gun over the edge, he kept firing. Standing up for a better angle, bullet shells flew out of his MK-17 clip. An unseen Revolution soldier must have waited low on the other side of the wall. In one motion he knocked the gun out of the CONTRA soldier's hand while, to Diamond's horror, thrusting a large dagger into his chest. The soldier let out a mortal scream. Diamond shot the enemy soldier twice in the head. He dropped onto the wall next to the dead NATO operator he'd killed.

Satellite watched, amazed at how many Revolution troops were dying to protect the building. How many aliens were on Earth? This *was* an alien army after all, not a rebel militia. The reptilian skin of The Revolution soldier continued to plague his psyche.

A loud sputtering noised started up. He turned to see two of the attack choppers pulling away. The other started in a spin; its back rotor smoked from a Rocket Propelled Grenade hit. The pilot maneuvered, trying to save the copter.

"That chopper's going down!" Colonel Ranin shouted.

Spiraling to one side, the top rotor blades faced the troops then snapped off like a throwing star and flew toward the CONTRA members. Satellite heard the *zweep, zweep, zweep* of the blade as it passed near him. The blade missed several CONTRA soldiers by a matter of feet and smashed into the side of the target building. The downed chopper exploded in flames.

"I see the rest of our team," Satellite said to Colonel Ranin. "They're breaking for it."

The Revolution was on their heels. Their extensive presence and all-out fight confirmed the target building's importance. Whatever the cause of the purple smoke, it must have been crucial to merit such a dedicated defense.

Satellite jumped the wall and followed Colonel Ranin into what was hopefully the final charge. They entered the thick of the fighting firing at the windows occupied by Revolution troops who shot back, peppering the ground with bullets.

Satellite glimpsed the tooth marks engraved on the side of Colonel Ranin's face. Blood had soaked through the bandage on his wrist. The colonel fought on to support the world's dream of peace. Men and women like him from both the IDF and the Palestinian Army struggled in similar battles across Jerusalem. The world had begun fighting The Revolution together—an enemy with objectives nobody fully understood. *The world will come together over this. I hope it's not too late.*

Satellite also hoped Lydia found a good reason to leave Jerusalem early and miss the action. *Not a chance.*

Raption explained to Breakdown and Red how Crosshill got hit when they reached him at the target building. "Look," he said, pointing. "It's Diamond and Satellite near the foot of the building, fighting their way to the front." They were within shouting distance to their fellow officers. Satellite looked right at Raption.

Raption was about to yell to him when a thunderous blast from the turret of an IDF Merkva tank decimated a Revolution firing position. The tank rounded the corner two blocks down flanked by IDF troops. Raption turned to see the tank with Israeli troops on either side of it, funneling down the street behind them.

Satellite crept across the street from the building, running low around to where Raption, Breakdown, and Red were. He panted hard and looked pale.

"Are you okay?" Red asked.

"When this is over, I'll be fine."

"We're gonna blow a hole in the side of this puppy," Raption said. "Front attack's too deadly. I want in that building *bad*. Come on, let's get to the side."

They moved out of site to the side of the building. Two CONTRA soldiers attached detonators to the wall and hid behind a garbage container away from the discharge. The detonation blew a clean hole to the inside of the building.

Raption and Satellite were first in, ready to fire. Raption spotted a dying Revolution soldier near the entrance trying to reach for his weapon and ripped five rounds into his back. Other soldiers were against the wall nearest the entrance, crawling to their deaths.

Satellite scanned the room, ready to fire at the first threatening movement. A patch of bloodstained white fabric amid the destruction caught his eye. Hunched and alert, Satellite progressed toward what he thought was a civilian. He inhaled sharply when he reached his destination.

"Lydia?" Satellites voice trembled.

He sprinted to the corner of the lobby and crashed down to the floor, mashing his knees on a pile of rubble and glass, never feeling the pain.

"How?" he asked bewildered, staring at his sister.

There she was, Lydia Lewis, in front of him—in The Revolution target building's lobby. Cut. Bleeding. Distraught. She just stared back at him. For a second time that day, Satellite couldn't believe his eyes. He embraced his sister tightly.

Lydia sobbed, "Nate? You're w-wearing weaponry and . . . armor. The same . . . u-uniforms as the captured soldiers. Prowess . . . she's still upstairs."

"What captured soldiers? Who is Prowess? What are you doing here Lydia?!"

"I have so much to tell you, Nathan," Lydia whispered to Satellite weakly. "There is poison in the air. You have to hurry. It will infect us all unless we hurry."

"We have protection. I have a mask for you and I'm going to take you home, Lydia. Just hang on." Satellite couldn't let go of his sister for a moment. They sat on the destroyed lobby floor holding each other until CONTRA and the IDF had fully secured the building.

Outside, the sky darkened completely. A light purple mist started to fall over Jerusalem. The world didn't know it yet, but The Global Revolution had begun.

Prowess made her way through an escape passage deep below the building. The tunnel exited miles away into the outskirts of Jerusalem where a black limo waited. Prowess dusted herself off. She would check in with Ripster and let him know everything went according to plan.

Then she would initiate the Assassination Agenda.

CHAPTER 29
TRANSMISSIONS
Colorado Springs: May 6, 2035

Colonel Michael Vickers watched the newscast in disbelief. His coffee cup was full, the steam gone, the drink untouched. Staring at the television screen, his stomach turned knowing the situation had entered a new phase.

"Honey, what's wrong?" questioned his wife, Danielle, striding through the kitchen, seeing her husband transfixed by the news.

"Bad things in Jerusalem. Breaking news. It's everywhere now."

Danielle packed their son's lunch while peering over at the flat screen. She sighed. A fifth grade school teacher, she tried not to monitor every emerging tragedy like her husband. Their son, Donovan, was having trouble at school.

"Honey, I've arranged a meeting with Donovan's teacher today. You remember, right?" Danielle asked.

"Yes, of course. Mr. Springer will listen to us and do nothing . . . again."

"You'll be able to make it this time?" Danielle set a small bottle of grape juice next to the lunch box on the counter, waiting for an answer.

Colonel Vickers didn't hear his wife. The newscast was reporting that Pentagon officials were blaming the crisis in Jerusalem on The Revolution.

"Honey!"

"Christ! Yes, I'll be there, dear." Colonel Vickers turned off the television and dumped his coffee out in the kitchen sink; he had twenty-five minutes until he needed to report for duty at his NORAD station. Donovan came downstairs. The colonel bent down and kissed his son on the forehead.

"Donovan, listen to me. People are always going to give you challenges in life. Making the best of things is something they can never take away from you. Bullies will come and go. Remember that—today and every day."

"Okay, Dad. I will."

"You're more special than you know."

The colonel patted his son on the head and kissed his wife goodbye. He watched them pull out of the driveway, then walked back to his home office. Sometimes he spent hours there: working on e-mails, preparing briefings, or planning upcoming high-profile visits to NORAD. As director of the Space Defense Operations Center, his government job included the detection, identification, and tracking of all manmade or foreign objects in space.

An Emissary had traditionally sought and held the position because of its dual purpose.

Typing in the code on the black safety box under his desk, Colonel Vickers opened the latch and removed his Emissary transmitter. Each Emissary kept one for secure communications and updates between Earth and Nerrial. Colonel Vickers had provided Magden with a new transmission from Lonthran— Nerrial's chief of Earth intelligence—the previous evening. That message would change the future for all of them. No response yet from Magden. Likely he wanted to talk things over with Joseph McBride first.

Colonel Vickers put the mobile transmitter back in its safe, happy that initiating the space transmission process from Cheyenne Mountain wasn't required that day. He had performed space transmissions to Nerrial dozens of times since his promotion to the position of overseeing the Starblazer program.

Nonetheless, initiating the sequence required perfection and several minutes of uninterrupted focus from inside a secret chamber within the mountain complex known only to Emissaries. Being the primary contact between Earth and Nerrial made Colonel Vickers nervous. Danielle was not a descendant of Nerrial and she did not know the pressure he felt. Sharing such secrets was forbidden.

Between 1961 and 1966, when the Soviet danger of Intercontinental Ballistic Missiles threatened the United States, the construction of the mountain complex was underway. Originally, NORAD was built within the Cheyenne Mountain Complex but later moved to Peterson Air Force Base.

Under a Top Secret program called Starblazer, a special unit of Emissary scientists worked on top of the mountain during the construction phase of NORAD. Nerrial's then chief Emissary, Calliden, used NORAD as the ideal construction project where an advanced communications system could be built within an Earth-based infrastructure containing enough high technology to support deep space transmissions. They built a communications portal—or COMPORT—into the rock at the peak of the mountain, which was capable of sending and receiving transmissions to Nerrial.

The Starblazer COMPORT could transmit up to fifty million light years through space. It used advanced, miniature nuclear reactors to generate the necessary power for a space-time continuum shift. Two closely neighboring TeraWatt magnetic fields initiated the reaction. The magnetic fields were of opposite polarity and very small in size. Their concentration created a space-time discontinuity, commonly known as a wormhole. The wormhole made it possible for energy to be sent from one point in space and time to another.

After the Starblazer program was complete, it took approximately three months for a transmission to cross deep space and reach Nerrial, a dramatic improvement in speed and quality, lessening the risk of deploying stealthy Starships to Earth for quick exchanges of intelligence which had resulted in numerous UFO sightings through the years. Colonel Vickers managed all incoming and outgoing messages between Earth and Nerrial. Next to Magden, he held the most critical Emissary position on Earth.

The colonel grabbed his keys off the fireplace mantel and readied for work. He laced his shoes and quickly polished them to a spit shine before locking the front door behind him. Outside, he stopped to admire the beautiful spring morning: blooming flowers adorned his patio and lined the gravel pathway to the driveway. Colonel Vickers focused all his senses on the pleasant distraction from the ugliness of world affairs.

He took two steps down the short gravel path—Colonel Vickers never completed his third step. The silencer kept the shot from waking the neighbors. A stream of blood filled the gap between the edges of the gravel path and newly planted flowers.

The Revolution assassin tucked the weapon back under his black coat and checked the colonel's pulse to make sure the Emissary was dead. Confident, he hopped the white fence next to the garage and strode through the backyard. A car waited in the alley. Once he got in, it pulled away and melted into morning traffic.

CHAPTER 30

MEMORIES OF A LEGEND
Washington, DC: May 6, 2035

When the Emissaries established CONTRA their suspicions were high that something was amiss on Earth, but the developments since the group's inception were staggering. Joseph McBride was overwhelmed by everything that had transpired. In only the past few days the secret world of Nerrial's Emissaries had collided with American national security—and now the Nezdeth. How the ancient past came full circle so suddenly was hard to fathom.

Images on the morning news of dead, unmasked Nezdeth warriors in Jerusalem confirmed the worst was true. No longer was there hope for doubt. The evidence was irrefutable.

Joseph stood on the Pacific balcony of Washington's World War II Memorial overlooking the Rainbow Pool and waterworks. He watched Magden arrive and sit on a park bench. No rush today for either of them. Both understood what was happening. The Emissaries didn't need divulgences from any government. Far greater things overshadowed Earth's circumstance than any federal employee could comprehend, even if they understood the basic truth.

Sandra, the president's trusted national security advisor, kept them in the loop as best she could. The president approved her reaching out to Magden after the contentious White House meeting. She promised an open door, agreeing to provide him with any new information on The Revolution she could. Her curiosity in something deeper in the Emissary code, something good, was hard to ignore. Joseph sensed she understood they mattered, but Sandra couldn't find out who they were, and they couldn't tell her. For now, receiving updates from Sandra was a privilege the Emissaries appreciated.

SHADOWS OF THE PAST

The Secret Service detail was in relative open force, following Joseph and Magden around Washington wherever they went and eavesdropping on everything they talked about. Magden had news, which prompted the meeting at the World War II Memorial.

The memorial was a favorite of theirs. That war changed so much on Earth, defining generations and nations while redefining the Emissary mission. Nerrial's earliest envoys on the ground quickly recognized Earth's inherent problems. Greed. Money. Power. War. The insatiable desire for each led to repeating mistakes and an eventual path to violence. Memorials were built while history was lost to the continuation of senseless feuding. The power struggles were never relinquished. War always returned on Earth.

Joseph walked slowly to Magden and sat next to him wondering if somehow, over the centuries, the same thing happened in Nerrial. Magden slid him a medallion with a blue outer rim composed of seven planets circling an inscribed depiction of Earth at its center and the number *1898* embossed in silver. Joseph recognized it at once. The medallion was a token of Emissaries handed down from their fathers, a lasting symbol of their purpose and the rarity of human life in the universe.

"Good morning, Joseph," Magden said, not looking away from his morning read on a digital reader.

"A beautiful one, notwithstanding what's happening."

The men sat silent for some time.

Magden's newsreader displayed breaking news and videos from across the world. The stories read like a collection of dire poems from the oracles of civilization's demise. Stark patterns of chaos were rendered in the havoc of The Revolution's destructive agenda. Executed with precision and controlled by beings this world could not comprehend, The Three worked with enemies of humanity to bring Earth closer to a mournful termination . . . unless the Emissaries could stop it first.

Most reports were devoted to coverage of various firsthand accounts coming out of Jerusalem and the violence continuing to spread throughout Palestine and Lebanon. As the Holy City continued unraveling on televisions around the world, rumors began to spread of biological and chemical war. Images of crazed civilians—some were calling them zombies—along with IDF defections, and multinational security forces fortifying their positions and publicly requesting evacuation, left a stunned global populace desperate for answers.

The world was fixated. Fears were mounting.

Several news reports included pictures of dead Revolution soldiers unmasked by journalists in Israel. Stories circulated of a massive government cover-up of genetic experiments; some hinted at an alien presence on Earth. The initial government reaction was denial, followed by the media's unanswered questions.

Amid the nonstop news coverage of the deteriorating Middle East peace was an online story posted by a man named Boris. He claimed he witnessed a massive firefight between NATO and Revolution troops east of Moscow, where Russia's notorious crime bosses had been killed. Reuters, CNN, and Station One picked up his post hours following confirmation of the mafia slayings.

Soon after, news agencies issued a retraction when the Kremlin discredited the story, showing its own footage of how the crime bosses were "brought to justice" by undercover Russian police agents. Russia's information ministry hailed the police operation as testament to their fight against organized crime. The mafia deaths received attention, as did other developments around the world. Together, these combined events exhibited a rapidly worsening international atmosphere of instability—all stoked by agents of The Revolution.

The Holy Land Accord celebrations unraveling in such dramatic fashion had the world media feeding almost exclusively on the hottest news story in a decade, leaving Joseph and Magden trying to decipher how far the Nezdeth manipulation of world affairs stretched.

India and China had exchanged artillery fire in a short but intense battle overnight on the disputed Himachal Pradesh border region. Indian territorial gains were brief as Chinese troops advanced to lost positions and announced plans to declare war. Commercial satellite imagery showed large movements of Chinese troops and hardware toward the Indian border. Half a dozen Chinese nuclear submarines were launched from the Yulin Navy base on Hainan Island. Indian missile forces and patrols were placed on high alert.

In South America, security forces lost ground fighting drug cartels and rebel paramilitaries. In most metropolitan areas, businesses were completely shut down. Civilian deaths increased and anger at regional governments unable to stop the violence—now reaching anarchic levels—mounted. Military commanders in the field reported difficulty in identifying enemy troop movements.

Brazilian forces discovered several massive underground tunnels on the outskirts of Ecuador. Photos of the tunnels reached the Internet and matched CONTRA's discovery in Colombia. Both Ecuador and Brazil sent investigative teams to explore the tunnels. Both teams disappeared without a trace.

Magden and Joseph feared the dangers humanity faced from the Nezdeth. They were well versed in the history of Nerrial's war with the Nezdeth. The militancy and ruthlessness of their ancient demonic enemy was responsible for over one billion Nerrial deaths during the War of the Star. Most of those killed were innocent families trying to escape into the countryside before Nerrial even had a military. Past conflicts on Earth paled in comparison to what the Nezdeth would do. Or was doing.

Nothing weighed more on the Emissaries' shoulders than stopping the Nezdeth from ravaging Earth. No military—no matter how advanced by Earth standards—could compete with the Nezdeth if they launched a full-scale attack.

A group of middle school children followed their chaperone past the bench where Magden and Joseph sat. The chaperone spoke in generalities about the Nazi regime, Japanese Empire, and the great American struggle almost a century ago. Joseph watched the children who were too far removed from that era, that time, to understand its significance.

Magden broke the silence. "We won't speak in code this morning. There is no longer a need. I received word in the night that a Triad has been completed. All three pillars of Nerrial's leadership—The Crown, High Council, and Adena Monarchy—met in the sacred ceremony and have agreed the secret should be revealed."

"What?" Joseph turned, shocked. "But the last Starblazer transmission was sent to Nerrial only recently. How could Lonthran have time to respond, let alone receive it?"

Across the memorial pool, two Secret Service agents cupped their hands over their ears, keenly following along. Magden ignored them.

"Princess Shia discovered evidence from one of our previous transmissions, which confirmed a Nezdeth presence here—The Revolution symbol found and photographed at the first Demon Lab and sent back in an older transmission. That symbol is from an ancient Nezdeth war tribe. We missed it somehow . . . One of the forgotten details from the War of the Star."

"How did Shia know?"

"The symbol was originally drawn in Exa the Great's accounts from the War of the Star. Princess Shia rediscovered it in Exa's book *Time of Legend*, confirming that the symbol from the Demon Lab matched."

"Right under our noses this whole time?"

"Not really, Joseph. That reference was from almost two thousand years ago and Star Command never confirmed a single Nezdeth war tribe was responsible for the invasion. That symbol never became a prominent part of any studies. It remained a footnote in Exa's account of fighting during the liberation of Cellcia. The Triad understood there was no other possible explanation for that symbol to appear on Earth unless the Nezdeth were here. It cannot be coincidence, thus, the *revelation* of the secret must occur. Nerrial will be made known to Earth. The Starforce is already approaching."

Joseph folded both hands across his chest and leaned back absorbing the situation and what it all meant. "It's going to finally happen. I . . . can't believe it."

"Believe it! It's what we've been waiting for. Earth is ready. And after all these years—so is Nerrial. There is one more disturbing premonition from this new Princess of Adena, and I must say…it's both brilliant on her part and worrisome for us."

"What is it?" Joseph asked, concerned.

"You may recall an old transmission some thirty years ago regarding the last Starforce battle with the Nezdeth?"

"Yes, faintly . . . a terrible occurrence. The Nezdeth landed on a planet outside the Whorvz perimeter established after the War of the Star. Tracked by the nearest Starforce fleet, the Nezdeth were encountered for the first time in hundreds of years. Their landing party was decimated, however they killed many Star Troops. A tragedy."

"That wasn't all. Three Starforce officers went missing after returning to Nerrial. They were described as going mad, delusional, and angry."

"I don't remember that." Joseph thought hard.

"In Nerrial it was a very big deal. The officers stole two Starwings and were thought to have died in the depths of space."

Joseph saw where Magden was going. "You're saying—"

"The Princess had a premonition that these officers might be 'The Three' we've reported of to Nerrial through transmissions. The Revolution ringleaders."

"Which is how the Nezdeth would have known about Earth's location in the universe . . . and about us."

"In all our knowing, it is apparent there remains much we don't understand. Those are the things we can't see. But if the Nezdeth could reach Earth without the Starforce knowing . . . Joseph . . . it means the Nezdeth have reconstituted their capabilities and we underestimated their cunning. More than this planet and our secrets on Earth may be compromised. Nerrial is at risk."

Joseph's body went numb. "The new war for the universe: It's already begun. The shadows of the past have returned."

Magden's left eye flashed as he openly displayed the sign of The Blessed for the first time. His eye gleamed bright and noticeable, even in the daylight of the sunny Washington morning. It would attract due attention from those they were sent to protect.

So be it.

CHAPTER 31
SHADOWS UNCOVERED
Colorado Springs: May 7, 2035

A lone Shadowhawk carried the Blue and Gray Team officers from Brussels to CONTRA headquarters in Colorado Springs. Their second missions were complete.

The Russian military had quietly escorted the Blue Team out of the country. To the team's surprise, nothing was confiscated. There were no interrogations. The dirty work was done: the EMP weapons secured and the mafia crime bosses dead. The Russians just wanted CONTRA out. The Blue Team was driven back to the same small Kazan airstrip where they tased the Russian police officers. The officers weren't particularly happy to see the NATO unit return, and swore and spat at them as they boarded a waiting cargo plane.

In Jerusalem, the Gray Team and IDF explored the target building that emanated the purple psychotropic drug. The main dispersing mechanism originated deep beneath the building and was locked away by thick and impenetrable iron doors. Air strikes were called in after it became apparent that the mist was driving Jerusalem's citizens into a maniacal state, but the damage had been done. The mist covered most of the city. Bedlam ensued and it was still spreading. Several Gray Team soldiers were infected with the poison and were restrained awaiting transport to a military hospital in Brussels along with the others who were wounded in battle.

"Everything that's happening . . . what does it all mean?" Lydia asked Satellite.

"It means you're going to need Top Secret clearance," he joked.

Lydia laughed, applying a new ice pack to her still swollen face. "This puffiness is improving, but I still look ugly."

"That's impossible, sis."

"Shadowhawk . . . that's what you guys call this plane?"

"Yeah, someone at the Pentagon came up with that."

"I like it. Better than a Dreamliner." Lydia paused for a moment, "Writing my book won't be quite the same. I don't even know where to begin now."

Satellite hugged his sister, glad she was alive and with him. "Remember when we were kids and I'd pretend to encounter the first alien on Earth?"

"And I was the first reporter to get the story."

"Funny thing, those skits in the family basement ran through my mind when I looked at that . . . thing. I knew what it was right away, even before listening to you describe the one you saw and what Prowess told you. Everyone else doesn't believe yet, but they will."

"Nate, let's visit mom when we get back. Can we do that together?"

"Sure, Lydia. I'd like that."

Raption sat next to Diamond. At times like this he hated that they'd decided to keep their relationship a secret. They talked about the world a lot when they were alone. Their conversations were so much different then. The darling Olympian sharpshooter from Iceland with a Californian beach bum turned jungle fighter—it seemed a perfect fit to Raption.

Girls came and went in the simpler times, when catching a wave, reading magazines, and slacking off filled the joyous days of his teenage life on the beaches of Santa Monica. Raption never imagined being an elite NATO officer. He never thought he'd meet someone like Diamond. She caught his eye and gave him a genuine, radiant smile.

These days, nothing was better than that look.

Like an uncut rose edging through the gates of an abandoned mansion, her desires conflicted with a sweet shyness. She told Raption he needed to stay patient with her. She thought it would be difficult to be romantic and feel secure in CONTRA showing affection with another officer. Guys had always been after Diamond for her stunning beauty, but Raption was the only male she'd ever felt a connection with. She told him that the night he gave her his first gift—diamond earrings.

The reason behind her codename was Raption's secret.

"That cut on your forehead is doing well," she said warmly.

"It's nothin'. I've had worse."

To his surprise, Diamond moved closer to him. She reached into her pocket and pulled out a square jewelry box Raption recognized immediately. Diamond opened it and there were the two earrings he'd bought her. She put them on and looked at him with a big smile.

Raption wasn't sure how to react. "Umm . . . "

Diamond put her finger to his lips, "I don't want to hide anymore." She kissed him deeply.

Nobody asked any questions.

Red slept on Justice's shoulder and woke to one of the quietest Shadowhawk cabins ever. In the entire surrounding calamity, her world was at peace with him. The experience in Israel and quiet calm of the warcraft brought clarity to her mind. One thought prevailed—the military wasn't the lifestyle she wanted. Red pondered all the reasons she had joined in the first place.

Early in her career, she worked as an UNSFOR medic in central Africa during the Resource Wars and witnessed the aftermath of a biological attack on a tribe of Sudanese peasants resting near a water reserve. The "precious resource" was worth more to local militias than their lives. Violence and war had surrounded her life ever since. Red kept telling herself joining Canada's military was worth it. Making a difference mattered, but she felt uncertainty instead. She wanted to do well. Those around her deserved it.

"Are you awake?" Justice asked.

"Sort of," she whispered.

"What's that mean?"

Red sat up. Tears welled. "I don't think I can do this anymore. Science, not war, is what I should be spending my career doing." She wiped her tears. "I'm not cut out for this . . . I'm sorry. I don't think I'm a good soldier."

"I've told you it's okay," Justice consoled. "What? You don't think command will reassign you to a lab if you requested it?"

"My command is Joint Task Force Two. I'm loaned to CONTRA, remember? They've made it clear, Special Forces don't draft their own assignments. I'd have to quit. With what's happening, they might force me to stay. It's too crazy for me. I can't—don't—want to keep going."

"You're better than you think. We'll work something out. I'm here for you regardless if you're wearing a CONTRA uniform or not. You know that."

"It won't be the same. I know that, too." Red began thinking of her life beyond CONTRA.

Grace didn't sit far from Battlestar. She couldn't take her eyes off him or stop wondering what made them alike. What happened in Kazan and Jerusalem was still sinking in. She wanted to write the bulk of the field report on these missions and took copious notes in Brussels as the wearied teams exchanged stories and videos of their battles. A shared feeling of CONTRA purpose surpassed all things. Something was happening to the world and they were definitely at the center of it. There was no doubting that now.

Grace prayed for Crosshill. He was fighting to stay alive in emergency surgery and had fallen into a coma. His wife and daughter were flown in from London to be at his bedside. The first sniper bullet missed Crosshill's major organs. The second slashed through the tunica media of an artery in his thigh. The life-sustaining vessel delivering blood from his heart had a quarter-sized hole in it. Grace couldn't imagine how his wife and daughter were faring.

When the Shadowhawks finally landed, Battlestar should have been tired but wasn't. He didn't sleep during the entire trip back and still felt fresh. He walked straight off the Shadowhawk to Commander Patton's old office. Grace trailed him. She seemed extra attentive and curious about something, but just followed along without talking. Battlestar's concentration was on finding Patton.

In flight, Decon informed Battlestar that Patton was called onto the base to debrief acting CONTRA commander Brownberg on the progress of the strike force, including the Third Company—Black Team—whose training had just completed. It would be Patton's last action before the Department of Defense escorted him off base permanently. Battlestar walked to Patton's office. The name on the door was taped over. He looked inside. Nobody was there.

Battlestar didn't understand what happened to merit the suspensions and didn't care at the moment. It was hard to think clearly until his one burning question was answered. He walked to the end of the hallway, passing a sign that read "Peterson Air Force Base, America's Space Superiority Wing— Globally Postured to Ensure Space Dominance." He went up a flight of stairs overlooking one of the training floors. Chairs had been brought in for a small ceremony—Black Team activation.

General Brownberg stood in front of the seven officers of the CONTRA Third Company, Black Team: Pridian of Spain, a psychological operations expert; Arashi of Japan, an intelligence specialist; Shade of Germany, an assassin; Outpost of Australia, a reconnaissance expert; Radaz of Croatia, specialized in amphibious assault; Doubleglock of the United States, a tactical warfare expert; and Burst of Denmark, a directed energy specialist.

Fifty CONTRA soldiers stood behind the officers. The pomp of NATO flags and speeches accompanied an ongoing ceremony. Battlestar didn't know these officers very well. He watched part of the ceremony in a daze atop the walkway still wearing his battle gear. Smudged with the blood of others, he held the aura of a seasoned warrior. Patton spotted him from below. They locked in a stare. The former CONTRA commander looked out of place in street clothing.

To Battlestar's surprise, his father stood next to Patton. He motioned toward the exit doors and mouthed, "Meet outside."

Battlestar exited with Grace. A warm breeze filled the air with the smell of honeysuckle and the promise of summer. His father and Patton waited next to a row of flagpoles. Two government agents watched over them from nearby. His father looked older and more worn from worry since the last time they'd seen each other months ago. Patton, who'd always been authoritative in uniform, appeared strangely ordinary in casual dress.

"Welcome back, Son," his father rejoiced, giving him an unusually warm embrace. "I always did my best to raise you."

His father's emotion caught Battlestar off guard. It was unlike him to be affectionate. "It's because of you I'm here, Dad."

"There's more to it than that—much more."

"I'm beginning to find there's more to everything."

The four exchanged greetings. Grace stood beside Battlestar who eagerly looked to Patton. "Sir, I have something important to ask you and it can't wait. I've known you for a long time. I used to hang around you when I was a boy and listen to your war stories from Afghanistan and Iraq. They meant a lot to me . . . inspired me to be strong and ambitious."

"You always had a lot of energy," Patton replied.

"I recall hearing something once, and only then—until this last mission. Sir, when I killed one of The Revolution ringleaders, he whispered something to me I couldn't understand right away."

Patton looked curious. "What did he say?"

"The last words from his dying lips were that I was Blessed and of . . . *Nerrial*," Battlestar said, studying Patton's expression.

Grace gasped. "You didn't report that in your field assessment?"

Patton looked to Joseph. "Then it's true. The Three . . . they are the fallen Starforce officers."

"Starforce officers? Lydia Lewis mentioned something about that in her debrief. What's going on here?" Grace blurted out in rare confusion.

Battlestar didn't understand the response from Patton and wanted a direct answer. "Sir, it took me a second to remember, but *you* said that word *Nerrial* once before. It was at the old house in Virginia. I was probably seven or eight."

"I recall the exact moment. It was the first time I met your father and visited the famous firepit in your backyard," Patton chuckled quietly.

"What *is* Nerrial?" Battlestar asked with the anxious curiosity of one who knows certain information holds a key to unlocking mysteries. Patton stared, appearing unable to speak, and looked to Joseph.

Battlestar turned to his father. "Dad? You made me go back inside that night, I remember that, too. This all would have fallen from my memory if I hadn't heard that word again. Please, tell me what it is and why a Revolution ringleader would say this to me."

Battlestar's father embraced him tightly. He whispered in his ear, "Meet us at the family lake house tomorrow morning. Be there no matter what. And bring Grace along. You will *both* be told everything."

His father backed away and held Battlestar by both shoulders, looking him in the eye with an openness never shown before. He then turned away, walking with Patton to the awaiting government agents. Battlestar watched them load into a car and drive off. He hadn't been to the family lake house in years. It always reminded him of his mother and the favorite picture of her he kept in his wallet.

Grace grabbed Battlestar gently by the arm. "Are you going to tell me what's happening?"

"It won't be long now, Grace." He looked at her with genuine care, knowing for sure they're lives were linked in a very special way. "Let's get ready—we're going on a little trip."

Magden rushed into Sandra Bethlem's office followed by three Secret Service agents. He'd called the emergency number she'd provided. The time for revealing all secrets had arrived. Two staffing aides were huddled around her computer screen wearing headsets, pointing, and typing fast into handheld devices. Information was coming in from all over the world.

Sandra stood in the corner of her office on the phone. She held up an index finger indicating she needed another moment. Magden waited patiently, understanding that a president's national security adviser dealt with many emergencies. The Secret Service agents lingered behind him, not moving an inch.

A minute later Sandra hung up the phone, vexed. She signaled the agents to leave and motioned her aides to do the same. Their swift exit left Sandra in her leather business chair, exhausted, alone with Magden who stood at the center of her office.

"Busy today?" he asked with more than a hint of irony.

"The secretary of defense is livid. The Navy just lost communication with its most advanced DDG destroyer off the coast of Cuba after it approached an unmarked container ship heading for the Port of Miami. That's never happened before."

"Disturbing."

"The Middle East situation is out of control. Nobody can rein it in. It's madness."

"In some ways it is."

"Among other things, the Chinese have a carrier battle group approaching within one hundred fifty miles of Hawaii and we've picked up one of their nuclear submarines near San Diego. They've been aggressively protesting our support to India over the latest border spat." Sandra leaned forward, putting her elbows on the desk, letting her head fall into her hands. "We don't know what their intentions are." Without looking up, she asked, "What can you tell me?"

"I must forewarn you, what I'm about to say will be hard to understand."

"Shoot." She leaned back in her chair.

"You are the first human on Earth to hear this."

Sandra's expression shifted from overwhelmed to curious.

"There is a human civilization inhabiting a solar system far beyond the reach of Earth's greatest technologies called Nerrial. Seven planets compose this system, all in livable distances from their sun, a Blue Star emitting exceptional energy and creating magnificent environments. The—"

"Just hold on a minute." Sandra raised her hand, chuckling. "What kind of joke is this?"

"I'm going to be blunt with you. Take it for what you will. I said it would be hard—"

"Are you on drugs? Don't waste my time because I don't have it. We have a crisis on our hands. We're on the brink of World War III, if you haven't noticed."

"It's worse than that," Magden continued, his voice firm. "Seventeen hundred years ago, Nerrial fought a war that changed the course of human history. A demonic alien race, known as the Nezdeth, launched a massive invasion to harvest the resource richness of our planet's envir—"

"Your planets?" Sandra questioned.

"My birthplace is Adena, the largest of Nerrial's planets. I came to Earth after my twentieth birthday."

Sandra rubbed her forehead in exasperation.

"The militaristic Nezdeth understood our Blue Star contained a special energy fueling the lush environments of Nerrial. Their home planet, Whorvz—on the opposite side of our galaxy—was starved and in despair, so the Nezdeth waged a ruthless invasion to occupy and horde our resources. We created a unified military called the Starforce to repel—"

"Stop this!" Sandra shouted again. She was angry now.

"Let me finish," Magden said resolutely, taking a step closer to her desk.

Sandra flung her pen to the side in frustration. "Finish. Be done. The quicker the better."

"The Starforce defeated the Nezdeth. Over fifteen hundred years later, in 1898, one of our exploration starships discovered Earth."

"Congratulations. I'm sure it was remarkable . . . just like every other time your starships find human life in outer space," Sandra's voice oozed with sarcasm.

"Not so. To this day, no other planet or solar system has been discovered with intelligent life, except Earth. And we have been searching for well over a thousand years. As such, Earth became the subject of highest intrigue to us. Most astonishing, life was human—same as Nerrial."

"The chances of that are *unthinkable*."

"You assume humanity is an organic anomaly," Magden fired back.

Sandra focused her eyes on him more closely. "You appear serious and this story is very well rehearsed. The previous codes federal investigators recorded were hard to figure out, but I can't imagine why you'd take the time to conjure something so outrageous."

"Because it's true! Early on, questions were raised if Earth should ever become a part of the Nerrial Alliance. Instead, it was determined we would monitor Earth without interrupting its natural progression. The mission was carried out in secret by Emissaries—like *me*."

"And how have we Earthlings faired, Magden?"

"Do not mock me." A glow appeared and flashed in Magden's left eye.

"How did you do that?" Sandra asked, jolting up in her chair. "What trickery formed that flash of light? How—"

"None. *Listen* to what I'm saying. The decision to proceed in secret was made in the first years after contact. Many questions still needed to be answered."

Sandra scratched her head, looking mystified.

"Great debate commenced about whether World War II was the moment to openly intervene with Earth and reveal Nerrial. Calls to stop the bloodshed and impose peace grew strong. Loss of human life was tremendous and the outcome not assured. Several covert Starforce operations were approved against the Nazis to ensure their defeat. We—"

"Where?" Sandra interrupted.

"On the Eastern Front and in support of Operation Overlord, the D-Day invasion. Two units of Starforce troops operated in secret, sabotaging Nazi communications, destroying select logistical targets, and, on one occasion, openly fighting a unit of the Sixth Panzer Division when they were spotted in the Ardennes Mountains near the end of the war."

"Interesting." Sandra sounded attentive for the first time.

"When the Second World War ended, the Cold War was debated with a passion. Unthinkable destruction loomed with the creation of atomic weapons. Emissaries were given the authority to become more involved in political and military affairs. Many Emissaries worked themselves into high governments to advise and recommend the creation of peacetime alliances and an increase in global cooperation. Those efforts succeeded early when the United Nations and NATO were formed."

"You're going to take credit for that, too?" Sandra questioned.

Magden ignored her. "Nerrial Emissaries have never been confronted . . . until you did so in the Oval Office."

"Why should I care about any of this nonsense?"

"We believe The Revolution is a product of the Nezdeth. Forces dooming Earth are on the move. No military—not even the great American armed forces—can match up with the Nezdeth if they launch an open assault. You would be crushed. You need us. You need to believe."

Sandra sat silent as if pondering something. Her eyes cringed. "Have you spoken to Lydia Lewis recently . . . or ever?"

"No. Why do you ask?"

Sandra glanced at her computer screen and swallowed hard as she rotated her monitor so Magden could see the image of an unmasked dead Revolution soldier. "This photo was sent to me by the director of the CIA. They're popping up all over the Internet. Hard to keep it classified with all the reporters swarming Jerusalem. The IDF delivered one of the dead Revolution bodies to Langley. The CIA can't determine what it is. They want to call it a human mutation but lab tests don't support that. What do you make of it?"

"That's a Nezdeth warrior, our ancient enemy."

Sandra stood up and rubbed her eyes. "Lydia Lewis was captured and released by The Revolution while reporting in Israel. She provided statements under oath and lie detection in Brussels. Some of what she recounted while captive matches your . . . story. She described one of these things alive as did Joseph's son Battlestar and that Italian CONTRA officer . . . what's her name?"

"Grace."

"To be honest, the fact these explanations corroborate scares me."

Magden could see Sandra beginning to accept at least some of the truth. He wanted to review the official CONTRA reports but was still forbidden. He'd speak with Battlestar soon enough. "Sandra, two days ago I received an important message from Colonel Vickers."

Sandra recoiled. "He's dead."

"Assassinated."

"How would you know?"

"Colonel Vickers was an Emissary. He was responsible for overseeing the communications between Earth and Nerrial. Before he was murdered, he sent me a final transmission. The Starforce is heading for Earth."

Sandra took her time to reply. "Do you know who killed Colonel Vickers?"

"Likely the same person or persons responsible for informing you of us. Someone within The Revolution is aware of our presence. Recent Intel indicates that The Three are former Starforce officers themselves," Magden acknowledged. "Three of them went missing over thirty years ago after going mad in a somewhat similar reaction to what's being displayed by innocent civilians in Jerusalem. It's only a theory. We don't know if it's true."

Sandra pondered a long while, staring at Magden. "I can't believe everything you're telling me."

"You don't have to. Look at your computer screen. Think about the underground base in Colombia and what's happening in Israel. These are *not* the outcomes of rogue experiments by a band of rebels perfecting genetic engineering. Perhaps the werewolves are, but *not* these beings. They are the Nezdeth. Run more lab tests. I guarantee you, there is no biological form on Earth to match those dead soldiers."

For the first time Sandra looked frightened by the viability of Magden's narrative.

Magden pushed, "You're dealing with an enemy far more advanced than any military force on Earth. The very existence of your planet is at risk. There are those in Nerrial committed to helping. We are Earth's final hope."

"This Nezdeth alien race could have annihilated us by now if they are as powerful as you say. Why The Revolution then?"

"Understanding its purpose has been our greatest difficulty and is the reason Nerrial leaders have shunned our warnings for so long. This is in the past now. The Starforce *is* on its way and Nerrial will reveal itself. War is coming, Sandra. The likes of which Earth has never seen. We must prepare together."

Sandra threw her hands in the air. "This just isn't plausible. I'm the national security adviser to the president of the United States, not the . . . the . . . galactic guru of the universe. Perhaps that's your title."

"I am chief of Emissaries on Earth."

"Fine. Whatever. I can't go to the president with any of this—I need proof!" Sandra pounded her fist on the table. "Show me something tangible of Nerrial and your Emissary society. Something I can prove to the president."

"As you wish." Magden was elated she was giving him a chance. "The proof you seek is at the peak of Cheyenne Mountain and in the depths of NORAD, called Project Starblazer. Emissaries developed the communications technology and infrastructure necessary for transmitting data to and from Nerrial by creating a wormhole in the space-time continuum, an accomplishment I know you've been unable to achieve. Examine the documents titled "Astron 1" in the Department of Defense Top Secret archives. Even *you* will need a cipher to unlock this digital file. Use one-eight-nine-eight when prompted, and then, in capital letters type in the word *vigilance.* This will unlock the cipher and guide you to the evidence you need."

Sandra seemed to teeter slightly on her feet. "I will do the research myself."

"Good. Don't delay. Colonel Vickers's temporary replacement at NORAD in the Space Defense Operations Center is not an Emissary. We need the ability to communicate with the incoming Starforce. We need that access back."

There was an awkward pause. Sandra finally said, "Very well."

Sandra watched Magden turn and go, quietly closing the door behind him as the Secret Service escorted him out of the White House. She got up and strolled to the refreshments cabinet where the outgoing national security adviser had left her an unopened bottle of Johnnie Walker Blue Label blended Scotch whiskey. At over one hundred fifty dollars a bottle, he speculated there would be a time when she'd need it, though this scenario was far beyond what he'd meant.

Sandra grabbed a crystal White House glass and sat back down behind her desk. As she poured a drink, her eyes wandered back to her computer screen. The demonic image staring back at her appeared more menacing than before.

"Earth under invasion," she muttered. "God help us."

Sandra threw back the Scotch whiskey and slammed the glass hard onto her desk. She grabbed her purse and headed for the Department of Defense Top Secret archives in the Pentagon.

EPILOGUE

St. Mary Lake, Montana:
May 8, 2035

"It's beautiful, like a summer postcard. A picture taken on the perfect day," Grace smiled, letting the wind pass through her outstretched hand.

"When I was a kid we'd come up here every summer—just me and my dad. He was always so busy with government work, but promised me a week at the lake each year. He kept that promise 'til I was in high school," Battlestar replied, anxiously adjusting the rearview mirror and checking if they were being followed. "We'd go hiking, fishing, or swimming the whole time. I haven't been up here since."

They had been driving nonstop since they slipped away from CONTRA headquarters in Colorado Springs, and were on the outskirts of St. Mary Lake in Glacier National Park, Montana.

"Wow. What about your father?"

"Nope. Him neither. He came here for me . . . I think, and memories of Mom. My parents found this spot on their honeymoon. Not a typical location. They didn't want extravagance, just somewhere quiet, peaceful."

"I can understand that."

"They fell in love with the lake and ended up buying a house right on the water. We're getting close to it. I remember this part," Battlestar recalled.

"'Going-to-the-Sun Road. Three miles to St. Mary Lake,'" Grace read aloud from a sign jutting out between two pine trees. "There is poetry to that. How can you go wrong with such good names? Behold—the American lake named after the Holy Mother herself!"

St. Mary Lake came into view below the steep decline of the McDonald Valley. Motor homes, campers carrying fishing poles, and bright-colored tents lined parts of the lakeside and marked the beginning of summer for outdoor enthusiasts. Douglas fir, limber pine, and Engelmann spruce trees surrounded the entire outer rim of the lake. Puffy white clouds parted in the sky above and a hot, dry sun shined on the emerald green waters below Little Chief Mountain.

Battlestar took a deep breath and recalled summer days swimming in the refreshingly cold lake; he wondered why his father had insisted that he and Grace travel all the way to Montana for their meeting. The question of Nerrial must be ominous to force his father into such secrecy. *And why should Grace be coming along?*

Grace had tried to convince him that his eye flashed brightly in Russia when he killed the bioengineered beast, or alien being, or whatever it was. It defied logic, as did not reporting for duty that morning. Instead, after Battlestar's reinstatement only one week prior, he was driving to the old family lake house for a meeting with his father and other suspended CONTRA officials. Justice would be disappointed. "I hope this is worth it," he whispered.

"Should we check the radio once more?" Grace asked.

"The news hasn't changed. Whatever's happening is getting worse in the Middle East. Besides, I have a feeling the information we're about to receive will answer most questions. My dad's not usually this . . . interesting."

Earlier news reports described a mobilization of the entire Middle East to thwart the spread of civilian violence incited by The Revolution. The Centers for Disease Control had sent in a high-profile team of scientists from its Division of Emergency Operations to investigate the mysterious happenings. They could not gain access to Jerusalem as multi-national security forces were in disarray within the city. Many emergency and military personnel had fallen under the influence of the mist. Troops outside the city had set up a quarantine zone. Nobody went in or out.

Battlestar turned off Going-to-the-Sun and headed down a dirt road toward the edge of the lake. He pulled in front of the driveway and cut the engine. Four cars were already parked in the gravel lot.

"Looks like we're not the only invites," Battlestar guessed.

He stepped out, crunching the gravel beneath his boot as his father appeared on the front porch to welcome them. He wore faded jeans and a green flannel shirt with rolled-up sleeves. Another man stood behind his father in a black suit. Battlestar thought the man looked familiar but couldn't pinpoint where he'd seen him before.

"Welcome home, Son." His father embraced him the same way he'd done in Colorado—warmer and more emotional than ever before.

"Hello, Grace," Joseph greeted.

"Director McBride," she nodded shaking his hand. "I'll still call you that, if it's okay?"

"In a way it is." Joseph smiled and turned to the man behind him looking to Battlestar. "Troy, you recall McDaniel Jessup from the night at the firepit— the night in question?"

"It's been a long time, hasn't it?" The man spoke with the same professional English accent and seriousness Battlestar could never forget.

"Oh," Battlestar said, remembering McDaniel had been present with Patton and his father around the firepit that October night in Virginia so long ago. "Mr. Jessup, sir. Pleased to see you again."

"Call me Magden, the both of you. It's *my* pleasure to welcome you here."

"Thank you, Magden," Grace replied cordially.

The four went inside where Grace almost toppled over. *"Mama! Papa! Cosa stai facendo qui? Il mio dio!"*

Grace's parents rushed to hug her. A flurry of Italian flew back and forth as the family hugged and kissed. Battlestar watched in awe and amazement. *Why were Grace's parents here?* Three other men and two women stood in front of the large rock fireplace that adorned the main room of the lake house. They watched the scene unfold but never spoke a word. Battlestar did not recognize any of them and, apparently, neither did Grace.

Battlestar stared at his father, waiting patiently for him to explain what was happening.

"Come Troy, let's get you and Grace a comfortable seat." Joseph walked them to the couch set to one side of the fireplace.

Battlestar glanced around. The lake house looked the same and, to his surprise, was very clean and well kept. The dark wooden floors were polished. The decor matched what you'd expect to find in a living room at a place like St. Mary lake.

Fishing poles, a miniature totem pole, and photos of wildlife covered the near wall. On the far side, a hand-carved canoe hung from the ceiling just above the window overlooking Wild Goose Island at the center of the lake. A thick wooden-framed oil painting of buffalo grazing in the open fields of Montana with Blackfeet Indians watching over them, ornamented the fireplace mantle. A coffee table constructed of driftwood was at Battlestar's feet.

"Troy. Grace," Joseph began with a smile, without introducing the other four people in the house. "Your lives are special . . . and they always have been. There are things we as your family have been unable to share with you, until now. The things that are happening around the world—"

"They bind us," interjected Patton from behind the couch, motioning for Battlestar and Grace to remain seated. He nodded to Joseph to continue.

Battlestar glanced at Grace's mother. Her eyes welled full of tears and her hands were clasped tight against her chest. Grace moved to the edge of the couch and ran her hand through the curls in her hair.

"Troy, my entire adult life I've kept things from you, things you've deserved to know but that I couldn't tell." Joseph looked Battlestar in the eye. "Your mother never left us the way I told you."

"What?" Battlestar jolted up off the couch. "Why would you ever hide *that* from me?"

His father held a hand up for him to be calm. "You were sleeping in your bed the night her time came. I opened your bedroom door and we quietly walked in together. She cried and cried, Troy, trembling—knowing it would be the last time she'd ever see you. Holding your baby brother in her arms, as a family we watched you sleep for the last time. It wasn't easy."

Battlestar felt very weak. He put his hands on his hips, buckled, and he fell to the ground on both knees.

"You need to breathe," Patton instructed.

Battlestar inhaled deeply and concentrated on breathing the best he could.

"Nerrial is a *place*," his father continued. "We are descendants of this place: you, Grace, me—everyone in this room. Your mother and I made the decision that your brother should be raised there. The last chance we had to get him to Nerrial, we took."

Battlestar was gasping for air, confused. His mind swirled in a torrent of emotions. Anger, frustration, and disorientation all mixed with a physical chest pain and lump in his throat that felt like he had swallowed a whole orange. The room spun.

Grace stood up behind him, fidgeting with her hands nervously. "Where is this place?"

"Far away. Very far," her mother struggled. "*Mi dispiace.*"

"Does Antonio know?" she asked.

"No, we have not told your brother. He is in the seminary and doesn't need to know as you do."

Battlestar struggled to compose his thoughts. Setting his hands on the coffee table he propped himself up and looked at the people next to the fireplace, then to his father. "How far exactly?" he questioned.

"Forty-six million light years away—in a galaxy within the Ursa Major constellation that Earth's scientists call NGC 2841—you'll find the Nerrial solar system," Magden stated.

"That's impossible," Battlestar gasped.

"Nothing is impossible," Magden replied. "That creature you killed was a

Nezdeth general. You are the first Nerrial warrior to kill one by sword in over one thousand years!"

The information made as much sense to Battlestar as geophysics does to a kitten. He could not comprehend its significance.

"So it *is* an alien invasion?" Grace asked. "Those things *are* aliens?"

"Nerrial's ancient and only enemy—the Nezdeth," Patton confirmed.

"I have a brother," Troy mumbled under his breath, not caring about the galactic implications of the Nezdeth at the moment.

"His name is Lonthran and he is chief of Earth intelligence in the Starforce," his father comforted.

Battlestar stood up. His legs felt like oatmeal. Shaking, he gingerly sat down on the couch again and pushed his hands over his face, wiping away cold sweat and tears. He pulled his hair for several moments and finally sighed. "Is that all you had to tell us?"

"I want to know more about Nerrial . . . and the Nezdeth," Grace urged.

Magden stepped to the center of the room in front of the fireplace and stared up at the oil painting of buffalos and Native Americans. "Nerrial is a solar system made of seven magnificent planets all as amazing as Earth. Billions of human beings live throughout Nerrial on Tettra, Denattron, Adena, Gendaron, Cellcia, Ourua, and Alowen. The planets sustain life and lush environments by a unique energy provided by our sun—a Blue Star."

Battlestar and Grace sat in stunned silence as Magden spoke.

"Seventeen hundred years ago, during what's called the War of the Star, the Nezdeth invaded, killing and imprisoning millions, ravaging our pristine environments, and threatening our very existence. Militarily superior, they horded our resources back to their desolate home planet of Whorvz, located on the opposite side of our galaxy. We had no established defense at the time... Nerrial's old age knew nothing of war. Utopian, free of internal conflicts, and far less advanced technologically. Over the course of this forty-year destructive confrontation, we became unified and determined to overcome the superior space and ground forces of the occupying Nezdeth."

"But if you had no defenses, how did you win?" Battlestar asked.

"We formed a joint resistance military called the Starforce. Most crucial to our efforts, an extraordinary scientist named Vigilance who revealed secrets of the Blue Star in our greatest time of need. He captured the energy of our sun in a Celestial Prism and Seven Orbs. These treasured artifacts were made sentient and helped the Starforce progress at an extraordinary rate. We began to research our populace finding that many of us possessed extremely high senses—they were called 'Blessed.'"

"Wait! Mama, Papa . . . you always told me I was Blessed. Is this what you meant?" Grace asked.

They nodded. "It was obvious with you," her father said.

Magden continued. "The Blessed have the ability to use their senses to achieve maximum human potential physically, spiritually, or intellectually. Greater strength, speed, wisdom, scientific understanding, and expanded psychological capabilities bordering on telepathy are characteristics. Premonitions are common. For Nerrial born, the sign of being Blessed is recognized by a flash of light in the left eye when adrenaline, acute emotion, or pending danger are felt or exerted. The light in your eye is a sign of being Blessed."

Grace smiled wide and nudged Battlestar as Magden went on.

"During the War of the Star, The Blessed began developing technologies to fight and win. Advanced laser and gravity weapons, air and space fighters, transports, and, later, destroyers. Even creating a robotic defense force called the Sentrix. In the end—through tragic suffering and loss—we endured and the Starforce prevailed. Nerrial has been at peace ever since."

The room was quiet for a moment. "How did *we* end up here and what do the Nezdeth have to do with The Revolution?" Battlestar asked, feeling an odd sense of renewal emerge from his bewilderment.

"If I may, Magden," Patton interjected.

"Please do."

Patton sat next to Battlestar and leaned forward close to Grace. "Nerrial discovered the existence of Earth one-thousand-five-hundred-twenty-four years after the War of the Star ended. That year was 1898 and the discovery happened by accident, startling the star scientists on an exploration starship traveling through the Milky Way. Jubilation followed at the discovery of intelligent *human* life. Earth was studied from space until a group of Nerrial explorers trained to live among its people. The explorers were called Emissaries—we in this room are their legacy."

Battlestar's jaw dropped. The information was starting to register. This was true.

"The original Emissary mission was to study and report on culture, technology, and environmental findings. Three groups of twelve visited in 1907, making first contact with Earth's humanity. They landed in Mexico, India, and Germany. High technology was hidden at all times. The first Emissaries quickly realized Earth was far behind Nerrial's advancements. The underlying focus on power and greed was disturbing to us all. Mostly, the constant conflict and war—human against human—troubled Nerrial."

"After World War I and World War II, Emissaries became more active in *influencing* Earth's political affairs alongside their continued observation. Magden's grandfather, Calliden, led this effort and gained endorsement from the High Council and Crown. The United Nations and NATO were created soon after by Emissaries."

"Jesus," Grace whispered as she crossed herself.

"What is the High Council and Crown?" Battlestar asked.

"Nerrial's power structure is split between three pillars: The Crown, The High Council, and Adena Monarchy. The Crown is a leadership figure whose primary task is to oversee the Starforce and work with the High Council. The High Council comprises seven Ambassadors—one from each Nerrial planet. The Monarchy is a complex process of selection whereby the lineages of royalty from Nerrial are elected to represent the citizenry."

"I have endless thoughts on what I'm being told, but what of The Revolution and the Nezdeth presence on Earth? This is nearest to our current reality," Battlestar insisted.

Patton thought a moment. "Somehow the Nezdeth evaded our space surveillance systems. Magden, your father, and I have been trying to warn the High Council of this since the discovery of the first Demon Lab. The formation of CONTRA was intended to either confirm a Nezdeth presence or disprove it."

"The Nezdeth are using The Three who are former Starforce officers turned minions," Magden remarked. "This was confirmed by you, *Battlestar,* when you told Patton and your father that the dying leader recognized you were of Nerrial. We believe these three fallen officers were poisoned after being captured during a Starforce mission outside of Whorvz three decades ago."

"Lydia Lewis!" Grace exclaimed. "I almost forgot! In her intelligence debriefing she recounted what the leader Prowess said to her. It matches things you're telling us. She said something of The Revolution on Earth splitting the Starforce...and acting as a *diversion* to the real threat of some distant place. Lydia couldn't recall the name, but said it started with an *n*. This must be Nerrial."

"The Starforce is too powerful for such a Nezdeth ploy," Patton stated.

"We cannot assume this," Magden argued. "The Nezdeth have proved their cunning already. Nerrial must be warned in addition to our preparations of Earth's defense."

"How much time until the Starforce arrives here?" Battlestar asked.

"Approximately three months," Joseph answered. "Lonthran sent us the message through what we call a transmission. Received by a communications portal built on Cheyenne Mountain named Project Starblazer, his message informed that Silverstar, the supreme Starforce commander, has dispatched two battle groups to Earth under the command of Gravitron—Nerrial's space forces commander."

"How many soldiers or spaceships is that?" Grace questioned.

"Enough to do the job," Patton finished.

A man ran down the stairs from the upper loft. Battlestar hadn't known that anyone else was in the house.

"Every network is reporting it!" the man shouted, his eyes blazing with fear. "Major ports are under attack across the world. It's open war! Werewolves and Revolution troops . . . there are thousands of them streaming off container ships! And Magden," the man gulped, "the Sentrix! The Nezdeth have them."

"What? NEVER!" Magden roared.

"There are pictures . . . it *is* them. Their designs modified," insisted the man.

"The Three . . . " gasped Patton, "Our most dangerous war technology . . . stolen."

"My God, they *will* destroy Earth and reinvade Nerrial," Joseph muttered. Going pale, he stumbled backward and fell to the ground.

"Father! No!" Battlestar yelled, running to his side.

Battlestar and Grace's CONTRA receivers beeped simultaneously.

"Let me guess, a Code Seven," Grace uttered, kneeling over Joseph at Battlestar's side.

"Destruction has begun," Joseph whispered, his face sagging with despair.

"Just relax, Dad. It's not over yet."

"These robotic machines—the Sentrix, they are massive, Son." Joseph grabbed Battlestar by the arm and squeezed hard. "Advanced weaponry like you've never seen. We stopped using them centuries ago. If the Nezdeth have them in large numbers . . . then humanity's survival is at stake."

Grace locked eyes with Battlestar. They shared a look of grave fear.

"The most powerful military in the universe is headed for Earth," Magden told them, his left eye glimmering. "We must hold the defense until they arrive."

"Then that's exactly what we do," Battlestar vowed, his left eye flashing bright.

APPENDIX

ACKNOWLEDGMENTS

Authoring a novel is a challenge for a first-time writer. Creating a stand-alone universe and completing its first installment required relentless determination. The effort to complete *The Contra Alliance Universe* and *Book One: Shadows of the Past* was exhausting yet enjoyable and full of interesting experiences. Collaboration with seasoned professionals to enhance its worth and quality produced an outcome I'm happy to present you with. I would like to acknowledge the key contributors and team members who have helped make Contra Alliance happen.

Alice Peck, my developmental editor and a gifted authority on improving a story's sequencing to achieve maximum impact, taught me how to approach the composition of fiction in a more choreographed manner. From subtle recommendations to reengineered scenarios and countless corrections, her signature is engraved within these pages.

Jessica Swift, my insightful proofreader/copy editor, tightened and polished this book, enhancing its readability and assuring the best prose was selected for delivering my intended story. Likewise, her oversight of the Web site's content assured ContraAlliance.com presents the universe, trilogy, and characters in their finest form.

Duane Stapp, the interior designer and typesetter of this book, stepped up to the plate in major ways. His design concept showcases the content of this book in a modern flavor—friendly to the eyes and attractive to the imagination. I am appreciative with great thanks for Duane's architectural contributions.

Joe Benitez, a wizard in the comic book world with talents that reach far beyond penciling, delivered the visual aesthetic of the universe in a poster spread titled *Discover the Universe* to near perfection. The piece contains most of Book One's main characters, done with precision making it the official artwork of *Shadows of the Past* and cover feature.

Drew Struzan, the legendary master of *Star Wars* and countless other classic Hollywood posters, painted an entrancing thematic window titled *Alliance Vision* that displays Contra Alliance on the iconic film path he is renowned for branding.

Marco Ciappelli, my fellow coffee shop aficionado and appreciator of Hermosa Beach, deployed Contra Alliance online in stellar form while enduring my laundry list of requests to go along with his fantastically constructed Web design.

Ian Shimkoviak, who must rank with the top national book designers, delivered a classic book jacket every marketer would be proud to promote. He and everyone else at BookDesigners.com are true professionals and highly recommended.

The wonderful team at Delta Printing Solutions—special mention to Jill Clark and Patt Davis—treat every client and project as if they were already in class with J.K. Rowling's *Harry Potter*. This organization—in book printing for over one hundred years—confirms my belief that serious authors should use traditional offset printers.

Special thanks: To Scott Mckinstry for getting me into comic books before my purest imagination was too old, and for providing the first peer edit of this book. To Victor Llamas and Edgar Delgado for superior contributions of inking and coloring on *Discover the Universe*. To John Marzano for his masterful injection of scientific realism on theoretical deep space communications. To Natalie MacLees for teaching me about blogging and designing the perfect backdrop to Alliance Command.

I would also like to thank Kyle Mahoney for his early graphic/Web support; Tina Brogi for being such an adept photographer; Chad Smith for protecting my legal matters; Dean Dimascio for being so responsive on pending promotional needs; Mat Broome for keeping me pumped about independent creativity; and Stephen King for authoring *On Writing*, which taught me the basics about authorship while leaving out all the BS.

Thank you to all Twitter, Facebook, and MySpace friends, and to all those driving the acceleration of the Internet technologies to provide infrastructure and access for entrepreneurs—notably Google and Amazon.

Many other friends, acquaintances, and even strangers have provided motivation, support, and shown interest along the way, encouraging me to finish *Shadows of the Past* and the entire Contra Alliance Trilogy—even when it meant staying home after work or on weekends while everyone else was "doing something."

Finally, I have to thank my parents for, well . . . everything.

CHARACTERS OF THE CONTRA STRIKE FORCE

-------------------- COMMAND --------------------

JOSEPH MCBRIDE
CONTRA Civilian Director, NATO Allied Command Operations, United States

MCDANIEL JESSUP (MAGDEN)
Director of NATO Allied Partnerships, United Kingdom

GENERAL PATTON (WILLIAM TAYLOR)
CONTRA Commander, U.S. Army Special Operations Command, United States

DECON (BOBBY CLARK)
Executive Officer, U.S. Cyber-Command, United States

-------------- FIRST COMPANY–BLUE TEAM --------------

JUSTICE (SHAWN RAPPORT)
Colonel, Army Rangers, United States

GIDEON (JEAN SINCLAIR)
Lieutenant Colonel, National Gendarmerie Intervention Group, France

GRACE (VICTORIA CABOZENA)
Major, External Information and Security Agency, Italy

XXPLOSIVE (DANIEL DIXON)
Captain, Naval Special Warfare Development Group – DEVGRU, United States

NIGHTSCOPE (CURTIS SPRINGS)
Captain, 1st Special Forces Operational Detachment Delta Force, United States

SANDSTORM (SHAH AKBAR)
Captain, Maroon Berets, Turkey

RAPIDFIRE (PATRIK REZEK)
Captain, Advanced Weapons Specialist, Czech Republic

SECOND COMPANY–GRAY TEAM

CROSSHILL (JOHN THATCHER)
Colonel, Special Air Service, United Kingdom

DIAMOND (ALEXA KRESS)
Lieutenant Colonel, Iceland Defense Force, Iceland

SATELLITE (NATHAN LEWIS)
Major, Air Force Space Command, United States

RAPTION (TYLER NORTHCUTT)
Captain, 4th Marine Expeditionary Brigade, United States

BREAKDOWN (ROBERTO CHAVEZ)
Captain, Army Special Operations – Green Berets, United States

WARSAW (KARL SLAWIK)
Captain, Operational Mobile Reaction Group, Poland

RED (KATE HURST)
Captain, Joint Task Force 2, Canada

THIRD COMPANY–BLACK TEAM

PRIDIAN (ISABELLA ZAMORA)
Colonel, Special Operations Command, Spain

ARASHI (ANAMI NISHIHARA)
Lieutenant Colonel, Central Readiness Force, Japan

SHADE (ERICH HEINKEL)
Major, Special Operations Division, Germany

OUTPOST (LAYTON THORPE)
Captain, Special Air Service Regiment, Australia

RADAZ (DRAZEN SKORIC)
Captain, Special Operations Battalion, Croatia

DOUBLEGLOCK (MARCUS FULCRUM)
Captain, Navy Seals, United States

BURST (RASMUS CLAUSEN)
Captain, Huntsmen Corps, Denmark

FULL PROFILES AND CHARACTER BIOS ONLINE AT
WWW.CONTRAALLIANCE.COM

ACRONYMS OF CONTRA ALLIANCE

ADS	Active Denial System
AFTAC	Air Force Technical Applications Center
ATGM	Anti-Tank Guided Missile
AWM	Arctic Warfare Magnum
C4ISR	Command Control Communications Computers Intelligence Surveillance Reconnaissance
CENTCOM	Central Command
COMPORT	Communications Portal
CONTRA	Counter-Revolutionary
DARPA	Defense Advanced Research Projects Agency
DCIS	Defense Criminal Investigative Service
DDG	Guided Missile Destroyer
DEVGRU	Naval Special Warfare Development Group
DIA	Defense Intelligence Agency
EMP	Electromagnetic Pulse
EU	European Union
FSS	Federal Security Service
GPS	Global Positioning System
GRU	Main Intelligence Directorate
HAZMAT	Hazardous Materials
IAU	Immediate Action Units
IDF	Israeli Defense Force
JLTV	Joint Light Tactical Vehicle
LAX	Los Angeles International Airport
MEMS	Micro Electro Mechanical System

MRPC	Mine Resistant Personnel Carrier
NATO	North Atlantic Treaty Organization
NCS	National Clandestine Service
NORAD	North American Aerospace Defense Command
NORTHCOM	Northern Command
NRO	National Reconnaissance Office
NSA	National Security Agency
PLA	People's Liberation Army
PACOM	Pacific Command
RPG	Rocket Propelled Grenade
SAD	Special Activities Division
SAS	Special Air Service
SEAL	Sea Air Land Forces
SOG	Special Operations Group
SOUTHCOM	Southern Command
UAV	Unmanned Aerial Vehicle
UFO	Unidentified Flying Object
UN	United Nations
UNSFOR	United Nations Stabilization Forces
WMD	Weapons of Mass Destruction

COMING SOON

The saga continues…

CONTRA ALLIANCE

BOOK II: BLUE STAR

War on Earth erupts. The Revolution unleashes
a shocking new enemy. Extraordinary allies join
the fight in a race against time.

The prequel trilogy

WAR OF THE STAR

BOOK I: TIME OF LEGEND

Discover origins of the Starforce. Experience
the Dark War as told by Exa the Great. Nerrial heroes
rise in the coming-of-age story that started it all.

CONTRA Alliance
Pinup Artwork Credit

Pencils by
Joe Benitez

Inks by
Victor Llamas

CONTRA ALLIANCE PINUP ARTWORK

Blue Team

Gray Team

The Revolution

The Nerrial

CONTRA ALLIANCE

UNIVERSE ONLINE

DISCOVER AND EXPLORE THE ENTIRE UNIVERSE THROUGH ALL NETWORKS

WORDPRESS: CONTRAALLIANCE.COM/ALLIANCECOMMAND

TWITTER: @CONTRAALLIANCE @ALLIANCECOMMAND

MYSPACE.COM: CONTRAALLIANCE

FACEBOOK.COM: TOMKOLEGA

WWW.*CONTRAALLIANCE*.COM

EXCLUSIVES ✦ ARTWORK ✦ CHARACTER PROFILES
NEWS ✦ INTERACTIVE